**Praise for the submarine novels**
**MICHAEL DiMERCURIO**

*BARRACUDA FINAL BEARING*

"DiMercurio knows his submarines, and the high-tech detail that he brings to [*Barracuda Final Bearing*] should delight fans of the genre. Especially impressive here are the futuristic methods employed by a Japanese infiltrating a new nation's atomic missile site, and the unique means employed by Japan to render that site useless. . . . Those who thrill to the blip of sonar and the thud of torpedoes will relish the author's latest deepwater dive." —*Publishers Weekly*

*THREAT VECTOR*

"DiMercurio really knows his subs. . . . His characters step right off the sub deck and onto his pages." —Larry Bond

*PIRANHA FIRING POINT*

"If dueling with torpedoes is your idea of a good time, you'll love it."
—*The Sunday Star-Times* (Auckland)

*continued . . .*

*PHOENIX SUB ZERO*

"Moves at a breakneck pace."
—Larry Bond, bestselling author of *Cauldron*

"A technothriller by a master rivaling Tom Clancy . . . exciting from first page to last."
—*Publishers Weekly*

"A good, suspenseful, and spine-tingling read . . . exhilarating."
—Associated Press

"Powerful . . . rousing . . . for Tom Clancy fans."
—*Kirkus Reviews*

*ATTACK OF THE SEAWOLF*

"Thrilling, fast-paced, action-packed . . . not to be missed."
—Associated Press

"As much fun as *The Hunt for Red October*, both as a chase and a catalogue of the Navy's goodies."
—*Arizona Daily Star*

"Superb storytelling . . . suspenseful action . . . Michael DiMercurio, a former submarine officer, delivers a taut yarn at flank speed."

—*The Viriginian-Pilot*

"Nail-biting excitement . . . a must for technothriller fans." —*Publishers Weekly*

"Gobs of exciting submarine warfare . . . with a supervillain who gives new meaning to the word 'torture.' "—*Kirkus Reviews*

*VOYAGE OF THE DEVILFISH*

"Those who liked *The Hunt for Red October* will love this book." —*Library Journal*

"A master rivaling Tom Clancy. . . . Cat-and-mouse games in the waters beneath the Arctic ice cap . . . building to a page-turning, nuclear-tipped climax." —*Publishers Weekly*

"Authentic . . . fresh . . . tense . . . a chillingly realistic firsthand feel." —*Kirkus Reviews*

**Books by Michael DiMercurio**

THREAT VECTOR
PIRANHA FIRING POINT
BARRACUDA FINAL BEARING
PHOENIX SUB ZERO
ATTACK OF THE SEAWOLF
VOYAGE OF THE DEVILFISH

# Michael DiMercurio

# BARRACUDA FINAL BEARING

AN ONYX BOOK

ONYX
Published by New American Library, a division of
Penguin Putnam Inc., 375 Hudson Street,
New York, New York 10014, U.S.A.
Penguin Books Ltd, 80 Strand,
London WC2R 0RL, England
Penguin Books Australia Ltd, Ringwood,
Victoria, Australia
Penguin Books Canada Ltd, 10 Alcorn Avenue,
Toronto, Ontario, Canada M4V 3B2
Penguin Books (N.Z.) Ltd, 182–190 Wairau Road,
Auckland 10, New Zealand

Penguin Books Ltd, Registered Offices:
Harmondsworth, Middlesex, England

Published by Onyx, an imprint of New American Library, a division of Penguin Putnam Inc. Previously published in a Donald I. Fine Books edition.

First Onyx Printing, March 1997
10 9 8 7 6

Printed in the United States of America



PUBLISHER'S NOTE
This is a work of fiction. Names, characters, places, and incidents either are the product of the author's imagination or are used fictitiously, and any resemblance to actual persons, living or dead, events, or locales is entirely coincidental.

*To the woman who gave me my life back,*
*the one I dearly love,*
*Patti Quigley*

## ACKNOWLEDGMENTS

With special thanks to Nancy P. Wallitsch, Esq., who is one of those rare people on this earth who are so amazingly good at what they do that it is an exquisite pleasure to watch them work. Nancy, of all those people, is the best.

Deepest thanks to Michael Perovich, who labored as much as I did delivering the book.

Heartfelt thanks to the Quigleys, who showed me what family really means.

Thanks to Matthew and Marla, who persevered through the toughest times, and gave me unconditional love through it all.

Thanks also to Bill Lord, who with skill and certainty, irrevocably and dramatically changed two lives for the better. His good deed will, in may ways, outlive us all.

And to living legend Don Fine, who opened the door to me and made all of this possible.

"CHAPTER II. RENUNCIATION OF WAR
ARTICLE 9. Aspiring sincerely to an international peace based on justice and order, the Japanese people forever renounce war as a sovereign right of the nation and the threat or use of force as a means of settling international disputes.

In order to accomplish the aim of the preceding paragraph, land, sea and air forces, as well as other war potential, will never be maintained. The right of belligerency of the state will not be recognized."

—ARTICLE 9 OF THE JAPANESE CONSTITUTION

"Rest peacefully, for the error shall not be repeated."

—JAPANESE SCRIPT ON THE GRANITE FACE OF THE PARK OF PEACE CENOTAPH, HIROSHIMA, JAPAN

"The United States is being utterly conceited, obstinate and disrespectful. It is regrettable indeed. We simply cannot tolerate such an attitude."

—Y. HARA, PRESIDENT OF THE PRIVY COUNCIL, DECEMBER 1941

"Both the United States and Japan are victims of forces they can neither control nor resist. The tragedy of this war, as in many of history's greatest wars, is that it will be fought by two altogether decent nations, neither of which harbors real ill will toward the other. Yet the fear that seems to dominate the human condition quite as much as love is supposed to will overwhelm the decency of each . . . if there is any hope in avoiding a second U.S.–Japanese war, it rests in our leaders becoming frightened."

"The vanquished seem repeatedly to rise anew, to try their hand at making history again."

"Everything happens twice."

—George Friedman/Meredith Lebard,
*The Coming War with Japan*

"Sooner or later, the United States must come to grips with the fact that Japan has become the leading industrial nation in the world. The Japanese have the longest lifespan. They have the highest employment, the highest literacy, the smallest gap between rich and poor. Their manufactured products have the highest quality. They have the best food. The fact is that a country the size of Montana with half our population, will soon have an economy equal to ours . . . The United States is now without question the weaker partner in any economic discussion with Japan."

—Michael Crichton, *Rising Sun*

"You are being offered a glorious way to die."

—Vice Adm. Ryunosuke Kusaka, Imperial Japanese Navy Combined Fleet, Chief of Staff, to Vice Adm. Seiichi Ito, Commander Second Fleet, prior to Operation *Ten'ichigo* (Heaven Number One), in which the battleship *Yamato* was sent on a suicide mission to Okinawa. As *Yamato* capsized and exploded, Admiral Ito chose to remain aboard, retiring to his sea cabin. Capt. Kosaku Ariga, commanding officer of the *Yamato*, likewise went down with his ship, lashing himself to an antiaircraft command station on the bridge.

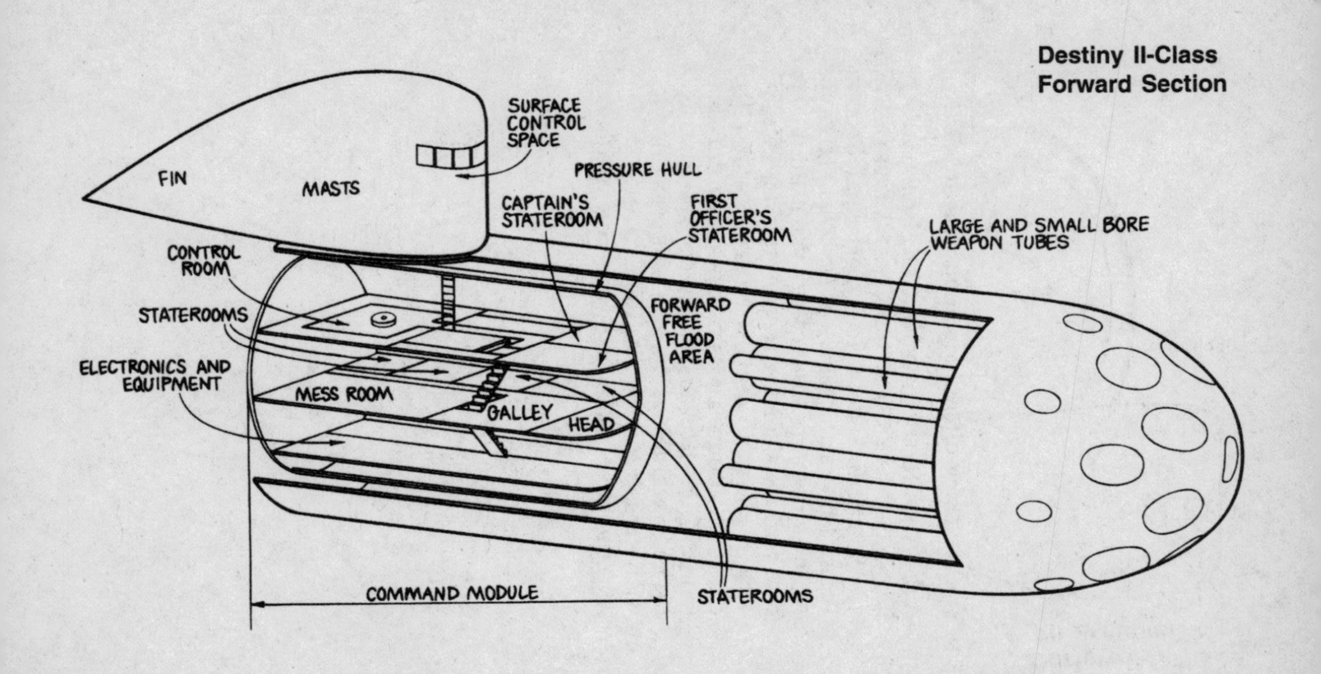
Destiny II-Class
Forward Section
SURFACE CONTROL SPACE
FIN
MASTS
PRESSURE HULL
CAPTAIN'S STATEROOM
FIRST OFFICER'S STATEROOM
LARGE AND SMALL BORE WEAPON TUBES
CONTROL ROOM
STATEROOMS
FORWARD FREE FLOOD AREA
ELECTRONICS AND EQUIPMENT
MESS ROOM
GALLEY
HEAD
COMMAND MODULE
STATEROOMS

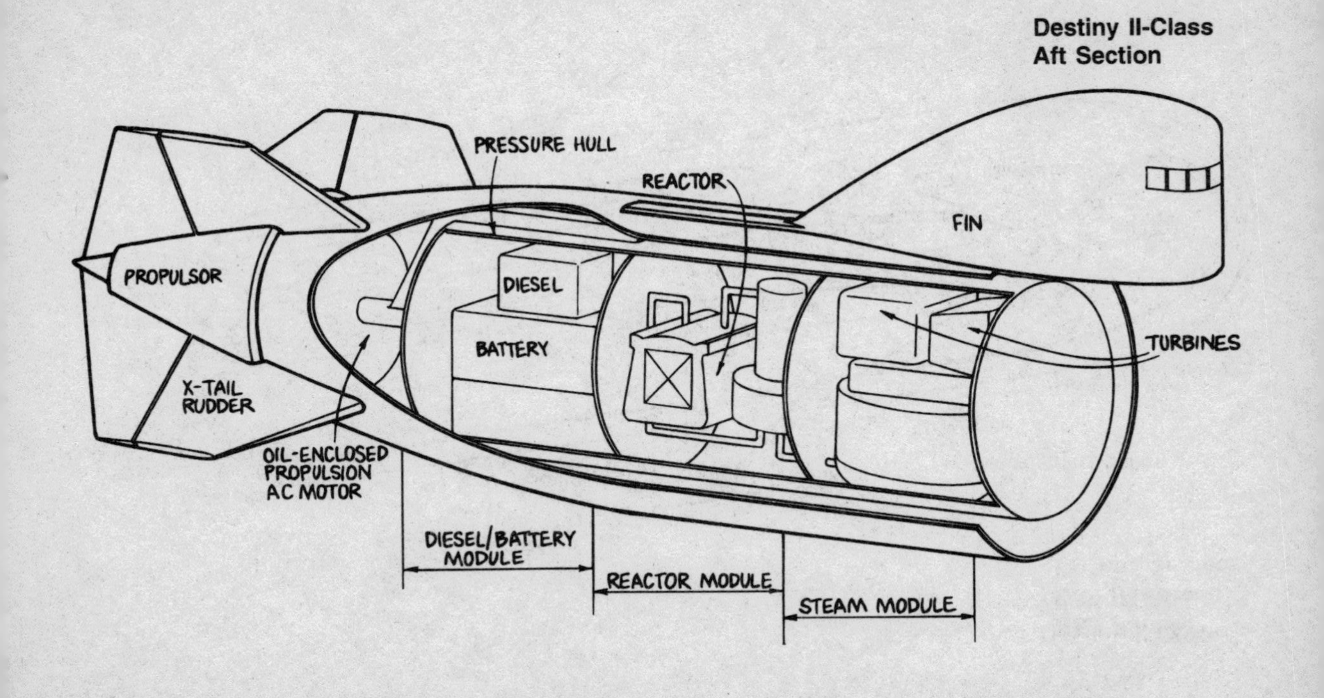
Destiny II-Class
Aft Section
PRESSURE HULL
REACTOR
FIN
PROPULSOR
DIESEL
BATTERY
TURBINES
X-TAIL
RUDDER
OIL-ENCLOSED
PROPULSION
AC MOTOR
DIESEL/BATTERY
MODULE
REACTOR MODULE
STEAM MODULE

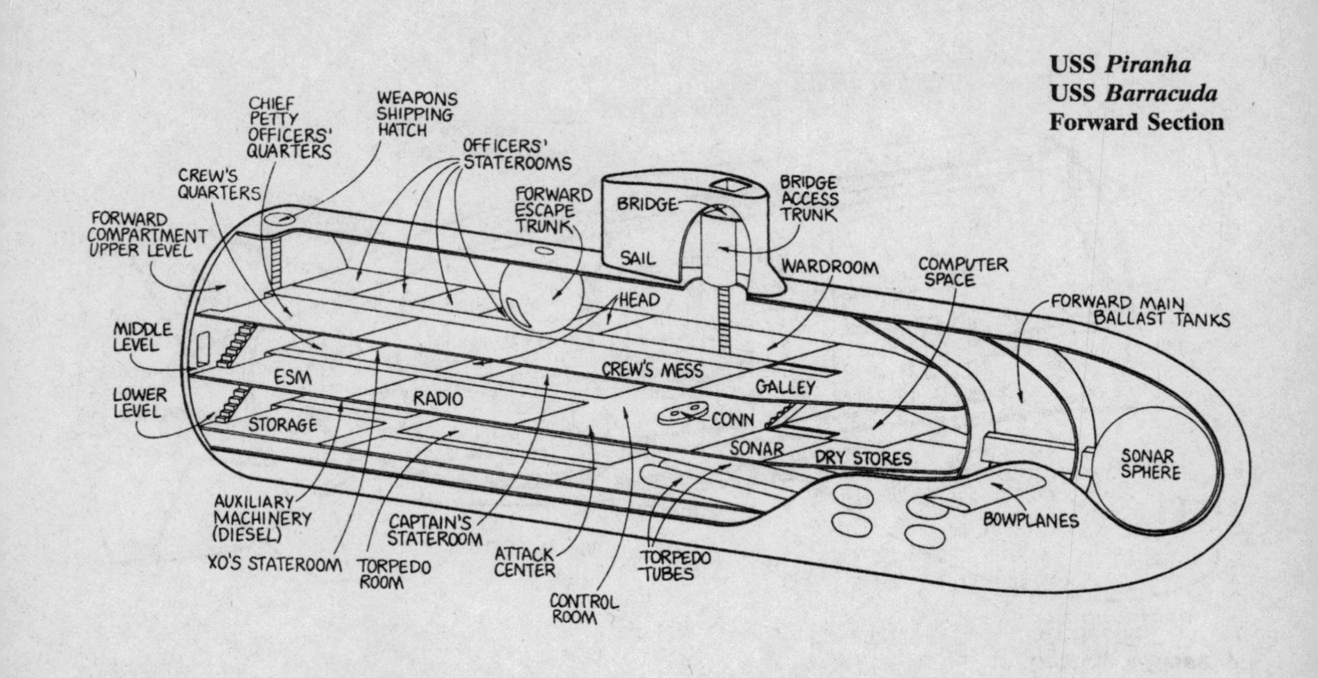
USS *Piranha*
USS *Barracuda*
Forward Section
CHIEF PETTY OFFICERS' QUARTERS
WEAPONS SHIPPING HATCH
OFFICERS' STATEROOMS
CREW'S QUARTERS
FORWARD COMPARTMENT UPPER LEVEL
FORWARD ESCAPE TRUNK
BRIDGE
SAIL
BRIDGE ACCESS TRUNK
WARDROOM
COMPUTER SPACE
FORWARD MAIN BALLAST TANKS
HEAD
MIDDLE LEVEL
LOWER LEVEL
ESM
RADIO
CREW'S MESS
GALLEY
STORAGE
CONN
SONAR
DRY STORES
SONAR SPHERE
BOWPLANES
AUXILIARY MACHINERY (DIESEL)
CAPTAIN'S STATEROOM
ATTACK CENTER
TORPEDO TUBES
XO'S STATEROOM
TORPEDO ROOM
CONTROL ROOM

**USS *Piranha***
**USS *Barracuda***
**Aft Section**

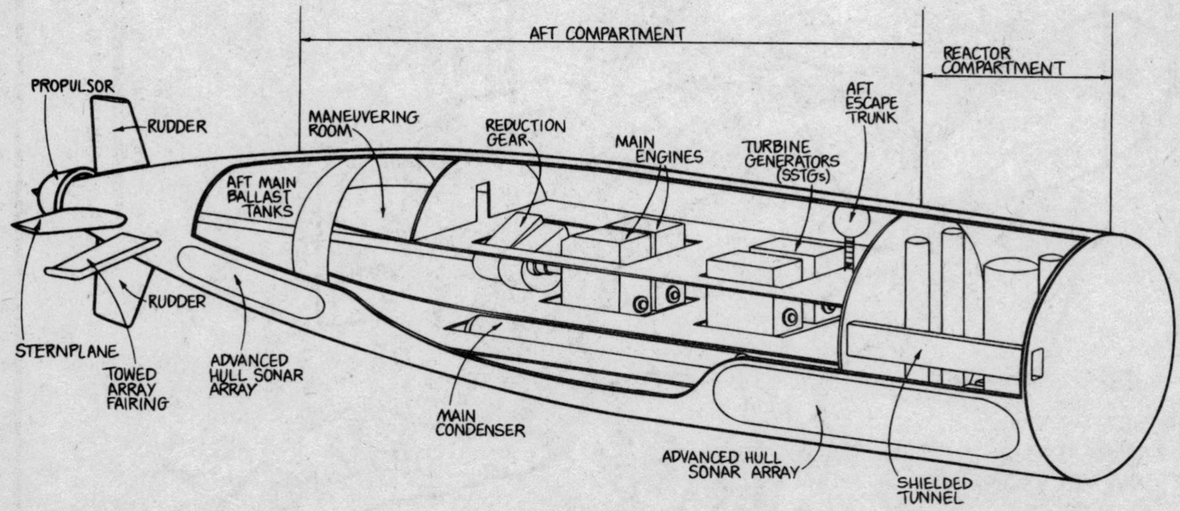

AFT COMPARTMENT
REACTOR COMPARTMENT
PROPULSOR
RUDDER
MANEUVERING ROOM
REDUCTION GEAR
MAIN ENGINES
TURBINE GENERATORS (SSTGs)
AFT ESCAPE TRUNK
AFT MAIN BALLAST TANKS
RUDDER
STERNPLANE
TOWED ARRAY FAIRING
ADVANCED HULL SONAR ARRAY
MAIN CONDENSER
ADVANCED HULL SONAR ARRAY
SHIELDED TUNNEL

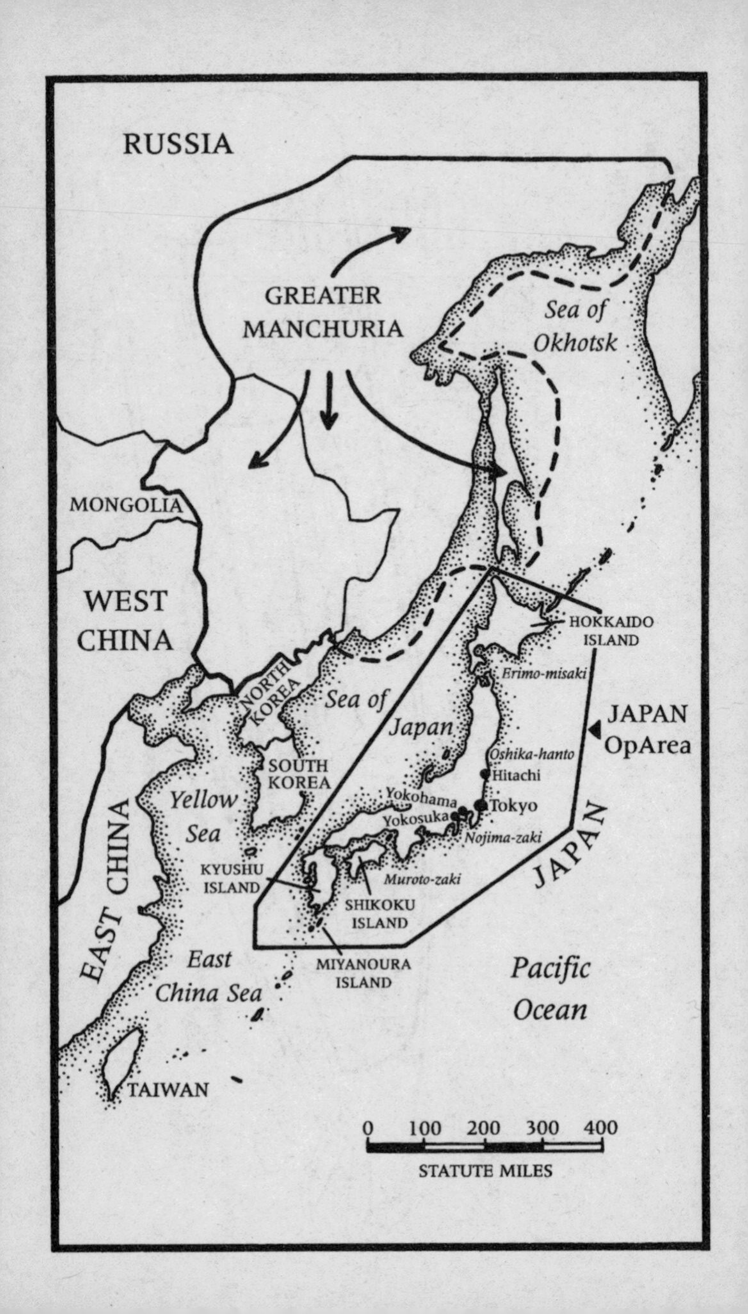
RUSSIA
GREATER MANCHURIA
Sea of Okhotsk
MONGOLIA
WEST CHINA
NORTH KOREA
Sea of Japan
HOKKAIDO ISLAND
Erimo-misaki
JAPAN OpArea
SOUTH KOREA
Oshika-hanto
Hitachi
Yokohama
Tokyo
Yokosuka
Nojima-zaki
Yellow Sea
EAST CHINA
KYUSHU ISLAND
Muroto-zaki
JAPAN
SHIKOKU ISLAND
East China Sea
MIYANOURA ISLAND
Pacific Ocean
TAIWAN
0 100 200 300 400
STATUTE MILES

# BOOK ONE

# HIROSHIMA

## SECRET NUKES ALLEGED

**Surrounded by Enemies, Poom Manages Without Military**

Edmund Tarawicz, World-Wide Press

Changashan, Greater Manchuria—Ever since the new state of Greater Manchuria was formed from the remnants of an ex-Soviet republic and an East China province, President Len Pei Poom has been considered one of the most brilliant diplomats of the decade. But persistent rumors have circulated that Len's organization of this fledgling nation was backed up by a seized stockhold of weaponry from the Russian Republic.

Although Len's administration has continued to deny such rumors, unnamed sources have reported the existence of a secret weapons depot in the Ozero Chanka valley north of the port city of Artom, formerly Vladivostok. What may be stored at the depot is unknown, but some political analysts assert that the facility maintains a cache of nuclear-tipped medium-range missiles, despite the nuclear exclusion treaties of the past fifteen years.

If Len does indeed have possession of nuclear weapons, it would certainly explain why he was able to ensure Greater Manchuria's survival in the face of the hostility of West China, the renewed nationalism of the Russian Republic and the second thoughts of formerly friendly East China, particularly in view of the fact that Greater Manchuria has essentially no army. . .

**InterGov**
Network E-Mail —Security Monitored—Top Secret/ Release 12

---

From: DirNSA R. Donchez
To: President/National Security Council
cc: Copy Protected/Distribution Controlled/Release 12
Serial: SM-TS/R12–04–0890
Date: 21 November
Time: 1653 EST
Subject: Manchurian Nuclear Weapons, Rumors Concerning

---

This EMail is a joint transmission of NSA and CIA. Issued under authority of R. Donchez, DirNSA, and B. F. Leach III, DirCIA.

Screen readout lifetime: 20 seconds.

1. (Unclass) Recent press reports allege the existence of nuclear missiles held by President Len Pei Poom in the fledgling state of Greater Manchuria.
2. (Secret) At the request of Presidential finding 04–17, CIA and NSA were directed to report on the possibility of nuclear missiles in Greater Manchuria.
3. (Top Secret) Details of the report are transmitted separately in EMail serial SM-TS/R12–04–0891 dated 21 November.
4. (Top Secret Release 12) Conclusion: There are no, repeat no, nuclear weapons held in Greater Manchuria.
5. (Top Secret Release 12) Despite Para 4, Len is managing by some unknown means to hold off the aggressions of the Russians, the West Chinese and the East Chinese. How this is being done should be explored immediately. CIA/NSA recommend the draft of a finding to authorize further intelligence operations to understand the dynamics of the border situation.

This message will self-delete.

IntelliVOX Transcription:

Date of Voice Mail: 21 November

Time: 0817

Initiating Party: A. Machiie

Initiating Location: Tokyo 27, Ministry of Information Suite 200

Security Level: Layer Fifteen

Destination Code: 05412

Destination Party: H. Kurita

Voice Transmittal:

Honored Prime Minister, this is Asagumo on Tuesday shortly after eight o'clock. I sincerely hope that you had a good rest. The meeting will be held in the central suite as you requested.

I am calling to let you know that we have confirmation from the Galaxy satellites that the weapons depot in Greater Manchuria is indeed manned and that our infrared micro-scan hints at the possible—but unconfirmed—presence of nuclear warheads. We are now uploading a mission request for a human agent deep penetration to confirm the presence of the warheads. The mission, as you suggested earlier, will be done with a Divine Wind Battalion warrior. Mission start time is estimated at eight to twelve hours after your authorization.

Once again, your instincts prove you correct, Honorable Prime Minister. I will see you shortly at the meeting. You have my sincere hope that your health remains well.

[End Transmision]

# PROLOGUE

**Sea of Japan**
**Altitude 20,000 Meters**

The cockpit shuddered as the ramjet engine shut down, fired its explosive bolts and detached, the pilot's flickering display showing the propulsion module tumbling into the sea below.

"Phase two," the pilot murmured in Japanese into his boom microphone. "Aircraft stable in full glide. Descending on glide path at nineteen thousand meters."

There was no need to maintain radio silence—the electronics saved the voice data, video camera images and avionics telemetry into a magnetic bubble memory and transmitted a compressed burst once every five to ten minutes on a constantly changing frequency with time-varying encryption codes aimed in a beam to randomly selected Galaxy multipurpose satellites. The communications suite was frontier technology, Japanese technology, the most advanced in the world. Maj. Sushima Namuru would continue to transmit despite the fact that this was the most secret human intelligence operation ever taken on by the Japanese Self Defense Force.

The cockpit hummed from the instruments and the gyro. Namuru half closed his eyes, at one with the airplane, which moments before had been a high-speed jet and was now gliding silently, its polymer airframe and fabric skin making it invisible to radar, its lack of an engine making it invisible to infrared scanners, its lifting surface shape eliminating much of the wingtip vortex swirl making the flight whisper quiet. The plane was a prototype, named Shadow-star by Namuru, the name resonant with meaning to him. For a moment he saw images of the morning, his goodbye to his wife and young son, the send-off party with his squadron of Divine Wind flyers, his time alone in the shrine, feeling his ancestors surround him, giving their approval.

He glanced at the tiny camera eye set in the overhead, the one that monitored him and his reactions, hoping that someday his son would see the video and have pride in his father. Namuru's reverie ended two seconds after it had begun, his attention now taken up in his display screen, its three-dimensional display of glide slope superimposed over the terrain model so real that despite working with it for years, Namuru was still tempted to reach out and touch the objects in the display. The screen was all Namuru needed to fly the plane—there were no windows to the world outside. The only thing the display was unable to do was allow a windowless landing approach; for that a pilot still needed a real view. But on this mission, Namuru's Shadowstar would not be landing.

The aircraft passed over the line marking Greater Manchuria's territorial waters, then soon flew over Greater Manchuria's coastline. Namuru shook his head slightly, amazed at how close this new barbarian nation was to Japan, just across the Sea of Japan, the state once divided between Russia and China, but now a united threat merely 300 kilometers from Japan at its closest point, the distance between Tokyo and the Greater Manchurian capital of Changashan only 1050 kilometers, well inside the range of the old Russian SS-34 nuclear-tipped missiles. The missiles were supposedly destroyed under the United Nations ban on nuclear devices years before Greater Manchuria's formation, but if they were, Namuru's mission would not have been ordered.

The intelligence brief, held an hour before his takeoff, detailed the satellite data that pointed to a nuclear-weapons storage depot in the sleepy railhead town of Tamga 200 kilometers northeast of Port Artom, the city the Russians had called Vladivostok. The evidence was frightening. That a *ketojin,* a savage, like Len Pei Poom could form a nation of barbarians so close to Japan could not be permitted. Especially if they were in possession of nuclear missiles . . . Namuru almost longed for decades past when the Soviet Union and China and America were too busy threatening each other to be a danger to Japan. But now that Japan was alone it would be up to him, Namuru himself, to give his commanders the intelligence they would require before taking action against this threat.

Namuru watched the glide path on the display. The glider had floated silently to an altitude of 5000 meters, completely undetected, now within twenty kilometers of Tamga. The computer flashed up the countdown to aircraft destruct. Scarcely a minute now. Namuru glanced at the pilot-monitor camera as he spoke.

"Phase three. Two minutes to aircraft destruct. As yet no sign of detection."

**Yokosuka, Japan, Twenty-five Kilometers South of Tokyo**
**Yokosuka Center**

"Please remain seated," the man in the business suit said, his voice quiet but full of authority. The officers in the command center remained at their consoles, glancing briefly, respectfully up at Prime Minister Hosaka Kurita as he walked slowly among the rows of equipment with his escort, Gen. Masao Gotoh, the chairman of the Joint Staff Council. Gotoh led Kurita to an isolated area of the dark room, the command corner, where an enlarged screen four meters wide and two meters tall flashed views fed by the defense computer network. The screen was split, one-half of it showing a helmet and oxygen mask, the only signs that a person was present the eyes, the other screen half showing a terrain model with superimposed computer graphics. It was gibberish to Prime Minister Kurita. Gotoh explained, his own eyes on the display.

"These are the transmissions from Colonel Namuru in the Shadowstar aircraft. We are seeing them at a five-minute delay from real time since the data is recorded, compressed and relayed at a burst to a satellite—that way it is unlikely he would be detected even against an advanced adversary. Against the Greater Manchurians, he is invisible. In a few minutes Namuru's aircraft will put him down near the Tamga weapons depot. We will be monitoring him as he executes his mission."

Kurita took a peek at his watch and settled into a leather command chair, his eyes unblinking as he took in the screen.

"What if something happens to him? What if he's caught?"

Gotoh smiled to himself, knowing Kurita had been fully briefed, but also knowing the older man liked richness of detail. Briefings alone were not enough for him.

"Colonel Namuru and the other Divine Wind Warriors have an implanted chip with a small chemical canister surgically placed in their abdominal cavities. On a signal from the satellite, the chip will release a small dose of poison into Namuru's body. Thirty seconds later he will be dead. There is no antidote."

The Prime Minister nodded. The two men watched the data display in silence.

"You can see him here preparing for the aircraft to destruct," General Gotoh said, the pilot's image busy in the cockpit.

Suddenly the screen image bounced violently, then winked out.

The Shadowstar glider sailed at 150 kilometers per hour, 3000 meters over the scrubby hills, four kilometers outside of Tamga. The cockpit's computer display numerals reached the single digits, rolled too quickly to one, then zero. The aircraft self-destruct sequence began.

The polymer of the airframe was as strong as aluminum when in solid form. Running through the skeletal structure of the framing were hundreds of small polymer tubes and capillaries, all of them connected to a foil-lined polymer tank filled with a mixture of sulfuric acid and several advanced solvents. A small cylinder of high-pressure nitrogen inside the top of the tank, on a computer signal, opened to the tank, the whooshing gas pressuring the fluid inside while a valve at the tank bottom snapped open, allowing the acid and solvent mixture to flow into the pipes and tubes and capillaries leading to the plane's airframe structural components. The walls of the tubes were machined precisely so that they would carry the acid to the remotest tubes just before dissolving themselves. The dissolving tubes then spilled the acid into the hollow regions of the airframe structures and along their outsides.

The polymeric composition of the airframe was chemically synthesized so that it reacted exothermically with the acid while dissolving in the solvents. Areas of the structure not directly in the wash of acid and solvents reacted from the heat of the adjacent melting structures, the acid molecules diffusing throughout the liquefying mass. Over the next twenty seconds, what before had been a network of solid curving beams and struts making up the shape of an airplane became a melting waxy semisolid, then a liquid, then finally as the reaction rate increased, a vapor. The airplane's lifting body shape melted into a large teardrop, the liquid flying off into the slipstream behind it, the liquid turning to a plume of gray smoke, until all that was left of the aircraft was the egg-shaped carbon composite cockpit module, now tumbling end-over-end to the rocky slopes below.

Inside the cockpit Namuru felt the aircraft shake, then tremble violently as the wings and tail liquefied and vaporized, the module encasing him spinning toward the earth. The g-forces of the spin knocked Namuru about the cockpit, straining his five-point harness, threatening to break his neck. Namuru wondered if the computer were still active. If it had malfunctioned in the breakup of the airframe, the cockpit module would fall dumbly into the ground below, shattering at terminal velocity of 160 kilometers per hour. He fought the dizziness of the spinning cockpit and the massive g-forces to reach his gloved hand for the manual parachute lever. He had just managed to brush it with his fingers when the explosive bolts blew off the drogue chute panel, ejecting a streamer from the rear of the cockpit module, stabilizing the wildly spinning egg until one second later the main chute blew out, luffing in the slipstream gale until it filled, the cockpit module settling below it. The cockpit egg now drifted gently down to the slope of a craggy hill a hundred meters below. Namuru had only a moment to inhale to clear his head before the module hit the mountainside, the impact considerable even under the canopy of the main chute.

Namuru hurried to punch the cockpit rupture button, knowing that the computer would wait only two minutes for him to activate it before self-destructing. The worst thing that could happen on this mission was his capture, and if he had arrived unconscious, the computer would kill him before allowing him to be taken. He pulled the cover from the rupture command switch and toggled it down and the cockpit module split in half, opening cleanly along a prescored material weld. The top of the module pulled up and away from the bottom on pneumatic cylinder struts, allowing a cold wind and diffuse but glaring winter light into the module. Namuru unlatched a case from the bulkhead of the capsule and hauled himself out into the cold of the outside and stepped away from the cockpit. Seconds later the module began to smoke and sizzle, burning until there was nothing left but a black molten pool of carbon, melted fiber optics and singed liquid crystal.

Namuru opened the case he had withdrawn and revealed a thick vest, full of pockets, heavy with explosives and the automatic pistol. He put on the vest and took out equally heavy pocketed pants that he strapped onto his thighs and fastened with Velcro seams. He kept his helmet on, since it contained two cameras, one that gave Yokosuka Center a view of what he himself saw, a second with a fisheye lens focused on his face. He pulled a small folding spade from a utility pocket and covered the smoking ruin of the cockpit and the parachute with earth dug from the rocky frozen ground. He stepped back after a few minutes, sweating despite the chill, realizing the job was far from perfect but still would only be noticed by someone stepping on top of it.

He ditched the shovel, pulled the pistol out of his vest, screwed on the long silencer and snapped a large clip into the gun. He then thrust the piece into a soft holster set into his vest and withdrew high-powered binoculars and a black rubber box with rounded edges about the size of a steno pad. The pad had heavy elastic straps on the back and a removable cover on the front that now revealed a liquid crystal display. Namuru strapped the pad onto his left forearm, then ran a small wire between his watch and the pad, switching the watch into digital compass mode, its satellite receiver turned to the orbiting Galaxy geostationary multipurpose satellite. A thumb pressure on the display turned the unit on, the display flashing a question mark. He raised the pad to his lips and whispered his password, which this hour was "blue." The display flashed to life, bright and colorful, although the light from it faded to black if the screen were observed even slightly off from directly in front of it at a distance of thirty centimeters.

"Nav display, vector to Tamga weapons depot," Namuru whispered to the pad. An overhead satellite photograph view of a hilly rocky region flashed onto the display, the scene showing an eerie depth from the three-dimensional effect. The green of the trees and ground cover were broken by several roads, a winding rail track and the roofs of several small buildings, with what appeared to be an expansive flat plateau among the buildings. A yellow grid flashed up over the landscape, with a blinking circle on the crest of a hill to the south of the compound. Namuru noted that the circle was within two kilometers of the center of the complex—and since the circle was his own position, he would have an easy hike to the base perimeter. He looked up into the cloudy sky for any sign of the sun, but it was buried in thick overcast. He made a full turn, looking and listening for observers in the scrubby growth around him. All was quiet. The pad computer aural sensors were tuned to pick out man-made noises and would alert Namuru by buzzing the flesh of his forearm, but until that function proved itself it was not to be assumed that it worked. After a last glance at the pad display, Namuru set off in the direction of the compound.

## Yokosuka Center

"So how will he get through the perimeter fence and security?" Prime Minister Kurita asked, watching raptly as the screen display jiggled and showed Major Namuru walking through the thick trees on the downslope of a mountain leading to the Tamga valley. The view on one panel of the display showed the trees and underbrush approaching the camera; a second panel showed a fish-eye-lens view of a puffy-looking face beaded with sweat, the eyes wide and hyper alert; the third panel revealed a grid superimposed on a bird's-eye view of the valley with a flashing circle nearing a fenceline surrounding a military compound.

"Not a problem," General Gotoh replied, glancing from the screen to Kurita's lined face, then back to the display. "Namuru has gas for dogs, a silenced automatic for human guards, shorting cables for electrified fences. We've spent six months training him in the use of every security measure we know. He's consistently penetrated them 78 percent of the time."

"Seventy-eight percent doesn't sound like it's passing."

"That is against Japanese technology perimeter security," Gotoh said, typing into a keyboard in front of his control console. "Against *gaijin* methods, he will be more than the equal of a security detail."

"Tell me again how he is going to get inside the bunker, if that is what it is."

"He'll shoot the guards," Gotoh said simply, his eyes still on the display, careful not to let a flicker of annoyance cross his face at Kurita's insistence on covering briefing material over and over.

"Does he have to do that? It would seem to imperil the mission, draw attention to the break-in."

"True, Prime Minister. But guards of nuclear weapons

are trained—conditioned is perhaps a better term—to shoot intruders. They call it Deadly Force Authorization. It means shoot first and forget the questions. The quickest way to penetrate the security around a nuclear weapon is to surprise the guards and kill them. Even then, one's life expectancy is numbered in the minutes, perhaps only seconds. That's why Namuru has the cameras. If he's shot we'll still have the data."

"What about the time delay? They might disconnect and destroy his camera before we know what happened."

"Unavoidable, I'm afraid, sir. But it is unlikely that if Namuru and his gear is captured that the *gaijin* Greater Manchurians could understand that he is transmitting. By the time they realized it, we would know all that Namuru knew."

In the panel monitoring Namuru's view a bush flashed close to the camera, then rolled away to reveal a length of fencing between two trees. The right panel showing the navigation display changed, a graph replacing the aerial photograph, the graph pulsing with circular curves.

"The fence is electrified with high voltage," Gotoh announced. The view from Namuru's helmet blurred as he approached the fence. Namuru's hands flashed in and out of view, attaching a cable to the fence, just before the fireball exploded and the screens again went blank.

Namuru looked at the fence as his computer pad flickered with the electromagnetic signature of 11,000 volts surging through the aluminum cable braided through the fence. What could be seen through the fence was limited, since there were more trees there and little else.

Namuru snaked out the electrical cables that were in the back of the heavy vest, uncoiled the heavy insulated wires, withdrew the lengths of copper rods half a meter at a time. He screwed the copper rod lengths together, until there was a two-meter-long copper rod, then attempted to force the rod into the ground. It went in halfway, then had to be tapped with a rubber mallet from another vest pocket until the rod was buried in the ground with only five centimeters protruding.

Namuru hid the mallet under a bush. At least after

this, he thought, much of the weight he'd carried in would be left behind. He took a cable and attached it to the top of the copper rod with a heavy copper clamp. The other end of the cable he attached to a large alligator clip, then stepped back to inspect his work. He unfastened the computer pad and digital receiver watch, his vest and his utility leggings so that most of the metal objects were removed from his body. He put on the thick 100,000-volt rubber gloves. His boots were already wrapped in insulating material, one of the reasons his feet were so uncomfortably hot.

He took a deep breath, studying the cable winding through the aluminum mesh fence. The idea was to get his cable attached to the live electrical cable in the fence, thereby grounding the voltage to the copper rod in the earth. The live wire would then short its potential to ground, either tripping the electrical circuit at the generator or melting the wire at the connection to the rod. If he did this right the power would blast through the grounding mechanism and disrupt the entire circuit so that he could cut through the fence. But if he mishandled the operation 11,000 volts of power would pass through his body. That had happened to one of the Divine Wind officers in penetration training. The high voltage had blown off the man's legs and one of his arms, stopped his heart and left him a smoking wreck. The training chief had cut the power, and the ambulance crew had revived the man, and he had actually lived for two days, the incredible pain of those days carved on his terrified burned features when they had buried him. A horrible way to die, a worse way to live. Namuru prayed, just don't let it leave me burned and maimed.

He lunged with the alligator clip and hit the high voltage fence cable with it. The fireball had no sound, only a fist of pressure. Namuru saw the light expand to the size of a zeppelin and surround him as it smashed into him and blew him off his feet and sent him flying into the woods.

"What happened?"

"Looks like he took a shock," Gotoh said, his voice a monotone. The screens remained blank.

"And he's dead?"

"Too early to say, sir." Gotoh had risen to hover over another younger officer at a neighboring console. The officer tapped furiously at a keyboard, stopping occasionally to manipulate a mouse, then typing again. "We're addressing the satellite now trying to get Major Namuru's cameras to work again. If we can reestablish a link with his instrumentation we might be able to determine what is going on."

The screen flashed a momentary broken image, then went dark again. Gotoh and Kurita waited.

"How long do we wait?"

"The mission brief calls for a four-minute delay before the satellite signals the chip with the poison canister in the major's abdomen," Gotoh said.

"How long has it been?"

"We were already on a five-minute delay from real time when the major got hit with the electricity. We saw it three minutes ago. I'd say Major Namuru has another sixty seconds before the computer aborts the mission and calls down to the chip to inject the poison."

The screen flashed, then held. The camera view from Namuru's helmet stared straight up at the sky, the boughs of two trees breaking the featureless clouds. The face-monitoring camera came up next. Namuru's face was burned on the left side, his eye gone, the flesh seared and melting. His right eye was shut and swollen.

"Prime Minister, I don't think we should wait for the mission computer. We should abort now. Namuru's gone."

Kurita stared at Namuru's burned and disfigured face. "I agree, General."

Gotoh gave the order to the officer on the control console, who nodded and made the commands as if they had nothing to do with killing a fellow officer.

"The signal is out, sir," the officer reported.

"He'll be dead in thirty seconds if he isn't already," Gotoh said.

Kurita looked up at the screen. "We need another plan. We still must find out if Len Pei Poom has nuclear weapons. He could be targeting Tokyo even now. "

* * *

Namuru was burned from the inside out. His flesh felt hot and running on his left side, his face aching and puffy. His whole body ached, he couldn't move. He concentrated for what seemed hours trying to move his right hand, finally able to move it upward. In the next ten minutes he used the hand to lift himself so that he was sitting up. He couldn't see out of his left eye. He reached for his face and felt the burned flesh, hard and crumbling. He crawled through the brush to find his watch and the computer pad. When he found them, the computer pad had melted into a puddle of plastic. The watch was also destroyed, the satellite above having given the signal to abort the mission. Which meant that his poison capsule should have been released and he should be dead.

Except that the electrical fireball must have fried the chip inside him. But if there had been enough power to kill the chip, there might have been enough to fracture the poison canister. It could be leaking even now, he thought. He had only hours to live—but then that was the whole idea of this mission.

He managed to stand, shaking when he finally made it. He took some water from his vest, then tried to put it on. It was too heavy and he was too weak. He would have to go in without it. He bent over the vest and pulled out the pistol, a spare clip, the two gas bottles, a small collection of electronic boxes and a small pack of film, then adjusted his helmet, wondering if the cameras were still operating. The circuits checked out—he should still be transmitting. He wondered if there was anyone on the other end. He stepped slowly toward the fence, saw the blackened hole the fireball had blown in it. He crouched down, walked through and limped to the trees, his strength coming and going erratically.

With the computer pad gone, he was operating on memory. The satellite photo had pictured a wide flat mound of earth, the kind used to conceal an underground bunker. The earth mound would be behind two rows of outbuildings from where he was, just beyond the trees. Moving through the trees to the far edge, he saw the outbuildings and began walking unsteadily through the exposed ground to the cover of the buildings. If the cameras weren't working, the mission was over.

The two black dogs running silently toward him were within ten meters before he saw them with his one eye.

"Prime Minister! General!"

The lieutenant from the command center, Gotoh saw.

"Sir, the major. He's alive. He's inside the compound—"

"General, what happened to the poison?" Kurita asked.

"I'm not sure, sir. Perhaps the electrocution damaged it."

"What else could fail on this day," Kurita mumbled. The two men hurried back to the command center, returning to the control corner they had abandoned minutes before. The left screen was unsteady with the blur of movement, the transmission fading in and out, the software freezing the image rather than allowing the display to go black during the short transmission interruptions.

During one short interruption Kurita saw the frozen image of the exposed fangs of a large black dog leering angrily at the camera as it lunged. The eyes were red and furious, the mouth hungry and lethal. Kurita unconsciously felt his throat.

The dogs had gotten too close. If he had still been able to use the computer pad, the motion detector would have alerted him to the animals ten seconds before, but that was in the past. In an adrenaline rush he grabbed a gas bottle with each hand, aiming as best he could with only one good eye, the streams of gas jetting out at the dogs in a loud blast, a white cloud forming around him. He clamped his mouth shut, hoping he could keep from inhaling the gas. The lab techs had assured him the nerve gas was active only on animals, not humans, but after seeing it demonstrated, he wondered. The dogs, already flying through the air to get to his throat, were dead before they hit him, the two bodies knocking him to the ground, the sounds of the dogs' gasping expulsions of breath in his ears as their bodies spasmed through reflex nerve actions.

Namuru got up, replaced the bottles in his belt and withdrew the automatic pistol. He was within ten meters of the objective now, the hump of earth covering the suspected bunker rising over his head. The slope of the dirt was too regular to be natural. There was definitely something buried here. Namuru closed the clump of trees at the edge of the earth embankment and had a momentary impression of the two armed guards in their helmets and flak jackets. Namuru sprayed them with a single silenced burst from the pistol, more than two dozen Teflon-jacketed rounds exploding inside their bodies. He had shoved the pistol into his belt, the barrel scalding hot, while the guards were still on their feet, slowly collapsing to the ground. As the two liquid thumps came from their impact with the earth, Namuru cradled the keypad entry box in his hands.

The keypad required a password numeric sequence be entered to open the blast doors of the bunker. Namuru pulled the cover off, reached into his belt for the electronic boxes, none of them bigger than a matchbook, and selected the proper one. He placed the box over the number pad, hit a button on the face of the box and waited. Twenty seconds later a small crystal display blinked as the box talked to the keypad. Finally the keybox surrendered, the heavy steel blastdoor groaning as it moved its rusted mass, one panel sliding right, the other left, opening into the darkness of the bunker. As it opened, Namuru pulled the pistol from his belt and dropped the electronic box, which was already sizzling and melting into a self-destruct sequence.

Namuru rushed into the opening, firing at the dim shapes of the inside guards, none prepared for an intruder. His eyes had begun to adjust to the darkness as he ejected the spent clip of the weapon and inserted another, the only replacement ammunition he had brought. He almost smiled as he saw the missiles in the dim light of the dusty overhead lamps. He stepped over the bodies of four guards for a better look, glancing up to see if he was being followed. So far all was quiet. He only needed another minute.

Namuru had spent years studying nuclear weapons. He could recognize and identify any production nuclear missile made by any nuclear power, past or present. And the missiles on the dollies in front of him were definitely old Russian SS-34's—medium-range ballistic missiles. Theater nuclear weapons able to reach any major city within 1500 kilometers. Most of the missile bulk was devoted to warhead rather than rocket fuel, which was why their range was so short. But Tokyo was only 850 kilometers away. It was not enough for him to identify the missile model, however Namuru's mission was to determine beyond any doubt that they were truly nukes, not just dusty hulks of the old SS-34s, or some unknown conventional model of the warhead with conventional high explosive mated to the SS-34's rocket stage.

All nuclear warheads, he knew, emitted neutron radiation. Especially an older Russian model. The neutron flux from the plutonium warhead would be enough to cloud a special filmstrip. Namuru stepped over to the weapon body, going through a yellow rope with the three-bladed circular radiation warning sign on it, and attached one of the filmstrips to the nearest warhead, then a strip on the next, and one on the furthest. There were at least twenty missiles in this end of the bunker and there would be no way to have time to test them all. Namuru counted to ten, then pulled the films away, crouching below the weapons. He put each film through a developer and waited another ten seconds, then held the processed film to the light. All three were clouded.

All three had been exposed to high dosages of neutron flux.

All three weapons had nuclear warheads.

*Which meant Manchuria could attack Japan and bring her to her knees.*

*Which meant that the war would begin in days when the high command attacked this facility.*

Namuru thought he heard a voice. He pocketed the films and ran out the blast door and into the open, amazed that his body could function after the electrical jolt, but then realizing he was operating on pure adrenaline. He ran past the outbuildings to the trees, and beyond to the burnt-out hole in the fence. There was noise now, a rising siren just starting off on the other side of the bunker, gathering pitch and volume until it howled, an old-fashioned air-raid alarm. He heard the roar of truck engines as he dived through the fence opening and made it back to the trees, where he had stashed his vest and leggings.

He was almost finished.

"So it is true," General Gotoh said.

"The weapons?"

"They *are* nuclear," Gotoh said to Kurita as both men watched the screen, Namuru's view of the missiles clear in his helmet-mounted camera. Namuru had apparently just gotten rid of the film and begun his escape. "Did you see the film? It clouded. Only neutron radiation can do that so quickly. And only nuclear fuel or nuclear warheads would do that. The SS-34s are live, sir."

"What happens to Namuru now?"

"We give him a medal. And we keep watching."

Namuru got the vest and leggings on and pulled the helmet camera out of the helmet by a coiled thread-thin wire, attaching the tiny camera eye to a limb on a tree, then backing away two meters so that the camera was looking at his face.

"Phase nine," Namuru said to the camera. "The weapons are SS-34s, at least two dozen of them. I have confirmed that they are nuclear. My extraction was successful but I am being pursued. This mission is now complete." Namuru listened for a moment, the sirens wailing behind him. He thought he heard footsteps in the underbrush.

It was time.

"To the victory of Japan," he said, and reached to the back of his helmet to pull the T-handle cord, down to his shoulder blade.

Kurita stared at the screen. Namuru's face was clearly visible, almost like a news reporter at a scene giving a description. The weapons were nuclear, he had said.

"To the victory of Japan," Namuru was saying as he pulled something down behind his back.

On the screen the explosion took Kurita by surprise. The detonation was severe enough to cause the transmission to freeze-frame several times as the satellite lost lock over the next second, the frames freezing the specter of Namuru's head being blown apart by his helmet lined with explosives. The screen shook as the vest apparently detonated, blowing the camera backward until the screen view looked up at the sky, then rolled over to look back toward the damaged fence. In a blur men could be made out running toward the fence, when the screen suddenly became snow and static, the static noise loud.

The officer at the control screen turned off the display.

"What happened?" Kurita heard himself say.

"Major Namuru's helmet, utility vest and leggings were fitted with explosives to blow his body apart. That way the Manchurians would have no way to identify him as a Japanese, not that their DNA-coding labs could ever match anything we have. The explosives also blew up his equipment so that there is nothing left for them to have that points to us. He was trained to detonate the explosives on camera so that we could verify that his self-destruction was complete. An excellent mission, Namuru did well," the general said.

"Next time, General, you might consider warning me that I will be witnessing a man's death in real time."

"Sir, it was not real time—it was on a five-minute time-delay."

Kurita realized General Gotoh would never understand. But it was time now for Greater Manchuria to understand. Soon they would know that having offensive nuclear missiles, violating the UN ban, so close to Japan would cost them dearly.

"Call Minister Machiie. Tell him to convene the Defense Security Council in one hour. Bring a disk of Namuru's mission but please edit out the last part."

"Yes, Prime Minister."

"And, General. Make sure your war plan is *very* carefully thought out."

"Yes, sir."

Kurita stared at the general for a long moment, then walked out, trying to banish the images of Namuru's death from his mind, but not succeeding.

# CHAPTER 1

## Chesapeake Bay

Rear Adm. Michael Pacino settled into the seat of the Sea King helicopter and stared out the window, the beautiful vista of the Chesapeake unwinding beneath him.

Pacino was only forty-two years old though he felt much older. He was tall, over six feet two, his frame slim but solid. He was still able to wear the uniforms he had worn when he graduated from the Naval Academy twenty years earlier; and from a distance he could be mistaken for a midshipman. Close-up the illusion continued for a moment because his almost gaunt face still had the shape of his youth, his emerald-green eyes sharp and clear, his pronounced cheekbones presiding over a straight nose and full lips. But then the clues to Pacino's age came into focus—deep lines at the corners of his eyes, crow's feet from staring out to sea or peering through periscopes, face tanned and leathery and losing the resilience it had once had, as if he had spent years in the sun, though actually the coloring was the result of severe frostbite he had suffered in an arctic mission that had gone wrong. The skin of his hands and arms was likewise damaged. His hair was thick but had turned white, not a single dark pigment remained of the jet-black hair he had once had. Rumor had it that the last mission he had commanded, so highly classified that even some of the brass weren't cleared to hear about it, had frightened the last of the black from his head. In any event, the effect of his skin, his white hair, and his gauntness made Pacino's rank of rear admiral seem less odd, since most men of his rank were twenty years older than Pacino.

Pacino's khaki shirt collar displayed the two silver stars of flag rank, and he wore a gold dolphin pin above his left breast pocket, a plain black phenolic name tag above his right pocket reading simply PACINO, and a white-gold Annapolis ring on his left ring finger.

In the seat of the big chopper, he wondered what Richard Donchez wanted to see him about. An hour before he had just taken the first bite of his working dinner with his aide, a young lieutenant named Joanna Stoddard, when his secretary came in.

"Admiral Donchez called from Fort Meade, sir," the secretary said. "He's sending a chopper to pick you up."

"He say what's on his mind?"

"He said he knew you'd ask and told me he wanted to give you an urgent briefing, and that all I could say was Scenario Orange. He said you'd know what that meant."

He had been startled to hear Donchez use the term "Scenario Orange." Adm. Richard Donchez—the "admiral" ceremonial now that Donchez was retired from the Navy—was the director of the National Security Agency, which had responsibility for electronic intelligence, whether by eavesdropping, satellite surveillance or any other nonhuman intelligence methods. The CIA had once had its own spy satellites until the Whitman Act reorganized the intelligence agencies, combining the old Central Intelligence Agency with the Defense Intelligence Agency, the new organization called the Combined Intelligence Agency. There had been momentum enough in the frenzy of government reorganization that Congress threatened to make NSA part of CIA, but Donchez's predecessor had called in favors from Capitol Hill and the result was an independent NSA with a meaty budget, a highly skilled staff and magnificent gadgets, among them the Big Bird III keyhole series satellites and several special operations nuclear subs. The subs gathered intelligence by driving close to a subject's shores and keeping an antenna up to listen for short-range clear transmissions.

It was this that made Pacino wonder what NSA Director Donchez was up to. The subs that reported to NSA could be one reason to call for him, since Donchez had to work closely with USubCom to deal with his special operations ships. But now that the *Dayton* was gathering intel in Tokyo Bay and the *Cincinnati* was doing the same in Port Artom in Greater Manchuria, the current trouble spots of the world, there usually would be little else official that Donchez would come to him about.

Which brought Pacino back to the top secret codewords "Scenario Orange."

*Scenario Orange* was the classified term for the possibility of war between the United States and Japan. War plans against other nations, even allies such as the UK, were routinely written, scrutinized and fed to a DynaCorp Frame 90 supercomputer for simulation and refinement. Until the tension surfaced between Greater Manchuria and Japan, those war plans would be expected to gather dust for the next half-century, but now things were very different.

The helicopter shuddered, the engine noises rising and falling again as the chopper neared Donchez's Fort Meade helipad, the compound nestled in suburban Maryland between Baltimore and Washington. It was getting dark by the time the helicopter made its final approach. The harsh glare of the helipad landing lights flooded into the cabin. Even before the pilot throttled down Pacino got up from his seat, grabbed his hat and held it against the rotor wash, waved to the pilots and stepped out into the cold night. His light working khaki jacket was no match for the cold front that had just moved over the area. At least it was no longer raining, he thought as he jogged to the edge of the pad, where Donchez was waiting, an unlit Havana cigar clenched in one hand, a smile crinkling his aging features.

Pacino smiled back as he approached. Dick Donchez had been Pacino's father's roommate at Annapolis decades before, the two men joining the submarine force together, always home-ported in the same town, usually taking shore duty at the same command. When Pacino was born Donchez and Pacino's father were both at sea, both under the polar icecap. By the time they came home, Pacino was two months old. His earliest memories of his father always seemed to include Donchez. He remembered countless Saturdays spent on his father's ship, the two Pacinos visiting Donchez's boat for a meal. Eventually when Pacino went to Annapolis, his father commanded the *Stingray,* berthed one pier over from Donchez's original *Piranha.*

When Stingray sank in mid-Atlantic from the detonation of her own torpedo—as the official story had it—Pacino was eighteen years old, a plebe at the Naval Academy. It had been Donchez himself who had broken the news to Pacino that the *Stingray* had gone down with all hands, and since then the older man had tried to fashion himself as a mentor and surrogate father to Pacino. Yet for twenty years Pacino had distanced himself from Donchez, perhaps, he admitted, linking Donchez to the sinking because he had been the messenger. Eventually Donchez had become a rear admiral in command of the Atlantic Fleet's submarine force, and hence Pacino's boss during Pacino's first command tour on the USS *Devilfish.*

Donchez had risen to command the service as Chief of Naval Operations, but afterward had left the Navy. There was nowhere upward to go. Donchez had always had an interest in intelligence work and had confided to Pacino that he wouldn't mind an appointment to CIA, which had always been tight with the upper echelons of the Navy, largely because of the spy duty that US subs had done in the past. But CIA was the personal fiefdom of Boswell Farnesworth Leach III, one of the previous president's cronies, not to be replaced for some time. Donchez had been appointed DirNSA, with the implied understanding that someday CIA would be his. That had been eleven months ago.

Donchez looked odd in a business suit, the gold braided stripes that once climbed all the way to his elbows now giving way to the Armani material. The last ten years had worn heavily on Richard Donchez, Pacino thought. It seemed each time he saw him Donchez had shrunk, until he was over a head shorter than Pacino.

He had grown thinner, his shirt collars no longer acquainted with his neck. Pacino remembered that Donchez's hairless head had seemed macho, but now that Donchez was older the baldness added to a look of infirmity that worried Pacino.

Pacino held out his hand to the older man, who pulled him into a bear hug, slapping his back. "Mikey, you look great."

"Uncle Dick, how you doing?"

"Same as always, Mikey. Glad you could come."

"My aide mentioned Scenario Orange." Pacino stated bluntly as they climbed into Donchez's staff car for the ride to his office. "What's going on with Japan?"

"I knew that would get your attention," Donchez said. "We'll talk about it inside the building. It's built against the possibility of eavesdropping. Security is better than the White House."

The limo drove through the dense forest of the complex, low brick buildings every few thousand feet giving the impression of a college campus, the resemblance broken by the fences, the security guards and the large antennae following the satellites overhead.

"Speaking of the White House, sir, how is the new president?"

"She's great, Mikey. I *mean* that. She can be tough, at times too tough, thinks she's Margaret Thatcher, or maybe she thinks she has to look strong as the first elected female President in the history of the country. But I can work with that. Hell, it's easier to back down an aggressive commander in chief than put backbone in a weak one."

The speech had come almost glibly, Pacino thought. The old man probably got asked that question all the time.

The car stopped at the front entrance of building 527, Donchez's new NSA headquarters. The floodlights were on, although it was not yet dark, showcasing the multiwinged building. From the front the protruding entrance wing was a truncated five-story pyramid done in brick and plate glass and copper sheathing, the copper just starting to turn an antique green.

"The copper reminds me of the Academy," Donchez said. "The rest is sort of modern without looking like a cookie-cutter office building."

Pacino looked at the low wide pyramid while following Donchez to the doors. The pyramid face was broken by a long row of plate glass set deep into a horizontal groove. The executive suites, Pacino figured.

"Where the hell did you get budget coverage for this? And it should have taken two years to build and you go from concept to finished building in, what, ten months?"

Donchez didn't smile. "Black programs, Mikey. Ultrasecret. We need the security—the electronic eavesdropping systems of our potential adversaries are getting too good, so we got the budget coverage in a hurry. But believe me, we're getting more than our money's worth here. You'll see."

Donchez's office on the top floor was even more of a showplace than his Chief of Naval Operations suite at the Pentagon. Along the wall were bookshelves filled with dusty volumes and some new books. The wall was covered with framed photographs, Donchez's old submarines, one showing the icepack with a black submarine conning tower broken through the ice, Donchez standing in front of it wearing arctic gear and a baseball cap with scrambled eggs on the brim—the old *Piranha* from the 1970s. Model submarines in expensive cases were set in the four corners of the room. Opposite the windows a bar was set behind wood panels.

Donchez threw out his cigar, pulled a new one from a humidor, walked to the bar and poured three fingers of Jack Daniel's over ice cubes in the highball glass and waved Pacino to one of the leather chairs, putting the drink on a side table and taking the neighboring chair.

"How are you, Mikey? I mean with the divorce at the same time you're trying to get your arms around the Unified Sub Command?"

Pacino knew he didn't come up by helicopter to discuss his divorce or how he felt about his job. He was right. Donchez reached into the table between them and pulled out a small keypad, flashing his fingers across it. The room grew dark as the polarized glass of the windows turned the clear glass black. A panel in the high ceiling opened and a screen came down in front of them. The room lights dimmed as a projection television flashed the emblem of the National Security Administration.

The image of the NSA dissolved to be replaced by a map of the north Pacific Rim. The banana-shaped islands of Japan were color-coded orange. The islands zoomed in while Donchez began with basics on Japan, facts about Prime Minister Hosaka Kurita, a brief history of Japan from the Shoguns to World War II through the trade problems of the late twentieth century to the isolation and trade wars of the twenty-first century's first decade. The briefing seemed to drag on.

"What about Scenario Orange?" Pacino asked.

"Part of the problem is Greater Manchuria," Donchez said, not directly answering, "but I'll get to that in a minute."

Greater Manchuria, Pacino knew, was a republic recently formed out of a chunk of land from Russia and another from China. Its ultranationalistic dictator was a problem for continental Asia, but a problem, so far as Pacino knew, with no connection with Japan.

Donchez went on. "If we look at today's global situation, it is very tense, Mikey. Scenario Orange is, I think, just over the horizon. We're going to have to fight them, and sooner than later. Here's why. Start with the lousy relations between us. Japan made the first mistake—their move for world economic conquest led them to try and buy too damn much. The final straw was their play to take over AT&T, IBM, Intel, Microsoft and General Motors. Jesus. And people once complained about hotels and movie studios and Rockefeller Center."

Pacino nodded. The news had broken one Wednesday morning just two years before, when overnight the Japanese government, through MITI, the Ministry of International Trade and Industry, had engineered a whirlwind takeover of the five most strategic corporations in America—and how they did it was a stunning lesson in secrecy and deception, the Japanese buying stock through third and fourth parties over months until the day they announced that their interest in the big five was controlling.

"The Fair Trade Bill that shut that takeover down cold was a slap in the face to Japan. You know how big they are on face. They apparently thought things would be business as usual. Suddenly anything with more than 10 percent Japanese content was illegal to import into the United States. Japanese goods might as well have been illegal drugs. We thought we were sending Japan a strong signal. They misinterpreted it, or at least they took strong exception to it."

"They landed on their feet, they went deeper into Asian and African markets and Russia is a prime market for them. The Russians would do anything to trade with Japan," Pacino said.

"They did *not* land on their feet, Mikey. They were hurt bad. They are mad as hell, and their anger is directed at the US. Even though what they did with the covert takeover attempts of our industries was unethical—not to mention damned hostile—the Japanese didn't and don't want to see it that way. To them our response was the economic equivalent of a nuclear bomb dropped by America—a total trade ban on Japanese goods in the US. It was a big hit in the pocket too. The US was a sort of cash cow for them. It went away overnight and no other markets can replace that, including Russia, which is still too poor to do important business with Japan."

"So far you're talking economics, Dick."

"All that historic national aggression we've seen before from Japan has been channeled once again into a military buildup. The manufacturing capability that once built cars for sale to America has been converted to defense. The so-called Self Defense Force—they don't call it an army, since an army is outlawed by their constitution—has increased in manpower by a factor of a dozen. The force's air wing has ten squadrons of the most advanced fighter in the air, the Firestar. And you know about their navy, the Maritime Self Defense Force. They were building a nuclear submarine for export sale five years ago, the Destiny class. Then they began building an improved version for themselves, the Destiny II class. They've built over a dozen of them. They're the most capable supersub since our Seawolf class. But from the little I hear from Leach at CIA, the Destiny II boats are head and shoulders better than Seawolf. And your aging Los Angeles-class subs are no match for it."

"I know, Admiral. But we could only get funding for two more Seawolf-class ships, the *Barracuda* and the *Piranha.* Until the new class comes off the drawing boards that's all we'll get."

"You'd better listen up, then, Mikey. There's worse news. Apparently there is now a Destiny III-class submarine. The Destiny III is unmanned, run by a computer."

"I had a quick briefing on that. From what I understand, it'll never work. The problems are endless. My people tell me it'll never go to sea."

"I hope you're right, but if anyone can make a robotic submarine work, it's the Japanese."

Pacino was restless. The briefing, troubling as it was, didn't seem to justify Scenario Orange.

"So, Dick, we had a trade war. The Japanese lost and have turned to other markets, including Russia. They've built up their military while ours has dwindled. That's not enough—"

"*Listen* to me and listen good."

Donchez clicked his remote angrily, and the map returned to an overhead view of the Far East. The new nation of Greater Manchuria, shown in blue, faced Japan across the Sea of Japan, the blue giant extending from North Korea north to the Sea of Okhotsk far north of Japan's Hokkaido Island. The northern island in Japan's chain, the disputed island of Sakhalin that had been Russian territory, was now part of Greater Manchuria. Greater Manchuria also included what had once been called Manchuria, a part of northeast China and far east Russia, but was now known as Greater Manchuria since it also comprised the Russian territory fronting the Sea of Japan, the slice of land once called Sikhote Alin, as far south as Vladivostok, now renamed Artom. Greater Manchuria was a state the size of Mexico hovering off Japan's west coast.

Immediately south of Greater Manchuria the state of East China, color-coded white, extended from North Korea south along the coastline to Vietnam, the strip of land 1000 miles wide, the larger country of West China in red still three-quarters the size of the former communist China had been before East China and Greater Manchuria had split off.

The screen zoomed in on Greater Manchuria, to the capital city of Changashan, then came down in satellite's-eye-view of the city center to the Presidential Palace. The image froze and bled into the face of President Len Pei Poom, who looked startlingly young to be the dictator of the new nation. He wore an officer's cap and a dark military uniform, but otherwise looked ordinary, someone who wouldn't be looked at twice on the street

"Len Pei Poom, Greater Manchuria's president, and his new republic are getting on a lot of nerves lately. I don't know if you knew this," Donchez said, reaching into his humidor and offering Pacino a Havana cigar, "since somehow we've been able to keep it from the press, but we've been bankrolling Greater Manchuria through Israel for the last five months."

"Why?" Pacino asked, taking the flame from Donchez's lighter. "I thought we were tight with East China since they broke off from the reds, and the East Chinese aren't too friendly with Len now."

Donchez lit his own cigar. "We want to maintain ties to East China, *and* Russia, *and* the Greater Manchurians. The balance of power is crucial to our interests in Asia. We don't want one big power there bullying everyone else and turning eastward toward us. Japan was weakened by the trade war, but now we see them building up their military, and now that Greater Manchuria is established, the Japanese see Greater Manchuria as a threat. Let me put it to you like this—Japan's aggressiveness and military hardware are the gasoline. Greater Manchuria, as a perceived threat to Japan, is the firewood. If we get a spark, we are in trouble."

"Wait a minute, why would Japan see Greater Manchuria as a threat?"

"Same reason they hated Korea. It's based on geography, politics, national psychology. Japan is highly xenophobic—they've *always* been distrustful of outsiders. And now this Len character surfaces, unites this nation right across the pond from Japan, and the Japanese are worried."

"That he'll invade Japan? Greater Manchuria's a land power, not a sea power. Len doesn't even own a canoe, that I know about. And he has his hands full with East and West China and Russia. What would he care about Japan?"

"The question is, what does Tokyo think of his intentions toward Japan? And it's more concrete than that. Did you know about the possibility of Len having nuclear weapons?"

"I read some of the speculation in the papers, but nukes have been illegal for years in Asia. I don't believe in ghosts or nuclear weapons in Asia."

"Leach of CIA thinks there are. Not ghosts, missiles. In Greater Manchuria. Leach was certain that the only way Len in Greater Manchuria was able to break off from the Russians and the East Chinese was by discovering a cache of nuclear-tipped SS-34 missiles. We were ordered by the president to find out. We found nothing. I concluded that Len had no nukes, *but* Len *did* manage to keep the wolves at bay with not much of an army. How?"

"I hope you have an answer to that question, Dick."

"Mikey, I think I made a mistake. I think Len *does* have nukes. And I think Japan, already threatened by the very idea of Greater Manchuria, knows about it. That's the match that's going to set Asia on fire. And it could involve us. Scenario Orange."

"Back up, Dick. *Why* do you think Len has nukes?"

"Yesterday, just as I was telling Warner's cabinet that Len didn't have nukes, we picked up a flurry of transmissions. We broke them all." The screen moved closer to Greater Manchuria, descending toward the terrain like a spacecraft returning to earth, the view closing in on Lake Ozero Chanka, a sixty-mile-wide lake set inland by a hundred miles. "This is the railhead town of Tamga. This place has mostly been abandoned. Or so it would seem. This looks like a perimeter fence and it surrounds some kind of armed camp, one we previously cataloged as closed, so we didn't pay any attention to it until all the transmissions came in." Satellite photos flashed by as Donchez spoke, one of them an overhead view of a compound with a perimeter fence and a large mound of earth, a sort of humped plateau. "The interception was lengthy. It boiled down to the Greater Manchurians going berserk that this place, this compound, was broken into. There were two repeated messages from the capital in Changashan asking if the 'stored units' were tampered with, and two replies that the units were fine. As to who broke in, the messages said it was a human agent who committed suicide."

"Possibly one of Leach's people?"

"No. I would have been in on a HUMINT penetration inside Greater Manchuria, especially a suicide mission, which we're not exactly big on commissioning."

"So who?"

"One of Kurita's men. The suicide at the end puts his marker on it. I'm old enough to remember when the Japanese invented the suicide assault."

"Did you check this place? Tamga?"

"Nothing we have can tell if there are nukes stored there. Short of going in like Kurita did, we won't be able to tell. And Kurita won't say."

"So what now?"

"First we make sure we're right. You ever watch *Conspiracy: Exposed* on UPX?"

"Sure. That nutcase Zap Zaprinski. I've never seen a journalist quite like him, if journalist is the word. What's that got to do with nuclear weapons in Greater Manchuria?"

"We're getting *Conspiracy: Exposed* to go into Changashan and try to get Len Pei Poom to admit to having nukes."

"How the hell are you going to do that? I mean, you are the director of the goddamned NSA but Hollywood doesn't care that you need intelligence. What's going on here, Uncle Dick?"

"Len will see Zaprinski."

"But Zap Zaprinski is a clown. He's shock journalism."

"Exactly. But Len doesn't spend much time watching American TV. Chances are neither do his advisors. And he's got bigger problems than who interviews him. Another thing—we don't *want* to send a serious journalist in, some Mike Wallace go-for-the-jugular reporter who'll antagonize Len and miss getting the scoop on the missiles."

"So you send in Zap. Will the UPX network let him go?"

"It's arranged. So, now, will Len talk?"

"The way I see it, the reason to reveal nuclear weapons would be to deter Russia and East China from attacking Greater Manchuria. But the reason to keep it quiet is more compelling," Pacino said. "If Len reveals nukes, Russia or East China might try to take them out. My guess is Len mugs in front of the camera to get sympathy from the West and holds his cards close to his chest on the alleged nukes. And at the end of the day we'll know nothing."

"But he may suspect that someone hostile to him knows already, based on the break-in. If so, we think he'll talk."

"So he talks. What does that do for us?"

"It should keep Japan from attacking the missiles, from attacking Greater Manchuria. If Len opens up to the world that he has nukes, the Japanese may pull back and we prevent a war."

"What if Len keeps his mouth shut? Or if we're too late?"

Donchez nodded. "Worst-case scenario, Mikey. Japan attacks Greater Manchuria. The world is sympathetic to Greater Manchuria and afraid of Japan. The West is called on to stop Japan. And next thing we know, we're up against a shooting war."

"Wait a minute," Pacino said. "Let's look at this another way. Nuclear missiles in Asia are bad news. Why would Japan attacking them be such a bad idea? Maybe we should just let them do that."

"Mikey . . . a little history. If Japan attacks Greater Manchuria, *and* they succeed, what next? Remember the

1930s? Japan needed resources and oil, so they took over almost all of Asia. If the world sits by and watches them attack Len, who's next? Korea? East China? They have the best military in Asia. Once they have momentum . . . the dumbest, most suicidal thing in the world would be to let them get away with this."

Donchez stood. "Mikey, you'd better stand by. Get your submarine force ready. You may be in a fight with the Destiny subs sometime in the next year, or sooner. There's no telling."

Pacino stood and Donchez started to walk with him to the door. "Where are you going? Back to Norfolk?"

"First I'm going to Groton. I've got something going on with the new *Piranha,* the Seawolf-class boat coming out of new construction."

Pacino knew Donchez would be interested, since he had commanded the first *Piranha,* hull number SSN-637, back in the late sixties.

"*Piranha.* I guess it's okay they reuse the good names. Still, it isn't the same. What's going on with her, anyway?"

"I'm outfitting her with Vortex missiles."

The Vortex had been Donchez's brainchild when he had been Chief of Naval Operations. The program had been cancelled after billions had been spent, the missile considered too lethal to its own firing platform. The test sub that had fired the missile had been Donchez's old decommissioned *Piranha,* now in pieces at the bottom of the Bahamas test range, the Vortex test-launch having blown the old sub apart. The missile worked, but a way to launch it from a submarine had never been found.

"Dumb move," Donchez said, shaking his head. "The firing ship always blows up. You should know that—"

"I do. But there's nothing wrong with the Vortex missile. It needs an outside launcher tube. I'm going to mount ten of them on the outside of *Piranha*'s hull."

"It may still blow a hole in the ship's hull."

"We'll test it when her new skipper shows up. I've scouted out a terrific captain to run the *Piranha.* You'd love this guy. Blood and guts. Smokes Havanas. Drinks Jack Daniel's. And he can drive a submarine like no one since"—Pacino paused, realizing he was about to say, "my father."

"Since you, Mikey, is what you're saying."

"Dick, this guy could kick my rear end."

"No way. What's his name?"

"Phillips, Bruce Phillips."

"I know him. Or at least his family. He could buy and sell us. Guy's got tons of money, old family money. And he gives it up to drive a sewer pipe."

"I'm about to put him under a couple tons per square inch in my attack trainer. And I'm going to simulate that he's up against a Japanese Destiny II class sub. I'm taking wagers that he'll come out on top."

"Well, I hope he's as good as you say he is. I wouldn't want my sub's namesake going to a paper-pushing type. So many of Wells's skippers couldn't shoot the broadside of a barn. You'd better clean up that force."

They were at the ornate entrance to the building. The black Lincoln waited, tailpipe vapors wafting over the car in the light winter wind. The two men began the checkout process at the security desk.

"I hope you know what you're doing, Michael." Pacino stared. Donchez had never called him that. "That Vortex missile's bad news."

"You know, Uncle Dick, I really miss going to sea," Pacino said, changing the subject. "Fleet command is nothing compared to conning a sub in combat."

"With all the tension in Japan, Scenario Orange may not be so far off."

"I have to doubt it, sir. But if the balloon went up and we got into a hot war at sea, I'd still be cooling my heels at USubCom headquarters."

"Not necessarily. Get your deputy to run the show landside and then go to sea with one of the boats. If you're going to command in a war, Mikey, you can't do it from the rear."

"I'm tempted to do as you say, but it wouldn't work, not with Wadsworth in charge."

"Watch out for Tony Wadsworth. He doesn't like you. Just another reason to take your show to sea. Sometimes submarines don't have time to come to periscope depth to communicate. It could give you the independence you'd need."

"I'll consider it, sir."

"Admiral Donchez, sir," one of the security guards called. "Urgent call coming in from the White House switchboard."

"Looks like you'll have to find your own way out, Mikey. Good luck."

Pacino shook the admiral's hand and forced a smile, ducking quickly into the staff car. The older Donchez got the harder it became to say goodbye to him, Pacino thought. He never knew if it was to be the last time he'd see the old man.

The new headquarters building faded behind in darkness and the trees. Pacino was so lost in thought about commanding a fleet from a submarine that he barely noticed when the helicopter took off and Fort Meade shrank below him.

# CHAPTER 2

**UNIFIED SUBMARINE COMMAND TRAINING CENTER**
**IMPROVED 688-CLASS ATTACK SUBMARINE**
**CONTROL ROOM SIMULATOR**
**NORFOLK, VIRGINIA**

Adm. Michael Pacino looked up from the briefing table, the chart computer display on it showing Tokyo Bay. Comdr. Bruce Phillips, the commanding officer of the 688-class submarine *Greeneville* walked in, looking tense.

"Commander Phillips," Pacino said, rising to his feet and shaking the younger man's hand. "Good to meet you. I know you're anxious to get on with it. I just want to let you know I want to see you succeed here. This *isn't* a test to remove you from command, as the rumors have it. I just want to see how you fight your ship. Are you ready?"

"Yessir."

"The scenario we'll be running is you against a Destiny II-class Japanese attack submarine outbound from Tokyo Bay. The Destiny is on the way to the deep Pacific to try and sink a US surface-action group. Your mission is to sink him before he can get by you and, obviously, to survive. Which won't be easy, because the Destiny II is one of the best there is. Your USS *Greeneville* is an older 688-class ship, but I'm convinced you can beat this guy."

"I'll try, sir."

"I'll be there only to observe. It's your deal. Good luck."

* * *

The announcement came over the loudspeaker.

> "OWN SHIP IS USS *GREENVILLE*, SUBMERGED OPERATIONS, EIGHTY NAUTICAL MILES SOUTHWEST OF TOKYO BAY. IN THIS SCENARIO, HOSTILITIES HAVE BROKEN OUT BETWEEN THE U.S. AND JAPAN. OWN SHIP'S MISSION IS TO SINK OUTBOUND DESTINY NUCLEAR ATTACK SUBMARINE COMING OUT OF TOKYO BAY EN ROUTE TO THE PACIFIC. BEGIN SIMULATION."

Admiral Pacino looked around. Something seemed wrong. He sensed it the moment he walked into the darkened control room. He tried to identify the source of his uneasiness but his thoughts were interrupted by the voice of the officer of the deck announcing, "The admiral is in the control room."

"Carry on," Pacino said, looking up to the periscope stand where Comdr. Bruce Phillips presided over his battlestations crew. "Captain Phillips, please go ahead."

"Aye, Admiral," Phillips said, turning away from Pacino to look at the control-room displays below him.

The room was completely dark, rigged for black, lit only by the backwash of light from the firecontrol console screens and the instrument faces mounted on the ship-control console, the periscope stand and at various points in the overhead. As Pacino's eyes adjusted to the darkness, he could make out the watchstanders crammed into a room the size of a small den. Three were in the ship-control station up forward, the seats and console arrangement looking like it had been transplanted from a 747 cockpit, except that instead of windows there were rows of instruments monitoring the nuclear submarine's course, speed, depth, angle, engine speed and control surface positions. Two men sat in leather seats on either side of a central console crammed with rows of switches and knobs, each man holding a control yoke exactly like that of an airplane. Behind the console an older heavier man leaned forward, supervising the first two. To the left was a large wraparound panel where another crewman sat facing rows of dials and switches, two large monitor screens set in the panel dimly flashing system-status displays with diagrams of pipes and tanks.

Behind the cockpit setup was the elevated periscope stand, the platform rising eighteen inches off the surrounding deck with polished stainless-steel railing enclosing it. The stand was called "the conn," since the officer of the deck controlled the ship from the platform. The two stainless steel poles penetrating the stand were the periscopes, both useless since the sub was too deep to see anything but darkness. On the conn Captain Phillips and his officer of the deck, a young lieutenant, stood side by side, the lieutenant unconsciously mimicking the older captain's stance and square-jawed squint at the room below.

On the starboard side of the conn was a long row of consoles, each with a television monitor screen. The row was the attack center, where the machines figured out where the enemy submarine was and programmed weapons to take him out. When Pacino had commanded a submarine the consoles were called the firecontrol system, before the separate ship's computers were linked and integrated, the row now part of a combat-control suite. Pacino looked at the displays on the console screens, surprisingly empty.

Aft of the periscope pedestal were two plotting tables, one used for navigation, the chart showing Tokyo Roads, the small islands and the main traffic approach channel into Tokyo Bay. The ship's position was marked with a glowing dot off the island of Inamba-Jima, barely over the hundred-fathom curve, very shallow water for a deep-draft submarine. The second table was crowded with two officers and an enlisted plotter, staring at a blank white sheet of tracing paper since there was no enemy to track.

On the port side of the periscope stand were rows of navigation equipment. Set into the overhead were radio control panels, television screens, chronometer indicators, cables and valves. One of the television monitors between the ship control area and the attack center was dark, since it played the view out of the periscope. The second was above the middle firecontrol console display and was lit in red and lined with what looked like vertical scratches—the sonar display repeater. Pacino looked at the screen, which showed that the sea around them was empty.

The crew seemed aware of him, yet was ignoring him, which gave him an odd feeling of being almost invisible.

Pacino glanced around the room again, beginning to feel plugged into the tactical situation, at one with the sea and the ship, the warm feeling he had once felt in his own control room on the *Seawolf,* but the warmth stopped as he realized that never again would he command a nuclear submarine, a job now reserved for the young. He looked at the captain, Comdr. Bruce Phillips, and envied him.

In stark contrast to Pacino, Phillips was short, with crewcut blond hair and a muscular build. The crewcut Pacino understood, since it was plain even in the dim light of the room that Phillips' hair had been receding. Phillips had shaved it all off close to the scalp some weeks before, but it seemed to look more natural now that it had grown a sixteenth of an inch. Phillips was in his late thirties and single, the latter unheard of for a submarine captain with all the social obligations of the job.

But then, Phillips had never fit the type, Pacino thought. He wasn't the conventional older, spare-tire-carrying family-man commanding officer. Phillips was independently wealthy, from an old Philadelphia Main Line family. The money, Pacino thought, might have been in part responsible for what made him different. He had a reputation for lack of caution, not so much uncaring as dismissive of safety regulations, impatient with bureaucracy, inattentive to fleet politics. The previous force commander, Adm. Dick Wells, had put it negatively to Pacino: "Phillips might at first seem like a good commander but he's unreliable, inconsistent and has an *attitude.* He'll screw something up and sink someday. He ran aground two months ago and the investigation is still ongoing. So far it looks like it was just bad luck, a double equipment malfunction, but bad luck follows sloppy sailors. I was going to recommend to the board of inquiry that we can him. There are too many good submarine officers out there to waste time on a marginal performer. Well, he's your problem now."

"How did he get command in the first place if he's so sloppy?" Pacino had asked.

"Usual story. Inflated fitness reports, he knew somebody on the selection board for commander, kissed up to his squadron commander. He'll snow you under until you look at the repair reports. His equipment is always breaking. His ship is dirty. When you ask him why, he just chomps on a cigar and squints at you."

Pacino wasn't sure whether to buy Wells's opinion, discard it, or see the same facts in a different light. Ten years before, someone on fleet staff might well have described Pacino himself that way. Except Pacino had never been sloppy; his equipment had been functional if not perfect, his decks tidy if not spotless, the Navy paperwork completed if not enjoyed. There was a distinction between bold and reckless. The question was, which was Phillips?

As if hearing his thoughts, Phillips squinted over at Pacino as he dug out a fat cigar from his khaki shirt pocket and put it in his mouth. He looked away to the sonar display, then reached for a phone. His voice was quiet, but Pacino picked up his conversation.

"Sonar, Captain, I'm about to brief the battlestations crew. Interrupt me if you get a detect." He put the phone back in its cradle and scanned the room, clearing his throat.

"Attention in the firecontrol team," he announced, his voice not deep but rock steady, grabbing the ears of every man in the room without having to shout. "Since the declaration of war with Japan on Friday the approach to Tokyo Bay has been clean. However, satellite photographic intelligence from an hour ago showed a Japanese Destiny Type-Two attack submarine getting underway from the Yokosuka piers. We suspect that his mission is to attack the USS *Ronald Reagan* carrier battle group outbound from Pearl Harbor. Our Op Order came in with the intelligence brief. Our mission is to sink the Destiny II immediately upon detection."

Phillips looked around the room, put the cigar in his

teeth and gave the rest of his speech talking around the cigar.

"Let me remind you all of the Destiny II's armament. He is probably carrying the new model of Nagasaki torpedo. It's a dozen tons of weapon, goes seventy-five knots compared to our forty, has an endurance of an hour and can sink us if it detonates within a hundred yards of our hull. There will be no outrunning that son of a bitch. So let's stay alert and put this guy on the bottom before he hears us. Officer of the deck, rig ship for ultraquiet. That's all, folks. Carry on."

Pacino put on a spare headset to listen in on the control-room conversation. He couldn't have said it better, he thought, looking up at the sonar repeater set high in the overhead of the conn above the middle firecontrol console. The trace coming down the screen was new.

"Conn, Sonar," crackled in Pacino's ear from the sonar supervisor, who manned the watch in the closet-sized sonar room forward of control. "New sonar contact on broadband sonar bearing zero one five, designate Sierra One."

"Sonar, Captain, aye," Phillips snapped, squinting. Pacino looked at the navigation display, realizing that bearing 015 pointed to the outbound traffic separation scheme from Yokosuka. Phillips met his eyes for a moment, nodded.

"Conn, Sonar, new contact Sierra One is operating on the surface, loud wake noises, no turn-count from his screw."

"Captain, aye," Phillips said, looking at the bearing line of the contact on the sonar screen set into the overhead above the conn. "Why no turn-count?"

"Sir, the screw appears to be a turbine-type screw, ducted propulsor. Contact is tentatively classified as a warship, submarine type, Destiny class, running on the surface. Conn, Sonar, we now have an increase in signal. Contact is putting out transients."

"Is it possible he's submerging?"

"Captain, Sonar, yes."

"Let's designate contact Sierra One as Target One, Destiny II-class attack submarine."

Phillips barked orders to the firecontrol team—weapon presets for the torpedoes in tubes one and two, speed changes, depth changes, calling for the bearing rate to the target. The ship settled down to a momentary quiet as the sonar and computer gathered data on the outbound Japanese submarine.

Pacino glanced quickly at the chronometer display above the firecontrol consoles, his experience telling him to turn now to get the second leg on the target, to zig zag the opposite direction and see how the direction to the contact, his bearing, changed. Pacino ached to give the order himself, when finally Phillips called out, "Helm, right fifteen degrees rudder, steady course east. Sonar, turning to the north."

"Helm, aye, my rudder's right fifteen, passing two eight zero."

"Conn, Sonar, aye," the sonar supervisor's anxious voice crackled in Pacino's headphones. "Captain, you're pointing the target, sir."

"I *know* fix that, goddamnit," Phillips said.

Pacino made a mental note to talk to Phillips about two things—that pointing the ship toward the contact when the range was unknown could cause a collision, and was a violation of fleet regulations, and second, that he'd better get his crew used to violating fleet regs, because in wartime the only rules were the ones the captain made up along the way. Obviously the sonar chief hadn't figured that out, but it was Phillips's job to prepare him. But then, how would he himself as a submarine skipper, the way he was six years ago, perform under the harsh light of an admiral's eye? Perhaps the same as Phillips, perhaps worse.

"Conn, Sonar, loss of contact! Target One has shut down, last bearing zero one eight."

"Dammit," Phillips mumbled. "What the hell happened?"

Phillips's executive officer hurried into the room. Lt. Comdr. Roger Whatney, Royal Navy, was on exchange while an American was second-in-command of a *Trafalgar*-class sub, all part of a pilot program to bring the two English-speaking nuclear submarine navies into a closer cultural alignment, one of Pacino's innovations since taking over the reorganized fleet. Whatney was short and slight enough to make Phillips look a giant. He was quick to smile, easy going, his enthusiasm a trademark. Today, however, he looked deflated, haggard. He stood next to Phillips.

"Where the hell did he go, Coordinator?" During battlestations Whatney would become the firecontrol coordinator, responsible to Phillips for the target's firecontrol solution. For the duration of the battle Whatney would cease to be called "XO"—shorthand for executive officer and would be simply "Coordinator."

"We lost the target, sir? Looks like he pulled the plug and went silent."

"Here's your headset. You look like crap."

"Thanks, Captain. A close encounter with pneumonia."

Phillips bent over the officer at the firecontrol console and spun the knobs set into the horizontal skirt of the panel. The lines on the display rotated and wiggled. "Coordinator, I'm thinking of putting a torpedo down the bearing line to his old position."

"Sir, loss of contact was two minutes ago. At his range, he could drive off-track before the torpedo got there even if he didn't hear it. And if he did, we're done for."

"Yeah, you're right. Sonar, any detect?"

"Captain, Sonar, no."

The room waited for the outbound Japanese sub to come closer, for him to get louder. Pacino watched the chronometer, thinking that he was probably going thirty-five knots at a range of sixty miles, with a detection range to the Destiny pessimistically at five miles, meaning it could be well over an hour before he got this far out. What would *he* do if he were in command. Drive in closer, he thought.

"Helm, left ten degrees rudder, steady course zero one eight, all ahead standard. Attention in the firecontrol team. We've lost Target One when he submerged. Present intentions are to get closer to him, get a quick detect, then drive off the bearing line to get a one-minute range, then fire a Mark 50 selected to immediate enable. After weapon launch we will clear datum to the south at flank and monitor the situation on the caboose array and the towed array end-beam. Carry on."

Gutsy, Pacino thought. This would be interesting. The time on the chronometer unwound for ten minutes until sonar called on the headsets.

"Conn, Sonar, reacquisition Target One, bearing zero one one."

"Helm, left three degrees rudder, steady course three zero zero. Commencing leg one when steady, Coordinator. You've got thirty seconds."

"Aye, sir."

"Sir, steady course three zero zero," the helmsman called from the ship-control panel.

"Mark leg one, Coordinator." Phillips tapped the soggy-ended cigar against his leg. Thirty seconds later the bearings were coming into the firecontrol screen and forming a rough line down the display.

"Got a curve, sir, recommend maneuver," Whatney said.

"Helm, right ten degrees rudder, steady course east."

Pacino waited, wondering how long it would be before the outbound Destiny heard them, wondering how long it would take a Japanese commander to put a torpedo in the water.

"Come on, Coordinator, you've got thirty seconds when steady."

"Steady course east, sir."

"Very well, Helm." Phillips's face seemed to be relaxing, lost in the situation, now seemingly unaware of Pacino's observation. "Weps, confirm torpedo settings tube one." The weapons officer sat at the far right console, the panel replete with function keys and a large silver lever.

"Tube one, outer door open, weapon warm, immediate enable set, medium speed active snake—"

Whatney interrupted. "Gotta curve, Captain, and a firing solution, range seven thousand yards, target speed thirty knots, target course one nine zero. Recommend immediate launch."

"Firing point procedures, tube one," Phillips called.

"Ship ready," the lieutenant next to Phillips reported.

"Weapon ready," the weapons officer said.

"Solution ready," from Whatney.

"Shoot on generated bearing," Phillips commanded, shoving the cigar into his mouth.

"Set," the officer at the middle firecontrol panel called, sending the target solution to the torpedo.

"Standby," the weapons officer said from the weapons console, taking the large silver trigger all the way to the left.

"Shoot," Phillips ordered.

*"Fire!"* the weapons officer said, his voice excited as he pulled the trigger to the far right.

Nothing happened. Pacino now realized what had been wrong when he had first walked into the room. The crew around him seemed not to notice.

"Tube one fired electrically, Captain," the weapons officer said.

"Unit one, normal launch," sonar reported. "Unit is active."

"Let's get out of here, Coordinator. Sonar, prepare to monitor the caboose array, we're putting the target in the baffles. Helm, all ahead flank, right ten degrees rudder, steady course south."

Pacino waited for the deck to tremble from the power of the main engines running at flank speed, but the deck was whisper-quiet.

"Sonar, Captain, what have you got on the caboose array?"

"Captain, own ship's unit is still in search mode. We no longer hold Target One on the caboose array. He's also dipping below threshold on the towed array end-beam. Loss of contact, Target One."

Phillips and Whatney shared a dour look. There was nothing now for them to do but get away from the Destiny and hope the torpedo hit him before he realized what had happened.

"Conn, Sonar, torpedo in the water! Rough bearing one two zero."

Pacino felt the acid hit his stomach. The Destiny had just fired a torpedo, a large-bore Nagasaki Mod Alpha.

They had almost no chance of evading the torpedo. It would be easier to outrun a bullet aimed at your head from a foot away. Pacino concentrated on Phillips to see if he would continue to function.

Phillips reached up to the sonar-repeater monitor and repeatedly stabbed a fixed function key, the monitor view changing with each button press until the caboose-array display flashed up. The caboose array was a recent innovation designed to allow the sub to hear contacts directly behind, since the machinery and screw made too much noise for the spherical sonar array in the nose cone to listen astern. The towed array, a long cable towing a ropelike set of sonar sensors designed to pick up narrow-frequency sound energy, was some help but was not intended to hear broadband irregular noises such as the screw vortex from a torpedo running due astern. The caboose array was installed to fill the gap. The teardrop-shaped sonar hydrophone assembly was about a half-meter across, big enough to detect some noises but not accurate in bearing because of the wiggling it did at the end of the towed array cable. And pulling the caboose caused drag on the ship, slowing her down.

Phillips would now need to make a decision—to continue to "drag the onion," as pulling the caboose array during a flank run was called, or get rid of the unit and go deaf, unable to know if the torpedo was still on his tail but at least speeding up the ship.

"Sonar, Captain, jettison the caboose and retract the towed array. Maneuvering, all ahead emergency flank at one four zero percent reactor power. Weapons officer, shut the outer doors to tubes one and two."

"We'll have to cut the wire, Captain. We won't know if the torpedo detonated on Target One."

Phillips made a sour face. "Cut the goddamned wire."

"Aye, sir."

"Conn, Maneuvering," a new voice said on the headphones, "making emergency flank turns now and one three seven percent reactor power, limited by overheating port and starboard main engine forward bearing temperatures."

"Cut in more aux seawater to the lube oil cooler," Phillips ordered.

"Sir, the valves are wide open, we're at max cooling."

"You got electrical loads running on the battery?"

"Motor generators are at max, Captain, we can't pick up any more kilowatts."

"Attention in the firecontrol team," Phillips said, his forehead beading up with sweat. His armpits were stained now, the cigar gone, a rivulet of sweat gathering liquid as it ran down his brow to his nose. "The Destiny has counterfired a torpedo. We've done everything we can to run from it at max speed. There is nothing more we can do except hope the Japanese torpedo runs out of fuel. Meanwhile, at least we have the pleasure of knowing our own Mark 50 is chasing the Destiny just as his weapon is chasing us. Even if he gets us, he's going down." Phillips stared at the room, the watchstanders staring at him, waiting for him to say the words that there was some way out of this. "That is all. Carry on."

Pacino looked down. The ride was still whisper quiet. Quiet until the sound of the incoming torpedo sonar beeped into the room. The enemy torpedo sonar was a high-frequency screamer, the pulses pounding into the skull of every crew member, the sound a terrifying screech. Suddenly the pulses changed to a siren tone, wailing up and down in frequency, getting louder.

Soon there was another sound—of the torpedo's screw whooshing through the water, the torpedo incredibly close to be able to hear that. There were perhaps only ten seconds to detonation.

"Conn, Sonar, torpedo is close, detonation any minute."

A loud, resounding boom roared through the room.

Bright fluorescent lights flashed, clicked and held, the light flooding into the control room. The firecontrol consoles, sonar repeater, chronometer and ship control instruments all went out. A huge voice spoke from the overhead.

"TORPEDO IMPACT. OWN SHIP DESTROYED. END SIMULATION. COMMANDER, WE'RE READY FOR YOU IN THE DEBRIEF THEATER."

# CHAPTER 3

**UNIFIED SUBMARINE COMMAND TRAINING CENTER**
**IMPROVED 688-CLASS ATTACK SUBMARINE**
**CONTROL ROOM SIMULATOR**
**NORFOLK, VIRGINIA**

Phillips was soaked in sweat, blinking in the light, the sudden fracturing of his reality confusing even though he knew it had been an exercise. Slowly, as if emerging from a darkened movie theater to bright daylight, the watchstanders left the room through the aft door, down a cinder block corridor to a small projection room. As they left it finally came to Pacino what had been wrong with the control room during the exercise—the *noise* was wrong. It just hadn't sounded like a real submarine. And the deck had never shaken during the high-speed maneuvers when it should have been trembling violently. He would have that changed later. The new attack simulator was another of his projects. Before, there had been attack trainers but they were just firecontrol consoles in a dark room. This simulator had the cramped arrangements of all the panels, the pipes and valves and feel of the real thing, but until he could pipe in the sound of a real control room and install vibration cells under the deck it would still just be another attack trainer.

When the men were seated, Pacino standing in front of the screen, the lights went out and the screen flashed up the view of Tokyo Bay. A blue dot appeared at the bottom southwest of the traffic entrance, a blue line trailing behind it showing where it had been.

"The blue dot is own ship," Pacino said, standing at

the screen with an electronic pointer arrow indicating the dot. "While you were waiting here the orange dot makes its way southwest out of the bay. As you suspected, it was a Destiny II class. Nice work in sonar, by the way. Commander Phillips was correct to attempt to get a shot out at the outbound unit when it was on the surface, since Destiny would have been deaf to an incoming torpedo, but I had her pull the plug early. As you can see, once Destiny is at sea submerged she is very quiet."

"I should have gotten the shot off earlier," Phillips said.

"Maybe," Pacino said, "but that wasn't the purpose of the exercise. I wanted you to see what you're up against when that unit goes under. It's quiet as a ghost. Anyway, you reacquired the Destiny here. Freeze frame, Chief." Pacino's arrow pointed to the orange dot, much closer, its history track longer now. "Give me an elapsed time, Chief, and pipe in the control-room conversations." The view froze and an elapsed time came up on the screen, showing *00:00:00.* "Okay, let's watch and then analyze it when it's over."

Pacino stepped back, watching the subs maneuver, the orange Japanese Destiny continuing southwest in a line, the blue US sub going west, Phillips's voice *commencing leg one when steady, Coordinator you've got thirty seconds.* The blue sub turned to the east, taking some time to come around, while the Japanese sub got closer and closer. *Shoot on generated bearing . . . set . . . standby . . . shoot . . . fire! Tube one fired electrically.* A new black track emerged from the blue dot, the fired torpedo, heading north to the Japanese orange dot. Almost immediately a red track came from the orange dot and pointed to the blue dot—the Nagasaki torpedo. The blue dot turned to run while the orange dot began to drive due east. Pacino watched, seeing that the red Japanese torpedo was dramatically faster than the black American one. The red track rapidly caught up with the blue dot until the blue dot flashed, pulsed and vanished.

"Own ship sank at time 6:41," Pacino deadpanned.

The screen view continued as the orange sub kept

going east, the black American Mark 50 torpedo going north to where the Japanese sub once had been. The two tracks made a cross as the black trace kept going north, the Japanese sub now miles to the east.

"The Destiny drove off the track of the Mark 50 and has lived to tell the tale," Pacino commented.

"Dammit," Phillips muttered, "we should have shot quicker."

"Let's spin it back to the initial detection, Chief. As you can see at the elapsed time of 00:50, the first leg is done and you're steady on the second leg. Nobody in this trainer has ever done that in less than one minute thirty." Pacino didn't mention the previous record was his own. "You did a great job on speed, Commander Phillips, going just fast enough to get the boat through a maneuver but not so fast that own ship noise would eliminate the signal from the target. Here at time 01:14 you're ready to fire. Torpedo is fired at time 01:27. That's thirteen seconds. Commander, if you had been in snapshot mode you could have launched in three seconds, which would have saved you ten seconds. Getting formal reports of 'ship ready,' 'weapon ready' eats time you don't have. Just command 'snapshot tube one' and the weapon's away."

"You're right," Phillips acknowledged.

"Chief, show us what happens if own ship fires ten seconds earlier," Pacino called out. The image reversed to time 01:14, and the torpedo emerged at time 01:17. The men watched the scenario as the same thing happened. The Japanese sub escaped, the American sub sank. Phillips sat up in his seat. "You'd have died anyway," Pacino said. "And those are my only comments. Well done, men."

"Admiral? Sir?" Phillips had raised his hand like a schoolboy in class. "Are you saying that the only thing we did wrong was shooting the Mark 50 ten seconds late, and even if we had fired earlier we'd be gone?"

"Looks like it, Captain."

"Then how the hell can we go to sea against the Destiny submarine and survive?"

Pacino paused. "This simulation assumes the Japanese crew to be nearly perfect, which, of course, they aren't."

"So in real life we might have won."

"Maybe. Have you heard of the Destiny III class?" Phillips shook his head. "It's completely computer controlled. A robot sub. There will be no inattention, no distracted captains. That's what you *might* be up against. And by the way, that's top secret, so you didn't hear it from me."

Phillips frowned and fished out a fresh cigar from his shirt pocket.

"Captain Phillips, I'd like to talk to you after you dismiss your crew."

"Aye, Admiral. XO, dismiss the men."

The watchstanders filed out until only Pacino and Phillips were left. Pacino's face grew serious.

"I didn't want to tell you while your crew was here," Pacino said, his voice a monotone. "How long have you been in command of the *Greeneville*?"

"Two years, Admiral."

"Well, Phillips, you're relieved of command of the *Greeneville*."

When Phillips had gone, Pacino had the chief turn out the lights and return the scenario to the time before the American sub heard the Destiny.

"Chief, can you reconfigure own ship to be a Seawolf class?"

"We think the program is almost right, sir, but I can't guarantee the results yet until we field calibrate."

"Can you reconfigure?"

"Yes, Admiral."

"Then do it." Pacino waited as the chief changed the computer simulation to make the American ship a Seawolf class instead of the Improved Los Angeles class.

"Admiral, own ship is now the USS *Barracuda,* Seawolf class."

"Begin simulation with the same signal-to-noise ratio."

The scenario began to run, almost the same as before, except the Japanese sub was detected at a range of

14,000 yards instead of 7000 yards. Pacino maneuvered the ship, calling commands into the overhead to the chief at the computer-control console. He couldn't help noticing that the fastest he could get a firing solution was two and a half minutes, sixty seconds longer than Phillips. He shot the torpedo, the Japanese sub moved off to the east and counterfired, and soon own ship sank and the Japanese Destiny emerged unscathed.

"Chief, rerun that simulation with Phillips's maneuvers superimposed, with his one-point-five-minute time to solution."

"Sir, should I take out Phillips's ten-second firing delay?"

"Yes, shoot faster."

The scenario played out again. Again the US sub shot the black torpedo, the Japanese evaded and counterfired. The US sub sank.

"This time increase the Mark 50 search speed to high," Pacino ordered, thinking the torpedo was too slow.

The simulation ended the same way. The American sub sank.

"Dammit. Chief, you got the ability to program in a Vortex missile as own ship's unit?"

The Vortex missile was an experimental hybrid combination of torpedo and missile, ran underwater on solid rocket fuel and traveled at 300 knots to the target. It was the fastest underwater device ever invented, guided by a blue laser and packing several tons of PlasticPac ultradense molecular explosive. It was accurate, fast and lethal. The weapon would have been used fleet-wide if not for two problems: one, the unit was huge and would not fit into an Improved 688-class submarine torpedo room; two, the missile had to be "hot launched" to be stable, meaning it ignited its solid rocket fuel inside the torpedo tube, and so far in every test it had blown up its own launching tube. In its last test in the Bahamas test range the unit had killed the target drone submarine *and* the launching drone submarine. The missile program, not surprisingly, had been abandoned.

"Admiral, we have an old program I wrote for the

Vortex, but, sir, that thing's a suicide weapon. It always blows up the tube."

"I know, I know, but configure it and let me try it."

"Aye, sir. It'll take a few minutes."

Pacino waited, thinking about Phillips and the expression on his face when Pacino had relieved him.

"I'm ready, Admiral."

"This scenario assumes a Seawolf class firing when Phillips got the solution, this time using a Vortex missile."

Pacino watched the screen, saw that the Destiny was detected at 14,000 yards, seven miles out, and that a minute and seventeen seconds later the Vortex missile was ejected from the tube. The result was dramatic. The firing dot, the US submarine, vanished as soon as the missile was launched, the chiefs black humor sneaking into the simulation. The missile track covered the ground to the Destiny in mere seconds. The missile hit the orange dot before it had time to fire back. The orange dot, the Destiny II class Japanese attack submarine pulsed, flashed and vanished.

Pacino stared at the screen, wondering how he could get the Vortex to keep from blowing up the firing ship.

Bruce Phillips walked slowly in the rain to the old turn-of-the-century Corvette, the blue convertible clean but ready for the used-car lot. He climbed in, wiped the rain from his face, cranked the motor to get the heater going and reached for the phone to call Abby while still in the parking lot of the USubCom Training Center.

He had known Abby O'Neal for almost two years, having met her at an international conference on maritime law he had been assigned to in a northern Virginia resort. Abby was a successful maritime law attorney. Phillips had approached her at a reception after her presentation. Her hair was long, sleek and midnight black with a sheen to it. Her looks were black Irish, her features soft, her eyes large and brown. But taking in his crewcut and rhino build, she obviously was thinking him a musclehead who knew nothing of the sea, his ill-fitting civilian suit giving away little about his career. The next day he had given his presentation on the effect of submarine warships on maritime law, and when he had finished she had come up to him and spent the next five minutes apologizing for the day before. Phillips had asked her out and they had been inseparable ever since.

Her secretary answered now.

"Braddock, Samuels & O'Neal, Ms. O'Neal's office."

"Hi, Sarah, is Abby in?"

"Hi, Skipper, she's just coming out of a meeting—here she is."

"Bruce, hi. How'd it go?"

"I lost my ship today."

"Oh. I'm sorry, honey, but you said those simulators are hell."

"No, I wasn't talking about the simulation. I got sunk in that too, but the admiral—"

"That guy you were telling me about, the maniac?"

"That's the one. He relieved me of command. I'm no longer in command of the *Greeneville.*" His voice was a monotone, as Pacino's had been earlier.

"Bruce, I can't believe it. What did you do that was so bad in a simulator? Or was this about the grounding? Was the simulator some kind of last chance?"

"Not quite, Ab. Get *this.*" And now his voice took on the excitement he felt. "Admiral Pacino took me off the *Greeneville* so he could assign me to the *Piranha,* that brand-new Seawolf-class boat coming out of construction in Connecticut, the one we saw in the Sunday paper. She's *mine* now! Pacino said I was the one he wanted driving it. He's taking me out to dinner tonight and flying me to Groton next week for the change of command."

Phillips waited for her to react.

"My God. That guy Pacino must *love* you."

"He just recognizes tactical brilliance when he sees it."

"Right," she said, laughing, "as long as there are no sandbars in sight."

"Well, if Wells were still USubCom commander I'd be relieved of *Greeneville* and driving a desk at the office of base security and car stickers."

"Congratulations, honey. Why don't you ditch the admiral and we'll celebrate tonight, just us?"

"You know I'd love that, but I better not. I'll be home early."

"I'll be waiting, Captain."

Phillips pressed the END button and dropped the phone in the console, stared at the rain washing the windshield and thought about how it would feel to command the newest submarine in the fleet. And suddenly it hit him that he'd be leaving his officers and crew behind, which dampened his mood. Well, perhaps he could convince Pacino to allow him to take Roger Whatney with him. Roger was now Phillips-trained. The two of them were a team, and Phillips didn't look forward to breaking in a new XO. He turned his mind to the things that needed to be done to turn his present ship over to her new skipper, put the car in gear and pulled out, heading for the O-club.

It had turned out to be a good day, after all.

# CHAPTER 4

**YOKOSUKA NAVAL BASE**
**YOKOSUKA, JAPAN**

Comdr. Toshumi Tanaka gripped the carved wooden handrails mounted on the edge of the clearing situated on the ridge overlooking the submarine piers of the Yokosuka Maritime Self Defense Force Base some 200 meters below the rocky ledge. The clearing at this spot had been groomed as a garden and meditation site. Below Tanaka's feet rounded stones were placed to form a cobbled area up to the handrails looking down the ledge. The spot was beautiful in the spring and summer, but in the fall the gloomy aura of it made it unpopular, which fitted Tanaka's mood. He glared out at the vista. Today he could only view the world through a haze of anger and frustration.

He thought of better times. When he was a small boy he had lived in a house by the sea, a house filled with laughter and love. His father had been a stern but caring naval officer, his mother happy to take care of him and his younger sister Onu. The elder Tanaka, then a junior officer, had been at sea much of the time, but when he was there the family was joyful. Toshumi and Onu spent happy hours playing and reading with their mother, waiting for the times when their father would return. All this until his eighth year when his father Akagi was asked to go on a foreign assignment in the United States and the Tanaka family had left Japan for America. Akagi Tanaka, a commander then, was sent to a small seacoast town in Maryland to teach navigation to the students at the U.S. Naval Academy. And from then on his son

Toshumi learned firsthand what it was to feel like a stranger, to be made fun of and feel humiliation. It had been a relief when he returned to Tokyo and his old friends, but four years after the family's return the Maritime Self Defense Force called on Akagi Tanaka again, this time to attend the US Naval War College in Newport, Rhode Island.

By then Toshumi Tanaka was a young teenager, watching the beautiful, rich American girls stroll the beaches and streets of the town, and knowing only rejection. Finally he convinced his family to allow him to go back to Japan and his friends. It was a happy reunion—abruptly interrupted by the news that his mother Orou was dead from breast cancer.

From then on Toshumi's life was a charcoal sketch, done in shades of gray and black. The pain of losing his mother would always be with him and he felt his father responsible. If only his father hadn't insisted on dragging the family to America, Toshumi reflected bitterly.

Two years later his father, now a captain with friends at the Maritime Self Defense Force Academy in Yokosuka, was able to secure an appointment for Toshumi, although Toshumi had begun to hate the navy, connecting it with his father, with the foreign assignments, with his mother's death. But to say no to this opportunity was to be forever behind his peers, at the bottom of Japanese society.

When Toshumi Tanaka finished school he had chosen to go into submarines, finding the surface navy boring, and found a natural, unsuspected talent. Tactically he was far ahead of his contemporaries and drove a submarine like it was part of himself. For the first time in many years he felt happy doing something; when he was driving a sub he could almost forget his mother's death, his anger at his father. He was promoted years ahead of his contemporaries from lieutenant to lieutenant commander.

As one of the youngest lieutenant commanders in the force, he was made the first officer of the first Destiny-class submarine intended for *Japanese* use—until then they had been manufactured for export sale. This had been the Destiny II class, the first submarine in the class, named *Eternal Spirit.* After two years in the building yards and three years at sea Toshumi was promoted to full commander and given command of his own new Destiny II ship, the *Winged Serpent.*

That had been only a year ago, and now he was a senior officer and submarine commander at age thirty-five. His father, Akagi, was now an admiral, the chief of staff of the MSDF, and though some outsiders thought that Toshumi's position was based on his father's commanding the force, those who knew Toshumi Tanaka also knew of his extraordinary talents for commanding men and his ship.

Tanaka forced his thoughts back to the present, forced his eyes to see the naval base stretching out to the horizon on either side. Below the ridge, piers pointed out to the bay, fingers reaching seaward. There was a large gap between the closest piers, with a squat outbuilding located half on the concrete of the pier, half hanging out over the brackish water of the slip. Tied up to the bollards on the seawall was a submarine, one of the Destiny III-class ships, the computer-controlled unmanned vessels.

Abruptly he heard footsteps behind him, and a shadow of a man materialized beside him. Tanaka did not turn.

"I thought I might find you here, Captain," a young voice said.

Still Tanaka didn't turn. His second-in-command, Lt. Comdr. Hiro Mazdai, was as different from himself as a first officer could be. Tanaka was the son of a navy officer, Mazdai was born to wealth, the son of a Panasonic chief financial officer and board member. Tanaka was raised on military compounds, Mazdai had never left Tokyo until he went to sea. Tanaka had sweated through five grueling years at the Self Defense Force Maritime Academy, Mazdai had breezed through Tokyo University. Tanaka was a loner, Mazdai was married to a beautiful Tokyo girl eleven years his junior. Tanaka was just short of 170 centimeters tall, almost towering for a Japanese, but slight, almost frail. Mazdai was short, stretching to reach 155 centimeters, solid and wide.

"The crew is ready, sir," Mazdai said. "We have completed the ready-for-sea checklist. All the weapons have passed their electronic checks."

Far out on the right, blue in the mist, their submarine, the *Winged Serpent,* lay tied up next to several other submarines of the Destiny II class. Down below, an odd-looking truck drove up. Several men in yellow suits jumped off the rear. All wore full helmets with clear faceplates and carried automatic rifles. A door in the pier building rose slowly, revealing bright interior lights shining down on the weapon-loading gear.

"We won't be going to sea," Tanaka said flatly to his second in command.

"Sir?"

Tanaka looked directly at Mazdai, disgust clear in his face.

"That Three-class down there, that robot sub is doing our mission. Our weapons will be removed as soon as that . . . thing is done being loaded."

"They took the mission away from us?"

The men in yellow suits surrounded the truck as it opened, splitting like a clamshell to reveal encased weapons painted yellow and magenta. Stencilled on the side of the capsules were large words, unreadable from that height, but Tanaka knew what they spelled: "DANGER—RADIATION HAZARD—PLUTONIUM."

"Some wizard at fleet headquarters has decided that an unmanned submarine is more appropriate in the land-attack role than our *Winged Serpent.*"

Mazdai paused, weighing his words. "Sir, you are telling me that *Winged Serpent* has been taken off the strike mission. We have lost it to a damned robot? And someone at fleet HQ downloaded our mission to one of the Three class."

"That, Mr. First, is correct."

"Do you think your father had anything to do with this?"

"Whatever, I doubt our orders will change."

"What are our orders now?"

"We pull into the loading bay and give back the Hiroshima missiles, then we go back to Pier 17."

Two hydraulic cranes had pulled up to the open clamshell truck beds. The men in yellow suits fastened lifting slings to either end of the first weapon. Behind the truck a flatbed weapon transporter waited, ready to move into the weapon-loading building. Tanaka noticed that the yellow-suited men's full-face helmets were connected to air bottles on their backs, precautions in case of a plutonium loss of containment.

"The Three class is flawed, sir. How can they trust it with a land strike?"

Tanaka shook his head. "I agree, but if the robot submarines prove themselves in a combat situation, the Two class will be phased out. They will claim manned submarines devote too much volume and weight to hotel accommodations. The computer-driven subs have no living quarters so they can carry more weapons. Command and control is supposedly more assured."

"Until, sir, the computer has a malfunction. And a computer-driven ship can only fight the way it's programmed. No midbattle learning, no human ingenuity, no intuition."

"And no wives at home to worry about, no babies about to be born, no monthly bills distracting the crews' minds. The computer never gets tired, it never longs for a woman, it never gets sick. It's just always there, driving the submarine. So goes the opinion of fleet HQ."

As they spoke, the cranes lifted out the first weapon canister and loaded it gingerly to the waiting transport bed, then turned their booms to pick up the second unit.

"You once mentioned inviting your father on the ship, sir, perhaps for dinner? Maybe together we could convince him."

Tanaka controlled his face to hide thoughts about his father. "Perhaps we will do that soon, but there is no time now."

The cranes lowered the second weapon to the transport bed. The clamshell truck closed and drove off, the cranes also departing. The men in yellow suits stayed behind, walking slowly behind the low transport, which rolled into the loading building and vanished into the portal. The rolling door came down, leaving the seawall area deserted except for two guards with their rifles at the ready.

"You'd better get back to the ship and inform the men about scrubbing the mission," Tanaka told Mazdai, who was astute enough to know when to withdraw and leave Tanaka alone.

All was quiet now on the seawall. Tanaka could visualize the Three-class submarine being nose-loaded with weapons. The loading building functioned as a caisson, sealing around the bow of the sub and draining out the water to leave the entire nose-cone area accessible for bow-in torpedo loading. Except the weapons being loaded into the unmanned computer submarine were not torpedoes, but Hiroshima missiles. For the land-attack mission that his *Winged Serpent* should have had.

After a sleepless night, part of it spent in the rain at his mother's memorial, he showered, dressed in a fresh uniform and called for his driver. Within hours he was back at the pier. Before he walked down its length, he stopped and stared at the scenario unfolding under the harsh lamps of the floodlights in the middle of the night.

Moored to the neighboring pier was the Three-class ship that had been loaded with the radioactive missiles the day before. The ship that was formerly called *Divine Firmament* had been renamed *Curtain of Flames*—presumably to inspire fear. In Tanaka it only inspired rage.

# CHAPTER 5

**TOKYO, JAPAN**
**KASUMIGASEKI DISTRICT**
**JAPANESE DEFENSE AGENCY HEADQUARTERS**

The black Lexus limousine rolled to a halt before the headquarters building, its powerful engine purring quietly at idle. Immediately a uniformed guard in a shining helmet with white gloves opened the rear door and snapped to attention in a rigid salute. A dozen other military guards holding rifles stood lined up on either side of a heavy gate set into the stone wall surrounding the building. Prime Minister Hosaka Kurita stepped out of the large car, past the guards, and through the gate, never acknowledging their existence. A step behind him Asagumo Machiie, the Minister of Information, walked and tried to keep up with Kurita. The prime minister was twenty years Machiie's senior, but seemed to have the physical strength of a man ten years younger than Machiie. Both men were dressed in expensive and conservative dark charcoal gray suits, starched white handmade shirts, and crimson ties, each with a tiny intricately detailed Japanese flag set in the red field. Their leather shoes were Japanese made, each pair worth the equivalent of a month's rent for a luxury Tokyo flat.

Prime Minister Hosaka Kurita was nearing sixty years old but had a tangible vitality to him. He could energize a room. His hair was mostly gray with only hints of its former black. Kurita was the grandson of the Imperial Japanese Army general who had commanded the invasion and occupation force in Indonesia. Kurita's father,

Noboru Kurita, had worked for MITI, the Ministry of International Trade and Industry, during the heady years of Japan's rise from the ashes of World War II to world preeminence in manufacturing and trade. The elder Kurita had become a deputy minister for semiconductors and was responsible for the successful Japanese penetration of American electronics markets. He was the architect of the Japanese takeover attempt of AT&T, Intel, IBM, Microsoft, and General Motors. Noboru had died of a stroke at his desk, laboring over the acquisition deal that should have made IBM a Japanese-owned company. Hosaka Kurita had mourned Noboru's passing, his bond with his father so strong that even now, nearly fifteen years later, he would occasionally mention to Asagumo Machiie, his minister of information, that he could still feel the spirit of his father with him, struggling by his side, watching over him, demanding performance from him.

Fortunately for Noboru Kurita, he had not lived to see the trade war with the US and Europe, and the eventual closing of Western markets to Japan. Kurita would never forget the day the US president had signed the Fair Trade Bill into law that made anything with Japanese content over 10 percent illegal to be imported or sold in the US and made Japanese ownership of corporations illegal, even repatriating—or expropriating—all real estate sold to Japanese owners. The nations of the European Union passed similar laws, some even harsher than America's. That month Japan turned into a poor nation, the cash river from the West drying up. That had all been four hard years ago, two years before Hosaka Kurita came to power.

Hosaka Kurita had followed his father's footsteps at MITI and had eventually himself been elevated to Minister of International Trade and Industry, perhaps because of his father's reputation there. But Hosaka Kurita proved able, becoming a member of the Diet's House of Councillors at the age of forty-six. When he was fifty-five, he became prime minister. In Kurita's mind his ascent to PM was not so much a result of his personal qualities as of his outspoken, passionate speeches against the

West and the United States in particular. Even so, his character and leadership were already legendary at MITI, his eloquence able to move the entire Diet when he was a member of that legislative body. His platform, his mandate and, he believed, his destiny was to bring Japan back to world prominence, as his father had done in the 1950s. Except that now Japan's *kokutai,* her national destiny, depended not on forsaking the sword for the factory but rather upon using the might of the factory to once more hoist the sword.

But as passionate and warlike as Kurita was, he was also conditioned in the ways of *on,* the special obligation of one holding power to those whom his power touches. He had listened countless hours to his father's words on *giri,* the network of obligational relationships, the endless mutual and reciprocal obligations borne by a leader. Kurita was at once assertive and certain yet humble and nonconfrontational. Kurita could give a speech urging confrontation with the West, and afterward seem to back down to the conflicting opinion of a colleague. Kurita was Japan. There was no Caesar in Japan, no pope, no king. Power was shared. Groups, not leaders, did the business of governing Japan. But ultimately those groups would listen to someone with the voice of destiny, and destiny seemed to sing through Kurita's throat.

They were only a dozen steps into the building when it opened into a vast rotunda, the dome peak over seven stories overhead. There Koutarou Iizuka, the Director General of the Japanese Defense Agency, waited with his entourage and the other council members. Prime Minister Kurita first greeted Iizuka as a father greeted a son. He beamed up at the younger man, his bow deep. Iizuka turned to Machiie, a warm bow of greeting passing between the men. Iizuka had also been to the university with Machiie years before. In fact, so had every other member of Kurita's Defense Security Council. The DSC met at the headquarters of the Japanese Defense Agency at any point of crisis that could result in military action. Kurita had formed the DSC soon after being voted PM, and the council was made up of the five inner-circle cabinet ministers whom Kurita most trusted.

The men were arranged by rank, determined by how close they were to Kurita. The PM and Iizuka greeted each of the other council members—Foreign Minister Yoshida, the stereotypical diplomat; MITI Minister Uchida, a hardheaded hawk; and Minister of Finance Sugimoto, the elderly, dispassionate financial wizard recently brought over from industry, from Sanyo. At the end of the row, a newcomer waited, an elderly man with what looked like great physical strength, white hair, white mustache and a starched white high-collared tunic with gold-braided shoulder boards, ribbons on his breast, a gold rope slung over his shoulder. His pants were starched and white, his shoes white as well. At the man's hip was a sword hanging off a gold hook that vanished into the tunic. The man's face was creased with deep wrinkles, the tanned skin taut. Rather than the usual Japanese dark brown, this man's eyes were light gray with flecks of green running radially from the irises. Some said he looked like a wolf.

"Admiral Tanaka," Kurita intoned as the men bowed to each other, "I am so glad that you were able to attend. Gentlemen, Adm. Akagi Tanaka, Supreme Commander of the Maritime Self Defense Force, will attend this meeting in addition to General Gotoh."

Standing a few meters from Tanaka was Gen. Masao Gotoh, the Chairman of the Self Defense Force Joint Staff Council, who functioned as the commander in chief of the entire military. Gotoh stood a distance from Admiral Tanaka, as if he wished to express a tacit disapproval of his own subordinate—remarkable within the tight framework of team cooperation inside the military.

The men walked into an ornate room with a huge rare tigerwood table taken from Indonesia in the last world war. On the wall were oil paintings of Japanese military conquests from the previous millennia all the way to the fighting for the empire in World War II. Shields and swords hung at the corners, while glass cases enclosed antique ship models, the battleship *Yamato* over four meters from bow to stern, its guns pointed at the conference table as if leveling fingers demanding action from the council. The room seemed to be designed for war plans. The prime minister used notes, since in the ancient tradition of *matomari,* the honored vehicle of group decision-making, the leader was first obligated to summarize an issue, showing no opinion, so that the group could begin to discuss it. Since confrontation was unheard of, each man would reveal his opinion slowly, one thought at a time. The momentum of consensus would build slowly, the brakes of dissenting opinions applied gently. As the men began to see similar patterns of thought among their colleagues, their opinions would become more safe to expose, until finally consensus would be reached. Once the leader established agreement, action would be taken.

Kurita stood and cleared his throat, his hands at rest at his sides. The ministers and military officers sat straight in their chairs, all eyes on Kurita. The hum of the presentation screen coming down was barely perceptible, accentuating the pin-drop silence in the room.

"Good morning, gentlemen," Kurita began as a map of Japan flashed on the screen. The Homeland was colored white. To the northwest Greater Manchuria was displayed in gray. "I hardly need mention the gravity of the Greater Manchurian situation. In the last twelve hours we have determined that here in Tamga"—a small dot in a valley near Lake Ozero Chanka pulsed in red—"is a storage depot for SS-34 missiles. General Gotoh will run the disk of our confirming penetration mission."

The disk played the scenes obtained from Major Namuru's mission into Tamga, up to the point where he said, "To the victory of Japan," when the picture was darkened. The soundtrack, however, continued, the dual explosions loud in the enhanced acoustics of the room.

The screen retracted into the ceiling. Kurita cleared his throat again.

"It is clear that the SS-34 missiles are nuclear tipped. It is also clear that they are twenty-four minutes' flight time away from us in Tokyo." Kurita looked around the room. "Minister Yoshida, do you have any thoughts?"

Yoshida, as foreign minister, was notorious for his relatively optimistic view of the world.

"It is most regrettable that there appear to be offensive instruments of war in Greater Manchuria. However, it is our responsibility to the people of Japan to remember that these weapons may not be aimed at Japan at all. They may not even work. The Russians no doubt left them behind. They are not even loaded into those underground silos. It would be premature, I suggest, to assume the intention of aggression only on this."

Kurita thanked him, turned to General Gotoh. "Obviously, intent is difficult to confirm. But as for the functions of the missiles—are they operational, General?"

"Prime Minister, the missiles are in perfect working order. Once manufactured they do not, after all, break. The bunker was climate-controlled, leading us to the knowledge that the missile-computer systems were being attended to. Furthermore, these weapons are not launched from silos as Minister Yoshida mentioned but from trucks. The missiles were preloaded onto launcher subassemblies inside the bunker. We can go back and review the disk if there is any doubt of that. The subassemblies need only be lifted onto a launcher truck to be ready to fire. A simple flatbed truck will suffice."

"So allow me to review, General. You are certain these missiles work?"

"I am, sir."

"And they have launchers?"

"They do."

"And the launchers will work?"

"We are certain of it."

The meeting went on for another hour while the opinions of the men in the room moved closer to the idea of a military strike, in spite of Yoshida's dissenting feelings. Finally General Gotoh made a move to review the arguments.

"So, gentlemen, if I might take this moment to summarize. I think we have reached agreement on several points. First, that there are offensive missiles in Greater Manchuria. Second, that these missiles are nuclear-tipped. Third, that the units are operational. Fourth, the missiles are twenty-four minutes' flight time from Tokyo. And therefore, fifth, if President Len has an intention of launching an attack on Japan, he will be successful.

Tokyo will look worse than 1945. Worse than Hiroshima and Nagasaki after the atomic bombs were dropped. To put it in perspective, the Hiroshima bomb had the equivalent of twenty thousand tons of TNT explosive. An SS-34 has over two million tons. Twenty well-targeted SS-34s would take our nation back two thousand years. Our descendants would live off whatever little land is not contaminated by nuclear radiation. Our promises to the people that Japan would never again suffer this humiliation and death will be turned to ashes along with the world's most advanced cities. On this, we are agreed, are we not?"

Kurita kept his face neutral. The men had agreed on the first four points. The fifth was Gotoh's opinion based on the consequences of a nuclear attack. But what he had said would need to be covered at some point, and perhaps it would be best to signify agreement and get the discussion of the memories of being bombed with nuclear weapons behind them. Since Japan remained the only nation to have been targeted and attacked by nuclear bombs, the national consciousness had remained sensitive to the issue. The antinuclear protests in Asia during the past decades had been heavily funded by Japan, and had succeeded in spite of rumors in the Western press that Japan itself was working on a new type of nuclear weapon.

Kurita began working his way around the table, asking each man present for an opinion, bringing out each minister's specialty. The minister of finance, Haruna Sugimoto, was asked what effect the weapon's presence alone had on the economy of Japan, and then what would happen to the economy if the SS-34s ever landed on Japanese soil. The MITI minister was asked about the effects on industry and how long it would take to rebuild the nation should it come under attack. Machiie was asked about the effects of an attack on the world's information network, and he had replied in much the same voice as did the MITI and finance ministers.

When all had spoken except Adm. Akagi Tanaka, who was not involved in the actual decision-making process but was present to give the council the benefit of his naval knowledge, Kurita stood.

"We have taken many hours to understand and explore the data before us—the fact of the existence of the SS-34 missiles and exactly what that means to Japan and the world around us. We now know the consequences of the use of those weapons, and we realize that those consequences are indeed grave. So grave that we are moved to ask the next question—what action do we now take?"

"Mr. Prime Minister, aren't we forgetting something?"

The room turned toward Foreign Minister Yoshida. Kurita bit the inside of his lip, but turned toward Yoshida and allowed him to speak.

"We have spoken about the weapons. We have spoken of what they can do. But for many decades we have been surrounded by such weapons. Before the revolution China had many such instruments of war, some no doubt reserved for Tokyo. Who could doubt Soviet Russia had even more? And the ships of the United States fleet that docked here for so many decades until the trade war, how many of them had nuclear missiles in their holds and magazines?

"But now, a small nation apparently has a cache of nuclear missiles, and the gods alone know how old they are. But I am willing to agree that they will work, so long as this body agrees that we know nothing of the *intent* of the owners of the missiles. China and Russia had no love for Japan, and we lived with the threat. The United States was supposedly an ally, and we lived with their weapons of destruction, even though they were the ones who murdered our children in the war."

Kurita was surprised that Yoshida had righteous anger in his repertory, but then realized it was another diplomatic tool, just like a smile or handshake.

"Yet now a nation that has offered no proof of hostile intent, no desire to hurt us, just a desire to live, just as we desire to, has managed to come into the possession of weapons of nuclear war. And while I agree that they are dirty and cursed machines, they cannot harm us without a malevolent nation to use them. And no facts have crossed this table attesting to the intent of the Greater Manchurians. I propose we simply ask the Greater Manchurians to remove the weapons. If they do, we can sell them military hardware, helping our economy and keeping them secure so they won't have to rely on the missiles. If they keep the weapons, we can expose them to the world and ask for UN help. Eventually the warheads would be turned over and destroyed in accordance with the Nuclear Free Zone Treaty. The crisis would be averted and we would lead our lives as before. Amend that—better than before, because by our actions we will show the world our moral character. And that may help to end this destructive trade embargo by the West."

There was silence in the room for some minutes after Yoshida spoke.

"Mr. Prime Minister, I'd like to say a few words, if I may."

"Please go ahead, General Gotoh."

"Minister Yoshida is entirely correct in his concerns about the intentions of Greater Manchuria. His proposal to ask the Greater Manchurians to remove the weapons has merit."

Kurita did not expect an opening toward Yoshida from his opposite number in the council.

"In fact, what we are proposing has elements of Minister Yoshida's idea."

Gotoh had the room's members entirely focused, in spite of the fact that the meeting had gone into its third hour.

"There are several possible uses for these missiles. As we have discussed, one use is for a preemptive strike against Japan. But another purpose is deterrence. Holding back the aggressions of the Russians, the East Chinese and the West Chinese, and theoretically the aggressions of Japan. I am getting ahead of our meeting agenda, and for that I apologize. The next order of business was to be—what should Japan do about these missiles? I will introduce that question now, because it addresses Minister Yoshida's concerns.

"Let us assume for a moment that the missiles are present for the purposes of deterrence. I personally do not believe this, because a nuclear deterrent only works if the enemy knows the weapons are there and operational. These missiles are secret. But let us go beyond that and recognize that there is a way for us to neutralize these missiles without the world knowing about them. We can surgically knock out these missiles while still letting Greater Manchuria bluff her neighbors into thinking she has a nuclear strike force.

"Again, I am arguing a point of logic I do not believe, because Greater Manchuria has kept these missiles a deep secret, but we can say for Minister Yoshida that there could always be plans to announce the presence of these missiles, turning them into a deterrent force. We have a way of striking these weapons so that they will be neutralized forever, in a way that there will be no telltale sign that the neutralization has come from us."

The room was silent. Kurita addressed Gotoh. "General, you seem to be saying that we can blow up these missiles and destroy them, but in such a way that no one will link the raid to Japan, is that correct?"

"Very close, sir. We can strike the missiles and make them useless. There will be no explosions. The missiles will not be physically destroyed but they will no longer be offensive weapons."

"You have a way to destroy these missiles without physical destruction? I think we are all confused, General."

Gotoh lowered the projection screen and tapped into the disk player. "This disk doesn't have a soundtrack, gentlemen," Gotoh said, stepping up to the screen with a pointer. A computer image of a cruise missile materialized on the screen. The missile grew until its nose cone filled the image and the weapon became transparent, revealing numerous components inside.

"In the last four years we have perfected a new weapon that causes destruction without blowing anything up. We call this missile the Hiroshima. The warhead itself is called the Scorpion. The warhead components are separate chemicals and gases that are dispersed into a cloud and react in midair to form a polymer emulsion—a glue, if you will. This glue rains down on the land below and adheres to every surface. Mixed in with the glue is this substance shown in the blue container. These are fine filings of plutonium, one of the most poisonous substances on the planet. The glue liquid and plutonium form a matrix that contaminates the area below the activation of the warhead. The effective zone of contamination varies with glue load, plutonium weight and missile altitude. We can dial in the area of contamination. Once contaminated, the area below, while physically the same, must be abandoned. Any human life in the effective zone dies from radiation effects. Other personnel entering the scene will die. An on-scene commander would soon deduce the cause of deaths in the effective zone, and the area would be cordoned off. Decontamination is not possible. The glue is essentially permanent, it doesn't wash off with water or chemicals. Nothing short of scraping every square millimeter with a chisel can clean up the area. If this weapon detonates over the Tamga bunker, the area will be condemned for many years and use of the weapons will be impossible."

The picture darkened and the screen retracted into the ceiling above.

"We plan to deploy a Hiroshima missile with a Scorpion warhead such as this against the Tamga weapons depot."

Foreign Minister Yoshida shook his head. "So you plan to deploy a nuclear weapon against the Greater Manchurians because they have nuclear weapons?"

"No, Minister Yoshida, that is not true. This warhead is not a nuclear weapon."

"It causes widespread radioactive contamination, killing the targeted city with radiation poisoning. It is a nuclear weapon."

"No. It is a plutonium poison weapon, and yes, it kills. But the target is not a city, it is a bunker. Anyone inside will be a professional soldier taking the risks that soldiers take. We estimate only two hundred casualties."

"Our people died at Hiroshima and Nagasaki from radiation. No Japanese weapon should exist that does this, General Gotoh."

"Our people also died in the Pacific from bullets and bombs and fires, Minister Yoshida. That has not stopped us from using and making bullets and bombs and incendiary devices. All this talk about the nuclear destruction in 1945 has to stop. That was three generations ago. It was war. That is what happens in a war. This scenario is very different. We are *surgically* removing a threat. There will be deaths, but no spectacular flaming mushroom cloud, no babies dying in their mother's arms, no shadows of pedestrians carved into the walls of buildings, no walls of flame for thirty miles from ground zero. It will not be a pretty scene inside the effective zone, but for this operation the effective zone will be a few hundred meters in diameter."

"A practical question, General," Kurita said. "The weapons are stored inside a bunker. How will this glue matrix contaminate them under the cover of the bunker roof?"

"First, the entire complex will be contaminated. No one will be able to get close, even if the weapons themselves are uncontaminated. But the ventilation systems will spread enough of the glue and plutonium to contaminate the surfaces of the interior. We have done tests. The missiles will be rendered useless."

Gotoh went on to explain technical details of the weapon, comfortable now that he was discussing machines instead of morality. After he had spoken for another twenty minutes, uninterrupted by Yoshida, Kurita called for a break. The council members filed out to consider. When the members returned, the meeting began where it had left off.

"So you believe an attack with these weapons is truly justified?" Yoshida asked Kurita directly.

"It is not just I, Minister Yoshida," Kurita replied to the foreign minister. "The council members believe it to be justified. If I understand the thinking of the group, they feel that the Greater Manchurian weapons are sufficiently offensive that their mere existence in an operational status, and within the unstable rogue government of this state, merit the contemplation of a military strike to make the missiles ineffective. You have brought up doubt that the Greater Manchurians intend to use the missiles. We share your troubled feelings, Yoshida-san. This will be the weightiest decision made by our nation since the preventive strike on the Americans at Pearl Harbor, and you are correct that it should be considered cautiously. But let me add that in war, or a prelude to war, there is much uncertainty. Allow me to liken this most serious matter to a chess game in which the playing board is partially obscured. Or to a game of poker in which the opponent's entire hand is obscured. We have peeked under the handkerchief hiding the board, Minister. We have seen several of our opponent's cards. We know things about him while he knows little about us. We must not waste this advantage.

"However, let me address one of your concerns. That of the reaction of Greater Manchuria should we attack their missiles. We have discussed a covert attack, and letting the Greater Manchurians guess who did the work. We have debated the impact of Japanese denials of Greater Manchurian accusations. We believe that if Greater Manchuria cried to the Western press about being attacked by Japan, the West would turn against us, in war as well as in commerce. And so far there have been no solutions to these problems. You do not want to attack Greater Manchuria's territory because they have not attacked us. We are worried that after the attack Greater Manchuria may use evidence of the strike against Japan. I have an answer to both problems.

"We should commission a diplomatic mission to go along with the strike. Minister Yoshida, your ambassador to Greater Manchuria—what is his name?"

"Nakamoto."

"Of course. Your Ambassador Nakamoto goes to President Len and tells him that Japan knows of his nuclear missiles and believes them to be offensive. Len will deny this. Nakamoto will say that Len must sign a nonaggression treaty with Japan in which Japan will control the missiles. Len will refuse. Nakamoto will demand that a Japanese military detail must be put in Tamga to oversee the depot and control the missiles. Len will again refuse. At this point the diplomatic delegation will depart to call Tokyo. That is when the strike will be executed. The diplomatic delegation will gather data transmitted by Tokyo and once the strike is a success, will meet again with Len. He will be shown the film of the bombing from the missile target camera. His own people will confirm for him what happened at Tamga. Nakamoto will tell Len that his refusal to help us led to the strike. But now Nakamoto will also tell him that Japan will keep the strike a *secret*—so that the missiles remain a deterrent to his immediate neighbors. In exchange, Japan and Greater Manchuria will sign the nonaggression treaty that he initially refused to sign. In the end, Japan has been honorable, telling Greater Manchuria what is desired, only attacking when there is no hope. After the attack, Japan offers to help Greater Manchuria keep her neighbors at bay. Nakamoto will offer to help Len build up his conventional military by selling him hardware at a special discount.

"As you can see, all parties win. The missiles will be destroyed, putting us at ease. Japan's honor remains intact, since we offered a diplomatic solution that was refused, leaving us no choice but a military strike. After the strike, the outstretched hand of Japan helping Greater Manchuria will transform a threat into an ally. In the years to follow, Greater Manchuria may well thank the heavens for the day we attacked Tamga."

"Mr. Prime Minister," Yoshida said, "if we use diplomacy we may well succeed where General Gotoh has predicted failure. If Greater Manchuria sees logic they will agree to the nonaggression treaty and Japanese control of the nuclear missiles. If that happens, we can avoid this horrible military attack."

"Gentlemen? General Gotoh?"

"Minister Yoshida, if Len Pei Poom signed a treaty that put those missiles under Japanese military control I will withdraw my motion for the strike. With one condition: that if the Greater Manchurians dissemble, if we suddenly lose communication with the missile-guarding detail, that the strike be executed. I must say that the chances of Len accepting Japanese Self Defense Force personnel at his secret missile depot, with the Japanese in control, is minimal. I do not think he will agree to it."

"But *if* he does, we must be prepared to stick to the terms of our own treaty," Yoshida said. "I don't want us to demand he sign a treaty and then watch us refuse to sign it ourselves. If our ambassador goes to Len with a peace treaty in hand I must know that Japan will be willing to live by its terms."

"Japan will abide by the terms of the treaty, Yoshida-san," Kurita said. "You write the treaty and make sure it is one we can live with. Len may sign the nonaggression pact, and this crisis is over. If he does not, we end the crisis by destroying the missiles. We then help Len by making sure his neighbors still think he has the missiles, and meanwhile we help him arm his military. And we help our own economy as well. In the end we may generate a large market in Greater Manchuria and receive their raw materials. I think we have taken a bad situation and turned it to our advantage."

Kurita went around the room soliciting opinions. Approval was unanimous. Yoshida merely nodded.

"There is more to discuss, gentlemen," Kurita said. "General, how will this weapon be delivered? And how will we control its launch?"

"We must ensure that the strike is effective. We plan on using two missiles. For absolute secrecy, these two units will be launched from a submarine already patrolling off the Greater Manchurian coast. Admiral?"

Admiral Tanaka stood. The screen came down and a map of the Sea of Japan materialized.

"We have placed a Destiny-class nuclear-powered submarine here off the Greater Manchurian shore. As you know, the Destiny-class submarines are quiet. They are nuclear propelled, so they will never need to surface after they leave port. The submarine patrols here off the coast waiting for the order from us to shoot the Hiroshima cruise missiles with the Scorpion dispersion-glue-bomb warheads. On receipt of orders to fire, the submarine fires the two cruise missiles and departs the area to return home. The cruise missiles come from the sea and fly close to the ground until they reach the target—

Tamga. Estimated elapsed time from receipt of orders to launch and missile detonation is less than an hour."

"Have we tested this method of cruise-missile launch?" Kurita asked.

"Extensively, sir."

"Very well. Has anyone any questions of the admiral or general? No? I recommend the council stand by to be reconvened later. I move we adjourn."

# CHAPTER 6

**CHANGASHAN, GREATER MANCHURIA**

President Len Pei Poom, if seen in civilian clothes, would not earn a second glance, being of medium height and weight, with thinning hair and a nondescript mustache. Which perhaps could explain why he was never seen out of a military uniform, his tunic resplendent with medals and a gold sash. Unlike most military dictators who wore the uniform of the fighting forces, Len's medals were genuine. He had been a career army officer his entire adult life, ever since a battlefield promotion in Afghanistan when he was eighteen and fighting a pointless war for what then was the behemoth of the Soviet Union. Later, in his twenties, he was detached from the Red Army to the United Nations forces in Ethiopia, Somalia and Bosnia, then repatriated to the Russian Republic Army for the Allied ground offensive against the Muslim United Islamic Front of God, which was an alliance of over two dozen Islamic nations led by a fanatical if charismatic dictator. Len was a mere major when Russian forces invaded northern Iran. He had been in command of an infantry company during the initial assault. By the time the decapitated UIF had surrendered, Len had been named a general, commanding the Second Combined Infantry Force that overran Tehran. In the interval he had lost every friend, every acquaintance, to enemy fire. The ground war had been a slaughterhouse.

No man could live through that war and not be changed, but circumstances were favorable to Len. In the years after his return from the Iranian front, the

Russian Republic had continued to fall on hard times. Len's home in the city of Chabarovsk, now renamed by him as Changashan, had been in a rebellious Russian republic. Len had become involved, slowly, since at first he had been regarded as a Russian general and not to be trusted. Within two years he had become the head of a revolutionary movement, determined to split off from greater Russia. He had learned the lessons of other earlier, less successful succession movements, and had managed to consolidate support from China, then in the middle of its own bloody civil war. Len had alternated use of diplomacy and threats. China ceded its Greater Manchurian territory just as the White Army was advancing on it, perhaps knowing that Greater Manchuria would fall to the Whites anyway, but Len had managed to hold on to it as the rebel Chinese fighters had turned toward Beijing. By the time the Chinese Red Forces had consolidated power and taken back Beijing, Len had wrangled Sikhote Alin from Russia. The latter feat was a masterful stroke of diplomacy, but it had boiled down to the Russians being distracted by their own problems far to the west, an economic collapse narrowly averted in the months that Len was shoring up the borders of his new state, one he had decided to name Greater Manchuria, a bone thrown to the Chinese that comprised half the land area of the region. Len's military at the time had been skeletal and poorly equipped, though heavily manned.

All that had been three years ago. Len had just begun to feel confident that the country might survive. The government he had constructed functioned, if crudely, but the people were fed and the trains ran, if not necessarily on time. But it was then that the crisis hit. The Chinese Civil War ended, with West China, the Reds, taking up central and northeast China and East China, the Whites, taking the eastern coastline. Not long after, the West Chinese, sharing a border with southern Greater Manchuria, decided they wanted their territory back, though it took some time for them to assemble their infantry and armored forces along the border. The Russians, with their worldwide intelligence network left over from communist days, saw the Chinese forces, and decided to mass their own armies at the western and northern borders of Greater Manchuria.

At one point Len believed that Greater Manchuria had only days of survival left. Appeals to the Western nations were greeted with monetary aid and advisors, but there would be no one to fight the war for them. Now, years later, the Western media credited Len with holding off both the Russians and Chinese without firing a shot, making him out to be a diplomatic hero. He had not been, but he had found a silver bullet. His aide, Col. Woo Sei Wah, had flown into Changashan and found Len despondent:

"I have news too sensitive for any radio circuit," Woo had announced. Len had not looked up from his desk. "The old Russian weapons depot at Tamga. We found missiles. Nuclear missiles. SS-34s, in perfect condition, their launchers all there and ready. There are enough weapons there to destroy the Chinese and Russian armies outside the borders and still have a half-dozen in reserve in case they come for more."

At first Len could scarcely believe the news, but as Woo's facts gathered irresistible force, what had happened became clear. The treaty banning all nuclear weapons in Asia had been signed by the Russian Republic as well as the other Asian nations. Something somewhere in the dusty, creaking Russian bureaucratic machine had malfunctioned, and a theater commander had failed to order the missiles turned over to the UN destruction committee. Apparently the mistake was never found. The Russians were not so stupid that they had forgotten about the nuclear missiles, but whoever the Sikhote Alin regional commander had been, Len knew *he* was an idiot. Through a combination of errors, the regional CO had neglected to report to the UN the Tamga facility. The mistake had to have been uncovered over the next year, since at some point the Russian army had evacuated the military bases and abandoned them, but Len's theory was that the regional CO had thought it better to abandon the missiles and gamble on them not being found than to call attention to his humiliating, compromising mistake. He had to have rationalized his decision with the thought that the untutored Greater Manchurians would never understand how to use so modern a weapon system anyway. Whatever his thinking, a cache of SS-34s was now in Len's quiver, and he used them wisely.

Woo Sei Wah had tried to convince Len to strike with the missiles, but Len had argued that two phone calls would be more effective. The first was to the Kremlin, in which Len had calmly informed the Russian president that he had the SS-34s, that if there were any doubts that there were SS-34s they should check the records and interrogate the former Sikhote Alin Regional Commanding General, and that his people knew how to deploy the missiles, and that, in fact, the armies massing on his borders were targeted by missiles one through seventeen. Before he hung up he suggested that the Russian president call the West Chinese Party Secretary and confirm the presence of the nukes. The second call took only minutes to be put through to the party secretary's office.

Ten days later the Russian and Chinese forces rolled back deep into their respective nations, and Greater Manchuria had survived unmolested ever since.

Until now.

Earlier that morning Colonel Woo had stood before Len's large desk, a storm cloud rolling over his face as he dropped a bombshell:

"The Tamga depot has been raided by a commando. The fence-line was breached. A single operative neutralized several guards, two killer dogs, opened the bunker's electronically locked door and visited the weapons for over two minutes. When he was done he left the way he came, then within sight of the fence hole committed suicide."

"The Russians?"

"No, sir. The *Japanese*."

"The *Japanese*? Are you insane? Why would the Japanese break into Tamga? And *how* did you make the determination that the raid was done by the Japanese?"

"General, we found a scorched reentry vehicle, some

kind of space capsule, two kilometers into the woods. The commando didn't cover his trail, as though he knew he wouldn't have to. At the fence there were several instruments charred beyond recognition. There was a penchant for self-destruction of the tools this man used, leading us to believe it was a suicide raid. The fence was penetrated, then the man managed to unlock an electronic security blast door. From everything we know, the Russians and Chinese don't have the technology to do that. Finally, the man blew himself up. All we found left of him were his feet inside his boots. The planning of the suicide mission leads us to believe that only two cultures could have done this—the Islamics or the Japanese. And why would the Muslims be concerned? Finally, the stature of the corpse indicates that the warrior was quite short. Likely Japanese."

"But *why* would they do this? Why are they worried about Tamga?"

"Have you considered the map lately, sir? If you roll it out and look at it from Japan's point of view, *we* are their new landward neighbors across the Sea of Japan. They likely see us as a threat, and *that* is the worst news we've had since the Russians and Chinese tried to invade us. If the Japanese know about our missiles, it is almost a certainty that they are threatened by them. Tokyo, after all, is only minutes away from Tamga by rocket motor."

"Why would I lift a hand against Japan?"

"Why do the Japanese hate the Koreans? Like Greater Manchuria, it is the proximity to their island, their *sacred* world. You know Korea is considered a dagger pointed at the heart of Japan."

Len had lapsed into silence. Woo waited, staring out the window at the city below.

"Do you truly believe the invader was Japanese?"

"I do. But perhaps you should see for yourself."

"And do you also believe this indicates a future hostile action by the Japanese against Greater Manchuria?"

"More difficult to predict, and based on less evidence, but the answer is yes."

"What is more likely, a protest to the UN or a strike against my missiles?"

"An attack."

"We must move the missiles—"

"No. Outside their bunker they would be exposed."

"But an attacker would have to find their redeployed location. We could hide different missiles in different places."

"You might buy time, sir, but taking the missiles from the compound makes them susceptible to one-man attacks of the kind that happened at the compound. It is one thing for the Japanese to find them, another for them to blow them up. Meanwhile, we have increased the base perimeter outward by two kilometers, we are installing infrared and radar motion sensors. The buffer zone is patrolled by killer dogs. The fenceline voltage has been boosted from eleven-thousand volts to one-hundred-twenty-four thousand. If you get closer than ten meters to it, every hair on your body stands on end. We have a system on the drawing board to put nerve-gas canisters on the perimeter fence posts, actuated automatically by an approaching intruder. In addition I am moving antiaircraft gun emplacements around the bunker itself. The blast door electronic lock has been replaced by old-fashioned metal-hardware locks."

"But a determined, technologically advanced enemy could still destroy the missiles."

"Perhaps some of them. But if even one remains, that enemy will suffer regret for a very long time."

Woo left then. He had saved Len's life on a battlefield in Iran five years earlier, which had only been the beginning of their partnership. Since then they had gone through much. Was it only prelude to much more? Len wondered.

# CHAPTER 7

**CHANGASHAN, GREATER MANCHURIA**

"This isn't like the Japanese," Len said, shrugging into his full military tunic as Lee Chun Wah held it for him. "They plan everything they do. Nothing spontaneous."

"Sir," Lee said, "it is a diplomatic delegation. They seem to be sincere."

President Len looked at Lee Chun Wah, his personal aide.

"Mr. Lee, you may, in my presence, accuse the Japanese of many things. But don't ever accuse them of being sincere."

"Yes, sir."

Len buttoned the tunic and concentrated on putting on his war face. Only minutes before he had been called by Lee, who relayed the fact that a Japanese diplomatic delegation headed by Ambassador Usume Nakamoto was en route to the presidential palace and had requested permission to convene with President Len. Unprecedented. Len would never have allowed it under normal circumstances, but he suspected that this must have something to do with the suicide raid on the missile complex.

He watched out the window as the door of the Lexus limousine opened, and a three-man diplomatic team disembarked, clearly one leader with two lackies, one of them carrying the leader's briefcase, the other holding a bulky metal suitcase. The leader stood by the car for several moments, smiling, bowing and shaking hands with the palace guards.

As the delegation was led into the presidential mansion, Len concentrated on what he would say. The video-link conference room, he decided, would be the room in which he would receive the Japanese. There they could be filmed unobtrusively, the video cameras mounted in the fabric of ornate and ancient oil paintings depicting wars on land and at sea. He could use the disk to keep the Japanese honest.

The intercom buzzed and Nakamoto was finally announced. Len nodded at Lee Chun Wah, and together they left the office and walked briskly down the hall to the conference room. Lee opened the door for President Len, who proceeded in.

The room was painted a deep shade of green to the railing, which was stained a dark brown and varnished to a glowing shine. Above the railing the huge oil paintings hung, the bloody scenes of battle shocking at first, then soon ignored. The room had no windows, its only furniture a wooden conference table with dark green leather set into the surface, several chandeliers casting a mellow light throughout the room. The place would be ideal for poker, an American ambassador had once joked. He had not known how close he was to the truth. Against the front wall stood Nakamoto and his aides. The Japanese ambassador, elderly and deeply wrinkled, broke into a grin, revealing uneven teeth protruding outward on top, inward on the bottom. He required only round wire-rimmed glasses, it occurred to Len, to complete the caricature of a Japanese from an old Allied World War II poster. Nakamoto began to bow, deeply, and Len wondered how he could go so far down without falling. Len continued to stand upright, refusing to bow, having decided to throw cold water on Nakamoto from the start. The Japanese were not going to steamroll him with their polite rituals, disarming their opposition and walking away winning the negotiation. That might work with certain naïve American presidents, but not a former battlefield commanding general.

"Please state your business, Nakamoto."

Nakamoto looked at the Greater Manchurian president with no change in his expression. "Honorable President Len Pei Poom, we have come to discuss a matter of urgency and concern to the Japanese people—"

Len sat down, not drawing his chair up to the table, as if he was about to leave momentarily. He looked pointedly at his watch and said nothing.

The Japanese ambassador sank slowly into a seat. "Your nuclear missiles, Honorable Mr. President."

"What?" Len sounded more indignant than surprised. In fact, he had suspected as much.

Nakamoto proceeded to open an envelope and spread out several black-and-white photographs of the inside of the Tamga facility, one of them showing the inside of the bunker. "These were taken from inside your facility."

Len refused to look down at the photographs. The Japanese gave him no chance to accuse them of spying. They began by acknowledging it. Clever. Nakamoto might look like a caricature, but that was clearly only on the surface.

"You admit it," Len said slowly, trying to recover.

"I merely advise you of a fact. The prime minister is gravely concerned."

"He has no need to be."

"We do not agree. We wish control of the Tamga facility to ensure our security. We will keep this private. We understand you have Russia and the Chinas to contend with. But we have, as I say, our concerns. The Japanese Self Defense Force will send a small force to guard the missiles. We must agree before you ever use them, and a Japanese team will fire the missiles for you if—"

Len allowed himself to laugh, although he saw nothing amusing. These people were serious.

"Sir, our only objective is to insure that Greater Manchuria not threaten Japan."

"My answer is that you go back to your embassy. Mr. Lee, see these gentlemen to their car."

"Wait, please, Honorable Mr. President Len. I request that you let me make a call to Tokyo. I have a satellite phone cell that will put me in video contact from here, if you will but allow it. Let me but put this matter to Tokyo."

Len began to shake his head, but an old saying by

Daniele Vare, an Italian diplomat, came to mind: "Diplomacy is the art of letting someone else have *your* way."

"Ambassador Nakamoto, you may make your call. I will be in my office chambers. When you are ready to talk again, pick up the phone in the corner and I will be back."

The rocky coastline approached rapidly and the missile climbed to forty meters in anticipation of a small cliff. The cliff approached at 600 kilometers per hour. At one instant the missile was flying over the sea, the next it was navigating over the rocky terrain of the Greater Manchurian wilderness. The missile continued on, following its programmed trajectory, dodging small mountains and trees and outcroppings of rocks, the land flying toward the video view at a dizzying speed.

Every few minutes the missile transmitted a burst communication to the Galaxy satellite, the transmission composed of video images of the previous five minutes along with missile-status parameters. The transmission was triple encrypted, meaningless tones to a hostile receiver, the first encryption by the computer onboard, the second encryption done by varying the transmission frequency across the spectrum in planned jumps so that a receiver could pick up the entire transmission only if he knew what frequency to skip to. And the frequency skips took place at random times, essentially making for a third encryption. The final precaution was the random-minute transmission intervals, so that a receiving station could not detect the telemetry during the outages between transmissions. The random transmission intervals were done so that a listener would not detect a transmission pattern and be waiting for a burst communication every five minutes, which would be too regular. The integrated system was highly stealthy and amounted to a full data exchange under conditions that normally would dictate radio silence.

The missile flew on, the afternoon sun beginning to sink in the sky. By sunset, the mission would be long over.

**CHANGASHAN, GREATER MANCHURIA**

Back in his office Len looked at Lee Chun Wah.

"What are the Japanese doing? Their offer seems almost deliberately insulting. They want my missiles. A Japanese team to make sure I don't play with my own toys, so to speak. And now they're on the phone. What are they thinking?"

"Only they know for sure. A not uncommon phenomenon for them."

"Any way of accessing the video cameras in the conference room? Getting an early read?"

"Afraid not, sir. We can get the disk in from the computer once the session is over, but we can't tap into the room now."

"Make a note—I want those cameras tied into my personal closed loop video. We may need to do this in the future."

"Yes, sir."

The phone rang. Lee Chun Wah picked it up.

"They are ready sir. And Nakamoto sounded shaken."

"Ambassador Nakamoto. What has Tokyo told you?"

Nakamoto looked up from the table to the standing form of Len Pei Poom. Len's directness seemed to be contagious. "Honorable Mr. President, Tokyo has decided to protect our nation. We must be rid of your threatening missiles." Nakamoto pointed to the display of a notebook computer on the table. The display showed land flying toward the video eye, trees and hills passing by at a tremendous speed. "With a nominal five-minute delay, this is the view out the targeting camera of one of the missiles we have launched at your Tamga facility. It will be arriving at the facility in approximately two minutes. We have one last chance to stop the missiles. Will you agree to sign a nonaggression pact with Japan, and agree to put Japanese Self Defense Force troops in command of your missiles?"

"*No.* And now, if there is nothing else, we will get you back to your embassy," Len said.

"You consider this a bluff?"

"I do."

"I will prove you are tragically mistaken, Mr. President."

Len noticed he was no longer the "Honorable Mr. President," but he was too angry to deal with it. What he desired was to reach over and snap Nakamoto's neck.

Len forced himself to watch the computer display as the video showed the sky, then the horizon, then an aerial shot of the ground approaching. He tried to show no emotion as he recognized the Tamga facility approach the view. All a Japanese trick—after all, the technology to fake this was well within their means. But then the compound continued to grow closer in the video display. Len held his breath.

# CHAPTER 8

**Tamga, Greater Manchuria**

The transmission came in from Galaxy satellite number three. The satellite identified itself, then issued a go code for the weapon to continue on its flight path for the target. If the message had not been received, the missile would have turned around and flown back out to sea and self-destructed. The attack could not take place unless the Japanese Defense Agency gave final confirmation within one minute of final arming and detonation of the warhead. But the message decoded to "DETONATE OVER TARGET AS PLANNED," and the missile made its final turn toward the target, now only one kilometer away over the ridge forming the Tamga Valley.

The warhead self-checks remained satisfactory. The missile armed the warhead detonator train, removing the safety interlocks from the system. It moved the canister of plutonium dust into proximity of the high-explosive cylinder so that the donut-shaped plutonium canister completely surrounded the explosive. The explosion cloud would not chemically alter the plutonium, but rather disperse it. Next to the plutonium canister high-pressure bottles of explosive ethylene gas were located, the gas pressure so high that a bottle failure alone could blow up half a city block. On the outside skin of the warhead were plastic bottles of vinyl acetate monomer liquid along with layered annular plastic bottles of other liquids, called "stardust" since they were miscellaneous additives that caused the polymerization to be able to proceed in the high temperatures of the fireball generated by the small high-explosive charge of the central detonator. The entire warhead was filled with inert nitrogen, which meant there was no stray oxygen to ruin the onboard chemicals or cause the ethylene to burn on warhead detonation.

Now fully armed, the warhead reported back to the missile computer that it was ready. The missile, at range to the target indicating half a kilometer, pulled up on the winglets and climbed for the sky.

The Tamga facility was now dead ahead by only a few hundred meters. The missile nose-cone video camera saw only the heavens above as the missile climbed, and when the altitude indicated a height of 1500 meters the winglets rotated to send the missile plummeting down over the target.

The video camera showed the facility laid out like a still-color aerial photograph, the afternoon sun casting the low shadows of the trees over the compound, which grew rapidly closer as the missile dived for the center, the humpbacked earthen bunker shown on the navigation files describing the target. The view continued to grow until the surrounding complex was gone, only the central buildings and the bunker in view, with one of the SS-34 missiles rolled out on the southwest side of the bunker, the shadows of people clear in the camera view.

Altitude 500 meters. The detonator, a small blasting cap, was energized by the missile-computer circuitry. Seeing the high voltage, the detonator exploded and caused the high-explosive charge to go off.

Altitude 450 meters. The high-explosive detonation rippled through the plutonium canister, the fireball reaching out to the ethylene bottles and rupturing them. Contained in the high-energy gases of the explosion were plutonium fragments and ethylene gas. The ethylene did not burn or explode, since the high explosive had already used its oxidizer, and there was no oxygen inside the warhead, only nitrogen. The blast circle then extended to the vinyl acetate monomer bottles and the stardust, the plastic material of the bottles vaporizing, the liquid, then atomizing and vaporizing as well, taking the aerosol stardust with it. The pressure pulse blew off the warhead skin, and the cloud grew, a sphere of high-pressure, high-temperature gases, the ethylene gas mixing with the vinyl acetate monomer in the high temperatures and reacting to form a vinyl-acetate ethylene copolymer—a liquid latex glue—which completed its reaction, using up the ethylene and vinyl acetate and stardust, the gas cloud finally cooling and changing from a sphere to a teardrop shape as it fell toward earth.

The polymer glue then mixed with the plutonium dust and rained down on the earth, the first droplets falling onto the ground of the bunker, the SS-34 missile that had been rolled out, and those standing by the missile.

After weapon one detonated, weapon two's warhead exploded, adding a second wave of plutonium-latex rain down on the compound below.

When the rain was finished, there was nothing left of either cruise missile. Weapons one and two, however, would live on in the lethal effects of their warheads.

Their missions were accomplished.

### Changashan, Greater Manchuria

Finally the video display on the tabletop flashed as the image of the compound vanished.

"That is it?" Len asked.

"The weapons are now destroyed," Nakamoto said. "I want you to know that many people argued against this course of action. None of us thought you would say no to us. It is regrettable that—"

"Nakamoto, now that your movie is over, you must go. My missiles are not for sale. But thank your prime minister for the interesting video. The special effects were outstanding."

"But, Mr. President—"

"I must go now. Mr. Lee Chun Wah will take you to the airport."

Len turned and left.

The forty steps to his office had seemed a lifetime as Len thought about the strange presentation by the Japanese.

When he opened the door to the office, Lee Chun Wah gestured to him rapidly.

"There's a phone call from Tamga, sir. The crew from the American television show 'Conspiracy Exposed'—the ones you sent to interview the base commander—want to talk to you—they said something awful is happening."

Len listened for a moment, knit his brows. "No one picked up. I only heard screaming."

# CHAPTER 9

**CHANGASHAN, GREATER MANCHURIA**

Len put the phone down, a dread beginning to fill him. If the Japanese had truly attacked the weapons, the survival of Greater Manchuria was at risk. In fact, Greater Manchuria might not exist a week into the future without the SS-34s.

A frantic knock came at the door. Intelligence officer Col. Ni Han Su rushed in.

"Sir, the video, turn it on, now!"

Len had spent too much of his life on battlefields to berate a junior who screamed at his superiors—a disciplined subordinate who behaved in this fashion did it for a very good reason. Len turned on the video to see an announcer from BBC Asia speaking, reporting on the destruction. The American reporters must have made their report before dying. The reality of the attack on his missiles was too clear.

"Get Ambassador Nakamoto back in the conference room."

"Sir, he's still there packing his equipment."

Len fairly burst into the room. Nakamoto looked up at him.

"Ambassador Nakamoto, you and your countrymen are treacherous felons. You come here, make impossible demands, and while I receive you, you stab me in the back, just as you did the Americans at Pearl Harbor while you talked of peace. You have attacked my missiles, which I have kept only for defense. You have killed my men and will blame this savagery on my alleged intransigence. I promise you that the world will know every detail of what has happened here."

"Sir, I will overlook your unreasoned outburst for now and urge you to realize that it is in your best interests, and Greater Manchuria's best interests, to keep this matter quiet. If so, Russia and the Chinas will not know you have lost your weapons. Japan will not, I guarantee you, speak of it. You keep your deterrent while Japan has its security, its freedom from fear of your former SS-34 nuclear missiles. This, sir, is the perfect solution."

Len looked at him in disbelief. "Surely you realize the world already knows. *I* have just heard it announced on the BBC. No more talk. You will be driven to the airport under escort from the palace guards. There you will meet the others from your embassy. You will all be put on a military transport and flown back to your island. God have mercy on your souls."

Len walked out of the room, motioning Lee Chun Wah to follow. Inside Len's office he gave his command to Lee while raising the phone to his ear:

"Go out to the airfield and see the commanding general of the air force at the tower. Allow the transport with Nakamoto and his people to get out over the Sea of Japan, but just on our side of the twenty kilometer territorial limit. When they are there, one of the escorting F-16's will blow them out of the sky."

Lee Chun Wah nodded, his face grim.

"And Lee, the disk of the meetings inside the conference room, copy and send to BBC. I want them on the air tonight. Unedited. We will let the world know *exactly* who the Japanese are behind their masks. Greater Manchuria may not survive but Japan will suffer with us."

Len stood, looking out the window at the approach to the palace's entrance. He could see Nakamoto's bent form walking to the limousine, then duck into it. The man looked old. It was later than he knew—his last day on earth.

The operator clicked into the connection.

"Yes, sir?"

"Get me the President of the United States."

**GROTON, CONNECTICUT**

On the other side of the world the early morning winter sun competed with scattered clouds, trying to light the landscape of the Connecticut countryside. Bruce Phillips took a breath of the northern air as he moved down the stair ramp from the Grumman twelve-passenger jet. The bare branches of the trees and weeks-old grimy snow might normally make for a gloomy scene, but to Phillips they added to the charm of this trip. He felt like a kid going with his father to pick out a Christmas present.

Admiral Pacino walked three steps ahead of him to the waiting staff car, where an aide stood by the open door. Phillips climbed in next to Pacino. The car drove toward the fence gate, the idling jet shrinking behind. For some minutes neither man said a word. Phillips looked out the window at the thick trees, their frozen branches waving in a cold wind.

"You ever heard about the Vortex missile?" Pacino asked, looking out his own window.

"Excuse me, sir?" Phillips moistened his lips, wanting a cigar but knowing it would not be proper unless his superior offered to let him smoke. All the more reason to be away from the top brass, he thought.

"The Vortex antisubmarine missile, invented four years ago for the Seawolf class," Pacino said. "The program was abandoned last year."

"I haven't heard the term, sir."

Pacino nodded. "I was involved early in the program, I keep forgetting its classification. When I worked on it the Vortex name alone was classified secret. The program was compartmented, limited distribution, codeword stuff. Anyway, Admiral Donchez came up with the concept—an underwater weapon that's a hybrid rocket and torpedo. It's solid-rocket fueled, blue-laser guided. Warhead is seven tons of PlasticPac explosive with a plasma yield equivalent to the effect of a small battlefield nuclear device."

"An underwater rocket? With seven *tons* of PlasticPac?"

Pacino paused, looking at Phillips. "You wouldn't happen to have any cigars, would you?"

Phillips grinned and pulled out two long Honduran cigars from his jacket pocket. "Sorry they aren't Cuban," he said, and passed the cigar cutter to Pacino, then his lighter, the emblem of the USS *Greeneville* worn by use. The back of the limo filled with mellow smoke.

"Anyway, the missile worked well. I was at a Bahamas test-range exercise when the Vortex made its preop trial. The firing ship was an instrumented 637-class attack sub, gutted of equipment with the Vortex launcher installed. The target sub was an old diesel boat similarly instrumented."

Phillips glanced at Pacino, squinting through the smoke. Pacino seemed sad, or nostalgic, or both.

"What happened?"

"The missile worked perfectly. Blew the target sub to iron filings. The blast made a water-vapor mushroom cloud that rained down on us for five minutes. I was deaf for three days."

"So why haven't we in the fleet heard about this miracle missile? It sounds like a silver bullet."

"Because the Vortex blew up the firing ship as well. There was nothing left of her. The solid-rocket fuel overpressurized the tube and the launcher burst open. The rocket exhaust blew the firing platform in half."

"Bad day after all."

"Yeah, you could say that."

"So why don't you launch this beast like a ballistic missile—propel it out the tube and *then* light off the rocket motor?"

"It's unstable. Spins around, the rocket motor goes off and water forces tear it apart. It needs the whole tube length for guidance."

Phillips looked at Pacino, wondering why the admiral was going on about a dead-end weapon program. When Phillips tamped out his cigar in the ashtray, the car had pulled up to a fenced-in gate. A large sign read DYNACORP INTERNATIONAL—ELECTRIC BOAT DIVISION. Pacino put down his window and passed out a bar-coded identification card to the guard, and Phillips reached into his wallet and handed over his own ID.

"State your business please," the guard said.

Pacino did and the car drove through the gate and around several small buildings, approaching a wide tall structure that was blue in the haze of distance. As they drew closer to the building a large sign loomed overhead: NUCLEAR SUBMARINE MANUFACTURING FACILITY—FAST ATTACK BOAT DEPARTMENT. The car stopped a final time. Pacino grabbed his white hat and climbed out of the car. Phillips got out, pulling his black overcoat collar up against the wind. From a door in the monolithic wall a short man in a double-breasted suit walked out, a uniformed naval officer following behind him. The man in civilian clothes had a goatee and mustache, his jowly face hanging down below the knot of a blue-patterned tie. The officer behind him wore a black reefer jacket with the four-striped shoulder boards of a navy captain. He was tall with graying cropped hair, an expression of distaste carved into the wrinkles of his face.

"Gentlemen," the civilian called heartily from forty feet away. "Glad you could make it!"

"Who's this guy?" Phillips mouthed to Pacino.

"Rebman, Doug Rebman," Pacino whispered back, "the DynaCorp vice-president of attack-sub shipbuilding. He's hard to take but he knows his stuff."

"And the captain?"

"Emmitt Stephens, superintendent of shipbuilding. As SUPESHIPS he has the unpleasant duty of hanging around with Rebman, but he got my *Seawolf* to sea from a drydock in four days when it would take a normal mortal four weeks. He's the best."

Rebman led them around the corner of the facility to an elevated platform overlooking a jetty four stories below. Phillips stopped dead in his tracks.

Pacino looked over at him and smiled. "Never seen the Seawolf class before, Phillips?"

Beyond the railing of the platform a submarine lay next to a narrow jetty, the hull bounded closely on either side by the protruding concrete structures. The ship was tremendously large, looking absurdly wide and fat. The hull was a flat black, the surface of it covered with foam tiles for quieting against active sonar pings. The conning tower, the sail, jutted straight up over the cylindrical hull, a triangular fillet joining the front of the sail to the ship below.

"She's huge," Phillips gasped. "I mean, she's at least ten feet wider in diameter than my *Greeneville.*"

"Meet the USS *Piranha,*" Pacino said. "SSN-23, third—and last—in the Seawolf class. Named after the original *Piranha* that Dick Donchez commanded in the 1970s. She's forty-two feet in diameter. She displaces over nine thousand tons, makes way on twin turbines cranking out fifty-two thousand shaft horsepower. The nuclear reactor is natural circulation cooled up to 50 percent power, that's thirty-two knots without reactor circulation pumps. Bruce, this submarine is quieter going full Out than your old *Greeneville* is at idle."

Pacino continued on, and before Phillips realized it, a half-hour had gone by, and he realized that something was different about the submarine. Where a few minutes before the hull had been black and unmarked, there was now a distinct white waterline mark circling the hull. He looked again, and noticed that the white line was rising further from the water.

"What's going on?"

"Dr. Rebman, please explain," Pacino said.

"We're lifting the hull out of the water," Rebman said. "For Admiral Pacino's ship alteration. We call it the Pacino ship-alt, Admiral."

"Lifting the hull out?"

"The ship is resting on blocks much like those on the floor of a drydock. This is a special jetty, Commander. The blocks touching the underside of the ship's hull are connected to a large metal platform, and beneath that we have steel columns about one meter in diameter. The columns are threaded and connected to motors below. There are twenty of them, and when we turn the motors, the columns turn and lift the platform out of the water, an inch at a time. Once the platform is out of the water the whole assembly can be moved into the assembly building. It allows us to move a submarine from its waterborne condition to inside the manufacturing bay in about four hours. That same operation to get a sub into drydock would take two to three days."

Phillips looked down at the jetty and saw that the sub had emerged from the water by another foot while they were talking.

"Let's go into the conference room, gentlemen," Rebman said. "We'll have a window view there. You can still see the ship coming out of the slip and into the building."

The four men walked inside to a hallway and then into a windowed room, one set of plateglass looking out over the jetty, where the *Piranha* was still quietly coming vertically out of the water, the other looking into the cavernous expanse of the manufacturing building. Phillips chose a seat where he could swivel his chair and see first one view, then the other.

Rebman doused the lights and started a disk presentation on the projection-screen wall.

"Commander Phillips, this presentation is for you as commanding officer of the *Piranha.* We put together this briefing about the Vortex missile, which I'm sure you're not aware of, when we moth-balled the program. Now the program is back."

Phillips looked to Pacino, who had a single finger over his lips, then watched the film on the Vortex program, observing computer views of the innards of the missile. He saw the missile test in the Bahamas when the missile was fired from one sub to see if it could hit the other. The screen view showed the explosion of the target boat as seen from the surface. The camera obviously had shaken as the shock wave hit, the enormous mushroom cloud rising from the sea as if a great beast had climbed out of the ocean, then the spray was raining back down again as the cloud dispersed. The target was obliterated, but then the film showed the slow-motion cameras depicting the inside of the firing ship, the film capturing the firing tube as it blew open, the flames pouring violently out of the tube, the screen going black as the recording camera was vaporized by the hot gas exhaust. A graphic came up, showing a cartoon of the missile in the tube and how the tube exploded, then widened to show how the rocket exhaust melted through the hull while the tremendous gas volume blew the hull open just as the missile had blown open the tube. In the cartoon the firing sub broke in half and drifted to the ocean bottom. After a few more words describing the final moneys spent on the missile program, the disk went blank.

"That was two years ago," Dr. Rebman said. "We thought the missile program could not go on. We put ten production missiles in a warehouse, archived the records and let the program die. Then Admiral Pacino called me. His idea to revive the Vortex missile is key to the alterations we will be doing to the *Piranha.* And that, Commander Phillips, is where you come in."

"What the hell are you doing to my ship?" Phillips heard himself ask.

"It's not quite your ship yet, Bruce," Pacino said, "but I'm glad you already feel possessive about her."

Pacino then went to the white wall, pointed his finger and traced a shape on it. As he did, the electronic white board turned his finger motion into a drawing, his finger acting as the chalk. The resulting shape was a submarine hull.

"Bruce, we know the Vortex missile needs to be launched from a tube to be stable. We also know it blows up missile tubes. What we want to do," Pacino said as he drew a small cylinder on the outside of the sketch of the sub hull, "is put the launching tubes on the *outside* of the sub. They will have blow-off caps at the aft end. When the missile launches, the outside tube won't blow up because the rupture cap at the back blows off and the missile leaves through the tube. The tube opens up at both ends and still acts to guide the missile in its first few milliseconds of travel. The missile leaves the external tube and moves on to the target. The sub then discards the tube and it falls to the bottom of the sea."

"Let me get this straight," Phillips said. "You're going to put these tube launchers on the outside of my hull?"

"Right."

"That's going to be noisy. It'll ruin the shape of the ship. All that work making the Seawolf class hydrodynamic and whisper quiet is down the drain. This tub will whistle and rattle and moan at cruising speed. An enemy boat will hear us coming five nautical miles away."

"Bruce, remember your failure in the simulator the other day? It was inevitable, though I didn't tell you so at the time. Your torpedoes had to miss. The only thing that would have helped was a Vortex missile. If you'd had one, the Destiny you attacked would have been dead."

"So would I when the Vortex blew up in the tube."

"Exactly, which is why they'll be on the outside of your hull, not the inside. The open-ended launching tubes with blowoff caps will keep the hull from rupturing. The problems with the Vortex are, we believe, fixed."

"Admiral, you mentioned them in the plural. You said *they'd* be on the outside of my hull. So do I get more than one?"

"I'm having ten of them put on the exterior of your hull. If we ever go up against Scenario Orange, you'll have ten silver bullets."

Phillips looked into Pacino's eyes, then exhaled and looked out the window at *Piranha,* now completely out of the water, the hull still drying in the cold breeze, the monster being moved slowly through the open door of the manufacturing facility.

"Admiral?"

"Yes?"

"You figure ten are enough?"

The massive hull of the *Piranha* lurked high above and behind the four men as they walked parallel to the hull to the east end of the bay. Phillips looked up at the black-painted cylinder dwarfing them. It was hard to believe that, with the ship this big on the outside, it would feel small on the inside.

By the time they reached the bow section, Phillips could see the racks with the stacked cylinders on them, the stenciling clear from fifty feet away reading MOD

BRAVO VORTEX. The men stopped near a weapon-loading tractor bed.

"Let's roll one of the missiles out," Pacino said.

One of the weapon-handling crewmen assembled two men to roll out the nearest Vortex. It took a few minutes, and during the wait Phillips saw the giant door of the facility begin to close, plunging the interior into gloom until his eyes adjusted to the overhead halogen lamps. Finally the weapon dolly pulled out one of the Vortex canisters. It was huge, almost four feet in diameter and fifty feet long.

"And how do you plan on putting ten of these things on the outside of the *Piranha*?" Phillips asked.

"You're going to look like you're wearing a bandoleer," Pacino said.

"Amazing."

"Admiral Pacino?" a young civilian asked, winded from trotting across the facility floor.

"I'm Pacino."

"Sir, an Admiral Donchez called and said he needed to see you at the White House within the hour."

Pacino looked startled. "Thanks. Emmitt, how soon can you be done with the alterations to the *Piranha*?"

"It's a month of work, Admiral."

"You know what I'm going to say, don't you, Emmitt?"

Capt. Emmitt Stephens smiled, resigned. "Yes, sir. You want the work done in a week with *Piranha* out of here on her own power. I'll see to it."

Pacino shook his hand, then Rebman's and waved Phillips to walk with him.

"What was that about a week, sir?" Phillips asked.

"Emmitt Stephens can work miracles. There's no reason you should have to wait a month to get your boat ready. I want you on the way to the Pacific by this time next week."

"Why, sir? What's going down?"

"Let's just say I have a bad feeling."

"One week. I can't believe it."

"Neither can I," Pacino said. "I was just going to ask

him to get it done in two. Good thing I kept my mouth shut."

"What's this White House business about, Admiral?"

"I'll find out in an hour. Bruce, don't be a stranger. I consider you my first line commander. Don't let me down out there."

Pacino clapped him on the shoulder and vanished out the corner door into the winter air. Phillips looked back up at the tail of the *Piranha* looming over his head, thinking about the admiral who had called him the best. He let his gaze roam over the Piranha's massive hull, and felt a mix of awe and near-sensual pleasure.

# CHAPTER 10

**WASHINGTON, D.C.**
**THE WHITE HOUSE**

Pacino was ushered into the Oval Office and led to a seat on a wide sofa next to Richard Donchez.

The room seemed much smaller than it had appeared on television. The desk was the same, the couch and chair arrangement the same, even the fireplace looked familiar, but the combination in reality was so close as to seem claustrophobic, although that could have come from the crowd in the room.

Pacino recognized Vice President Al Meckstar, the dark-haired Hispanic-looking boy of politics, his looks deceptively youthful. Now in his early forties, Meckstar had joked he would dye his temples gray if that would lend him more credibility. Meckstar sank into the sofa opposite Pacino and Donchez, next to Secretary of State Phil Gordon. Gordon was thin, a marathon runner who had joined government directly out of Harvard, although little of his education or elite background seemed to have rubbed off on him. His eternal smile and joking cheerfulness were so thick as to seem affected but they were not. His political instincts were matched by none; his success at State was eerie. Someone had remarked that Gordon could have been a time traveler back from the future armed with detailed history books, so accurate were his intuitions about foreign heads of state.

At the end of the opposite couch Steve Cogster, the National Security Advisor, stretched his awkwardly long legs. Cogster was an oddball. Donchez had once told Pacino he did not trust him. Impeccably turned out in a pinstriped suit, imported silk tie, and sparkling wingtips, Cogster was as tall as Pacino, with thinning blond hair, slightly buck teeth, and oval-shaped lenses in wire-framed glasses. Cogster was famous for his soft-spoken arguments in public, coupled with his flaming E-mails and memos so caustic his own staff had nicknamed him "the Blowtorch," passing his acerbic E-mails throughout State. Even Donchez had received a few winners at NSA. It was rumored that Phillip Gordon kept a file of Cogster's most acidic memos and passed them around Friday afternoons. Some said that Gordon even had some of them framed in his office and only took them down when Cogster or the president visited him at State. Donchez had once remarked that Cogster would not be a good man to have as an enemy, but having him as an ally did not seem particularly beneficial either. The Blowtorch was just that, best to stay out of the flame path.

In the end chair, near the fireplace, the director of the CIA sat with his legs crossed, his pale hairy flesh exposed over sagging socks. Boswell Farnesworth Leach III was bald, his face was red, his teeth either capped or false, his manner earnest. But Donchez had once characterized him as a snake. There were too many backs in Washington bearing Leach's knives, Donchez had said. Leach seemed to be the one person in government that Donchez loved to hate. Leach never signed his name, only used his initials, "BFL." Donchez had indicated to Pacino that Leach's intelligence estimates were usually inaccurate—not because of the failings of the CIA itself, since the information and analyses coming into Leach's office were sound, but because Leach was so arrogant that any intelligence assessment that didn't fit his predetermined notions would be rewritten to fall into line with his world views. Nonetheless, his intel assessments had been oddly correct in recent months, which had prompted Donchez to tell Pacino that "BFL" stood for "Blind Fucking Luck."

Noticeably absent was the Secretary of Defense, the elder statesman of the group, Bob Katoss, the pipe-smoking sixty-five-year-old who refused to wear suits, only cardigan sweaters and open-necked shirts. The political cartoons regularly depicted him wearing bunny slippers with the outfit. Katoss was from the old school, refusing to suffer fools, refusing to smile at those he did not respect. In short, refusing to be a politician. Donchez considered him a breath of fresh air; Pacino wasn't so sure; he wondered if the man's pugnacious exterior perhaps fronted for an inadequate intellect and a cold heart. Katoss had been retired for five years, his detractors frequently said, and in fact, at this critical meeting, Katoss was unapologetically on vacation in the Bahamas. Pacino was glad for the man's absence and wondered why President Warner had chosen him, but then who knew what political obligations she had had?

The Secretary of the Navy was likewise missing, President Warner having sent him on a mission to Africa with the chief of Naval Operations, Adm. Anthony Wadsworth, a tough black man, an inch taller than Pacino and who at 250 pounds had been a boxer at the Academy. He and Pacino had crossed paths a decade before when Pacino's first submarine, *Devilfish,* had been involved in an exercise against Wadsworth, who then was a full captain and the commanding officer of the aircraft carrier *Eisenhower.* Pacino had had orders to sneak up on Wadsworth's carrier and act as the aggressor submarine, and Wadsworth's antisubmarine warfare ships, the destroyers and frigates, were tasked with finding Pacino and *Devilfish* first. The exercise signal that the operation order specified was a flare, purple smoke, to be fired from *Devilfish*'s signal ejector to indicate that the submarine was shooting torpedoes at the aircraft carrier. Wadsworth hadn't planned on Pacino getting in close, since he was scouring the seas around the *Eisenhower* with S-2 Vikings and the towed array sonar systems of his escort ships. It had taken Pacino all day to set up to penetrate the antisubmarine net around the carrier but he finally had sneaked in past the outer barriers and had gotten in close. He could have simply launched a series of purple flares from the center of the task force, but somehow that didn't seem enough. Pacino had maneuvered *Devilfish* directly beneath the *Eisenhower,* steamed up on her port side, the opposite side of the ship from the island and bridge. Pacino had launched a purple flare from the signal ejector, filming it from the periscope as it arced high in the sky and landed on Wadsworth's flight deck. The carrier flight-deck crew had panicked, not expecting the burst of purple smoke from out of nowhere. The crew had treated it like a fire, stringing out hoses, alarms blaring. Pacino had gone deep, increased speed to flank and pulled away from the carrier. then when he was a mile away, had come back up to periscope depth and taken a panoramic photograph of the *Eisenhower,* the purple smoke obscuring half the deck, frantic firefighters scrambling to put out the flames.

Back in port after the incident, the squadron commander had called Pacino to his stateroom on the tender and chewed him out for a quarter-hour. Wadsworth had apparently put up a stink about Pacino violating safety rules with the flammable smoke grenade, not to mention violating the OpOrder *and* showing that a lone submarine could humiliate the carrier battle group's antisubmarine defenses and get close enough to poop a flare onto the carrier's deck, which, of course, was the idea. All that saved Pacino's career was that at the time Admiral Donchez was Commander Submarines US Atlantic Fleet, and had admired Pacino's gutsy move. But even Donchez had taken Pacino aside to tell him to save his aggression for real combat and not embarrass politically connected senior officers. When a few months later Wadsworth had held a reception on board the *Eisenhower* for the fleet staff, one of Pacino's junior officers had presented Wadsworth with a framed four-foot-wide blowup of the periscope photograph of *Eisenhower* with her deck half-obscured by purple smoke, the crosshairs on the picture leaving no doubt who had taken the photo. Another junior officer had snapped a shot of Wadsworth looking at the huge photo, his mouth wide open in shock and anger. That photo had been framed and hung on the bulkhead of *Devilfish*'s wardroom. The incident had been somewhat typical of Pacino's approach to life and to command before the arctic mission

Donchez had sent him on, the one that had led to *Devilfish*'s sinking. The years before that ice-cap mission now seemed so remote as to be from somebody else's life, but the fallout from them was still real, including Wadsworth's feelings about Pacino.

Pacino emerged from his reminiscence to look at Donchez, closeted as he was with men who were as difficult for him as Wadsworth was for Pacino. Sitting in the chairs next to Leach were Air Force general Felix Clough, the outgoing Chairman of the Joint Chiefs of Staff, and Army general Kurt Sverdlov, the newly nominated chairman. Pacino knew Donchez and Clough shared a professional dislike that went back decades, based partly on each man's disregard for the other's service. But Clough was a lame duck, and Sverdlov and Donchez seemed to be forming a close working relationship, Sverdlov apparently realizing that having a friend at NSA could help him. Meanwhile, Donchez was no longer in the Navy or in competition with Sverdlov the way he had once been with Clough. Pacino knew that Donchez hoped that when Leach was gone he would inherit CIA, and from that point on, the Blowtorch notwithstanding, he would have a seamless, functional network surrounding and leading up to the president.

As if cued by Pacino's thought, President Jaisal Warner swept into the office with aides in tow, her low-voiced orders flying to each until she reached her seat and dismissed them. The men in the room all stood as if someone had called them to attention. Warner waved them to their seats. Pacino tried not to stare at her, but wasn't successful.

Jaisal Warner was only in her second year in office, yet it was already a charmed administration. Warner had come into office almost unopposed, the previous incumbent withdrawing from the race for reasons of health, his announcement coming just after Warner was nominated. His party's nomination was a tired old senator who was in the race for show. Warner's campaign had focused on her energy and competence as the remarkably successful governor of California, where her hard-nosed leadership had pulled the state out of severe financial troubles. After the governorship she had become the state's junior senator yet had been named to the Armed Services Committee, making news with her proposals on revolutionizing the military. She had become something of a media darling, as well as of even the military and the American people over a period of ten years. Her campaign slogan still graced the bumpers of countless cars, the green letters proclaiming on a white field: JAISAL WARNER—JUST GET OUT OF HER WAY. Even her name was symbolic of her rise to power—the name Jaisal was Indian for "victory."

Her first hundred days in office had been a thunderstorm of activity as she cleaned house in the government, eliminating half the government bureaucracy and replacing the administrators with handpicked replacements. She made the cover of *Time* three times in two years, one caption reading: JAISAL CLEANS UP, the next: WARNER'S MACHINE, the third: GOVERNMENT NOW WORKS! the last in capital letters with an exclamation point. Warner seemed to live for crises, Donchez had once remarked to Pacino. She often quoted wartime leaders, her favorites Winston Churchill, the two Roosevelts, Eisenhower, even Nixon, but her clear number one was Margaret Thatcher.

Warner stood now in front of the large chair at the desk end of the couch-and-chair arrangement. She was in her late forties, and remained a very beautiful woman. She wore a dark suit, the skirt midlength, with a cream silk blouse, a small diamond necklace at her throat. Her hair was cut in a bob, the straw color graying but attractive. Her hands were graceful, her fingers long and unadorned by rings. Her husband had died when she was in the Senate, and she had never remarried, all her energy pouring into her job. Her eyes were dark and unreadable, but the lines around her mouth seemed to indicate her concern. When she spoke, her voice was clear.

"Good afternoon, gentlemen," she said. "Please sit down." She remained standing herself. "I assume you're all up to speed on what's happened in Greater Manchuria. I think you should all see this." She nodded at an aide, who passed out folders. Pacino opened his, finding an advance copy of the next week's *Time* magazine. On the cover was: JAPAN STRIKES AGAIN. Pacino opened the old-fashioned paper magazine, this version the one that would be sold on the newsstands. Magazines had gone digital four years before so that they could be downloaded onto a WritePad personal notesheet computer, but some people, particularly the over-fifty generation, preferred a hardcopy to hold in their hands, so the glossy paper version continued to be published. A photo of Kurita was shown, the caption quoting him as saying Japan had nothing to do with the attack. Another picture showed the Japanese Ministry of Foreign Affairs spokesman issuing the statement that the bombing was justified to eliminate the threat of the nuclear weapons in Greater Manchuria, making Kurita an instant liar. The lack of coordination of the Japanese government was astonishing, as it added even more to the picture of Kurita as a treacherous operative. Next was a story on the growing sentiment of Americans to "do something" about Japan, the bar graphs showing the burgeoning anti-Japanese sentiment. A final article profiled the US military, showing the possible military options that could be used against Japan. No one had attacked the US directly, but the mood of America now approached the intensity of feeling immediately before Pearl Harbor, if *Time*'s graphics were to be trusted.

"So, let's talk about how I see what's going on here before we open this up to discussion," Warner said. "First, Japan, feeling threatened by Greater Manchuria because of the possibility that Greater Manchuria could attack Tokyo, decides to take out the Greater Manchurian nuclear weapons. Next, Kurita is exposed doing what he denies.

"I suggest two ways of looking at this. One, the Greater Manchurian nuclear weapons were dangerous and destabilizing. The Japanese in one sense did our work for us." Warner rubbed her eyelids, looking tired for a second. "Now the nukes are gone and the East Chinese or the West Chinese or the Russians may invade Greater Manchuria and take over their territory. One headache gone, a bigger new one replaces it. This is unacceptable for us, we need a real balance of power there, not one all-powerful Far East nation.

"Now focus on Japan. We can say, for argument, that Greater Manchuria had no intentions of threatening Tokyo whatsoever, that their missiles were a deterrent to Russia and the Chinas. The attack by Japan on continental Asia is another example of Japan's new militarism. Let's look at the last five years. We essentially stopped trade between Japan and America. Europe followed suit. Japan was hurt, and badly. They turned their industrial strengths into rearming, building up a threatening military."

Pacino could almost hear in Warner's words Donchez's briefing. She must have liked it, found it convincing, because here she was speaking just as Donchez had a few days ago.

"Next we see a Japanese strike against an Asian nation. They took matters into their own hands rather than consulting with the rest of the world. Our response now is critical. If we look the other way, we encourage Japan to keep using its military. Some of my advisors indicate that in another five years or less, Japan could well invade continental Asia and expand. They would have an empire greater than in 1941. And that means China, Korea, Greater Manchuria, Indonesia, southeast Asia, all of it, *back in aggressive Japanese hands.* By then, there would be no stopping Japan without a major bloodbath involving another world war. On the *other* hand, we could move in and stop this *now,* and turn the tide. How many of us would argue, if we could go back in time, with stopping Hitler when he tried to make his move into the Sudetenland? We could have averted World War II. An early confrontation avoids a later war, if we learn *anything* from history. So, in spite of Japan's military strength, or because of it, I believe we should seriously discuss a military option. I am also open to other options. I'd like to go around the room now and ask each of you for your opinion."

Warner was famous for this approach, Pacino thought. Her advisors hated it, but it allowed her to get to a decision quickly at the risk of generating great conflict among the cabinet. Warner was convinced she could manage the clashing egos, but the recent resignation of the attorney general had shaken the administration, and his replacement had yet to be chosen.

"Alex, you get the honor of speaking up first."

Alex Addison was the soft-spoken chief of staff. He was fiercely protective of the president and her schedule but otherwise—as Donchez had described him—he would mostly be a good guy to have a beer with. He was short and balding but trim and well-dressed, still in his suit coat while the rest of the men were in shirtsleeves.

"Thank you, Madam President," Addison began so softly that Pacino had to strain to hear. "I think we should hammer the Japanese. We've always been reasonable with them, but now they need to be taught a lesson—that they can't just attack a neighbor without retribution."

"Short and strong and to the point, Alex. What about the people? Remember Vietnam. Do you think the voters feel as you do?"

"Yes, Madam President, though I'd leave the specifics of a military option to the pros." Addison nodded at the generals and to Pacino. "Indeed, I believe the people are very tired of the way we have tiptoed around Japan."

"We cut off nearly all trade with them after they tried to raid AT&T and IBM."

"Right, and they still flourish."

"It has hurt them—"

"And they are more dangerous than ever. I believe the American people would support a military option."

"Thank you, Alex. Al?"

Vice President Meckstar cleared his throat and stretched his neck.

"Well, we can't just go in there bombing and shooting. We have to have a clear objective. We have to figure out what we want. I'd say our position should be that we are going after Japan to dismantle their military. After all, their own constitution prohibits them from having a military."

"We blew off that rationale during the Cold War with

Russia," National Security Advisor Cogster said. "Kind of hard to invoke it now, over a half-century later."

"Getting back to our objective, Al?" Warner prompted.

"Yes. We want the Japanese to dismantle any more of these dirty radiation bombs, decommission their navy and sell their fighter planes. They won't do it, so we help them."

Cogster interrupted, "You're talking about an invasion. Does anyone here remember their freshman year history? This is the country we dropped two nuclear weapons on to *avoid* invading."

"Good point, Steve," President Warner said to Cogster. "Well, Phil, it's time for some of your inimitable wisdom," Warner said to Secretary of State Phil Gordon, walked to the back of the desk, parted the curtains and stared out at the city.

"I've been thinking about this for some time," Gordon said. Pacino leaned forward. "If we go in for an invasion, we go too far. We lose—millions killed, loss of prestige. If we do nothing, we do too little. Much too little. Loss of world respect, administration appears weak—"

"That's not going to happen," Warner said, her voice momentarily rising. She frowned, hearing it.

"Absolutely not, Madam President. So we're walking a tightrope, as usual. The middle course seems the best all around. We put up a blockade around Japan. Nothing goes in. Nothing comes out. They'll be in serious domestic turmoil within three months. Before that happens I believe they'll let us inspect their weapons, even allow us to take away the nastier ones, quietly let the air force and navy decline. By then, some new crisis will come up, the revolution in India and that wild man Nipun, and we can let Japan save some face. We mostly need to worry about how to prop up Greater Manchuria for the next month or so."

"Great," Cogster said. "Our best option according to Phil is to starve the Japanese. The little children starve to death on the APN network, bellies all swollen, tears coming down their sweet dirty faces, and it will be *our* fault. Or worse."

"Worse?" Warner asked.

"Yes, ma'am. The Japanese could well come out fighting. That *is* their heritage and history, after all."

"And what would they do? What is their capacity?"

"Perhaps our Admiral Pacino should answer that question," General Clough said.

The people in the room all turned to stare at Pacino. The moment he had dreaded. Well, time to get on with it, he thought.

"Since setting up and enforcing a blockade is an act of war," he began, "we had better remember that the Japanese have a blue-water navy made up entirely of submarine assets. Their air force is formidable. Several squadrons of Firestar fighters. As I'm sure General Clough knows, the Firestar fighters are considered more than a match for our F-16s, F-15s and F-14s. The F/A-18 stands a slight chance, and the AFX advanced fighter has technology almost as good. Almost. As far as the Maritime Self Defense Force is concerned, half of the subs are the new Destiny III class, computer-controlled and extremely quiet. The other half are the Destiny II class, the earlier manned vessels. Also quiet and lethal. Just one of these submarines lurking off the coast of Japan would make a battle-group commander think twice about setting up a blockade. But it's more than one. There are almost thirty of these killer subs. Some are being built, some are being repaired or refitted, but our latest estimates show between twenty-two and twenty-six vessels."

"So?" CIA director Leach asked, speaking up for the first time, while looking at his fingernails. "The Japanese may have some nice toys, as you say, but I understand their robot subs are problematic and—"

Warner broke in. "Admiral Pacino, you called a blockade an act of war?"

"Madam President, as far as international and maritime law are concerned, a blockade is exactly that. We would be as much at war with Japan, legally, as if we'd invaded them."

"That's true, technically," Phillip Gordon said, surprised at Pacino's fairly arcane knowledge for a military man. "We could introduce a resolution to the UN that specifies sanctions against Japan, no one trading with her at all, unless Japan allows a UN team to inspect and dismantle all the other radiation weapons, as well as ordering Japan to eliminate her air force and navy. The trouble is getting key nations to go along with the sanctions. We've had conversations with Vorontsev's people."

Vladimir Vorontsev was the new president of the Russian Republic.

"And?" Warner prompted.

"Well, we need to consider events in Russia as well as those in Japan. Russia and America, as you all know, have grown further apart over the last fifteen years. Russia's governments have been steadily more authoritarian. The Russians are poor. If we set up an effective economic embargo, Russia will abstain from voting for sanctions in the Security Council. It will be an opportunity for them to cozy up to a power, to Japan. Russia has the oil, ore, and lumber that the Japanese need. If we put sanctions on Japan, Russia will still trade with them. They'll see it as win-win. They get trade and reduce their own risk of being invaded themselves by Japan. Bottom line—Russia will keep Japan resupplied even after the UN votes sanctions. So sanctions will mean nothing. We are back to a blockade now, which would eliminate a Russian resupply."

Pacino looked at her, almost seeing through her attempts to seem almost naïve, a posture that made the men speak their minds more than if she revealed her own opinions.

"Furthermore," Gordon said. "If we are slow to put up a blockade around Japan, the Russians would resupply Japan, neutralizing the sanctions. We would have a very tough time effecting a blockade two weeks from now, with the Russians already supplying Japan—it would mean a confrontation at sea with the Russians. If we go ahead and set it up *now,* the Russians would think twice about running it."

"You'll still have to wait," Pacino put in. "The carrier battle group operating in the Pacific under Exercise Pacific Thrust is a long way from Japan. Seven days at tactical-approach velocity from the inner waters around Japan."

"So, Admiral Pacino," the president said, "you are saying the blockade would be an act of war. And Phillip, you're saying that without it, sanctions are useless, because there's a new Russian alignment toward Japan."

"Exactly," Philip Gordon said. "Another damned tightrope."

"Admiral Pacino, how would you recommend proceeding?"

Thin ice, Pacino thought. With Wadsworth in Africa, he was being asked to recommend the Navy's advice during a time of crisis. If he were wrong, Wadsworth would crucify him. If he were right, Wadsworth would be just as angry for taking the political spotlight from him.

"I'm sure Admiral Wadsworth would be better to—"

"Admiral Pacino," Warner said, iron in her voice, "*I've* asked your recommendation and I want to hear it. I didn't ask Boxing Tony, I asked you."

"Yes, well, I see it like this. The fleet is a week out of Japan. We should do our work now in the UN, as though sanctions will work. We get State to work on Vorontsev to hold back, even if it means giving him some trade benefits, making him whole on the money he'll lose. Then we take out every Japanese Galaxy satellite in orbit, all ten of them. Our submarines sortie from east and west, seek out the Japanese fleet and sink their submarines. Our aircraft carrier air arm takes on the FireStar fighters, one hopes with a covert night raid that catches them on the ground. Or General Clough's Stealth fighters could go in to neutralize the air force. And if we're quick about it, we could use air attacks to neutralize some of their submarines, because once they're at sea, they'll give us a hell of a fight. We can claim that the strike is done to bring Japan back into compliance with their own constitution, and that we have to take that step because the Greater Manchurian missile attack shows that they can't be trusted with a military. By that time the USS *Ronald Reagan* is in the immediate waters off Japan and we can enforce our blockade. The Russians, I suggest, won't fool with us when we have Japan surrounded. But just in case, I recommend we also send the other battle groups to sea." Pacino reached into his briefcase for his WritePad computer. "The carriers *Abraham Lincoln* and *United States* are in Pearl Harbor, being fueled and loaded out now. They can be ready to go to sea tomorrow on your orders, Madam President. In addition we can assemble a European force with the French carrier *De Gaulle* and the Royal Navy's *Ark Royal,* both of them accompanied by their escort forces. The Brits and French are visiting Guam now and they can load out, fuel up and get underway within thirty-six hours. The Royal Australian Navy has a small force that could come up from the south. By Christmas, if we're *quick,* we could have Japan encircled."

Warner waited for comments, and when there were none, looked hard at Pacino.

"Admiral, you are saying you would hold off the Japanese until the first carrier battle group is closer, then take out the Japanese surveillance and communication satellites, then attack and blow up the Japanese air force and submarine navy, *then* set up the blockade. Is that how you see it?"

"Yes, ma'am. We should be deliberate about it, but we should hit the Japanese with a knockout punch now and make our demands later."

"And if they fight back?"

"Madam President, they *will* fight back. This is exactly what happened just before the Japanese attack on Pearl Harbor in 1941. We cut off the flow of their oil, they were backed into a corner. Once in the corner, they fought to get out, among other things. And they'll do it again."

"So you're saying we are heading for war?"

"I'm saying that Japan is an island nation. It's like a scuba diver, if you will. If we cut off its air, it can either die or fight back, and the Japanese aren't likely to lie down and die."

"And so?"

"The *Reagan* task force is accompanied by two 688-class submarines. If the Japanese deploy their submarines in force they could conceivably overcome the 688 subs and sink them. After that, the surface force would be easy pickings. There are a dozen admirals in the navy senior to me who would jump down my throat for saying this, but it's true—the only *effective* antisubmarine warfare device is another submarine. Destroyers and frigates and helicopters and P-3 patrol planes are good, damned good, but good won't wash against the Japanese. Their subs and crews are the best. Their technology is on the cutting edge. Their sub is the latest generation built. Even our Seawolf class was designed a decade and a half ago, and we only have two of them. The Destiny class is equal to, if not better than, the NSSN, our new submarine being designed."

Leach shook his head. "You sound like your counterparts did during the Cold War—'The Russians are better than we are, they have all the best stuff, they can kick our tails.' Then when it came to it, their military was revealed to be overstated and we'd spent our national product on guns, defending against an alleged tiger bear, forgive me—that was a paper tiger going flat broke."

Pacino said nothing. Leach, the head of the CIA, had no business holding his job with such an attitude. No wonder Donchez couldn't stand him.

"Dick?" President Warner asked Donchez.

"My opinion on the issue is that Japan is once again threatening all of Asia, and the world demands something be done. Our people think *we* should do something about it. Our response to this must be governed by the best interests of America. And by Japan's peculiar response to threats of force. Here's what I mean. Al was right when he said we need to have a clear objective, something more than pie in the sky. We must know what we want and be willing to take only that, nothing less. The American people must buy into that objective before we act. And I think the objective is to walk away from this event with Japan's radiation missiles destroyed, their submarines and fighters reduced in number to what they really need for home defense. This would involve international inspectors or advisors on Japanese soil. Now—here's how we do that . . .

"We have to realize that the Japanese famed national pride would be a casualty of this operation. These people will die before they'll accept some of what I am suggesting. They will fight, so we must be prepared for that. We must expect a violent reaction to a blockade. I think Admiral Pacino has it right—we need to do a coordinated attack on the Japanese Galaxy satellites, encircle Japan, keep Russia out of the scene, whatever the cost, and take on the Japanese air force with ground attacks or air-to-air combat. We will have casualties and lose some of our force strength. Once the blockade is in place, I fully expect the Maritime Self Defense Force to come out fighting."

"Why?" Leach said. "Just because you and Pacino think it's 1941? That was then. This is now, for God's sake."

"Same cultures. Same ocean in between. Same island economy in Japan. Same worldview in America. They have guns and ships and airplanes. We have guns and ships and airplanes. Three generations later, and it'll come down to the same fight."

Warner turned toward Leach. "Brian, what's on your mind?"

"Well," Leach began in his faintly singsong voice, "I think we've all missed the point here. We're already talking about war, how we'll do it, what the bad guys will do, what the public will think." Leach crossed his legs, the hair showing on the skin of his ankles. He pulled a pair of half-frame glasses from his shirt pocket and perched them on the end of his nose. "We haven't discussed diplomacy yet." Leach now looked over his glasses at Phillip Gordon, secretary of state, as if denigrating him for not doing his job. "We haven't discussed nonmilitary options yet. I think we should have our ambassador there explain some simple facts to Prime Minister Kurita. Facts such as—we have the power to completely bottle up the Japanese islands. We can blow up their entire military. Madam President, I suggest we get smart. Ask politely, spell out the facts. I believe the Japanese will cooperate—*they don't want to lose face.* I urge you to consider that."

Warner paced, finally stopped, again in front of the window.

"General Sverdlov," she called. She had yet to ask the opinion of the incoming nominee for Chairman of the Joint Chiefs. Sverdlov was a young-looking general, short with a full head of straight, fine brown hair, teeth so smooth and white as to seem capped or coated, and a perpetual smile. With his recent ear operation he was rarely seen without a ball of cotton in his right ear, and he had stumbled slightly on the way in, his equilibrium thrown off. Pacino had met him at several Pentagon parties, and they had gotten along well, although Sverdlov's second wife had seemed a bit young and flirty.

Sverdlov blinked and rubbed his chin, his teeth appearing as he smiled.

"You know, Madam President, when a cancer patient goes to a surgeon, the surgeon recommends surgery. An oncologist recommends chemotherapy or radiation. A faith healer recommends prayer and herbs. A tree surgeon, he pulls out a damned chain saw. If you put a situation like this in front of the Navy," Sverdlov pointed to Pacino and Donchez, since Donchez had once been the Chief of Naval Operations, "they'll recommend blockade. The Secretary of State will urge diplomacy, and CIA and NSA will recommend spying for more information or a covert operation to assassinate the prime minister. But the call for diplomatic means from CIA and the call for a military operation from State tell me that *this* situation is far beyond routine. So now you want the overall military view, knowing I'm an Army professional." Sverdlov flashed a dazzling smile, neutralizing any thoughts of the crowd around him that he was being pompous. "I'd say blockade now if we had the carrier battle groups closer to Japan, but I do not want to advise that until our forces are in position. If we announce a blockade and the Russians run goods to Japan, it'll be damned hard to set up a blockade piecemeal and stop the Russian resupply. If we just send in an ambassador to threaten Japan, we appear weak to them and the world. I suggest a compromise."

Pacino smiled to himself. It was no wonder Sverdlov had managed to work his way to the top—as a military man he was a master politician. Which made Pacino wonder about the future of his own career, with his bull-in-a-china-shop approach, and with Wadsworth gunning for him.

"Let's do this," Sverdlov went on. "For the next two days we say nothing. No comment. The Navy makes announcements and gets into the news with a massive deployment of the fleets out of Pearl Harbor. The battle group at sea heads directly for Japan, and the other battle groups follow suit. Five days of steaming later, the Japanese Galaxy satellites show all this firepower headed their way, almost there. The first battle group is already in position. We let the Russians do what they want, with a notice to them that at noon on Day Zero, something will change. Then, only then, our ambassador comes knocking. He says he's got a face-saving deal in mind for the Japanese. The deal is, we slip in some UN inspectors, we put in at Port Yokosuka with a battle group, and what's in it for the Japanese is that we will let them back into our trade markets, slowly and quietly, and in two weeks this all drops from the news and we go on."

"What if Kurita says no?" Warner asked, a warm expression directed at Sverdlov. Obviously Warner was one of Sverdlov's many champions, Pacino thought.

"That would be crazy, though I admit the Japanese sometimes look that way to Western eyes. Okay, so let's assume they turn us down. All the better for us, because then we have no choice but to set up the blockade. And we do, but our ships just watch the commercial boat traffic for a day, let the reality sink in. We ask Kurita one last time. He says no again. We announce that for one week we will blockade Japan. We start our stranglehold and let them feel it. We ask Kurita again. Again he says no. We keep up the blockade. Every week we ask. When Kurita says no, we'll publish that to the world. Then the starving people are *his* fault. Eventually, I believe we'll work it out."

"Thanks, General, very interesting. Now, Mr. Cogster?"

Cogster cleared his throat and uncrossed his legs. "General Sverdlov seems to have the situation analyzed. Although we haven't answered the one question we should have asked at first. What happens if we just do nothing? Why do we feel we have to solve every international squabble in the world? What's Greater Manchuria to us? What is Japan to us?"

"Alex, what do you think of Steve's playing, I assume, devil's advocate?"

Alex Addison, Chief of Staff, lifted an eyebrow and rubbed his nose. "Well, I think the answer's obvious, Madam President. If we do nothing we announce to the world that we're the Great Britain of the twenty-first century, a former world power, no longer a player. Greater Manchuria is a good friend to have because of its location and resources, its counterbalance to Russia and the Chinas. And Japan is a problem to us. If we let them get away with this, that is a slippery slope. Japan then would have a blank check to use their illegal military any damned way they want. And then finally, our popularity figures will literally go negative. The public wants action. If we want to be here in two years to finish your good work, we'd better give Admirals Pacino and Wadsworth some orders."

"Steve?" Warner asked expectantly. Cogster looked at the shine of his shoes.

"I have to say that I don't think the Navy is adequately represented here. We have a junior flag officer who commands submarines, and I mean no disrespect, Admiral Pacino, we've all heard about how brave you are, your Navy Cross and all those other medals, but you do have a sub man's point of view. Your worries about Japan's subs are a case in point. Maybe they're no big deal. I don't know, but I'd like to hear what Admiral Wadsworth has to say about this."

"Okay, Steve," Warner said. "But what about Admiral Donchez, who was chief of naval operations just two years ago?"

Cogster smiled tentatively at Donchez. "Yes, ma'am,"

he said, looking at Warner for the first time. "That was then. Two years ago. This is now. Wadsworth is the officer responsible for the Navy. I say let's get his input."

The Blowtorch speaks, Pacino thought, while trying to keep his face impassive.

"Well, Steve, you do have a point, but we need to put a plan in action now. Can we raise Admiral Wadsworth on the videolink?"

Warner waved over a staffer who took four other staffers and began scurrying in and out of the room while the occupants shared an uncomfortable silence. Pacino turned on his WritePad computer and began scribbling on the one-page display. With his finger he drew a line vertically down the center of the page and on the left wrote "Blockade" and on the right "Delay." The notes below each were his ideas for orders to the combined submarine force for each decision. By the time the videolink was ready with Wadsworth, Pacino felt he had the embryo of a plan.

Wadsworth wore whites, in contrast to Pacino's dress blues, since Wadsworth was in tropical Africa. Warner briefed Wadsworth on the situation as if he hadn't heard, then informed him of the recommendations of the men in the room, eventually outlining Pacino's ideas. Wadsworth's face tightened at the last. Finally Warner asked the admiral his opinion.

"It's difficult for me to believe Admiral Pacino would want to attack Japan without provocation. That is a dangerous recommendation. He apparently feels that our carrier battle groups are no match for the Japanese submarine force, and, Madam President, that is just his parochial submariner attitude. The Japanese forces' reputations are overblown. They have high technology, *and* the bugs that go with it. Their planes have low reliability and their submarines don't always work. Let's not make this decision based on guesses. I recommend we use the diplomatic solution, and we should keep the USS *Reagan* force Japan-bound, and I do want the *Abe Lincoln* and *United States* sent to sea toward the northwest Pacific, but no threats, no talk of blockade. Let's let diplomacy work."

"Thank you, Admiral," Warner said, beginning to look weary. "Steve?"

"Ma'am, it's up to us to do the right thing. Admiral Wadsworth's sober and responsible recommendation is the right thing."

"Admiral Pacino?"

"Yes, ma'am?" Wadsworth was having his revenge, and at what cost?

"Do you agree with Admiral Wadsworth?"

This was it, he thought. Either he bought into what he believed was a flawed plan and watched it fail, or he publicly disagreed with Wadsworth and was quietly relieved and retired from the Navy ten days from now when Wadsworth came back and built up a case against him. Which would be easy—he had, after all, lost two ships in five years, albeit in combat, but nevertheless, it was a dual black mark. Pacino looked at Wadsworth's puffy face on the video screen and decided he didn't want to be part of a Navy with a Wadsworth in charge. He had had a wonderful career, and every career had to end. In the military, that came about by death, disability, resignation or retirement. And retirement could be voluntary or forced. Perhaps resignation held more dignity, particularly when the politics of flag rank became too much. He thought about his waterfront house over the Severn River, facing the Naval Academy, about his dreary office at the base in Norfolk, about the fact that for the rest of his career he would probably just command one office after another, never again giving rudder orders aboard a nuclear submarine. That duty was reserved for younger officers. So what was left for him? No longer eligible for submarine command, the rest of his career would be a series of meetings like this one. With that thought, Pacino made his decision.

"Madam President, not only do I completely disagree with Admiral Wadsworth, I'm willing to put my reasons why in a memo to you. Admiral Wadsworth, I'll be sure and have a copy on your desk for when you return from Africa. If we do as Admiral Wadsworth suggests, the Japanese submarine fleet will put to sea as soon as they see our carrier battle groups coming, which they will if we aren't going to knock out their surveillance satellites. When the battle groups are finally in position, the Japanese sub force will put our surface ships on the bottom the minute we say the word 'blockade.' If we want this operation to *work,* we have to sortie the fleet, hit the Galaxy satellites, attack the sub bases and air force bases, and blow away their planes and ships—and all within a six-hour interval—and tighten the rope around Tokyo's neck. If we fail to commit to that level, Admiral Wadsworth's surface sailors will be drinking seawater. And I suggest history will remember the men in this room—and in our videolink—as cowards and failures."

There was a shocked silence in the room. Wadsworth heard Pacino on a two-second delay. As the words registered a storm came over his face. Pacino no longer cared, and ignored the video display and the recording camera. Donchez's face was a study in mixed emotions. Pacino didn't care about that either. He began packing his notes in his briefcase.

"Admiral Pacino," President Warner said, her tone neutral, "I think perhaps it would be best if you got yourself back to your office. The rest of us need to talk to Admiral Wadsworth. Thank you for your time. *And* your outspoken and candid opinion."

Pacino stood and nodded to Donchez, then followed one of Warner's staffers out of the Oval Office. He doubted he'd ever see the inside of it again.

# BOOK TWO

# BLOCKADE

# CHAPTER 11

**Washington, D.C.**

Pacino walked swiftly from the first floor of the White House east wing through the door held open by a Marine guard, who snapped to attention and saluted. Pacino ignored him. He could hear the clicking sounds of his aide's footsteps behind him. He ducked into the back of the borrowed staff car and waited for Lieutenant Stoddard to climb into the front.

He was stonily silent all the way to Andrews Air Force Base, where the car was ushered past the fencing and guards to a gray-painted swept-wing jet, a twelve-passenger Grumman SS-12. Pacino left the staff car behind and rushed into the aircraft, dumping himself into the midcabin executive seat. Joanna Stoddard scurried up the ladder. He could hear her muttering to the pilots and stealing an anxious look at Pacino. The sounds of the jets whining didn't soothe him as they usually did. He stared out the window, furious, mostly at himself for being so tactless. As a submarine commander he had been known for brash action, but that was a different world, he told himself. He had just spoken up before the president of the United States to say that his commanding officer, the Chief of Naval Operations, was so wrong that his recommendations would be against the best interests of the country. Way to go, he thought.

After a statement like that Admiral Wadsworth would have no choice but to fire him. There was no way that Pacino's insubordination could be allowed.

The jet neared the runway's end and throttled up, the turbines spooling up to full power. Usually Pacino liked to sit in the cockpit for the takeoff, to watch the runway hurtling at the windshield. Not today. He continued to stare off into the distance as the runway vanished underneath the plane, the beltway rushed by below, then the city as Washington faded away to the northwest, the aircraft bound for Norfolk. The jet would never climb above 10,000 feet on this trip, since the two cities were so close, but by car it would be three or four hours in rush-hour traffic to get back to the Norfolk base, and by jet it was perhaps a half-hour door to door. As the jet flew on, Pacino considered his now limited options.

He had at most ten days. Wadsworth had every right to fire him on the phone or send a written message relieving him of command. But he had come to know Tony Wadsworth's style, and the man seemed to enjoy personal confrontation—hell, he'd once been a boxer. Wadsworth had fired several subordinates before, the stories legendary, and every time he did, he had done it in person, his face millimeters from his subordinate's nose. Which meant that Pacino had until Wadsworth returned from his African tour, maybe ten days from now.

Except there was always the possibility that Wadsworth would return early after the meeting with the president, which could cut Pacino's time down. The president might take him out of the office of Commander Unified Submarine Command, putting him behind a desk somewhere in the Navy's bureaucracy. But somehow his gut feel was that he had enough rope to hang himself, and that would amount to ten days. And there was a lot he could get done in ten days. He waved at his aide Joanna Stoddard, who came over and sat next to him.

"Call Norfolk," he said without preamble, "and get Captain Murphy and Commander McDonne to the office." Murphy was the deputy USubCom commander for operations, and McDonne was the deputy for administration. "I want them waiting for me when we get in. And make sure the car is standing by at the airfield."

"Yessir," and fairly vaulted herself forward to take care of the orders.

Pacino returned to looking glumly out the window.

Richard Donchez cleared his throat and tugged at his collar. It had been painful to watch the self-destruction of a career he had hand-built over twenty years. Pacino had been stupid. Stupid at sea was one thing—even the sea was more forgiving than the politicians—but stupid in the Oval Office was fatal. And it made no sense, because Pacino, despite his brashness, was still attuned to the way the world worked. Donchez had witnessed him biting his lip a hundred times when he'd had other opportunities to be less than tactful. Pacino had never stepped out of line, over the line, like this. Which made him wonder whether it might have been intentional. Maybe Mikey didn't want to play with the big dogs anymore. Donchez resolved to talk to Pacino as soon as the meeting ended. There might be some things he could do, but holding back Tony Wadsworth would be a Herculean task. Donchez had heard that Tony, in the boxing ring, had gone undefeated his senior year at Annapolis.

"Well," President Warner said after the door slammed on Pacino, "that has to be the most up-front statement by a military officer I've ever heard. In the meantime," she said, turning back to the group, "we are left with the decision on what we will do regarding Japan." She paced from one side of the office to the other, then stood behind Alex Addison's seat. "Here is what I want done. First, Admiral Wadsworth, and Generals Sverdlov and Clough. The aircraft carrier battle group that is closest to Japan—I want it to keep going at top speed to get ready to set up a blockade. When that force is closer, say five hundred miles, I want to be notified. The other groups, with the other two carriers, should be sent to sea as fast as possible. I want an update every six hours on where we stand with those forces. Clear?"

"Yes, ma'am," the senior officers in the room said at once, Wadsworth's acknowledgment delayed by the video lag.

"Mr. Gordon, get with our ambassador to Japan. His name is—"

"Pulcanson. Chesty Pulcanson."

"Oh, I remember him. Good." Pulcanson was six feet five inches tall and weighed at least 250, a ruddy-faced Texan who had a presence imposing enough to fill a ballroom. "Get Pulcanson to request a meeting with Kurita. Have him tell Kurita to accept the UN resolution—which I'm sure will be passed by then—allowing for inspectors to dismantle the Hiroshima missiles and to take control of the Japanese air force and navy, because if he does not, the US will enforce the embargo by military means."

"Yes, ma'am," Gordon said.

"That's it. I want this group ready to come back and continue this meeting at a moment's notice. Don't anybody leave town. Admiral Wadsworth, I'd like you to remain a moment, please."

**UNIFIED SUBMARINE COMMAND HEADQUARTERS
NORFOLK NAVAL BASE, NORFOLK, VIRGINIA**

Pacino crashed into his office and slammed his body into his leather chair. The oak desk, a relic from John Paul Jones's command *Bonhomme Richard,* was covered with papers laid out for Pacino's signature, the gasoline that fueled the fleet's bureaucracy. Pacino hated to see the desk like that. He wanted to see an ocean of bare wood in front of him, uncluttered by blotters, pen sets, staplers and, most of all, *papers.* He had lectured the staff that with the new computer systems, with the four-year-old WritePad computer, there should never be a need for hardcopies. The WritePad Systems were radio-networked to a national megafile server in earth orbit, so that any newspaper or magazine could be accessed with a click of a finger on the flat paper-thin surface. With the support of officers like Pacino, the WritePads were linked into a defense megafile server, so that messages that before were sent on radio circuits and printed down were now sent by electronic mail to individual WritePads. Paper was mostly obsolete. So why was it still everywhere? With a quick motion of his hands he swept the pile off the desk and looked up at Joanna.

"Where the hell are Murphy and McDonne?"

"Sir, they just arrived. They were out inspecting Eighth Squadron until—"

"Just get them in here." Pacino bit his lip, wishing he had some bad habit like smoking that could calm him down. He couldn't remember ever losing his control like this. He had been on the business end of half a dozen warshot torpedoes and twice as many more Chinese depth charges. Now, after having words with his boss he was acting like a plebe being hazed at the academy. Hell, he had served under psychotic Rocket Ron for two years, knowing there were at least five times he had almost punched him out, knowing also that Rocket Ron had been trying to provoke exactly that in order to find Pacino's limit, one time succeeding as Pacino had left the submarine in the middle of the day and gone home to drink half a fifth of Jack Daniel's. But now, with the end of his career imminent, he found that he wanted that career. Death was all in a day's work, but facing ignominious demotion or retirement was not something he could deal with. He fought for control. He owed Joanna an apology.

"Admiral," Murphy's gravelly voice called, at the entrance to the office. As soon as Pacino saw Capt. Sean Murphy, his tension evaporated. He and Murphy went back decades. They'd been roommates at Annapolis from sophomore year on. They had double-dated when Pacino had first met Janice, who had introduced Sean to Katrina. Now, twenty-five years later, Katrina and Sean had two children, Janice and Pacino had one, although Katrina and Sean were inseparable while Janice and Pacino were filing for divorce. But their professional lives had been just as close. They had been aboard the same subs during their junior officer and department head tours, both men teaching at the academy during the shore tour in between. Six years before, Murphy had been in command of the USS *Tampa,* then the newest

Improved 688-class attack sub, which had been taken hostage in the Bo Hai Bay outside of Beijing by the Red Chinese. Pacino had been commissioned by Admiral Donchez to take the then untested *Seawolf* into restricted waters and rescue the crew of the *Tampa* in a mission so classified that only the president's inner circle were aware of it. Murphy had taken two bullets and almost died, but after two years of physical therapy he had regained his strength. Murphy was tall and lanky, blond and tan, his skin wrinkled around his eyes, his voice a deep growl from an old smoking habit. He looked good, a slight smile haunting his lips, his blue eyes dancing with the same mischief they had held when he and Pacino had pulled pranks on the first-class midshipmen when they had been lowly plebes.

"Murph," Pacino said, feeling like hugging his ops officer. He reached out and grabbed Murphy's hand and gripped it hard, Murphy's own grip painful, their old ritual. "Have I got a deal for you."

"Oh? Where are you sending me now?"

"That's the deal—you're staying home. Where's CB McDonne?"

"Sir!" McDonne called from the door.

"You're late," Pacino said goodnaturedly. "Get your butt in here."

Carl B. "CB" McDonne waddled into the office and shut the door. CB was the deputy commander for administration, the workhorse who made the trains run on time, kept the orders flowing to the ships of the fleet, tended to the requests coming up from below and the orders going down from above. CB loved it, every paperwork nightmare of it. If Pacino's personality were a photograph, CB McDonne would be its negative, yet they got along as if they were brothers. CB had come to the admin post as a "hard labor" tour, done to improve his fitness report, to rehabilitate him for problems he had had in the past trying to get command of his own sub. Part of CB's problem was his weight. He defined obese, and the Navy doctors disqualified him for sea duty until he could lose over a hundred pounds. It would be a challenge to find a McDonne body part, at least one that was visible, that was not fat. The man was nearly spherical, and bald. The absurdly generous flesh, however, covered a razor sharp intelligence, a steel-trap mind that remembered everything. He could quote whole paragraphs from the Reactor Plant Manual like southern Baptist preachers could quote scripture. He had once memorized operating instruction 27, "Normal Reactor Startup," a procedure that was over forty pages long, and had recited it to his wardroom while they tallied up his errors. He had promised the junior officers that he would buy them each one beer for every mistake. The bet had cost him quite a party, but it had come to only two sixpacks each. Twelve errors from a memorization forty pages long.

Not surprisingly, there was something of an edge to McDonne's sense of humor, which seemed to be easing now that he had been with Pacino for a year. In addition, his daily six-mile walks were beginning to melt off the bulk. Although still ponderously huge, McDonne's uniforms were starting to hang on him.

"About time you got in here," Pacino said, shaking McDonne's huge hand. "Sit down, gentlemen."

For the next twenty minutes Pacino outlined the debate with the president and her men, including some of what Wadsworth had said. He finished with: "Listen up. I'm going to sea. CB, I want a call put in for transportation to the aircraft carrier *Reagan*."

"What's on your mind? We need you here. Or in Pearl. At sea you'll be tied up by the other officers in the battle group. You'll need to get permission to transmit, and your radio messages will be scanned by the surface pukes."

"Hold on, Murph. I'll get off the carrier as soon as they can helicopter me to one of the battle group's escort submarines."

"We won't be able to transmit to the fleet, and—"

"It's not we, it's me. You both are staying here at HQ. You'll be running the operation from here. Here's your big chance to show that you've got what it takes to wear an admiral's stars. And as usual, you get the job description first, much later the rank and the title. CB,

I want you to help out Captain Murphy with this to-do list."

"Aye aye, sir," the men said, puzzled. It was not to be part of the briefing why Pacino intended to send his orders from the radio room of a forward deployed submarine, as Donchez had suggested. With Wadsworth coming back, the only way Pacino figured he could remain in command was by staying away from the man. Wadsworth could only relieve him at sea if he could prove Pacino was doing something flagrantly wrong. In an office, Wadsworth could unseat him for having a messy desk.

"Guys, we have a very unusual situation here. You're both going to have to live outside your comfort levels. We'll all be very uncomfortable in the coming weeks. Particularly if the president orders us to blockade Japan. Now here's the deal—CB gets me something to take me to the USS *Reagan* as soon as we leave this meeting. I'll put together a message to the force commander saying that I need to get out to one of his attack subs. I'll put the draft of that on the megaserver in your admin directory, CB. You get it in the right format and throw it out to the *Reagan* with immediate priority. Now, which subs are assigned to that battle group?"

McDonne, who had been scribbling, his finger whirling across his WritePad, stopped and tapped a fingernail at a software button displayed at the top of the notepage display. A menu flashed onto his page, and he selected another button, until finally the information he sought blinked on the display.

"*Pasadena* and *Cheyenne.*"

"Who are the commanding officers?"

"*Pasadena* is run by a Jackson Vaughn—"

"Lube Oil Vaughn," Pacino said, grinning. "Murph, Lube Oil was with you on the *Tampa,* right?"

"Good man," Murphy said, looking at the far wall, but lost for a moment in a memory.

"He was my XO on the *Seawolf.*" Lube Oil Vaughn was damned good, Pacino thought, feeling some guilt for not keeping up with him.

"*Cheyenne* is commanded by one Gregory Keebes. I think he was also on the *Seawolf* with you, Admiral."

"Navigator. Smart guy, cool as they come. Unflappable. While I'm out, Sean, you're in command. We've got some new priorities. Everything you were doing before this meeting, I want you to forget. Drop it. No reports, no paperwork, no wives' bake sales. You need to stay absolutely focused."

Pacino's intensity was getting through to Murphy, who on the outside looked calm but his finger tapping his thigh gave him away.

"Here are the priorities. Number one. Get the USS *Piranha* to sea."

"She's ready now, sir," Murphy said, puzzled.

"No. We just put her into the Electric Boat manufacturing barn to be fitted out with Vortex missiles."

"Has someone figured out a way to keep them from blowing up their own tubes?" McDonne asked.

"Yes, but EB has a month of work to do and I gave them a week. You have to get that down to five days, six max. I want Bruce Phillips at sea yesterday."

"Where's he going?"

"Get him to the Japan surrounding waters. Which reminds me, we're going to start calling that chunk of ocean the Japan OpArea. And for the submarine force, we need an operation name for this . . . blockade."

McDonne pinched the flesh around his throat, his habit when thinking hard. "How about Operation Steel Trap or Operation Stranglehold or Operation Airtight?"

"No," Pacino said. "I want something that sounds almost Japanese. Let's call it Operation Enlightened Curtain. This blockade is a curtain around Japan that will give her leaders something to think about, a curtain of enlightenment." He didn't wait for their approval. "Okay, next priority. Get the rest of the sub force to sea. Send a flash message, sub force to Defcon three. CB, what's that mean to you?"

"All repair availabilities are canceled. Tenders and shipyards stop all work. Crews button up any systems they're repairing. All leaves are canceled. All personnel to be within an hour of their ships. All ships are to be ready to get underway within two hours. Every submarine loaded with torpedoes and cruise missiles. The ready-status ships are already fully loaded out."

"Send the order. Defcon three, all submarines in the Unified Submarine Command."

"Aye, aye, sir."

McDonne scribbled on his WritePad. He stroked a software button and the scribbled handwritten notes became block letters, machine typed. Pacino scanned the message.

"Start an authenticator system."

"That normally doesn't happen until Defcon two—"

"Start it anyway."

McDonne wrote on the message, Pacino read it.

131912ZDEC
FLASH FLASH FLASH FLASH FLASH FLASH
FLASH FLASH
FM COMUSUBCOM
TO ALL FAST ATTACK SUBMARINE
UNITS USUBCOM
SUBJ READINESS CONDITION/OPERATION
ENLIGHTENED CURTAIN
SECRET

AUTHENTICATOR BRAVO FIVE ECHO
//BT//
1. (S) SET DEFENSE READINESS CONDITION (DEFCON) THREE.
2. (S) AUTHENTICATION:
3. ADMIRAL M. PACINO SENDS.
//BT//

Pacino looked at the message and nodded.

"All we need is the authenticator," he said. "Break it out."

The two men in front of him suddenly became serious and formal, standing up at attention.

"Break out the authenticator, aye, sir. Commander?"

"Aye, sir."

They left the room briskly, shutting the door behind

them. While they went to the safe-within-a-safe, locked inside a vault that held top-secret material, compartmentalized material and codeword material, Pacino waited.

War, he thought, hadn't happened yet, but the ball was rolling and picking up speed.

# CHAPTER 12

**OVAL OFFICE**
**WASHINGTON, D.C.**

President Jaisal Warner frowned at Admiral Wadsworth on the videolink screen.

"Tony, what about Admiral Pacino's statement?"

"Madam President," Wadsworth said slowly, quietly, his accent flat and Midwestern now that he addressed the president, although he had a tendency to slip into a dialect of Mississippi African-American when addressing subordinates. "I think Pacino is out of line. I want a USubCom commander I can work with. Pacino, frankly, is too parochial. All he sees are submarines. I'm coming back right now to begin the selection process for Pacino's replacement."

"Tony, about Pacino being too focused on enemy subs . . . he did mention the FireStar fighter squadrons."

"Yes, but he has overlooked the power of our surface fleet. I have major antisubmarine equipment at sea right now, all at the command of the *Reagan* battle-force commander. Just because Pacino's power base is a bunch of sewer pipes doesn't mean the rest of the world's navies have lethal submarines that should make us tremble."

"Admiral, Pacino pointed out the specifics of what he's worried about. The Destiny III robotic submarines, the Destiny II-class—"

"Ma'am, the Destiny classes are more often than not at their piers. We don't believe they're threats to us."

Warner sighed, the weight of her office falling on her all at once. There were times that she seemed surrounded by men who didn't want to listen. During times like these she asked herself, "what would a man do?" and the answer was usually the same. A man would take charge and give orders. Even Iron Jaisal Warner would rather build a consensus, which was why she asked her subordinates for their honest opinions, and all she received was conflict and resistance. Especially in this case. There was something about Pacino she liked. It was a presence, a certainty he had. He focused on the issues, not the politics, not the possible political gains he could make. Other than Dick Donchez, he alone in her administration was like that. It added up to something she hadn't sensed in a long time, and it was almost hard to admit it, but when Pacino was in the room offering a blunt opinion, Warner felt safe. Yes, safe, that was exactly the word she had been searching for. There was something about the young looking but white-haired admiral that reminded her of her own father, a New York City policeman, a street cop. It was elemental, naked, a certain fearlessness her father had had. In his career he had been forced to shoot two criminals, both times exonerated by the boards of review. She had known he had felt terrible about it, but it made her love him all the more, because when he was around, no one could hurt her. Her father shot criminals, he made the streets safe. And there was that quality in Pacino. He was something of a world cop, making the hostile seas safe, making her job safe. He would not fall to Tony Wadsworth's ax. She took a deep breath.

"Admiral Wadsworth, about Admiral Pacino . . . I want you to make damned sure you don't lose Admiral Pacino. He has a good head. I like his style. This administration has plans to promote him, whether it means demoting or retiring certain other naval officers. Am I clear?"

"Yes, ma'am."

"I don't want to hear that you've put him in charge of paper clips in Guam."

"Yes, ma'am."

"And I want a position paper from you addressing Admiral Pacino's memo in detail, saying *exactly* why you believe he is incorrect. If you still do."

"Yes, ma'am."

"And I want you to send Pacino a message, and I want you to copy me on it. This message will go out within the hour."

"Yes, ma'am."

"It will read that Pacino has full authority with respect to his submarines to pursue the best possible resolution of this crisis. He is to work with the commanders of your surface battle groups, but he will also be independent and of equal operational rank."

"Ma'am, you'd have to promote him to vice-admiral to do that, and that can't be done without congressional confirmation."

"Then put a recommendation on my desk for his promotion. I'll take care of the rest. And another thing, Tony. Stay out there for the duration of your planned trip. I don't want the world to see us running around looking panicked, especially with this upcoming action off of Japan."

"But ma'am—"

"No buts, Tony. You're staying. Pacino is to have the authority I have prescribed. Understand?"

"Yes, Madam President."

She wondered, as she cut off the videolink, whether he did.

**USubCom Headquarters**
**Norfolk Naval Base, Norfolk, Virginia**

Pacino looked up as Murphy and McDonne came in the room. Their serious faces indicated the authenticators had shocked them into the awareness that this was no longer one endless drill, that the filmy boundary between peacetime and wartime had just been crossed.

Murphy held up the authenticator, so that both he and McDonne had it in sight at all times, since the little foil packet was so secret it was under two-man-control. Never in its lifetime, from printing to destruction, would an authenticator be under the control of one man alone.

And for good reason, since one man with an authenticator could start an all-out war. Once Pacino set Defcon two, not a single unit of his sub force would listen to him or follow his orders without a valid authenticator.

Murphy held out the authenticator packet, the size of an Alka Seltzer foil container, and put it in front of Pacino.

"Sir, it reads as authenticator number bravo five echo." The name of the authenticator matched the one they had described in the subject area of the message to the fleet.

"Very well," Pacino said. "Open the authenticator."

"Open the authenticator, aye, sir," Murphy said, opening the packet. A simple piece of cardboard was inside with the code "XC83JOEM" written in block letters. "Sir, authenticator reads x-ray, charlie, eight, three, juliet, oscar, echo, mike."

"Very well," Pacino said, "insert the code into the message, verify it and transmit."

It took some time to get the message out. The men reassembled in the seating area.

"Sir," Murphy said, "we've got as priorities getting you to sea, getting *Piranha* to sea, setting Defcon three. And then what?"

"Inspect the ships. Atlantic coast ships first. Talk to every skipper behind closed doors. Tell him what we know."

"Aye, Admiral."

"We have a contingency warplan for Scenario Orange for blockade erupting into war, correct Sean? I remember doing revisions on that."

"Admiral, we rewrote that eighty times."

"Good thing we did, because here we go. Brief the skippers on the OpOrder, which will be out of the Scenario Orange contingency-planning manual. How are the plans going for my trip to the *Reagan*?"

"Joanna's got UAirCom working on it. Probably get a ride out of Pearl to the *Reagan* on an F-14."

"Not good enough." Pacino growled. "Get me out of Norfolk on an F-14. The SS-12 would be too slow."

McDonne grabbed the phone on the end table. He

whispered something to Joanna, then put the phone down. "She'll go to work on an F-14 out of Oceana. The jet will come to you here at the airstrip, fuel up and be idling when we're done. I assumed you'd be leaving after this briefing, sir."

"Is my seabag ready?" Pacino kept a closet full of uniforms, submarine coveralls, at-sea sneakers, underclothes, shaving kit and reading disks, which had replaced books with the widespread use of the WritePad. He could have it packed for a sea trip within minutes.

"Should be ready in five minutes."

"Brief the East Coast sub skippers on the warplan, then get them to sea, full deployment. I want them deployed to the Japan OpArea."

"Panama Canal?"

Pacino considered. The canal passage was much faster than going around the horn or going under the polar icepack, but transiting the canal meant that Tokyo's Galaxy satellites would see them coming. Which could be a good thing, except Pacino didn't want them to know the exact number of subs that would be coming at them.

"Let's start this out right. Give each captain the option. If they want to go under ice, let them. If they want the canal passage, okay. Just tell them I want them there in one piece as fast as they think they can make it."

"Sir, polar passage is risky. And slow this time of year."

"I know. But a few skippers will take it, anyway."

"What would you do, Admiral?"

"Murph, I'd take it through the canal. It's faster."

"Sir, doesn't giving them an option make it look like we don't know what we're doing?"

"Wrong, it makes it look like we trust our commanding officers. Don't micromanage these guys."

"Aye, sir."

"Once the Atlantic boats are away, get the Hawaii ships to sea. Brief their skippers first, then get them going."

"Yessir."

"When everyone is there in the Japan OpArea, I'll be positioned to help the fleet. At that point your job, Murph, is to feed me as much information as you can to help me make decisions, and in the absence of word from me, make the orders to the fleet that you believe you need to. There's only one thing."

"Sir?"

"No one, *no one,* is to countermand any of my direct orders but the president. Not Wadsworth or anyone else. And if someone tries to give you orders of any kind to relay to the fleet, I want you to refuse, unless it is authorized by President Warner *in person.* And Sean, I don't care if you have to go to jail to carry out that order."

"I don't understand, Admiral."

"There's a reason I'm going to sea aboard one of our subs. I want you to think about that and what I said before."

"Aye, sir." Murphy no longer looked confused, just concerned.

"Now, let's work on a way to get all the USubCom authenticators out to the *Reagan* with me."

"We'll put them in a double-locked case, the same way we get them from the manufacturer to our safes, then have the F-14 pilot sign for them, then the radiomen aboard the *Reagan,* then the chopper pilots and the top-secret control officer aboard your final sub."

"Make it happen."

"Yessir."

"And Murph. About the *Piranha.* Get yourself up there personally. Visit there every twelve hours if you have to, between briefing skippers. But get that sub out to sea."

"Admiral," Joanna interrupted. "Your aircraft is at the naval air station and your car is waiting out front. The bag is packed and aboard the car."

"Gentlemen, good luck. Keep me covered, Sean. CB, give Sean your max support."

Pacino shook their hands, wondering for a moment if he would ever see either of them again.

**NORFOLK NAVAL AIR STATION**
**NORFOLK, VIRGINIA**

Pacino got out of the staff car and walked across the concrete apron to the waiting F-14 Navy fighter jet, impressed by the size of the plane. He was dressed in a flight suit and parachute. Joanna carried the case of authenticators and his flight bag and stowed them with the ground technician. Pacino returned Joanna's salute, then shook her hand. She vanished into the car and watched from the window. Pacino turned to the pilot, a young officer with a name patch reading SHEARSON and a flight helmet in the crook of his arm, the name on the flight helmet reading TUBESTEAK.

"Good afternoon, Admiral, I'm Lt. Brad Shearson. We'll be on the way as soon as I can brief you on the trip."

"Fine, Shearson. What's your handle there from—after-hours exploits?"

"No, Admiral. I just eat a lot of hot dogs. I survived on them all through flight school. Admiral, you ever flown in a Tomcat before?"

"Never."

"Let's get you in the cockpit, first, sir."

Shearson pointed Pacino to the wheeled ladder to the cockpit high above the concrete. Pacino looked down over the top of the wings of the two-engined craft with its twin tails, the wings extended outward but designed to be pulled in tight into a delta-wing configuration. It was astonishing how big it was. Pacino swore it was bigger than his twelve-passenger Gulfstream. He looked down into the cramped cockpit, the seat little more than an olive-drab section of canvas stretched across aluminum tubing. A flight helmet sat on the seat, shiny and new, two silver stars across the top, the words PATCH engraved in black letters.

"Compliments of the squadron boss, Captain Tomb, sir. He said he knew you at the academy."

Pacino smiled, remembering. "Tell him I said thanks."

"If you'll climb in, sir. That's good."

Pacino stepped into the cockpit, feeling like he was stepping into an electronic canoe, the side consoles and front display bursting with toggle switches and function keys, the display glowing electronically green. Pacino was careful to avoid hitting any of the electronics of the consoles, and found himself sitting deep inside the airplane, the sills of the cockpit rising all the way to the top of his shoulders. He felt like a child in an amusement park ride, too short to see out. He was completely surrounded, enveloped, by the consoles and screens and displays of the rear cockpit. He pulled on the flight helmet at Shearson's prompting, further sucked into the tight world of the aircraft. Now that he was here, he thought, the interior of a nuclear submarine would always seem roomy by comparison.

"Now, sir, let me strap you in. This is a five point harness. The release mechanism is here. Now, see this lever here?"

A red ribbon attached to a pin was attached to a yellow and black striped lever set deep into the bulkhead opposite Shearson.

"I'm pulling the pin out of it. It's armed now, sir, so be careful not to touch it. That's the manual canopy release, just in case we need to eject and the automatic sequence doesn't blow off the canopy. There are two ways to eject, Admiral. The first way, the better way, is to pull that cord above your head. See it?"

A yellow and black bungee cord was wrapped into the ejection seat headrest, two loops of it extending out on either side of Pacino's helmet.

"Can you grab that for me? Good sir. If we need to punch out, you pull that cord down to your crotch, all the way down, and the curtain in the headrest will come down over your head. The curtain protects your face and head while it keeps your elbows in tight."

"What's the other way?"

"See the D-shaped ring by your crotch? You can pull that up, but it's not as good. Your oxygen mask and helmet would be ripped off in the slipstream, and there's no guarantee for your face."

"Why is it here then?"

"If we're in a high-g spin, even Hercules might not be able to lift his arms up to the curtain cord, so the second one is down low."

"Comforting thought."

"Yes, sir. Now, if you pull the curtain down, count to fifty by thousands and you'll be out of the plane. It only takes three seconds, which is how long it would take you to count to fifty when you're pumped up with adrenaline."

"Okay."

"Now, if I want you to punch out, I'll call 'eject, eject, eject,' and out we go. If you're unconscious, you're going anyway."

"Great."

"Water bottle is here, snack pack is over here, and this is the urine bag. You put this tube around your thing and let go, then seal it like this. It goes into this pouch when you're done. Just make sure the velcro holds it in the outer pouch, sir. Spilled urine can mess up the avionics."

"I'll be careful."

"Last piece of advice, sir. If you have gas, there's no such thing as being polite aloft. I recommend you try to fart out anything you feel, as hard as you can. Otherwise the altitude will give you one hell of a bellyache."

"I can handle it."

"Vomit bags are in this pouch. Whatever happens, do not throw up in your oxygen mask. The rule is, you have to clean up your own, even flag officers, sir. Sorry."

Pacino laughed. "Let's go."

"I'm arming your eject mechanisms, so be careful."

Shearson pulled two more ribbons attached to pins and stowed them, then donned his helmet and climbed in. The canopy came down over their heads, and Shearson waved down to the technician standing on the concrete below. Pacino could hear the whining sound of the port turbine coming up to speed. It took some time for it to spool up, until it caught, the noise and vibration less than he'd expected. A minute later the starboard turbine came up. The jet started to move, inching along the taxiway. Shearson's voice chattered brief bursts of numbers to the tower.

Soon they were at the end of the runway, and the turbines came up to full power. The noise of it was deafening. Shearson released the brakes and the jet surged forward. Soon the ground below, the line marking the runway's edge, and the hangars and buildings of the air station were streaking by impossibly fast. The world outside was a blur, the vibrations from the plane indicating that they must be going at least 150 miles per, maybe faster. The jet stayed on the runway for a long time, far past the speed when it should be able to fly, Shearson keeping it tight to the pavement. Pacino felt a moment of alarm when he saw the lights at the runway's far end approaching, but then Shearson pulled up, and the aircraft, with its extra velocity, rocketed upward, hurling Pacino far back into his seat, his head feeling four times as heavy as usual. He tried to turn his head, and it was an effort, and when he looked out the canopy, all he could see was blue sky, turning darker and darker.

"You okay, Admiral?"

"Fine."

Pacino reached into his flight kit for his WritePad. He turned it on and removed his nomex gloves.

"Okay if I talk to my WritePad?" Pacino asked Shearson.

"There's a switch on the port console under intercom. Select it to receive only."

"What's next?"

"Well, we'll be over the wilds of Canada in a few hours. We'll go supersonic then to make up some time. Up over the pole is the shortest route. We'll intercept an A-6 tanker over Alaska and get some gas. By the time we're over the *Reagan* task force it'll be dark. We'll be making our approach at night. And the weather is closing in. We've got a tropical storm brewing in the Pacific. Pearl weather says it's going to develop into a typhoon but it should miss the Japan seas."

"Okay, I'm killing the intercom."

Pacino turned the WritePad on, intending to write his memo to Warner, when his E-mail indicator flashed. He double-clicked into the electronic mail and saw the message to him from Wadsworth, the admiral ordering that he take full initiative in the pursuit of the Japanese operation, that he would be of equal operational status to Adm. Mack Donner, the *Reagan* task force commander and overall commander of the Japanese theater blockade operation. How could he be subordinate to Admiral Donner yet on an equal operational status to him? Pacino scanned the message again and noted that it was copied to President Warner and Admiral Donner. Very strange.

A second message was from Admiral Donchez, wishing him luck, commending him for getting to sea. Nowhere did Donchez mention the meeting in the Oval Office. Several other E-mails were addressed to him, one from his son Tony, one from his attorney in the case of his coming divorce. The one from Tony he read and savored, the one from the attorney he stashed for later.

Pacino brought up the voice processor and spoke to the WritePad. The oxygen mask muffled his voice, the computer display printing question marks. He unlatched a hook of the mask and began to mutter into his display, his words appearing on the screen, the context-sensitive software distinguishing between alternate spellings, Pacino occasionally correcting it. He reread what he had written, edited it and sent it as an E-mail to President Warner, copying it to Wadsworth, his own staff and Donchez, with a forwarding message to Donner including his arrival time. He also took Wadsworth's message about his "equal operational status" and sent it to Donner, thinking that maybe Mack Donner could better interpret it.

Pacino next turned to the battle plan. From the WritePad's tactical section he pulled up the chart of the Japan OpArea and the Scenario Orange Warplan, Annex A, the plan for a naval blockade of the islands. He began marking where each Pacific submarine would take station, most off major Japanese ports, some along the shipping lanes, others patrolling sectors unconnected with shore infrastructure. The Atlantic fleet boats would arrive later by at least a week, so the Pacific boats would have to hold the islands down. When the Atlantic ships arrived there was more depth, but nothing changed fundamentally, at least not until the *Piranha* arrived.

Pacino looked at the chart and the plan, trying to find the flaw, and determined that if there were one, it was the failure of the president to order a preemptive strike against the Japanese air forces, submarines and satellites. But that was the shape of Warner's comfort level. Pacino just hoped that her comfort zone would be big enough to allow his force to prevail.

# CHAPTER 13

**YOKOSUKA NAVAL BASE, YOKOSUKA, JAPAN**
**JAPANESE MARITIME SELF DEFENSE**
**FORCE SUBMARINE**
***Winged Serpent*, SS-810**

Adm. Akagi Tanaka was led down the length of pier 23 by the senior rating, past the ships of the Destiny II class tied up along either side of the concrete path, to berth 5. The *Winged Serpent* was tied fast to pier 23 by eight doubled-up lines. A gangway extended from the concrete pier to the top surface of its hull. The ship was stubby and broad, its fin reaching high into the sky, its hull vanishing astern into the waters of the slip, the X-tail of its rudder protruding above the stagnant water. Akagi Tanaka looked up at the towering fin, the windows set into its surface from the interior control space. He tried to suppress his feelings of awe, the ones he invariably felt on entering his son's submarine. It was important not to reveal feelings of awe or deference when dealing with Toshumi. Not that a father should withhold these emotions, and for a different son or his own son at a different time Akagi would have been effusive in his praise and enjoyment of his son's command, but Toshumi was not one who could accept praise from his father. It was as if his son needed harshness and confrontation from his father. It would always be between them, this separation born of Orou's, Akagi's wife's, death, for which Toshumi blamed his father.

Akagi walked across the gangway, returned the salute of the sentry, and ducked into the door in the side of the fin. Inside was an area crowded with a ladder and cables and valves and pipes, smelling of lubrication oil. He put his foot down on the first rung of the ladder and began to lower himself into the hole in the ship. The enclosure of the hatch enveloped him, the light above receding as he came down the ladder until he landed on the deck four meters below. He looked at the passageway, trimmed in Indonesian tigerwood, which led aft to the control room and forward to the staterooms of the captain and first officer. On either side of the passageway was a door, one labeled COMPUTER ROOM, the other RADIO. A steep stairway led below. The rating continued forward, knocked on the door labeled CAPTAIN'S STATEROOM. A muffled voice called for them to enter. The rating opened the door and stood aside.

Akagi found himself in his son's stateroom, the walls bare, the room empty of papers or charts. It looked as if it had been emptied out so that one crew could turn the ship over to another. In fact, it reminded him of the staterooms on the Destiny I class just before they would be turned over to the purchasing crew. The rooms had been tidy but empty of personal effects. That his son's room was so bare and cold was alarming to Akagi. It was as if young Tanaka's stateroom was as cold as his heart.

Toshumi gestured to a seat at the conference-sized table. He did not stand, but looked up from his handheld computer display.

"It is good to see you again, father," Toshumi said.

"And you, son."

Toshumi's expression remained neutral, his eyes focused on his father's, the gray irises darker in the unnatural light of the stateroom's fluorescent lights.

"You said you had business with me, father."

Akagi found his briefcase and pulled out a computer the size of an envelope. He muttered to it, the displays flashing in response to his voice commands. He scanned the notes on the screen, then looked up at his son.

"Yours is the first vessel in the flotilla to be briefed. You are the senior commander of this flotilla."

"Since the other flotilla is made of Destiny IIIs, will you be briefing them too, or is your computer doing that for you?"

Akagi concentrated on the display before him, the steel in his son's voice noted but unacknowledged.

"Since last week the United States' aircraft carrier battle group headed up by the Nimitz-class carrier *Reagan* has been on the way to the northwest Pacific. The day of the bombing of Greater Manchuria the *Reagan* task force turned westward to a course that is on the great circle route directly toward Japan. Since then they have steamed five hundred kilometers closer. Presently they are within a thousand kilometers of the Home Islands, close enough for their fighter planes to attack our fighters and submarine piers. And Tokyo. The *Reagan* task force, in effect, is in our front yard. Since then our Galaxy satellites have detected heat blooms aboard every warship in Pearl Harbor, with some ships starting to get underway. Even the foreign visiting ships are starting up their engine rooms."

Toshumi's face showed only disgust. "Father, I told you we should station a Destiny III outside the northwest side of Hawaii. You rejected my advice. You relied on dumb satellites for your information. We could have intercepted unguarded communications and known the Westerners' intentions by now."

"That still is not necessary. We have intercepted cellular telephone calls from Pearl Harbor and the vicinity. The fleets are getting underway. We believe that they intend to encircle Japan. The United Nations has voted sanctions that would choke us if they were enforced. Fortunately Russia will be supplying us through this crisis. However, the American ambassador to Japan held a conference with Prime Minister Kurita this morning. He threatened to construct a blockade around Japan."

"What were the terms?"

"The ambassador called for UN troops on Japanese soil to supervise the disassembly of all radioactive weapons. In addition the Maritime Self Defense Force would be relieved of its submarine, the SDF would have its FireStar fighters removed, and Japan would never again have an offensive military."

"What did Kurita say?"

"He stalled for time and sent the ambassador on his way."

"And we have orders?"

"Yes. All submarines are to put to sea. If you stay in port, you could come under air attack. The FireStar squadrons will be scrambled to civilian airports scattered throughout the countryside. That will take away our immediate vulnerability to air attack."

"What about the incoming fleets?"

"This flotilla will take station off the Home Islands to wait for the arrival of the first battle group. The other will penetrate the deep Pacific and set their courses to intercept the battle groups coming from Hawaii."

"You are sending the *machines* to intercept the surface groups? Won't they get lost? And even if they make it, how will they fight?"

"Toshumi, the same men who trained you to fight a submarine programmed the Destiny III vessels. It is true that the manned vessels are considered more reliable, which is all the more reason to keep them here, the eventual destination of the deep Pacific aircraft carrier fleets. If the Destiny III flotilla fails, there still remain the manned vessels."

"Do we have orders to attack?"

"No. Kurita will be kept informed, and he will issue any such order to me directly. I will then relay it to you."

"Dammit, father, the first thing the West will do is knock out our Galaxy satellites. Then how will you communicate? This is so typical of the thinking of the men who never had to go into combat with—"

"Commander!" He got Toshumi's attention, but his son's face was a locked door. "We have contingency plans should that occur. We have a new Galaxy satellite ready for launch in the Guayanas. To back that up we have patrol aircraft with transmission gear loaded aboard. After that we have the third contingency, and that is the commanders of the Destiny II submarines. In the absence of orders, should the blockade be confirmed to stop the Russian traffic, you as senior commander will have the authority to order the other submarines to attack the surface forces."

"What about the American submarine force? They will come too. It will complicate the operation if we have to deal with threats from the surface and subsurface simultaneously."

"What do you want?"

"Advance permission to sink any hostile submarine contact."

"No. Such orders will come from Kurita at the same time he orders commencement of hostilities against the Western surface forces."

"Typical."

"Commander, I find your attitude most irritating."

"And I find your obsequiousness to those in power most irritating."

"I can have you relieved of command."

"When you find a better submarine commander to run this ship, you won't have to relieve me, I'll leave."

It was times like these that Akagi missed Orou the most.

"Son, there was something I wanted to tell you, but after our words, it seems silly and sentimental."

"What is it?"

"It seems that once again, three generations later, we are headed for destruction. Once again, we Japanese have picked the wrong enemy."

"The Americans?"

"No. Ourselves."

### Northwest Pacific

During the F-14's refueling with the A-6 tanker it had been up to Pacino to guide Shearson's probe into the refueling hose receiver. He had called out instructions, as Shearson had taught him, until Shearson, blind, was able to put the probe into the receiver. It was almost comically sexual, but Pacino was too preoccupied to comment on it.

After refueling they flew on into the darkness high above the dense clouds, the cockpit bathed in starlight. Pacino stared out of the canopy at nature's beauty. Closer to the ground, the problems were more real. As if proving Pacino correct, Shearson's voice clicked into the intercom.

"Admiral, bad news. The tropical storm has turned north. By the time we're on approach to the *Reagan* it'll be only a few hundred miles away. They're thinking of upgrading it to a typhoon. Fairbanks weather is showing some heavy stuff, they're recommending we turn back. There's nowhere to divert to if we go much farther. Admiral?"

"Yes, Lieutenant?"

"Did you copy that?"

"Yeah. Lieutenant, they're holding dinner for us aboard the *Reagan.* I think we should show up."

"Sir, you realize that if we can't set down on the *Reagan,* we're going to have to ditch the plane. We ditch in calm weather, it's a swim date at Club Med. We ditch in the dark, it's only fifty-fifty that we'll get picked up until the next morning. A night in the water means it's us against Jaws and his brethren. We ditch in a typhoon, you might as well break out your survival pistol and eat a bullet. The chances of survival are zero point zero. You copy that, sir?"

"Yes, Brad. For what it's worth, I've spent more time in a life raft waiting for a chopper than some folks have spent in the Navy."

"Well, sir, if we lose this airplane you'll have to stand with me at the board of inquiry. And if we lose ourselves you'll be standing with me at the pearly gates. If you can handle that, I'll put us on the deck of the *Reagan* or as close to it as anyone can get."

Far below them, lightning flashed in a cloud, momentarily illuminating the world below.

## PIER 23
## YOKOSUKA NAVAL BASE, YOKOSUKA, JAPAN

Comdr. Toshumi Tanaka climbed the ladder two rungs at a time to the surface control space. He climbed the final steps to the surface control space, the light from the sun blinding after being below in the belly of the submarine.

The crew in the surface control space greeted him but Tanaka barely heard. He looked out over the lip of the fin and saw that out in the deep channel the manned Destiny II-class submarines, *Soaring Cyclone, Winter Dragon, Perfect Voice* and *Godlike Snowfall* were already underway, but each of them holding in the waters of the deep channel. On the starboard side of the *Soaring Cyclone* tugs were maneuvering the Destiny III-class ship *Ring of Fire* in close in preparation to being lashed to the manned submarine. The Destiny IIs would be tasked with towing out the unmanned submarines into unrestricted waters; the Three class did not have the capability to navigate near the shore. Tanaka shook his head, the flaws of the Three class so obvious yet so apparently hidden from the high command. Out in the channel *Soaring Cyclone* and *Ring of Fire* were now tied together and began to make their way slowly down the channel to the sea. Next the *Winter Dragon* took on the *Circle of Death,* the *Perfect Voice* was tied up with the *Sphere of Doom,* and *Godlike Snowfall* was saddled with the *Cycle of Fear.* Tanaka's *Winged Serpent* was next.

He turned to the deck officer, Lieutenant Commander Kami, and snapped his fingers for the electronic chart, a notesheet computer that was a half-meter by thirty centimeters, large enough to display all of Tokyo Bay in large scale. The ship's position, pulled down from the Galaxy orbiting overhead, was flashing next to the projection of Yokosuka pier 23. Tanaka studied the track out to the channel and from there to the sea. A flash of his fingers on a software button on the display created a window in the chart picture, the window showing wind velocity, tide direction, soundings through the channel, current data and the weather forecast. All but the last were routine. Tanaka stared at the weather prediction, and stroked the key marked MORE, the subsequent pages of the weather forecast displayed on the screen. Another key was marked SAT. PHOTO. Tanaka selected it, and a photograph from the overhead Galaxy satellite flashed up, the photo showing the earth, the whirling cloud taking up half the area shown, the typhoon developing into a violent storm. Their own mission would be, he decided, unaffected by the approach of the typhoon. It would only move into the vicinity of the Home Islands if it kept moving along its present course, and its speed would not put it near Japan for another three days. Even if it were to continue on its present course at its current speed, *Winged Serpent* would be long submerged at sea. At 200 meters keel depth, the most violent typhoon would not be felt—the ship would be rock steady, only feeling the waves above when the ship ascended to mast-broach depth.

But while the typhoon might not impact their mission physically it might set it back tactically. Communications during the storm would be unreliable—only a dry antenna mast could receive radio communications. The incoming surface group would have free passage, since even Nagasaki torpedoes could not hear through the interference of the high-sea state.

Tanaka pushed aside such thoughts. He had to focus on getting *Winged Serpent* to sea.

"Mr. Kami," Tanaka said, taking his binoculars from the deck officer, "are you ready to get underway?"

"Yes, Captain, request permission to get underway."

"Very good, then, Deck. Take us out and take the *Curtain of Flames* alongside."

"Yessir." Kami, a short husky officer originally from Kobe, took up the headset and boom microphone from the control panel that ran along the forward lip of the surface control space, there some ten meters above the top of the hull. "Control room, surface navigation space, report motor status."

The control panel indicator light lit up, the yellow lamp showing the control room's voice circuit energized.

"Surface nav, control, AC motor breaker shut, motor energized."

"Very good, control. Shift motor control to the surface control space."

"Aye, surface nav, motor control is released to surface nav."

"Very good, control." Kami hit a selector toggle on the control panel, tying his headset with the deck crew. "On deck forward, cast off all forward lines." Kami watched as the deck crew hurried to let go of the lines holding the bow to the pier. The current drove the bow outward from the concrete pier, the brackish slip water opening up. "On deck aft, cast off all stern lines." The deck crew scurried to toss off the lines to the men on the pier until the last line was off and the ship was free. "Lookout, the flag, please." Behind the surface control space, the lookout hoisted the banner of the rising sun high atop a steel flagpole, the flag flapping loudly in the wind.

Finally, Tanaka thought, the ship was underway. A rare sense of contentment invaded his habitual bitterness. If there was one happiness left to him, it was this—taking his ship away from the landbound, petty and officious men of the base to the freedom of the sea, where there was only the crew, the ship, the sea and the enemy. He must write that into haiku, he thought. It would make a fine poem.

"Control, surface nav," Kami announced, "I have remote control of the motor, ordering dead slow ahead." Kami grabbed the throttle lever and gently moved it forward until the motor tachometer read ten revolutions per minute. He looked aft to make sure the wake was making froth astern of the pumpjet propulsor, that the motor was rotating the turbine in the correct direction. The ship began to inch ahead, the pier beginning to slide slowly away. "Control, surface nav, I have remote control of the X-tail and am maneuvering into the channel."

Kami took the throttle lever back to STOP, the ship continuing to glide into the channel, then as the fin became even with the end of the pier he rotated the X-tail rudder-control wheel clockwise to right fifteen effective degrees of rudder. Slowly the ship turned into the channel. Kami added power again, driving the pumpjet back up to 30 rpm to push the ship into the channel, then pulled the throttle back to STOP and zeroed the rudder. The ship glided to a halt in the channel. Far ahead Tanaka could see the twin shapes of the fins of the Two- and Three-class ships steaming to sea lashed together. The water of the channel foamed peacefully against the hull, the *Winged Serpent* motionless in the seaway.

Tanaka looked toward the west, where the sun was setting over the ridge and felt himself move into a new era in his life, realizing that his hours of contemplation on the ridge were over. The feeling was a deep certainty. It was perhaps only the side-effect of the knowledge that he was embarking on a wartime mission—assuming the orders from the high command to attack the threatening surface group ever came in. Politicians always seemed to have a way of lying and cheating their way out of trouble, avoiding whenever possible the simple course of using the guns they had spent so many yen on. This navy would easily prevail if only it were given the chance, he was convinced.

Soon it would be nightfall. With a sense of urgency, Tanaka pulled his radio from his belt, making sure it was tuned to the tactical frequency.

"Portmaster, this is Unit Sunshine. What is the status?"

"Sunshine, Portmaster, hold your position. Your passenger is on the way."

"Tell him he has ten minutes. Then I'm leaving without him. Your tugs can take him to sea then."

"He'll be there in five, sir."

Tanaka clicked twice on the transmit key. A tug horn sounded a mournful blast across the water of the harbor, the last light of the sun winking out on the ridgeline. The operation to tie up the *Curtain of Flames* alongside the *Winged Serpent* had to be accomplished before the dark came—it would be too dangerous and there weren't sufficient lights on the tugs to perform the operation in darkness. Finally the tugs pulled *Curtain of Flames* away from its pier and steadily towed it to the deep channel.

Both tugs were made up to the helpless Three-class' port side so that it could approach *Winged Serpent* on its starboard side. As the light dimmed, the Three class came up alongside, the ratings from the tugboats standing on its deck ready to toss over the lines. It was such a waste of resources to have unmanned robotic ships, Tanaka thought, although it was useless and frustrating to go down that path of thought. Still, it irritated him that once at sea his crew would have to risk their lives, in moonless pitch blackness, to disconnect the lines linking the two ships.

Curtain of Flames was now within twenty meters, the tugs pushing her slowly closer.

Tanaka sighed, looked at his watch. If not for the Three class he had to haul to sea, he would be well on the way to the dive point by now. To the point where life became worth living.

# CHAPTER 14

**New London, Connecticut**

Bruce Phillips opened the door of the motel room's suite, knowing that to call it a suite would be stretching the truth. The motel was called the Dolph-Inn, a play on the submariner's dolphins displayed in a crumbling concrete statue in front of the motel office. The room was dark, the two small windows covered with heavy floral print curtains, the walls done up in trailer-park dark paneling, two double beds on one wall, a kitchenette with a Formica table in the other corner, a couch with a coffee table and television, the old-fashioned square-screen type. Phillips hadn't used the kitchen or the television since he had checked in the week before. He had spent sixteen hours a day at the manufacturing facility trying to push the working crews to get the *Piranha*'s Vortex missiles done sooner. Sometimes progress seemed lightning fast, but most of the time the work got done at a glacially slow pace. He could go nuts in the building yards, he thought. It was a good thing the detailers had never sent him to new construction—his ships had always been well used, not old but worn in, like a pair of favorite deck shoes. So familiar and comfortable that they were preferable to new ones.

It was now dark, in the late afternoon. Usually he got away from the ship from dinnertime until about eight in the evening, when he would go in to catch the tail end of the swing shift. He'd take that until two or three in the morning, then yield to Capt. Emmitt Stephens, who liked to come in at three A.M. to keep the graveyard shift motivated. Phillips would spend the next hours at the motel sleeping, then go back in at noon to meet with his new crew. While he was with the crews putting the missiles on the hull of the sub, his executive officer Roger Whatney was butting heads with the crew, then spending an hour or two briefing Phillips on what the men were like. Phillips was starting to get the picture, but it was coming slower than he wanted, names not yet connected to faces. Not a good situation, given the fact that he would need to take the vessel into hostile waters and soon.

He sat on the bed and took off his soiled coveralls, slowly peeling them off his aching body. He forced himself to stand, wondering if he should take a shower or just collapse in the bed. He opted for the shower, turned on the spray red hot, stepped into the steamy water, the tension leaving him slowly. He was in so long he was turning red, when he thought he heard pounding. It would be typical of the day to have some moron trying to get into the wrong room, he thought, turning off the water as he grabbed a towel and trailed water all the way to the door, the pounding loud and insistent now. He wrapped himself in the towel, opened the door.

"What?" he said as he threw open the door.

"You always greet a lady like that?" Abby O'Neal said.

Phillips's mouth literally hung open. He stared at her, amazed not only at her presence but at what she was wearing. She had come in and dropped her heavy overcoat on the floor. Beneath it she wore a miniskirt with a skimpy tank top.

"Ab, what the *hell* are you doing here?"

"Okay, where is she? In the shower? You were doing her in the shower?" She came up to him, stole his towel and hugged him, and covered his mouth with hers.

Phillips wasn't complaining, but he could hardly take it all in. Self-possessed Abby O'Neal was not one to show up unannounced in a seedy motel room, least of all wearing call-girl clothes. She majored in business suits and workout clothes. A miniskirt and tank top . . . ?

"This is Abby O'Neal's evil twin, right? Where's Abby?"

"Right here," she said, hitting the light. She maneuvered him to the bed, her mouth on his, her hands on him, pulling him closer. Her clothes dropped to the floor, more by her hands than his. She had him on his back as she climbed on top and drove him into her. He shut his eyes, then opened them to see her face, her eyes half-shut. Her lips were parted, her breathing coming in gasps.

It seemed like forever, it seemed like a heartbeat. He lost himself, lost the Navy, the *Piranha,* the Japanese, the Dolph-Inn, and for an achingly sweet moment there was only Abby and him, and the boundary line where he ended and Abby began had become blurred in his union with her.

"I have to go to sea," he was saying to her.

"I know, that's why I'm here, idiot."

Phillips pulled on jeans and a T-shirt. Abby wrapped herself in the bed's comforter. He went to her rental car and got her overnight bag, from which she pulled out her sweatshirt and torn sweatpants that she'd cut off into shorts, her comfort clothes. Once they were settled on the couch, he pressed her for what was going on, stealing a glance at his watch, knowing that with her there it would be a miracle if he went back into the manufacturing facility. It wasn't that she wouldn't let him, it was that when she was with him he didn't want to do anything but be near her, talk to her, touch her hair. He told her she would be responsible for *Piranha* being late to sea, and she said "good."

"So, what's going on, really?" he asked.

"I heard from some people in Norfolk. They say this Japanese thing is heading for a confrontation at sea. Maybe war. And that it was going to be a submarine battle, because the Japanese navy is all submarines, and I knew you were getting ready to go to sea, and I knew you were working around the clock, and, not being stupid, it hit me. This ship is the newest in the fleet. You're going out there to fight—"

"Well, no one knows if—"

"Bruce, don't patronize me."

"All right. Yes, we're going to sea, we'll probably do nothing but go in circles around Japan, and if you want to know the truth, by the time we get there this will all be over. The Pacific fleet boats will probably be force enough, and I seriously doubt that anything will come of this whole thing. It's a tempest in a teapot." He pulled her toward him and stroked her hair.

She looked up at him, eyes looking into his. Of course, she didn't believe him. She sank into the couch and into him.

It was ten hours later that he was able to pull himself away from her and go back to the ship.

## NORTHWEST PACIFIC

The F-14 tossed in the violence of the storm. The clouds around them were black, the rain pounding against the canopy. When the intercom came on Pacino could barely hear it, even though Shearson was screaming.

"Admiral! We're not going to make it!"

"I thought you said we didn't have enough fuel to divert. I thought we'd had to commit to the carrier." Pacino could barely get it out.

"Sir, we don't. But if we're going into the drink we'd better do it outside of the radius of the storm, and goddamn well upwind where it's already been. If we ditch in this sea we'll last minutes, maybe less. We'd better decide now, because we've been dodging the bigger storm cells and it's been burning our fuel. We only have enough gas to make one approach. That's not enough for the book. We need to have at least a half-hour reserve or we're supposed to abort."

"No, Shearson. Take it in. As long as you have navigation capability, you get this plane in to the carrier."

Pacino waited, the plane beginning to bounce so hard it slammed his helmet against the port sill, then the starboard. Directly above them a flash of lightning exploded. The plane jumped, Shearson struggling for control. The plane dived, then took a starboard roll, then a sharp port spin. The lights of the instruments were dark, Pacino realized. The lightning must have hit them. Shearson managed to pull the jet out of the spin but the cockpit was blacked out.

"Have you lost power?" Pacino asked, wondering if the panic he felt was in his voice.

"I'm bringing it back, Admiral. Lightning tripped the instrument bus off the line."

The glow of the dim cabin lights came back on. It felt as if the plane were flying sideways instead of forward. The sensation got worse, as if the jet were upside down.

"Brad, are we flying okay? If feels like we're slipping sideways. Now it seems like we're upside down."

"It happens, sir. After a while being tossed around like this, your inner ears get confused. Down becomes up, left feels like right. If it'll help I'll bring up an artificial horizon on your display aft."

The display came up, the ball in the center of the screen representing the horizon, the superimposed wings of their own plane showing the craft diving slightly. A gust of turbulence hit the plane, tossing Pacino into the side of the cockpit. The horizon dipped to the left, the right wing turning toward the earth. Shearson brought the wings level again. Seeing the instrument seemed to help a little.

"How far to the carrier?"

"About fifteen minutes, sir. We're descending now. But I'm telling you, I can't do this on instruments. If we have no visibility lower than a thousand feet, we're scrubbing the landing."

"No we're not. I mean it, Shearson. I don't care if you smash this thing on the deck, you get me to the *Reagan.*"

**Tokyo Wan**
**Thirty Kilometers West of Point Nojima-zaki**
**SS-810 *Winged Serpent***

Comdr. Toshumi Tanaka watched as the linehandlers cast off the lines from the *Curtain of Flames* and let the heavy manila ropes sink into the sea. The cleats on the deck of the *Curtain of Flames* had automatically released the lines now that they were at the mouth of Tokyo Bay and into the deeper waters of the Pacific. The *Curtain of Flames* barely had enough sense to put its rudder over to port to pull slowly away from *Winged Serpent* without smashing its stern into Tanaka's ship. Tanaka watched as the *Curtain of Flames* steamed off to the southwest, on its way to intercept the closest American aircraft carrier battle group. Once again, the Three-class computer ship got the choicest mission, while *Winged Serpent* was to take station in the Sea of Japan to make sure the Russian shipping to supply the Home Islands was not interrupted.

Tanaka boiled with frustration. The Sea of Japan was the last place he would put the *Winged Serpent.* Such a capable, well-trained crew aboard a magnificent submarine of the Maritime SDF should not be wasted on such a ridiculous mission. But he could let none of this attitude show on his face or in his manner.

Besides, he would be too busy to think about it in a matter of minutes. They were at the dive point, time to get the ship submerged.

## NORTHWEST PACIFIC

The F-14 bounced all the way down into its descent. Pacino looked back at the wings, both of them flapping so hard that he was sure they would break off at any minute.

The altitude on the display board kept unwinding, now at 10,000 feet. The artificial horizon swirled and jogged as the wind tossed the aircraft. Pacino kept his eyes outside, trying to find the lights of the carrier. Shearson was on the radio to the *Reagan,* trying to put the plane down on the deck of the ship, which would be tossing on the high seas.

The rain seemed to get worse as they passed below 5000 feet, the blasting noise of it louder than the jets.

The altimeter continued to unwind, the artificial horizon still swirling. They were running on vapors, with fuel enough for one, maybe two passes.

Pacino strained his eyes for lights and found nothing but the driving rain reflected in Shearson's landing lights. The plane took a dramatic bump upward, Pacino's stomach left in the footwells, then an equally impressive dive. Shearson's nose pulled right, then left, then right again, then another bump up and a slam down. The jets outside were whining, then screaming as Shearson powered up, then whispering again as he throttled back. It occurred to Pacino then that he was going to die, and he had absolutely no control over the situation. This was entirely different from being shot at by a torpedo. At least then he had a submarine under his command, a horse beneath him, but now all he could do was ride, crash and drown.

He glanced at the altimeter and saw that they were at 900 feet, lower than the requisite 1000 to see the carrier, and there was nothing ahead of them but rain shimmering in the landing lights. He looked ahead, straining to see the lights of the carrier. He tried to ignore the onset of vertigo as the plane took another thrashing, bouncing sideways and then up and down and up again. The odd feeling of flying with one wing down came, then became worse as it felt like he was hanging from his harness upside down in the plane. He kept trying to ignore the feeling, pounding on his helmet to see if that would help his inner ears, but it did nothing.

They were too low and there was no sign of the carrier—he saw lights. "Brad! There! The carrier!"

"I don't—"

"Fifteen degrees right!"

"Roger," Shearson said, turning the plane.

The maneuver swirled Pacino's inner ears. The rain continued to blast at them, the thickness of it in the landing lights making the tossing deck of the *Reagan* hard to see. Shearson continued to row the throttles, the engines throttling up and down, the wings dipping and twisting as the plane rolled to fight the storm. As the deck got closer, the plane lurched violently.

"Port engine flameout!" Shearson called. "We're on one engine. I'm going around!"

"No, goddamnit!" Pacino yelled. "Take this bitch in now!"

Shearson didn't answer, just kept on the glide slope, the plane swaying as he tried to keep it on the descent with just one engine. Almost there. Pacino could see the lights dancing in the shimmering rain, until he noticed the numbers on the island were wrong, all wrong.

He glanced down at the instrument panel and saw the artificial horizon and nearly choked. He shouted into the intercom, "Brad, we're upside down! You're coming in upside down!"

Shearson pulled the plane through a two-g maneuver, as much as he could do with a single engine. Pacino's head spun.

It took almost fifteen minutes for Shearson to set up and approach again, this time the artificial horizon showing them right side up.

"Admiral, we're showing zero fuel. I've only got one engine. If we lose it on the glide slope we're going down. Okay. Here we go."

The deck of the carrier floated toward them, ghostly in the rain, the lights dancing around them as they approached in the storm. Shearson goosed the starboard engine, it screamed for a moment, then died.

Pacino didn't need to be told. They were out of fuel on the final approach to the deck, the plane now one big glider. At least, he thought, they wouldn't catch fire.

Shearson had come in high, with the thought of the low fuel situation in mind. Pacino saw the deck of the carrier flying toward them. The right wing dived for the deck, caught on the surface and disintegrated. The remainder of the jet rolled, the deck coming toward the cockpit. By the time the canopy smashed into the steel of the deck, Pacino had already lost consciousness.

**USS *Ronald Reagan***

"Admiral Donner, sir, the news isn't good."

"Go ahead."

Mack Donner, vice admiral, USN, was the commander of the carrier action group and the Japan operational theater. His official title was Pacific Force Commander, but in the acronyms and abbreviations that the Navy lived by, he had become merely the PacForceCom. He was of medium height, balding, with remarkably smooth skin for a fifty-five-year-old. His round baby face always wore a pleasant, open expression. He was a capable mariner, an empathetic leader, a decent tactician and a better than average politician. Most importantly, Mac Donner knew his weaknesses, both in relation to dealing with his people and to deploying his equipment. With a decent team surrounding him, Mac Donner was a winner. With an average team, the odds were not so good. But Donner listened and his sailors and officers loved him, which was more than most leaders could say. As the ship's captain spoke, Donner watched his eyes. The ship's commanding officer, Capt. Robert Petrill, was low key and professional, with an underlying toughness.

Donner was in his stateroom, a cavernous room with three portholes on the 0-4 level, a large head with a shower and a conference table. The room was almost spartan in its neatness, not a single paper or disk on any horizontal surface. The lights were on low, as it was just after midnight local time. The ship was taking twenty-degree rolls and twenty-five degree pitches, the waves outside mountainous. Donner wore khakis, his three stars gleaming on the collars, the only neat thing about the uniform after a long day.

"The pilot is dead. His name was Brad Shearson. Know him?"

"No. What about Admiral Pacino?"

"Out cold in sick bay. Doc thinks he'll pull out of it. A concussion and some scrapes and lacerations."

"I want to be notified as soon as he comes to."

"Aye, sir."

Four decks below, Pacino opened his eyes and grabbed the sleeve of a corpsman.

"Get me Donner. Now."

**DynaCorp International, Electric Boat Division
Groton, Connecticut**

"Even the boss used a limo to get to EB from the airport," McDonne said. "This chopper is going to raise eyebrows. Congress will accuse the Navy of joyriding."

"Ask me if I give a goddamn." The admiral had given orders, Murphy had commandeered the supersonic SS-12 and several jet helicopters, and he had used them to follow those orders.

The chopper made the approach to the Electric Boat helipad, the pad lit with bright lights. The sun wasn't due to come up for another forty-five minutes. Murphy intended to see what the place was like during the slowest part of the day, immediately before the dayshift started.

He walked swiftly into the manufacturing building, the security captain alongside them. Murphy came through the main door in the manufacturing bay and walked swiftly along the length of the hull until he came to the working crew. In the center of the men was Capt. Emmitt Stephens in oil-stained blue coveralls and a hardhat. The man was shouting orders at the controller of the bridge crane high above, the team standing on the scaffolding at the hull where the next Vortex missile tube was about to be lifted and set. The atmosphere was tense, the bay coiled like a spring.

McDonne and Murphy stood in the chill of the bay watching Stephens work. Fifteen minutes slipped into a half-hour, then forty-five minutes. Finally, the missile launcher had been lifted up to its position on the flank of the hull and welded into place. Murphy counted. There were five launchers on the starboard side. He walked under the *Piranha* hull to the port side until he was hemmed in by equipment and looked up. There were five launchers done on the port side. When he returned to McDonne he found a commander standing next to McDonne, his khakis bulging with arms of a stripjoint bouncer. The commander and McDonne saluted, Murphy returning it.

"Commander Phillips, sir. Bruce Phillips."

"So this is your ship. When's she going to sea?"

"Dayshift will be putting her back in the water. My crew is ready to go now. Ship systems will take a day to line up—"

"Line them up at sea," Murphy said.

"Sir, the precritical checklist alone would normally take a week. This reactor's only been in the power range twice."

"Phillips, get *Piranha* to sea this evening."

"I can't start the plant that fast. It'll take fifty to sixty hours. Anything faster could make the reactor run away."

"Take the ship to sea shutdown. I'll get a tug to take you into the sound. Your core will be cold iron. Go ahead and do your pull and wait startup in the river and the sound until you get to the fifty-fathom curve."

"What good will that do?"

"It'll keep your infrared signature cold. We'll put some cellular phone calls out in the local area that your ship is a target for a live torpedo-firing exercise."

"What are you saying?"

"If we can convince the Japanese satellites that the tug is towing your hull to sea so you can be a target, they won't know you're coming."

"What difference does that make?"

"It might keep you from being targeted before you can get to the Japan OpArea. And maybe they won't do a lot of thinking about what those bulges are on your hull."

"And how am I supposed to get out to the OpArea with a dead reactor?"

"I recommend you submerge the ship when it's dark, with the diesel on the AC buses using the snorkel mast. That way your infrared signature will be minimal and the Galaxy satellite that's orbiting directly overhead won't see a hot reactor submarine going to sea, one with a lot of suspicious bulges on the hull, one that is definitely a Seawolf class. If they don't know you're coming, they can't get to you early."

"If I'm going into combat in the OpArea, why should I worry about what's out there?"

"Because Admiral Pacino wants all ten Vortex missiles in the OpArea, not three, not one, ten. Get there quietly. Undetected."

"Is this your idea or Admiral Pacino's?"

Murphy looked at Phillips and lied.

"Pacino's. I don't have it in writing but he gave it to me on a secure VOX transmission on the way to the forward deployed carrier air group."

Phillips looked up at the *Piranha.* "Okay, we're getting underway tonight. Anything else?"

"I'll check back with you this evening."

"If you call after sundown you won't get me. I'm not transmitting anything to anyone once I toss off the lines. You want me, send me a message on the broadcast but don't expect an answer."

"How will you be going to the Japan OpArea?"

"Under the polar icecap."

Murphy was impressed. "Good luck. Come on, McDonne."

They walked away, Murphy stealing a last glance at Emmitt Stephens, now joined by Commander Phillips, as they worked the crew loading the Vortex missile into the tube they had just erected onto the hull.

**NORTHWEST PACIFIC**
**USS *Ronald Reagan***

"Well, Admiral, welcome aboard the USS *Ronald Reagan.* We don't have many VIPs who crash-land to get here."

"Mac, how long has it been?"

"About five years, Patch."

Pacino was set up in his visiting admiral's stateroom, certainly not as glorious as Donner's, but with two portholes, a civilian-sized bed, a small round four-piece conference table and a head that was more impressive than anything ever built into a US submarine. It would be damned hard to leave it to go to one of the battle group's submarines. Particularly given the comfort of the stateroom's bed, where Pacino had been ordered to stay until the doctor gave him a follow-up examination.

"How's Brad Shearson?"

"They left that news for me to tell you, Patch. I'm real sorry. Shearson didn't make it."

Pacino looked up at Donner. Another life lost from his orders. He said something to Donner but couldn't remember it. He was dimly aware of the doctor coming in and injecting him with a syringe, and darkness closing in on him despite his fighting it

**USS *Piranha*, SSN-23**
**ELECTRIC BOAT DIVISION, GROTON, CONNECTICUT**

"Any questions?" Phillips asked the assembled crew in the ship's mess, all of them dressed for December weather, the heat in the room making their parkas that much more uncomfortable.

"Sir," a chief asked, "how long to get to the Japan OpArea?"

"Going under ice, maybe two weeks, maybe less."

"I've been stuck under the ice before, Captain, back on the *Chicago*. It wasn't great."

"Well, it's not gonna happen to us. Next."

"Yessir," Lt. Pete Meritson said. Meritson was the sonar boss and the most senior of the junior officers. Phillips said that Meritson had the sweetest disposition and the most pleasant face, that it was a shame that he wasn't selling used cars—he'd have made millions. Meritson was more than a pleasant presence on board the *Piranha*. His intellect was penetrating. With the modern sonar systems now being installed on the Seawolf class, it was more common that the "bull" lieutenant, the most senior and trusted of the junior officers, be a sonar officer than the main propulsion assistant to the chief engineer. In this case Meritson was the man for the job. He had been an electrical engineer at Cornell with a specialty in electronic communications, the major that was sailing so many graduates into the highest paid engineering jobs as the WritePads and cellular phones became as common as telephones had been in the previous century. But he had chosen to join the Navy, without the service paying a nickel of his education, just up and sauntered into a Navy recruiting office one day, spent three months in an officer-training program and a year in nuclear-power training and sub school, and scarcely a year after graduation was a submarine officer. The enlisted men joked that he was possibly the only one aboard who had paid for his own schooling, and was still doing "hard time" on board the submarine when he could be out making money.

"Go ahead, Meritson."

"Sir, what exactly are we going to do when we get there?"

Phillips looked around the room as if wondering if it were secure enough to say what he needed to say.

"Gentlemen, the only reason I'm going to answer that question is that when we're done here we're going to sea." Phillips called the chief of the boat over, the COB, Chief Hanson, a torpedoman, a country boy. "COB," Phillips said, "collect all the cellular phones, every goddamned one of them." Cellular phones were controlled more carefully than anything else aboard, the submarine force becoming security crazed after several SEAL operations had proved that the subs' cellular phones were giving away too much. Only official ship's phones were allowed aboard. Anyone caught with their own cellular unit lost it to the COB until the ship made port again.

"Okay, here's the deal. Just before the executive officer and I reported aboard we ran a special simulation against a Destiny II-class submarine, trying to sneak up on the SOB. Guess what? No matter what we did, we lost." Phillips let that sink in for a moment. "Now, that was with an improved-688 class, but Seawolf ships are only marginally better against the Destiny. Let's face a fact, gents—if we could buy Destiny II submarines we'd fill our piers with them and sell off these 688s and Seawolfs to the highest bidder. They're that good. But we've got something that can neutralize even a Destiny." Phillips paused for effect. "The Vortex missiles we're carrying like a bandoleer are the ultimate antisubmarine weapon." As long as they didn't blast their rocket exhaust through the hull, he thought. "Which means we're the cavalry. If the sub force goes up against the Destiny ships in combat, and I hope to hell they don't, we'll be there to put them down."

"Skipper," said Roger Whatney, the Royal Navy executive officer in RN sweater with its soft epaulets and lieutenant commander's stripes, the star missing, a loop of braiding replacing it, "if there are more than ten Destiny subs we could be in for trouble."

"Spoken like a gentleman, sir," Phillips said, unconsciously imitating something Whatney was fond of saying. "Now, if we can get on with it, let's get this pig to sea. We've got to make the best time ever made to the Bering Strait. I've got a feeling that our people in the Japan OpArea are going to need us."

**NORTHWEST PACIFIC**
**USS *Ronald Reagan***

"Admiral, I'm sorry I lost it last night," Pacino said, standing on the bridge next to Donner's admiral's chair. The waves were still pounding the ship, the other ships of the surface action group invisible in the storm. The glass windows of the bridge were drenched with rain. Three Plexiglas wheels set into the front plate glass spun at high rpm, throwing off the rain, the only clear view of the sea ahead. The officer of the deck stood at the radar console, his visual sight nearly useless.

"Patch, after nearly augering into the deck and totaling yourself, it's very understandable. How are you feeling?"

"Seasick, sir. I need to get out to one of the submarines, the *Pasadena* or the *Cheyenne.* As soon as possible, sir."

"Patch, I don't want to burst your bubble, but have

you seen it out there? We're grounded. Ain't no choppers going to be flying in this weather."

"When's it going to calm down?"

"We've got another day of this to go. But there's more bad news. By the time this weather clears we'll be in the Japan OpArea and there won't be any helotransfers. You'd better read this." Donner handed Pacino a message, classified top secret/special compartment/codeword *Enlightened Curtain.*

Pacino read through the message, quickly at first, then read through it a second time. It was a confidential message from Warner and Wadsworth. Ambassador Pulcanson had met twice with Prime Minister Kurita. The first time Pulcanson had laid out the deal—that UN troops would take station on Japanese soil, that their initial actions would be to supervise the dismantlement of the radioactive weapons, the second the deactivation of the nuclear cores of the submarines of the Maritime Self Defense Force, the third the selling off of the FireStar fighters. Kurita had been noncommittal, Pulcanson had been firm and told him he had a day to provide an answer. Two days later Pulcanson had returned. Kurita's answer was no better than before. He didn't say no, he didn't say yes.

Warner had had a meeting with the National Security Council. She had ordered Donner's force to set up the blockade. They were going in to stop the flow of all commercial traffic into Japan.

"This will be the first act of war of the new century. And maybe the worst."

"Oh, hell, Patch, we did this a ways back with the Cubans and it prevented a war."

"That was the Cubans, and the Russians. These are the Japanese. Go back to your history books, Mac. The last time we cut off the oil to these people they used it as an excuse to sink our fleet. They'll do it again, they'll fight. We shouldn't just put a ring of warships around Japan, we should hit them *preemptively.* If we sail off their coast they'll nail us with everything they've got."

"I don't think so, Patch. This will last a week, maybe a month. The other carrier groups will get here and then the Japanese will have to see reason. We'll be home in a couple of months—"

"Mac, I'm telling you. We should hit the Galaxy satellites *now*. We should sortie every goddamned airplane we have to bomb the FireStar squadrons and the Destiny submarines. Then and only then, we should blockade the islands. It's the only way."

"I think you're forgetting the antisubmarine warfare capabilities of this surface force, Patch. Now let me give you a piece of advice."

Pacino stared out into the rain.

"Why don't you go below and meet with Commander White? He's the submarine liaison officer. He could use a boost. You both must come from the same school, you sound like a broken record."

Pacino went below. It was going to be a long war, he thought. Or a very short one.

# CHAPTER 15

**Electric Boat Division, Groton, Connecticut**
**USS *Piranha,* SSN-23**

Comdr. Bruce Phillips dumped eight heaping teaspoonfuls of instant coffee into the Big Gulp cup and poured an entire pot of boiling water into it. He filled a second Big Gulp cup with ice, stirred the instant coffee, then dumped the hot coffee into the iced cup. He pinched his nose, put the cup to his lips and drank the liquid down in one go, gagging as it went down. He looked over to find the XO, Lt. Comdr. Roger Whatney, staring at him, shaking his head.

"Well, Skipper, I hope you're planning on taking both those cups to the bridge with you. You'll need them to dump the used coffee in when your body's done with it."

Whatney had a point, he thought. He yawned and glanced at his Rolex, wondering why the hell he had neglected to sleep in the last twenty-four hours. Part of it was Abby's visit.

"What's the status, XO?" he asked Whatney.

"Well, sir, we've got enough exceptions to our rig-for-sea to fill a three-inch-thick three-ring notebook. I don't know that I'd ever recommend doing this, if not for your orders from Admiral Pacino."

"How bad is it?"

"Here's the rundown, Skipper," Whatney said. "Starting aft, we have no main engines. Propulsion is on the emergency electric propulsion motor. The electric plant is only fair because we're long overdue for a battery charge. The electrical turbines are as dead cold iron as the main engines, the steam plant is cold, the steam generators are in wet layup and the reactor is shutdown in the fiduciary range, completely nonvisible."

Phillips shook his head. Nonvisible reactor power meant that it would take days for reactor power to come up to the power range, unless they added enough reactivity to it that it might come up uncontrollably, little more than a fission bomb. All the publicity about reactors not being able to explode like atom bombs only applied to tame natural uranium cores in civilian industry. Navy cores were fueled with highly enriched bomb-grade uranium, reactive enough to blow the hull fifty stories in the air and scatter enough radiation to wipe out a three-county area. The core designers called it a "prompt-critical-rapid-disassembly." Phillips called it an explosion.

"Anyway, the reactor plant is at about a hundred degrees. It'll take a long time to warm it up to operating temperature. The pull-and-wait startup will take forty-five hours if we do it by the book, the plant startup another couple hours."

"Well, we won't be doing it by the book, I can promise the engineer that."

"Eng won't like that."

The engineer, Lt. Comdr. Walter Hornick, was a by-the-book procedure man. He and Phillips had already had words about the reactor startup.

"Fine, he'll just have to deal with it. What about the forward systems?"

"The combat-control system is in good shape, navigation systems are go, ship control is ready. The diesel generator is up and running so we're divorcing from shorepower now. The only question is the reactor."

"Maneuvering watch stationed?"

"Fully, sir. We're ready to go."

"Tugs?"

"Waiting at the mouth of the slip."

"Is the ship fully waterborne?" Phillips said, asking about the platform and blocks that had supported the submarine as it was slowly lowered into the Thames River at the manufacturing slip. Was the ship still resting on the blocks, or was it afloat?

"Yes, Captain. The platform is two meters below the keel."

"Watertight integrity checked?"

"Yessir. We're not leaking from any of the systems the yard worked on or from anywhere else."

"Have the engineer come up to the wardroom."

Whatney acknowledged and left. Phillips made another tall cup of chilled instant coffee and had halfway gagged it down when Chief Engineer Walt Hornick stepped into the wardroom. He grinned at Phillip's coffee-drinking method as he poured himself a steaming cup of fresh-brewed Columbian into a mug with the *Piranha*'s emblem painted on it, the ship's symbol the inevitable toothy fish with the eyes of a menacing wolf.

Hornick was tall, thin, too thin, mid-to-late thirties, with all his hair, a curly black mass. He looked much younger than his years, spoke gently, but what Hornick missed in the fire-and-brimstone area he made up for with cranial power, a brilliant Villanova graduate in mechanical engineering. Hornick had a memory that amazed Phillips, not only in his grasp of procedures and technical manuals but with his men, with the engineering plant's history, with everything that crossed his desk. His style of giving reports, however, could send Phillips up a wall. Whatney had described it to Phillips one night in the manufacturing bay.

"Skipper, don't ever ask Hornick what time it is."

"Why not, XO?"

"He'll build you a watch."

Phillips's and Hornick's styles diverged in other areas. Hornick was a straight arrow, the likes of which Phillips had never seen. In the week since Phillips had taken over *Piranha,* Hornick had repeatedly declined to go out for beer at the local strip joints. Some of the married men weren't into that either, but Hornick seemed genuinely uncomfortable at the thought of discussing ship's business in the company of exposed female breasts. Phillips, on the other hand, did his best thinking in that environment.

"Well, Eng, how do you feel tonight?" Phillips felt his

pockets for the stash of Cuban cigars but didn't pull one out, knowing that Hornick would be annoyed by it.

"I feel like I'm ready for bed, Captain. This whole startup has got me worried."

"You mean the emergency power range approach, the emergency heatup rates, the emergency steam-plant startup?"

"Yessir. The plant could blow the roof off. How then will we get to sea? This ship has been critical all of twice, once for the initial crit, once on sea trials, and even then we never got above 35 percent power."

"Yeah," Phillips said, sinking into the leather-covered bench seat at the end of the table. An idea began to dawn on him. "What would you do, Walt? You'll be a commanding officer in a few years if anyone listens to me. What would you do to start this ship's reactor and steam plant?"

It was another language for Hornick, another culture, to imagine that he was someone other than the ship's engineer. He took a deep breath.

"Well, sir, I'd—"

"Tell you what, Walt. Here, sit down right here." Phillips stood, walked to the end of the table and pulled out the end chair, the chair that was reserved for the captain. Hornick looked stricken at the thought of sitting in the captain's chair.

"Sit down, that's an order." Phillips pulled his silver oak-leaf insignia off his collar, pulled Hornick's gold colored oak leaves off and traded, putting the full commander's pins on Hornick's collar, the lieutenant commander's pins on his own. He pulled the pin off his left pocket, the anchor in a circle of laurel leaves, the capital ship command pin, and pinned it to Hornick's pocket. Then he left the room, shut the door quietly and came in again.

Hornick was embarrassed completely by Phillips' role playing.

"Sir, really—"

"Sir? Captain, sir, you wanted to see me, sir? You remember me, sir, don't you, the engineer? You wanted to talk to me, sir? About the reactor startup, sir? How should we do the startup, Captain?"

Roger Whatney picked that moment to come into the room with a metal clipboard that held the radiomen's WritePad encrypted computer notesheet, the one used for radio messages that were highly classified and needed to be electronically signed before they could be released to Phillips' personal WritePad computer. Whatney took a look at Hornick in the captain's chair wearing the accouterments of command, then over at Phillips wearing lieutenant commander's insignia, and he pulled the radio WritePad back from Phillips and instead offered it to Hornick. He did not even do a suggestion of a double-take.

"Captain," Whatney said to Hornick, "you'd better initial this and get to the bridge. Have you given the order to start the plant yet? By the way, the admiral wants us at full power in three hours, submerged and underway."

Another reason Phillips wanted Whatney aboard as his XO—the Brit could practically read his mind. Phillips and Whatney looked at Hornick, waiting.

"Oh, all right, sirs. Engineer," Hornick said to Phillips, "perform an emergency approach to reactor criticality, when critical perform an emergency heatup, then start the engine room with emergency warmups."

"Aye, aye, sir!" Phillips tossed Hornick a salute.

Five minutes later Hornick was back aft wearing his proper uniform, as Phillips was swallowing the last dregs of the iced coffee. The navigator came in then, carrying a rolled-up larger version of the WritePad computer, this one big enough to display a chart. Lt. Comdr. Scott Court was a tightly wrapped Annapolis grad with a starched uniform, spit-shined shoes, his academy ring always in evidence. Phillips considered Court maybe the "greasiest" officer he'd ever met, the term a relic from the academy and used to describe men who oiled the wheels of their own political progress. Still, Court was friendly, confident, smart and even-handed with his department. But then Phillips had the feeling that if he were not Court's superior officer, Court would not give him the time of day.

"Here's the chart display, Captain. You wanted to go over it?"

"Have a seat, Scotty," Phillips said to Court, again sprawling into the end bench. Court put the navigation display on the table. The chart showed the Thames River in the vicinity of Groton and New London, its approach into the Fisher's Island Sound through the Race and into Block Island Sound, and from there into the Atlantic.

"We'll be towed out along this track. I'm trying to figure out where to submerge on the diesel," Phillips told him.

"How much room do you want, sir?"

"At a keel depth of eighty feet snorkeling, it would be nice to go down to 150 feet if some traffic came by—"

"You'd have to secure snorkeling and run on the battery while starting up the reactor, Captain."

"It wouldn't be pretty, but even if the engineer is running a main feed pump on the diesel and we have to pull the plug to go deep, he'd just stop the pump and stop the steam draw. Hornick could recover from that, don't you think?"

"Skipper, thank God we've got Walt back here. I doubt anyone else could handle this."

"Okay, 150 feet, with a margin of another 150 feet, that's 300 feet or fifty fathoms."

"That's shallow, sir."

"Fine, sixty. Where's the sixty-fathom curve?"

Court touched a software function key and danced with the software until the depth curve he sought highlighted itself. "Right here, Captain."

"No way, that's too far out. Give me fifty fathoms . . . not much better, but that's the deal . . . Weather holding up?" Phillips was sneaking *Piranha* out of town under the cover of darkness and an overcast sky, all the better to keep the watchful eye of the overhead Japanese Galaxy satellite from looking down at them.

"Both good and bad, sir. It's started to snow, hard. They're calling for a foot of snow, and then it's going to turn to freezing rain and sleet. The snowstorm will keep us hidden from the Galaxy upstairs, but visibility is closing down on us and that makes this trip doubly dangerous. We'll have trouble seeing the merchant traffic, and they'll have problems seeing us."

"Maybe we should keep the tug longer, stay on the surface and run the diesel until the reactor's warm."

"I don't know, sir. The Galaxy machines can see an infrared heat trace through heavy clouds, maybe even through this storm. I like the idea of getting down under as soon as we can. I liked even more the idea of getting the reactor plant up fast."

"I may spend some time aft with Walt when we're starting up."

"Sir, please don't. That'll just slow him down. Walt likes precision and plans. You being back there isn't part of his . . . plan."

Phillips smiled. "You've been hanging with Walt for a while, now, right, Scott?"

"Sir, Walt is different but he's damned good. You tell him what you want, and once he agrees he delivers. He's not your typical military type."

"Is there a typical type?"

"My wife thinks so. She says all my friends and I are walking military robots."

"What do you think?"

"I think we wear uniforms and are trained to behave certain ways, and on the ship we're a team, but the test is when we're up against a situation we haven't been trained for, and we go on our own. That's when I think we'll prove that we're about as far from robots as you can get."

"Is that good or bad?"

"Captain, it could go either way."

"Guess I should get to the bridge. Is the pilot here?"

"On the tug, sir. It's waiting for us in the river."

"Let's get the hell to sea."

# CHAPTER 16

**NORTHWEST PACIFIC**
**585 NAUTICAL MILES EAST-SOUTHEAST OF YOKOHAMA**
**USS *Ronald Reagan***

Pacino had asked for Donner to come into flag plot, away from the bridge and other ears, so he could talk to him about how they would work together on the blockade. Once that was done he'd assemble the submarine operations people in a room and take over from the submarine operations officer. Then he'd get on with Sean Murphy and go over the fleet deployment. It was already 1000 and Pacino had a mountain of work to do before noon.

The worst of the typhoon had passed through during the night. Pacino had spent the storm in his rack, the motion of the ship, which made him seasick when he was up, had the opposite effect on him when he was lying down. The waves had actually rocked him to sleep and he had slept beyond his wakeup notice, but no one had cared. No one but Donner even seemed to know he was on board. With the storm, the accident with the F-14, the sedative and the jet lag, Pacino had needed the sleep. He had awakened feeling so much better that for a moment he almost forgot about Brad Shearson, but the memory of their flight came back and landed on his conscience with a resounding thump. If he had waited a day the kid would have lived.

Pacino looked out the starboard windows at the horizon, the sea calm now that the storm had ceased. The sky was overcast, but the glare from the brightness was giving Pacino a headache. The other ships of the battle group steamed in formation, the beauty of it breathtaking, the precision, the guns and missiles and radars of the sleek surface ships a powerful display of naval might. Looking at them, Pacino for the first time felt that the blockade might work out. He turned away from the starboard window and looked at flag plot, a room the size of the bridge on the deck above. The room's windows were as panoramic as the bridge's, the floor space taken up with plot tables and conference tables. Now that charts and papers were replaced by WritePads, the room's broad tables were somewhat out of use. In Pacino's experience on submarines, which were so cramped for space and volume that the eye never focused on a distance more than fifteen feet away, the openness and wide view from flag plot seemed luxurious, almost sinful.

Finally Admiral Donner came in, dressed in fresh working khakis with no decorations on his uniform other than his surface warfare pin and his three silver stars.

"Morning. I see you're still with us. How do you feel?"

"Better. After last night anything is better."

"Good. Listen, you'd better take a look at this. Seems things are picking up steam."

Pacino squinted in the glare to see the writing on Admiral Donner's WritePad.

"Warner wants to start the blockade *tonight,*" Donner said.

"But we're not in position yet. We've got another twelve hours of steaming to get us within fifty miles of Honshu, and that's just the east side of the islands. We have to get the Sea of Japan task group on the other side of the islands to interdict shipping from the west. That'll take at least another day—"

"President Warner has maps, she knows where we are and the timing of getting in close. Admiral Wadsworth is working on it with her."

Wadsworth strikes again, Pacino thought.

"Mac, what the hell is this? We can't set up a blockade that fast. What kind of a blockade would that be? By this evening the Sea of Japan will still be wide open."

"I thought something like this might happen, Patch. I sent your submarines on ahead a few hours before you landed, if that crash on the deck can be called a landing. I should have told you when you were up on the bridge last night but I figured once you talked to Paully White, the sub-operations officer, you'd come back up here to the bridge to scream about it. But you were down until now."

Pacino realized he should have checked in and met the submarine-operations officer, the man aboard the carrier who was responsible for the tasking of the two submarines traveling with the battle group. But he had been too exhausted and sick to go below and had left it for today. Once again Pacino cursed the fact that he wasn't in command of a submarine anymore. On the sub, his information network surrounded him. Now here he was, his information screened by Donner, who kept him in the dark to avoid his anger, hiding behind an operations officer when he was supposed to be as heavy in planning the operation as Donner was. He would have to work on Donner, Pacino thought, deciding to get in touch with Sean Murphy as soon as he left the bridge. The Hawaii subs, the Pacific Fleet submarine force, should be well on its way by now, he thought.

"You detached my submarines without informing me, Admiral. I'd appreciate it if you'd keep me in the goddamned loop. Sir."

"Sorry, Patch, but don't forget, technically those submarines are under the operational control of the battle group, and since I'm the force commander they report in to me."

"No, Admiral, those ships were to out-chop to my command. I'm the USubCom force commander, and as of last night those ships are under my op-comm." The jargon meant the ships left the battle group and got a new boss, Pacino, the evening he arrived on the carrier.

"Okay, Patch, fine. They're your boats and under your command. Okay? It's just that you had a hell of a night with the accident and the sedative, and the doc thought you might be down for a while, which you were, and we were steaming as before."

"Where are my ships?"

"The *Pasadena* and *Cheyenne* have been running at flank all night. They'll be in the western OpArea, in the Sea of Japan, by the time the blockade starts."

"Mac, we may be in a hurry to play this ball game, but why would we agree to kick off with only two players on the goddamned field? The whole point of a blockade is to be *visible.* That takes surface ships. No blockade is credible with subs alone. And the Japan OpArea is crawling with their Destiny-class ships. With our boats running in there at flank speed, they'll be eaten alive."

"Those are the orders."

"Admiral, my subs need release to sink the Destiny subs in the OpArea. You've given that order, I assume, sir." Pacino braced for the worst.

"Those aren't the rules of engagement, Patch, and you know it. The blockade setup is that, first, Tokyo and the world is notified that as of nineteen hundred hours today, no merchant shipping is to cross the boundary of the OpArea, or as Warner's calling it in public, the Exclusion Zone. Then, as of seven o'clock tonight local time, we sink anything crossing the boundary, going in or out. There's nothing authorizing us to attack the military of Japan."

"Let's ask, Admiral. We've got to get that request on the wire now. If my boats are out there, they could be targeted by Destiny subs. And since you sent them in at maximum speed, they made a hell of a racket getting there. The whole Japanese Fleet knows exactly where they are. They won't last after the first torpedo."

"What do you want this to say?"

"That we want to be released to strike at any Destiny submarine the minute we detect it, and that Tokyo should be told to withdraw their submarines or we'll attack."

Donner scribbled on the WritePad, and Pacino read. "Fine."

"I'll send it as a joint message from PacForceCom and USubCom/PacForce. How's that?"

"Great." Pacino was still angry but he tried to keep it from showing.

**Northwest Pacific**
**USS *Barracuda***

The phone buzzed by the side of the rack. Capt. David Kane lifted a mucous-encrusted eyelid, found the phone, pulled it out of its cradle and dragged it to his ear.

"Captain," he croaked. He felt older than his forty-five years, the forty-fifth birthday hitting him much harder than he had anticipated. He had been having another nightmare about it, the room filled with black balloons labeled "over the hill" while he looked in a mirror and saw deep wrinkles, bald head, gray mustache, himself bent over a cane. He was glad that the phone had interrupted the dream. He glanced at his watch, the face reading 3:15, trying to remember if it was set for Hawaii time, local time, Greenwich Mean or Tokyo time. He managed to recall ordering the ship's clocks set to Tokyo time so that when they got to the Japan OpArea their bodies would be adjusted to the light cycles outside. There was nothing worse than coming to periscope depth in a dark submarine with your body thinking it was two in the morning only to find that when the scope cleared the sun was shining from high in the sky.

"Captain," he said again, wondering if he'd dreamt the phone had buzzed.

"Yessir, Captain, Officer of the Deck. It's zero three fifteen, sir. I'm calling to request to come up to periscope depth."

Kane had trained his junior officers, on night wakeup calls like this, to make him dig for information. If the officer of the deck did a data dump on him, he'd be back asleep by the end of the OOD's report.

"Okay. Any contacts?"

"No contacts, sir."

"Present status?"

"Depth one five zero feet, speed six knots, course west, sir."

"Reason for PD?"

"Broadcast, Captain. Also we need to check the inertial nav against the GPS signal."

"Last broadcast was when?"

The ship was required to come up to periscope depth at least once every eight hours to get radio messages from the ComStar satellite that orbited in a geostationary orbit over the Pacific. The satellite would transmit messages in a ten-second burst every fifteen minutes, whether anyone was there to hear them or not. Usually while they were up, the periscope antenna would pull down the signal from the navigation satellite, the global-positioning system.

"We were up at twenty-thirty last night, sir. It's time."

"Very well, Off'sa'deck," Kane said, slurring the title, "take her up to PD and get the broadcast and a nav fix. Then get us back down and speed back up to flank. We're late."

"Aye, sir, periscope depth, broadcast, nav fix, deep and flank."

Kane recradled the phone and shut his eyes again, sleep washing comfortably up over him, the dreams coming slowly, but then he was in his backyard dressed in a clown suit at his daughter's birthday party, his wife Becky handing him a beer, the kids squealing in delight. The party melted into a beach where he and Becky were alone in the moonlight and she was reaching for him, a devilish look in her blue eyes. He could feel her long fingernails as she drew them across his flat stomach to his waistband, her playful laughter mixing in with the sounds of the waves on the sand. He felt her fingers plunge into his bathing suit and gently stroke him, then pull him out. She began to kiss him. His eyes rolled back in his head, Becky's mouth working until sweat poured down from his temples and—

BOOM BOOM BOOM.

"Radioman, sir, messages for you."

"Goddamnit." Kane sat up in the rumpled bed. The radioman came in with the metal clipboard with the official WritePad. Kane glanced at the messages, the ones classified with codeword *Enlightened Curtain* first in the queue. It looked like the blockade would proceed ahead of schedule. Kane initialed the messages, drawing his finger over the surface of the WritePad as if using it for a pencil, the computer drawing lines as his finger sketched his initials over the pad.

The radioman left and Kane sank back into the rack, feeling the deck take on a down angle as the officer of the deck drove the ship deep again and increased speed to get back on their planned track to the Japan OpArea. He shut his eyes and felt sleep overtake him again, but this time lovely Becky was gone, the dreams dominated by the ocean, its depth and darkness, storms at sea, dark rain. He tossed and turned all the way to the next phone call from the control room.

**Sea of Japan**
**SS-810 *Winged Serpent***

Comdr. Toshumi Tanaka was still awake in his stateroom, reading the message traffic about the coming of the American Navy's carrier battle groups. One of the messages was from his father, addressed to the entire Destiny force at sea in the waters near the Home Islands. The message read that the approaching battle groups might attempt to set up a blockade, but no matter what happened, no submarine was to attack or molest any incoming American unit—even if there were American submarines approaching in close. Admiral Tanaka allowed the Destiny force to shadow the Americans, but even at that he was being cautious, ordering the Japanese submarines to remain outside a half-kilometer distance from any American ship.

It was ridiculous, the younger Tanaka thought. He was in the middle of thinking about how he would change those orders when a knock came from the door to the head Tanaka shared with his first officer, Lt. Comdr. Hiro Mazdai.

"Come," Tanaka said.

"Evening, Captain. Is everything satisfactory?"

"Fine, Mr. First, why?"

"I was in the head and saw your light on, sir."

"Anything on your mind, First?"

"The crew is uneasy, sir."

"About the American battle groups?"

"No, Captain. I think it's just the situation."

"Explain."

"Sir, our Two-class manned ships are in the waters of the Home Islands. Our Three-class ships have set sail for the deep Pacific—and for the near Pacific, where the closest incoming aircraft carrier group is approaching. Only two things can happen. Either our fleets engage or they don't. Either the Americans shoot at us and we shoot at them, or we return to our separate ports with all of our weapons still aboard."

"First, is there a point to this?"

"Just that, one could say if we go down the path of shooting, both sides may lose. At first we should prevail. The Americans will be sunk. But they will send more ships. We will return to port to get more torpedoes. One can only hope the Americans run out of ships before we run out of torpedoes. Our own ships will take losses, some of us will die. The American fleets will be hurt worse, but America has an air force too. Will they not fight back, bomb our country, maybe shoot their missiles at us, drop paratroopers onto our soil? How long can we fight? How long will we watch our children and women dying? Some, sir, say we were wrong to attack Greater Manchuria, that we should say so now. They say it is a new century, that it seems wrong to fight the same fight we did in the last."

"Are you speaking for yourself or others?"

"Sir, I am an officer of the Japanese Maritime Self Defense Force. I will do my duty to the day I die. I will follow my orders. I will shoot torpedoes at hospital ships if ordered. I will blow up this submarine before allowing it to be captured, if ordered. I am an officer, but I am also a man. The time for Samurai warriors is over. Our leaders have not realized that."

"That's quite a speech, First. I had no idea you felt this way. I order you to keep these opinions to yourself. Failing that, I will shoot you myself. Now get out."

Mazdai returned to his own stateroom. Tanaka stared at the door, amazed and angry. Did others in Japan really think this way? Mazdai's argument had no attraction for him. Mazdai had not lost his mother, the one person who loved him on this earth, to the uncaring, incompetent and hurtful Americans. Mazdai had not spent his young years being spit at and taunted by Americans. Mazdai had not been forced to live with them, with their disgusting food and arrogance about being the best country in the world, the one and only world power. Mazdai had not had to suffer their vicious racist attitudes toward Japan, toward all people of color.

Toshumi Tanaka had, and even if his torpedoes didn't make the world a more peaceful place for flower-loving Mazdai, they would at least even the balance sheet. The torpedoes were named Nagasakis for a reason. The cruise missiles were named Hiroshimas for a reason.

To hell with the Americans.

# CHAPTER 17

**Block Island Sound**
**USS *Piranha***

Comdr. Bruce Phillips scanned the horizon with his binoculars, searching for the lights of merchant ships, fishing boats or pleasure craft, although there was no way a yacht would be out tonight. The blizzard was the worst Phillips could remember since he was a child, back in the storms of '93. The snowflakes were the size of nickels and quarters, fogging his binoculars, getting inside the collar of his parka.

He dropped the binoculars and stared out at the fog, cursing the slowness of their journey. Somehow, though, it seemed fitting that a trip under the polar icecap would begin with a blizzard. The fog obscured vision, the horizon coming in, then receding again. The fog and the snow and the late hour made the Sound dead quiet. The only sounds were the dull rumble of the tugboat's diesel engines, the thudding roar of *Piranha*'s own emergency diesel generator and the wash of the wake against the hull.

The *Piranha* was moving at little more than five knots, her diesel running to provide power to start the reactor. As soon as the Sound was deep enough, he would order the ship to cast off the line to the tug and he'd submerge the ship. It would be a hairy operation taking it down on battery power alone.

"Control, Captain," Phillips said into his boom microphone, "mark distance and time to the fifty-fathom curve."

"Captain, Navigator," Court's voice replied in his single-earpiece headset, "forty minutes to fifty-fathom curve, distance three point three nautical miles."

"Present sounding?"

"Forty-one fathoms."

"Very well." Phillips looked at the officer of the deck, Lt. Peter Meritson. "Well, Pete, what's Deanna think of all this?"

"I told her it was no big deal."

Phillips looked over the lip of the sail to the port side, the Vortex missile canisters ruining the flow of water around the ship, the missiles half the length of the submarine. They were certainly ugly, he thought, wondering if the missiles would work. He looked back over at his sonar officer and officer of the deck.

"Yeah, but what does she think?"

"She thinks I'll be wearing a flag at the bottom of the Sea of Japan."

"She said that?"

"No, Deanna actually said, 'Be careful, honey, I'll worry about you,' but her tone of voice said 'You're not coming back.' It's a bit much for her to take."

"What's Deanna do again?"

"She's a nurse. Takes her show on the road, makes rounds of older folks' homes."

"Tough job. Hope she's not going out in this weather."

"No, she's at her mothers'."

Phillips sighed. "Let's get this bucket of bolts ready to submerge, Pete. I'm laying below. Rig the bridge for dive and shift control to the control room."

"Aye, sir. I'll see you in fifteen."

Phillips took off the headset and handed it to Meritson, then took a long look around at the sea, shrouded in fog, the snow drifting heavily, densely down and vanishing as it hit the water. He consciously took a deep breath, tasting it, knowing that his air for the next days or weeks or months would be canned, flavored with ozone, sweat, sewage, oil and garbage, as well as carbon dioxide, carbon monoxide, amines and other chemicals used inside the ship. The breath exhaled, Phillips raised the deck grating and lowered himself into the rigged-for-black tunnel, the vertical tunnel's lights extinguished so they would not ruin the officer of the deck's night vision. Blindly Phillips came down the long ladder, passed by feel through a smooth lip of a hatch and further down into darkness. Inside the ship now, there was still blackness surrounding him. He felt for the blackout curtain entrance, pushed through it into the dim red wash from the upper deck passageway red lights. The red light that made the ship look ghostly.

He went down through the center of the ship past the opening to the crew's mess, past the chief's quarters—the "goat locker" it was called, in reference to the age of the ship's senior enlisted men—down a steep set of stairs to the middle level. There in the stairwell was a large hatch leading aft. The lights in the tunnel were bright white, the red no longer applying, the difference between the ship's operating habits starkly different for the forward tactical sailors and the aft nuclear-trained men. Phillips stepped through the hatch and into the bright reactor compartment tunnel, a narrow corridor through the shielded reactor compartment. This was the only access through the space, since the nuclear reactor was so radioactive and gave off such powerful neutron radiation. The tunnel had a central hatch that went into the reactor compartment. The hatch dogs were locked and chained with a second lock, since anyone making their way into the compartment would not survive more than ten minutes when the reactor was critical. At the end of the tunnel Phillips stepped through a hatch into the middle level of the engine room then up a ladder to what was properly known as the aft compartment upper level or ACUL for short. The upper level held the steam piping on its way to the electrical turbines and the main engines, as well as the upper few feet of the electrical generators and the main engine turbine casing. Further aft, the top of the reduction gear's casing poked through the deckplates, requiring Phillips to walk around it until he came to the door to maneuvering, a large and soundproofed, heavily air-conditioned space, the maneuvering room, where the reactor and steam plants were controlled. He pressed the intercom button and announced himself, then opened the heavy door and walked in.

The room was freezing. Walt Hornick stood in the center of the space, staring at the reactor plant control panel over the shoulder of the reactor operator. Next to Hornick was his main propulsion assistant, the MPA, a senior lieutenant named Katoris, a bone-thin blond officer who looked like he should be walking the hallways of a high school rather than the passageways of a nuclear submarine. Phillips walked next to Hornick and scanned the reactor-control panel. Phillips looked at the position of the control rods; they weren't moving. On the surface of the console a Plexiglas cover was lifted off a black rotary switch marked MANUAL SCRAM. The reactor operator's hand was on the switch while his eyes were on the panel. Nothing seemed to be happening.

"Well, Eng, pretty slow day here?" Phillips said.

Hornick didn't budge, not even to look at Phillips. When he spoke it was in a quiet mutter.

"It's an emergency approach to core critically, and the start-up rate meter might jump at any second. We're standing by to try to scram the plant manually if that happens, but more than likely a failure of the protection circuitry would find us blown to pieces back here before Bronson there could hit the scram switch."

"How did you do this?"

"We calculated the estimated critical position of the control rods for the core based on the core life—it's new and highly reactive—and the fission product poisons from the last operation—minimal since we've been at low power on our two previous start-ups—and the length of time we've been shut down. All those factors have tolerances and errors, so we backed off about 5 percent on the reactivity of the core. Once that was done it was checked and triple-checked. I did my own calculation and confirmed the reactor chief's calcs. The book is not all that specific about this, but I took the liberty of taking the reactor-protection circuits to maximum sensitivity—the voting circuits are out, so any one channel of the protection can scram us out—but that's all I can do."

"Eng, can we talk privately?"

Hornick looked half-panicked at the idea of leaving the reactor plant control panel, but Phillips waved him to the door. Hornick glanced nervously at Katoris, then followed Phillips to the door and out of the space into the wider expanse of the engine room.

"Sir, I think I should be back in—"

Phillips interrupted with a finger over his lips. He put his arm around Hornick's shoulders and started walking him slowly forward. "Walt, I could give you a long lecture about cost versus risk, about the risk thresholds of wartime operation, about the prerogatives of command, but I'm not gonna do any of that bullshit. We don't have time for that crap." Phillips took two Cuban cigars from inside his wet parka, unwrapped both and clipped the ends off them, handing one to Hornick.

"No, no, sir, I—"

"Come on, it'll put hair on your chest," Phillips said, squinting. He plugged one of the cigars into Hornick's mouth, lit his own, then put his lighter to Hornick's cigar. Hornick mechanically puffed the cigar to life, cringing at the smoke in his eyes.

"Now, where was I? Oh yeah, risk. Now Eng, you're more senior than Court, right?"

"Yes, Captain."

"So that makes you third in command, right, after me and Whatney?"

"Yessir."

"Good, good." Phillips took a puff of the Cuban and looked at Hornick, dipping his head in encouragement. Hornick took a puff, frowning, blowing the smoke out. "Now, you being third in command, I can tell you things that I couldn't really tell kids like Katoris, right? I mean, you're not gonna go blab them to your stateroom mates after watch, right? Okay, then here's the deal. How's that stogie?"

"Not too bad, sir," He took a puff.

"Okay, picture this, Walt. This ship is doing a Coast Guard kind of mission. You know what the motto of the Coast Guard is?"

"No, sir." Phillips still had his arm around Hornick's shoulders, walking him to the forward end of the space.

"The Coast Guard motto, if I remember it right, is this—'You have to go out. You don't have to come back.' That sound familiar?"

"No, sir."

"Well, here's why I thought of that, Walty-boy. Pretty good cigar, I think." Phillips puffed a smoke ring at the overhead. Hornick had the cigar clutched between the knuckles of his fist, looking like an old pro. He took a puff and blew it into the overhead, squinting slightly at the smoke, but the expression of pleasure winning out over a frown. Suddenly Phillips dropped his arm from Hornick's shoulder, clenched the cigar between his teeth, and with both hands grabbed Hornick's shirt and brought him in close, his eyes wide open.

"Walt, this ship ain't likely coming back. Those Vortex missiles might open up the hull. Or the Japs may be able to run from them. Our own torpedoes may not work so hot against those Destiny-class boats. But I don't have any plans for next month, Walt. If we come back with a ship under us, that'll be like winning a sweepstakes. If we come back, or half of us do, and the boat's on the bottom of the Pacific, I'd call that a good day. If this ship becomes our coffin, you and me and the crew in Davy Jones's locker, that's going to be shooting par. If it's a bad day, we don't even make it into the Pacific and we get stuck under the icecap and stay there. And if it's a totally bad week, we blow up the core on initial start-up. So do you see what the game is looking like, Walt?"

"I see your point, Captain."

Phillips dropped the maniac act and straightened out Hornick's shirt, then stood off to the side and puffed the cigar, looking down at the deckplates for a moment as he collected himself.

"So, Walt, what do you say? You only have 95 percent estimated reactivity inserted into the core. I think you should crank it up to 100 percent. I need power and I need it an hour ago. Once that goddamned needle comes out of the start-up range, you can heat this bitch up and we can be in a full-power lineup in five minutes. Yeah, it may blow up, but you know what? I won't even put that in your fitness report, I promise. You've got total amnesty today, Walt. So I'm not going to order you to do this, it's your call, it's your plant. But I would sincerely like to get reactor power this century. Can you do it for me?" Phillips looked up at Hornick, a sad expression on his face.

"Skipper, it would be my pleasure," Hornick said, clamping his own cigar between his teeth. "You give me a half-hour and I'll give you main engine shaft horsepower, all fifty-seven thousand of them."

Phillips clapped Hornick on the back. "Good man, you let me know." He winked at Hornick and ducked through the tunnel hatch and vanished. Hornick smiled, shaking his head, then walked quickly aft to the maneuvering room.

The reactor tunnel's forward hatch opened out into the forward compartment middle level. After the bright lights of the engineering spaces, the forward compartment's red lights seemed strange. Phillips followed a dogleg in the passageway to a central passage that went past his and Whatney's staterooms to port, the electronics rooms—radio and countermeasures—to starboard, the passageway stopping at a door labeled CONTROL ROOM—AUTHORIZED PERSONNEL ONLY. Phillips went in, the space crowded with watchstanders, and hot. The room was larger than the *Greeneville*'s control room, but even though *Piranha*'s control space was the full width of the ship, over forty feet wide, it still seemed cramped.

"Navigator, sounding please!" Phillips shouted, the cigar still clamped in his teeth.

"Forty-nine fathoms, sir."

"Close enough. Off'sa'deck, where's the officer of the deck?"

"Here, sir." Meritson's voice was muffled as he was hugging the thick periscope module of the type-twenty periscope, the scope extending from the overhead all the way to the well in the deck of the periscope stand. The module would be hot, at least 105 degrees from the electronics it bristled with. An hour at the periscope would leave the front of a man's shirt wet with sweat—the reason periscope time was known as "dancing with the fat lady."

"Status, please."

"Yessir, the bridge is rigged for dive, control is in the control room, I have the watch, ship is rigged for dive with the exception of the forward escape trunk hatch. I have two men topside ready to cast off the tug line on your orders."

"Very well, coordinate with the tug, come to all stop and cast off the tugline."

"Aye, sir."

Phillips was beginning to smell progress now. It took five minutes, but finally *Piranha* was officially on her own, on her diesel engine, her reactor still in a coma, but without tugs.

"Off'sa'deck, submerge the ship to snorkel depth," Phillips called. The order began a flurry of activity. A phonetalker called for Phillips.

"Captain, Engineer on the one-jay-vee phone."

Phillips reached for the phone. "Captain."

"Engineer, sir. Reactor's critical, performing an emergency heatup now."

"Excellent, Eng. How did it go? Any overpowering?"

"No, Sir, it came right up to one decade per minute, just like you said."

"I didn't say anything, Eng, that's your start-up. Remember that, Walt. Now, how long till you're answering bells on the mains?"

"We're at thirty degrees per minute, that's about twelve minutes to the green band, then we'll warm the steam plant. I'd say another twenty minutes."

"Battery?"

"Holding up, but don't give it more than four knots."

"Aye. Hurry up, Eng."

"Yessir."

Phillips found a seat in the captain's chair aft of the periscope stand, the "conn," from which the ship was controlled. It would be a long night, he thought.

Submerging without the reactor! The last thing he thought he'd be doing with the newest ship in the fleet, but then, if it kept him from being peeked at by the

Galaxy satellites so much the better. He settled back into the chair and watched Meritson submerge the ship, the vessel sinking slowly into the Atlantic as the main ballast tanks gave up the air. Soon, he thought, he'd be driving on nuclear power. He waited, puffing the cigar.

# CHAPTER 18

**NORTHWEST PACIFIC**
**USS *Barracuda***

The deck trembled with the power of the main engines at flank speed. Capt. David Kane walked into the wardroom, crowded with officers waiting for his briefing.

Kane was taller than average, slim, with a full head of dark hair and a tan. When the ship was in port, he would be on the beach, running, walking his dogs or hanging out with his wife Becky and his daughters. He was famous for being the Pacific Fleet captain who worked smarter, not harder. His face was chiseled, the high cheekbones set above thin cheeks and a strong square chin. When he had been at Annapolis he had been the six-striper, the brigade commander. He had met his wife while a first-class midshipman, when he and his friends had written to a Playboy centerfold model, the letter written as a prank, but after two months she had written him back. After they corresponded for a few weeks they decided to meet, choosing a Georgetown bar. After that it had been all over for Kane. He had proposed to her on that first date, and she had just laughed. During their spring break they had flown to Bermuda, and on the beach one twilight he had popped the biggest ring he could finance into her hands, and this time she didn't laugh. In fact, she had cried. They had been engaged for two months when Kane had been interviewed for the nuclear-power program by Admiral Rickover, the famed father of the nuclear navy. Rickover had managed to shoehorn a nuclear reactor into a submarine, an engineering task that should have taken fifteen years, but

Rickover had done it in three at a fraction of the cost of the estimates, and with an impeccable safety record. When his USS *Nautilus,* the first nuclear submarine, went under the polar icecap, his nuclear navy had been the envy of the world. He had pledged to Congress that not a single naval officer would be admitted to his program unless he personally approved of him. Every single candidate would be interviewed personally. Once Rickover flunked someone, there was no appeal.

Rickover had called a very nervous Kane into the office. Submarine duty was all he wanted to do in the Navy. Airplanes held no fascination, and surface ships made him seasick, many of them stinking of diesel fuel, the amphibious fleet a flotilla of rustbucket ships that carried unwashed Marine troops into combat. Aircraft carriers particularly irritated him, since it was the worst of two worlds, a surface ship that acted as a bus for a bunch of arrogant pilots. He had gone into Annapolis for the free education and the status, but as graduation approached he could only see himself being a sub driver. Now that he was finally in Rickover's office, it sank in that Rickover could easily say no to him, as he had done with 40 percent of the applicants. The man who had the interview two before Kane had left the office with glazed eyes.

"What happened?" Kane had asked him.

"Rickover told me I'm too shy," the midshipman had said. "He told me I had thirty seconds to piss him off."

"What did you do?"

"I stood on a chair. I was going to piss on his desk but he looked at me like I was an idiot, and I couldn't even do that. I couldn't get the piss to come out. Rickover said that even my cock was too shy, and he told me to get the hell out."

"That was it?"

"No. He has this four-foot-long shiny model of the *Nautilus* on his desk. I picked it up and smashed it into a thousand pieces. One of the fragments broke and nicked his hand. He was bleeding onto his shirt."

"Holy shit! You broke the admiral's ship model? What did he do?"

"He said, 'Get the hell out of here,' but then he stopped me. I turned around and he looked at me like he was going to kill me, and he says, 'Goddamnit, you're hired!' I guess I pissed him off enough."

Kane had wondered what test Rickover would have for him. He was ushered into the office and told to sit in a wooden chair in front of the admiral's desk. He found it was true—the front legs were truly shorter than the back legs. Kane had felt the bile of nerves rise in his stomach. Rickover was short, slight, wrinkled and old. He mumbled over at Kane something Kane didn't understand.

"Excuse me, sir?"

"Why, did you fart?" the admiral said. "I *said,* your class standing sucks. Your grades suck. You've been showing a flat or declining trend since your youngster year. Yet they appoint you brigade commander second set. And I notice that you're ever so pretty. That must be why. It certainly isn't your wits, is it, Mr. Kane?"

"I think I—"

"Oh, you don't fucking think at all, that's your problem. Look at this. Look at it! Would you accept you into my program?"

"Sir, yes, I have a 3.78 grade point average in ocean engineering—"

"Ocean engineering. What do you study, fishies? Good Lord, what's the academy coming to? Okay, Kane, I'll just make this easy on both of us. I don't like jocks and I don't like stripers. You sit in your admin offices and drink coffee and put midshipmen on report and carry a sword and get the girls, yessir. You have a girlfriend, Kane?"

"Yessir."

"Are you engaged to her?"

"Yessir, we're supposed to get married the week after graduation."

"Show me her picture."

Rickover looked at Becky's photo. He showed no enthusiasm.

"Well, you call your little girlie friend—I'm sorry, your fiancé—and tell her you're going to put off your wedding until after you pass all the way through my program."

Kane looked at Rickover. The training pipeline was over a year long, and Becky and he had made their plans.

"Here's the phone. Go ahead. Call her. Tell her you're putting off the wedding to make sure you won't be distracted in my program."

"Yessir." Kane dialed. Becky's voice came on.

"I'm putting you on the speaker phone," Rickover said. He punched a button and Becky's silky voice came over the speaker.

"David? What's going on?"

"Honey? I'm here with Admiral Rickover right now, and you're on the speaker phone." Kane waited, Rickover glared.

"Becky?"

"Yes?"

"How are the wedding plans going?"

"Great, David. You know that. Why?"

Rickover hit the mute button, and whispered, "Go ahead, tell her." He punched the button again. The connection was back. Kane could hear Becky breathing.

"Oh, nothing, sweetheart," Kane had said. "Listen, Becky, I was just calling you up to tell you that I'm going Navy air. I decided to be a pilot after all. Nuclear subs are for the birds. That's all, honey. Bye."

Kane hung up the phone and stood up, assuming the interview was over. The decision had not been that difficult. A choice between Becky and his career was not a choice. He'd take Becky any day. He'd swab the decks of an aircraft carrier's heads if it meant marrying Becky. Rickover could shove it. He walked to the door. Admiral Rickover didn't say a word until Kane had put his hand on the knob.

"Oh, Midshipman Kane?"

"Yes, Admiral?"

"You're hired. I expect you'll prove yourself to be one of the best nuclear officers who's ever been in the program. Good luck to you, sir." Rickover's tone was almost fatherly. Kane was stunned. He just stood there, looking at Rickover as if he'd been frozen to the spot. Suddenly Rickover looked up from his work, surprised to see Kane still standing there.

"Get out! Get the fuck out of here!" Kane opened the door and ran all the way to the debriefing room.

Kane had gone on to be the youngest submarine captain in Squadron Seven in Norfolk, commanding the *Phoenix,* which had been torpedoed in the Labrador Sea during Operation Early Retirement in the Muslim War. With the help of an unmatched crew, Kane had managed to get *Phoenix* back with most of the men still alive. For his acts during the war he had been awarded the Navy Cross and offered the new ship *Barracuda,* the second Seawolf-class ship to roll out of the building yards at Electric Boat. After nursing *Phoenix* back to where she could be towed out of the northern waters, Kane was ready to quit the Navy. The admiral who had offered him command of *Barracuda* had looked stunned when Kane had said, "I don't think so, Admiral. It's over. I'm done going to sea."

But the sea was not yet done with him. Maybe it had been *Phoenix*'s outstanding luck. Or maybe it was Admiral Rickover's blessing. *I expect you'll prove yourself to be one of the best nuclear officers who's ever been in the program.* Or perhaps it was Admiral Steinman's request that he take command of *Barracuda.* But for whatever reason, Kane missed the sea, missed submarine duty, and found his life had less weight, less meaning without a ship under his feet. In spite of the separation from Becky, the element of risk, there was just something about it he couldn't live without. He couldn't stand the idea that he'd never again hug a periscope module as the ship swam out of the deep and approached the silvery bottom sides of the waves, the view out the scope foaming and clearing, the horizon coming into focus after hours of living in darkness. He even missed the smell, the lack of sleep, the dirty sheets. It was crazy, but finally even Becky couldn't stand it any more, insisting that Kane's mooning over the lack of a submarine command was driving her crazy. She had given him a phone and said, "Call Admiral Steinman, right now, and tell him you're taking command of that submarine, or else you're out of *my* program. You got that, mister?"

Steinman had laughed so hard he could barely breathe. When he recovered, he told Kane it had only been a matter of time, that he had kept the commanding officer slot open for him. Kane had hung up, feeling the tiny bites of wetness at the corners of his eyes. Becky had jumped right on it.

"David! You're crying!"

"I am not," he'd insisted. "There's dirt in my eyes."

"Yeah, just like there was dirt in your eyes when Vicky was born. Come here and give me a hug, Captain Kane. What's the name of the ship?"

"The *Barracuda.* Nice name, huh?"

"Only the best for you," she had said, holding him.

Kane stood now in front of the gathered men in the wardroom, his crew, aboard his submarine. They were the best crew at sea, even better than he had had aboard the *Phoenix.*

"Good morning, gentlemen," he said, his favorite opening for a briefing.

**NORTHWEST PACIFIC**
**USS *Ronald Reagan***

"Well, Patch, it's time," Donner said, staring out to sea with his binoculars.

The sun had set an hour before, the last traces of twilight fading now. The carrier was closer to Japan, but there had been no time to coordinate or set up the blockade.

"The interdiction effort begins in the Sea of Japan," Donner said. "There's a Russian supertanker coming in from South Korea loaded with oil and heading for the oil terminal at Niigata on the western coast of Japan. We're scrambling four F-14s to fly out to her and keep her from crossing into the Japan OpArea."

"Mac, you really think that supertanker's going to pull back because of some F-14s?"

"If he doesn't he's going to get a hull full of torpedoes. And Japan is going to get a very nasty oil slick."

"You'd better tell the captain of the supertanker that. What about the men aboard?"

"Don't worry about that, Patch. There's no way that supertanker is going to run that blockade. No way."

"Admiral, I've told you this before, but we need surface ships. We need a cruiser to fire shots over the guy's bow and pull up alongside with deck guns pointed at the bridge and board the ship, physically take the helm if you have to and turn that ship around. Otherwise the whole crew is going to buy it."

"Patch, he'll turn around."

"Admiral, god*damn*it, you're not listening to me."

Mac Donner's tone was icy as he stared at Pacino. "I'm *listening,* Admiral. Now what the hell do you want to say?"

"If that supertanker doesn't turn around, we have to shoot him. If we let him through the blockade fails. So you put my men in the position of firing torpedoes at a civilian ship. My men will want to surface and rescue survivors."

"No. That would give away their position. The satellites will see that and lead the Japanese submarines there."

"First, Admiral, we should have blown those goddamned satellites away days ago. Second, if that supertanker gets torpedoed, every ship in the Pacific will know where at least one submarine is, it's where the supertanker went down. Third, I don't want my men killing civilians."

"Get off it, Patch. They have lifeboats. The Japanese can rescue them. Now quit being an old lady and—"

"I still say a destroyer or cruiser with guns is the way to do this. Let this goddamned tanker in, Admiral. When we have some surface ships over there, we'll stop the next merchant ship."

"No. My orders are specific. The blockade begins now. Don't make me request to relieve you, Admiral Pacino."

Pacino took a breath and let it out. "Aye, aye, sir. I'll send the order. On your command, if the tanker doesn't turn around, we'll shoot it. And no rescue of the survivors."

"Very well."

"I don't think so. *Sir.*"

# CHAPTER 19

**ATLANTIC OCEAN**
**USS *Piranha***

Bruce Phillips stood smoking his cigar while standing on the conn looking down on the diving-control station. The control room was rigged for black, all lights out, only the glow of the instruments at the ship-control panel illuminated. The screens of the fire-control consoles of the attack center were dark, the rig for reduced electrical not allowing them to be powered up. The ship rolled gently in the waves, still at periscope depth at the mouth of Block Island Sound, now legitimately in the Atlantic, the sea beneath them still perilously shallow. Behind him Peter Meritson was dancing with the fat lady, rotating the periscope through endless circles, searching for the lights of close surface ships, fishing boats, anything that could collide with them.

The ship had no power to get deep if something came by, some ferry ship or misdirected container ship, and not only was there no power, there was nowhere to go; there was barely enough water beneath their keel to allow them to be submerged. They were in sixty fathoms of water, and if Phillips had gone by the book he would not have submerged until he had a minimum of 600 fathoms. But then, submerging without a reactor up and running, snorkeling on the diesel, with only bare steerageway for power, was in gross violation of the standard operating procedures as well.

"Off'sa'deck, you hear anything from the Eng?"

"Sir," Meritson said, his voice muffled by the periscope module, "his last report was four minutes ago. He had turbines warmed and was shifting the electric plant."

"CONN, MANEUVERING," Walt Hornick's voice blasted from a speaker in the overhead, "ELECTRIC PLANT IS IN A NORMAL FULL POWER LINEUP. RECOMMEND COOLING THE DIESEL."

"Maneuvering, Conn," Meritson said into his boom microphone, still rotating the periscope through his surface search, "cool the diesel."

"COOL THE DIESEL, CONN, MANEUVERING, AYE. ESTIMATE MAIN PROPULSION CAPABILITY IN TWO MINUTES."

"Maneuvering, Conn, aye."

"Let's go, Eng," Phillips said. "Hey, OOD, let's pull the plug on cooling the diesel. I don't want that damned satellite upstairs seeing the exhaust."

"Aye, Captain. Maneuvering, Conn, from the Captain, we are going to secure snorkeling." Meritson turned the periscope so he could shout at the chief of the watch, up at the ballast-control panel in the forward port side of the room. "Chief of the Watch, secure snorkeling!"

"Secure snorkeling, aye, sir." The COW picked up a microphone to the circuit-one public address system, his voice booming throughout the ship.

"SECURE SNORKELING! RECIRCULATE."

Walt Hornick's voice replied on his speaker: "SECURE SNORKELING, RECIRCULATE, CONN, MANUEVERING AYE."

Phillips waited impatiently, walking to the aft rail of the conn and peering down on the navigation display, a horizontal wide-screen display that projected the chart where they were on a glass surface. The depth beneath them would stay shallow for some time. Usually a sub departing from Groton would be steaming at twenty knots on the surface for twelve hours before reaching the continental shelf, where the water depth fell to thousands of feet beneath the keel. Phillips would be steaming at twenty knots with less water under his keel than a full hull diameter. But that was nothing compared to what would happen when they got under ice.

Hornick's voice squawked on the speaker again, this time his voice sounding almost cocky.

"CONN, MANEUVERING, MAIN ENGINES ARE WARM, READY TO SHIFT PROPULSION TO THE MAIN ENGINES."

Meritson did not wait for further orders—Phillips had already made his orders for this moment.

"Helm, all stop," Meritson called. "Maneuvering, Conn, shift propulsion to the main engines."

The orders were acknowledged and for a moment a lull came in the room.

"CONN, MANEUVERING, PROPULSION SHIFTED TO THE MAIN ENGINES, READY TO ANSWER ALL BELLS, ANSWERING ALL STOP."

"Conn, aye, Helm, all ahead standard."

"Ahead standard, Helm aye," the kid at the diving station's helmsman's wheel called. "Maneuvering answers all ahead standard, sir."

"Lowering number two scope," Meritson said, retracting the instrument. "Mark sounding!"

"Nine zero fathoms, sir."

"Dive, make your depth one five zero feet."

Even with several hundred feet beneath the keel, the bottom was uneven, rising up to ten fathoms in places, many of the humps uncharted. Phillips continued looking at the chart, then glanced at his watch. Within a few hours they would be steaming in the open deep Atlantic. Then all he had to worry about was the polar icecap and the Japanese.

**NORTHWEST PACIFIC**
**USS *Ronald Reagan***

Pacino left the bridge and headed for ASW Operations. Comdr. Paully White looked up from the intelligence plot on a large area WritePad, startled to see Pacino.

"Boss," White said in his Kensington and Allegheny accent. "What brings you here? I thought you were up with Admiral Donuts up there."

Paully White was in his late forties, his hair dark and thick, his frame trim. He was something of a comic, a frustrated stand-up comedian, in a place that had no humor, at least none directed toward him. Paully White got very little respect aboard the *Ronald Reagan*.

Neither the surface sailors nor the pilots had good words for the submarine officer. They were happy that the battle group had two escort 688-class submarines there, and they knew that someone had to coordinate them, but the surface-group officers, when they saw Paully, had to face the fact that there were enemy submarines out there, that the battle group was vulnerable to them, and that only Paully's submarines could keep them clean, in spite of the billions spent on surface ship antisubmarine warfare—the destroyers and frigates with their multiple sonars, their ASW standoff weapons, their Mark 51 torpedoes, the S-2 twin-jet Vikings that patrolled the sea for submarines with their blue-laser detectors, magnetic anomaly detectors, sonar buoy detectors and Mark 52 torpedoes, the LAMPS III Seahawk helicopters with their dipping sonars and their Mark 52 Mod Alpha torpedoes—*all* of it was an attempt to combat enemy submarines from above, and it was an attempt that fell short. Because in the end the only thing that could counter a quiet and stealthy hostile submarine was a quiet and stealthy friendly submarine. So many men in the surface battle group had devoted their lives and their careers to trying to prove otherwise and had failed, that when Paully White walked their passageways with his gold dolphin pins gleaming over his left breast pocket he was silenced, ignored. At the wardroom table he could tell a joke, a good one, and he would hear nothing but the clink of silverware on china. Paully, in fact, was the most unpopular man aboard, and desperately looked forward to going back to sea on board a fast attack submarine.

"Hi, Paully," Pacino said heavily. "Admiral Donner is kicking off the blockade. It looks like we're carrying the ball on the first play." Pacino described the basics of the operation and directed White to get some messages out to the *Cheyenne* and the *Pasadena*.

"*Cheyenne*'s here, *Pasadena*'s here. They've both been lurking off the major shipping channels. I'll have to move *Pasadena* but that still puts her here when the operation goes down."

Pacino tried to stay focused, but the way this blockade was happening was foreign to him. One thing that never showed up on a submariner's report card was "works well with others." In spite of all the exercises favoring joint-operations, there was something about the Silent Service that developed independence. Having the operation managed by someone who barely understood submarines was damn frustrating.

The room reverberated with the earsplitting roar of a catapult launch of an F-14, the engines of the fighter roaring in full afterburners as it cleared the deck.

The sooner this operation was over, the better, Pacino thought.

There was still light left, the sun just going down into the sea, as Comdr. Joe Galvin waited on the deck of the *Ronald Reagan*. He was the last of the four F-14 pilots to get to the catapult. The other three for this mission had just been launched. He had watched them sail down the cats, float uncertainly over the sea for a second before deciding to fly up and away from the carrier. That moment when the deck ended and the sky began was always the worst, with the exception of crashing back down on the carrier's deck. His turn was coming up. He went through the prelaunch checklist, rotating his control surfaces, checking his switch lineup, radio comm circuits, cabin oxygen, hydraulics, health of the engines. The deck officer put up the aft blast shield and signaled for Galvin to throttle up. Galvin applied his brakes and brought the throttle keys to the forward stops, hearing and feeling the turbines spool up to full thrust, the roaring power of them electric. He could never experience that sound and that feel without an excitement almost sexual.

The turbines were steady at full thrust, temperatures and pressures normal, fuel flow in limits. Galvin took the keys to the right, passing the full thrust detents, and took the throttles all the way to the firewall. Aft, the diffusers at the jet engines' exhaust were clamping down, the gas velocity out the nozzles increasing while raw jet fuel was injected into the hot exhaust, reigniting and doubling the engines' thrust. Full afterburners. The roar of the jets grew louder, the engines now half-jet, half-rocket, the F-14 trembling on the deck of the windward-bound aircraft carrier, the carrier's own speed at forty knots designed to help him keep flying once he cleared the deck.

The deck officer and catapult officer were waiting on him. He looked up from his panel and gave the deck officer a salute. In return, a gesture to the pilot and a signal to the cat operator, the deck officer leaned forward, his legs far apart, until he crouched forward, while taking his orange wand and swinging it through a giant overhead arc as if throwing a tomahawk in slow motion. His wand came all the way down to the deck, then came back up pointing forward, the gesture graceful and exhilarating, a combination statement of "good luck up there, sir," and "hit the catapult, cat operator."

The catapult kicked in, the high-pressure steam driving a trolley that pulled on Galvin's nosewheel. Galvin was thrown far back in his seat from the acceleration, the world around him dissolving into a blurred tunnel of gray and blue. In an instant the jet was shot like a bullet off the deck, the catapult trolley disconnecting, the acceleration gone, the jet hanging in space trying to fly but almost hesitating as if confused, the jets still shrieking on full afterburners, the ocean waiting below to swallow him up, but finally the aircraft won and the ocean lost, the jet accelerating again, Galvin swinging the wings to a port roll as he turned out of the carrier's path.

Beneath him the USS *Reagan* sailed on, majestically plowing through the sea, her stern kicking up a wake that trailed her for five miles. Galvin climbed to 8000 feet in slow spirals, catching up with his flight of F-14s, then falling into formation as the flight leader, taking the jets to the northwest, diving down low as they approached the Japanese coastline. The mission profile called for them to fly in the grass, taking the shortcut over the island itself to get to the Sea of Japan on the other side. Galvin wondered if they would be met by FireStar fighters. The land came closer, the F-14s now at Mach 1.8, the wings swept back, altitude eighty feet, the supersonic jets kicking up a huge roostertail wake. The Japanese were about to see the US Navy in action, Galvin thought. Soon they were feet-dry over Japanese soil, the ridges and valleys flying at him as they sailed in at treetop level, the occasional rice paddy and collection of houses flashing by, their inhabitants standing outside, children pointing up at them. Now the coastline approached, the west coast of Honshu Island, and again they were feet-wet over the Sea of Japan.

Another twenty minutes of flying low over the sea and the ship, the target, was in sight. The supertanker was huge, as long as the *Reagan,* so full of oil that its waterline was almost all the way up to the gunwales, its bow wave plying back far into the twilight. There was just enough light to make out the name on the bow—the block letters spelling PETERSBURG.

For the first time during the mission Galvin broke radio silence and spoke into the microphone, his radio selected to the bridge-to-bridge VHF frequency.

"VLCC *Petersburg,* this is the flight leader of the US Navy aircraft formation circling your bridge. I say again, this is the flight leader of the US Navy aircraft formation circling your bridge. Do you read me, over?"

**SEA OF JAPAN**
**USS *Cheyenne***

Comdr. Gregory Keebes wore a blue poopysuit that was faded and old, the pants legs too high over his black socks and faded canvas loafers. He had a crewcut and sported horn-rimmed black glasses. He stood now leaning on the railing of the periscope stand and replaced the phone in its cradle. The radio chief had just told him the orders that had come in.

"Officer of the Deck," Keebes called, "man battlestations."

"Man battlestations, aye, sir." The OOD was Lt. Frank Becker, former right tackle for Navy's varsity squad, a hulking youth with a good head, though in Keebes's opinion something of a whiner. "Chief of the Watch, man battlestations."

"Man battlestations, aye, sir." The COW, a young slick-haired, wire-rimmed-glasses–wearing youth in a blue poopysuit, reached for a coiled microphone and clicked it on. His voice poured from the circuit-one speakers throughout the ship. "MAN BATTLESTATIONS." He unclicked the mike and partially stood to get to the general alarm, a small lever in a panel in the overhead, found it and rotated it clockwise. The blaring BONG BONG BONG of the alarm rang throughout the ship. He clicked the circuit-one microphone one more time. "MAN . . . BATTLESTATIONS."

Keebes clicked a stopwatch on his neck and waited for the crowd to arrive in the control room. He leaned over the chart table and saw the flashing dot where they were presently located, the ship channel pulsing in yellow, the position of the target, a VLCC supertanker called the *Petersburg,* there in the shipping channel some twenty miles to the northwest, approaching the boundary of the exclusion zone, the edge of the Japan OpArea.

"Off'sa'deck, take her deep and flank it at heading three one zero. Once you're down lay out a course to the target."

"Aye, sir. Dive," Becker called to the diving officer, "make your depth five three zero feet. Helm, all ahead standard."

"Five three zero feet, aye, sir."

"All ahead standard, Helm aye, maneuvering answers all ahead standard, sir."

"Five degrees dive on the sternplanes," the diving officer ordered, his seat set up between the control seats of the flight-deck arrangement, the man in the left seat the sternplanesman, the man in the right seat controlling the rudder and the bowplanes and responsible for the ship's angle. "Five degrees down bubble, bowplanes down ten degrees."

OOD Becker's view out the periscope grew closer to the waves. Keebes looked up into the overhead at the television repeater, wondered if the approach of nightfall would make the blockade that much more difficult. How hard would it be to shoot the target at night, with darken-ship rules, he wondered. Still, it was hard to believe the tanker would really try to run the blockade, though the threat of submarine attack might or might not work. The view from the scope, displayed on the repeater monitor in the control room overhead grew so close to the waves that the sea splashed up on the view, the white foam obscuring vision, then the cross-haired reticle focused up on the underside of the waves, bits of seaweed floating by the view.

"Lowering number-two scope," Becker called, aligning the view directly forward and retracting the instrument with a rotation of the hydraulic control ring set into the overhead. The module vanished into the scope well, the smooth stainless-steel pole coming down afterward, riding all the way down into the well until the scope was fully retracted.

Keebes looked up from the chart as Becker leaned over the table with him, the two men calculating the course and speed while the ship dived for the depths.

The deck leveled out.

"Sir, ship's depth five three zero feet."

Becker called to the helmsman, still looking down on the chart table.

"Helm, all ahead flank, right two degrees rudder, steady three one zero."

The deck began to tremble. The room began to fill up with watchstanders, the lone firecontrol tech manning the four consoles of the attack center replaced with four officers. The executive officer Mike Jensen arrived.

Lt. Comdr. Mike Jensen was a Stanford grad, a thickly muscled black man with an open face, a coathanger grin and an easy Southern California manner. His laugh kept ship's morale high, as did Jensen's girlfriends when he threw a wardroom party. He drove a Porsche, owned an airplane and gave glider lessons. A shark jaw graced the bulkhead of his XO stateroom, but the shark had its own trophy, a piece of Jensen's leg from one of his scuba dives.

Keebes and Jensen were as different as two men could be. Keebes was raised on a Pennsylvania farm. He had gone to the Naval Academy without the slightest idea of what he would be getting into. For him the Navy had been a vehicle for a college education. He found that he neither loved it nor hated it. He was a loner, quiet, enjoyed engineering and his weekends studying at the library. The librarian and he had become friends, and after knowing Louise for four years, on the eve of graduation, he had asked her if she wanted to go with him to the Smithsonian in D.C. One thing slowly led to another. Keebes had then passed his Rickover interview and gone nuclear, leaving Louise for the sea. She had moved to Virginia Beach on her own, showing up on his pier one day when the *Buffalo* was coming into port. Fifteen years and two kids later, and Keebes had never looked at another woman. He had wondered, though, if he would ever command a sub, since on his executive-officer tour the captain decided to take a disliking to him. That captain had been a drinker, a partier, with a mistress in every port. He had tried to deice Keebes, but Keebes wanted no part of it.

Fortunately for Keebes the new admiral in command of the reorganized Unified Submarine Command, Admiral Pacino, had interviewed him after reading through his record and taken him to a battle simulator. After a sweaty eight hours of simulated approaches with an unfamiliar control-room crew, Pacino had offered him command of the *Cheyenne.*

"Captain, battlestations are manned," Jensen now reported.

"Very well," Keebes said. He stepped up on the conn and addressed the control-room crew.

"Attention in the firecontrol team. We've just received orders to intercept a supertanker that may try to run the blockade. We're setting up to position ourselves on the north of the supertanker's track as it crosses the exclusion-zone boundary. We'll be at periscope depth with a solution to the supertanker. A flight of F-14 jets is on its way to intercept the supertanker and turn him around. If he turns around we'll go deep and wait for the next violator of the blockade. If he's stupid and doesn't believe we're here, we'll get orders to put some torpedoes in him."

Keebes looked around at the watchstanders.

"Chances are that he'll turn around, but we'll be doing an approach on him anyway. Carry on."

The watchstanders turned to their tasks. Keebes glanced up at the sonar display, waiting for the supertanker to become visible on the screen.

# CHAPTER 20

**Sea of Japan**
**SS-810 *Winged Serpent***

Comdr. Toshumi Tanaka stood in the center of the control room of the *Winged Serpent,* the square room's center dominated by the periscope control center. The starboard forward corner was the electronic section devoted to ship control, the starboard aft quarter the reactor controls, the port forward section laid out for navigation. The most crowded was the port aft corner, weapons and sensors control. The control room was electronically connected to a control system, the "Second Captain," a neural network-layered control system that was only one development-generation behind the computers that controlled the Destiny III-class ships. The Second Captain was able to control the ship and function without a crew—not very well but with adequate programming it could fight its way out of a battle. Tanaka preferred that it just take orders and leave ship command to the people.

On the Second Captain's sensor display now were several jumping, undulating curves, a second display showing the curves to be a Los Angeles-class nuclear submarine lurking in the shipping channels. Probably sent to enforce the blockade.

"Program the two Nagasakis in tubes one and two for the enemy submarine and open the outer doors on tubes one and two."

**ATLANTIC OCEAN**
**USS *Piranha***

Bruce Phillips lay on his rack with his arm over his eyes. The phone from the conn buzzed.

"Captain."

"Off'sa'deck, sir. Sounding is 600 fathoms. We're legal, Captain."

"How long to the Labrador Sea?"

"By the morning, sir. Are you going down?"

"I think I will."

"Good night, sir."

Phillips put the phone back, and without opening his eyes peeled off the poopysuit and got under the covers. He yawned and fell asleep before he shut his mouth again. In his dreams he wore a sombrero and carried a machine gun, a bandoleer of bullets hanging off each shoulder.

**SEA OF JAPAN**

"VLCC *Petersburg,* this is US Navy flight leader. Do you copy?"

Finally the captain of the *Petersburg* spoke up, his speech clear and understandable through his Russian accent.

"This is the captain of the *Petersburg.* What do you want?"

"Sir, you are standing into danger. You are two miles from the exclusion boundary set up by the United States of America. Japan is now under blockade by forces of the US Navy. You are ordered to reverse course and turn away from Japan. Do you read me, sir?"

Silence on the radio.

"I say again, you are standing into danger," Galvin repeated.

Still no answer.

"VLCC *Petersburg,* I am warning you that you are now one point five miles from the exclusion boundary.

You are running the blockade set up by forces of the US Navy. You are ordered to turn back now. If you fail to turn around and reverse course our nuclear submarines will be forced to fire on you. Do you read me?"

"This is the captain of the *Petersburg*. I am within my rights under international law. I am turning off this radio."

Galvin continued to try to radio the *Petersburg* for several minutes, but finally the supertanker crossed the line of demarcation of the exclusion zone. Gavin switched his radio to the tactical-control frequency.

"Uncle Joe, this is Aunt Sue, over."

"Go ahead, Sue."

"We're unable to win the game. Over."

"Roger, Sue, we'll clean up. You can leave for backstage now. Out."

Galvin dipped his wings and turned to the right, flying his formation away from the supertanker, far enough away to see it clearly as the twilight got darker.

**USS *Cheyenne***

The scrambled satellite UHF secure-voice circuit, the NESTOR, was piped into the conn on a red phone handset. Commander Keebes had the red phone on his ear, the conversation playing on the overhead speakers for the crew to hear.

"Cousin George, this is Uncle Joe, over," the speakers crackled.

"This is George, over."

"Cousin George, Uncle Joe, authorization bravo six delta reading victor, mike, tango, five, four, mike, I say again, authorization bravo six delta reading victor, mike, tango, five, four, mike. Break. Commands from Grandfather Pete as follows. Immediate execute—Cousin George to clean up the garage, I say again, Cousin George to clean up the garage. Break. Over."

Keebes read back the transmission to the phone from

the notes taken by Jensen. The transmission ended after the other end confirmed that the message was correct.

Keebes looked up at Jensen. Two officers walked in with the sealed authenticator packet and opened it on Keebes's orders. The B6D packet had a piece of paper inside reading VMT54M, the authentication on the radio transmission.

"It's valid. Okay, attention in the firecontrol team. We've just been ordered to shoot the supertanker. We'll do this with a periscope approach. Horizontal salvo, tubes one and two. Carry on." Keebes looked around at the crew. "Captain on the periscope."

Frank Becker stepped away from the periscope. "Zero nine zero relative, sir, low power on the horizon."

Keebes put his eyes on the periscope eyepiece, the rubber of it warm and slick with Becker's sweat. Through the crosshairs and range marks he could see the supertanker, Target One. He rotated the right grip, increasing the power to high. The bridge of the supertanker grew to giant size, the windows shining warm yellow light out, the navigation lights of the tanker still illuminated.

"Observation, Target One," Keebes called.

"Ready."

"Bearing, mark!" Keebes called, and punched a button on the periscope grip.

"Bearing one seven five," Jensen called.

"Range mark, six divisions, high power. Angle on the bow port ninety."

"Range, two thousand yards."

"Firing point procedures, Target One," Keebes called from the periscope. "Horizontal salvo, tubes one and two, one minute firing interval."

"Ship ready," Frank Becker reported.

"Solution ready," Jensen said, bending over the consoles of the attack center.

"Weapon ready," the weapons officer reported.

"Final bearing and shoot," Keebes ordered, his periscope crosshairs on the supertanker's midsection. "Bearing . . . mark!"

"Bearing one seven six," from Jensen.

"Range mark, six divisions, high power. Angle on the bow, port ninety five."

"Two thousand yards and set," Jensen called.

"Standby." The weapons officer took the torpedo firing trigger to the nine o'clock standby position.

"Shoot!" Keebes ordered.

"Fire!" The weapons officer took the trigger to the three o'clock firing position.

The detonation slammed Keebes's eardrums, the high-pressure air venting inboard from the torpedo firing mechanism two decks below.

"Tube one fired electrically, sir."

"Tube two, final bearing and shoot," Keebes ordered.

The crew went through the same routine for the second torpedo, the air pressure pulse slamming Keebes's ears as the torpedo left the ship.

"Tube two fired electrically, Captain. Both units are active and homing."

"Very well, energizing periscope videotape."

Keebes kept the supertanker on the periscope, waiting for the torpedoes to impact.

### SS-810 *Winged Serpent*

"Sir, the American submarine just launched a torpedo."

"Confirm it's not aimed at us." Tanaka said.

"No, sir, it would appear he's shooting at the merchant tanker."

"Let's take it up to mast-broach depth."

"Sir, we have Nagasaki torpedoes one and two locked onto the American. Should we prepare to fire?"

"No. We're not authorized, Mr. First." Tanaka mounted the steps to the periscope-control stand, seated himself in the periscope-control chair. The assembly looked almost like a motorcycle, the front wheel replaced by the optics module and the pole of the unit. "Ship control, mast-broach depth."

"Sir."

The *Winged Serpent* came up slowly, the deck inclining, the hull creaking as the ship came up shallow.

"Second torpedo launch from the American submarine, sir."

"Periscope coming up." Tanaka hit the control-function key and the stainless steel pole came out of the fin, the light piped into the hull by fiber optics and reassembled in the optic module. The actual mast did not penetrate the hull of the ship, yet with the fiber-optic transmission, the view looked good enough, as if he were looking out an old-fashioned optical periscope.

The view was dark, only a faint glow coming from the waves far above. Tanaka hit the fixed function key to rotate the control seat and the view above began to rotate just as his seat rotated on a circular track on the platform. The shimmering glow on the waves grew nearer, the moonlight coming down from above, until finally the glow got closer, individual waves now clear in the view. Tanaka rotated more quickly, needing to see the surface as soon as the periscope cleared.

The periscope suddenly broke through, the horizon showing up, if still blurry, from the rotation of the platform. Tanaka slowed the rotation and looked out for close contacts. There were none, only the supertanker in the distance, heading away to the southeast as it made its way to Japan.

Satisfied that there were no other ships on the surface, Tanaka studied the supertanker.

"Sonar shows the torpedoes pinging on their target, sir."

Tanaka saw the supertanker explode before sonar heard it. The white mushroom cloud blossomed into an orange-and-black flame cloud as the oil hold detonated. Tanaka could feel the blast shaking the ship as the shock wave traveled through the water.

Then the second torpedo hit.

"Mr. First, you should see this," Tanaka said, not wanting to watch anymore.

Mazdai looked out the periscope, watching the supertanker on fire. The Second Captain displays showed the view out of the periscope, the flames rising miles into the sky, the supertanker sinking, breaking in half, the bow vanishing from view, the aft section going down by the forward section, the superstructure, when it was visible, tilting upward as the ship drove into the sea. More of the hull vanished underwater, until all that was visible was a part of the superstructure and the stern, the huge screw and rudder pointing to the sky, the structure lit by the light of the fires from the oil. Soon that was gone too, the ship sinking and taking with it most of the flames, the remaining oil slick still flaming but at a fraction of the brightness of the supertanker.

It had taken ten minutes for the supertanker to explode and disappear.

"It's over for us," Mazdai said as the ship went deep again, the order given to avoid fouling the periscope optics on the oil slick. "They sank a supertanker—"

"Don't panic, Mr. First," Tanaka said, his voice flat. "There are still the Russian airlifts to resupply us. It may not be enough to keep us prosperous, but with the airlifts Japan will survive."

**NARITA AIRPORT**
**TOKYO, JAPAN**

The first missile hit the FireStar fighter escorting the Russian Ilyushin transport on final approach to Narita International Airport. The transport was the first of the planes to be flown from Russian Republic airfields in support of the Japanese. The pilot of the transport, Col. Ushi Valenka, saw the runway ahead by only a half-mile, the lights of it guiding him down. He saw the missile from the Americans hit the FireStar escort. The moron flying that fighter had taken Valenka's missile. Valenka looked over at the port wing, where the second FireStar fighter was escorting the flight into Narita Airport. As he watched, a flame trail slammed into the FireStar, which exploded in a spectacular fireball a single wingspan away, pieces of the FireStar falling into the fields below.

Valenka concentrated on the runway ahead. He was almost there. If he could get the airplane on the ground, could he fly out, or would the Americans try to blow up the airplane when it was empty and leaving Japan? The lights of the runway threshold came toward him. He throttled up, his altitude too low, trying to keep his mind on the landing gear that would soon hit the runway, trying to keep the airplane in the center of the concrete strip.

The missile hit the Ilyushin below the tail, blowing it off. The airplane dived for the deck, the runway coming up swiftly and smashing into the windshield. The cockpit blew apart, and Valenka's brief luck gave out as well. The fuel in the wings exploded in a fireball that rained down on the runway, the missile explosion still spending itself. Nothing was left of the Iluyshin or of Valenka but smoking metal parts lying in flames on the runway.

**JDA HEADQUARTERS**
**TOKYO, JAPAN**

"So may I assume we are in agreement?" Prime Minister Hosaka Kurita asked.

Adm. Akagi Tanaka sadly realized he had no real argument to offer Kurita. History and destiny had once again led Japan to this threshold of war. Tragic, but how could he suggest they not fight? The die had been cast. All he could do was fight honorably and pray that his son, Toshumi, survived.

# BOOK THREE

# WINGED SERPENT

# CHAPTER 21

**Sea of Japan**
**SS-810 *Winged Serpent***

Tanaka had kept the American submarine under surveillance since the sinking of the supertanker. He had been called to mast-broach depth by an emergency transmission on the extremely low-frequency radio, the set able to receive radio signals even though the antenna was deep, the radio waves generated by a powerful set of huge antennae on Japan's northern coastline. The ELF radio waves, since they were such low frequency, took a long time to send a signal, one alphanumeric symbol taking three minutes to be received. The two-number signal was received into the Second Captain, which called Tanaka in his stateroom.

Tanaka walked into the control room and ordered Mazdai to bring the ship to mast-broach depth. He waited until the ship's UHF antenna in the periscope received the emergency transmission from the director of the JDA.

*Unrestricted warfare against the Americans.* Tanaka would start with the sub that sank the supertanker.

"Battlestations, Mr. First."

**Sea of Japan**
**USS *Cheyenne***

"Secure battlestations, XO. Station normal underway watches. I want a section-tracking team stationed in control at all times, though, for the rest of the time we're in the OpArea."

"Aye, sir."

Keebes returned to his stateroom, shut the door behind him and dropped the portable sink behind the door. He ran water in the basin and splashed it on his face. He thought he would throw up.

How many men had he just killed? The images of the sinking supertanker would not fade. He shut his eyes for a moment, never aware that if he had opened them, if he had been able to see through the bulkhead of his stateroom, through the hull of the ship and through seven miles of ocean, he would be staring at an incoming Nagasaki torpedo bearing down on him.

"Nagasaki in tube one is away, Captain. Lining up to fire unit two."

"Wait one, Mr. First," Tanaka said. "Let's see what the American does."

The control room crew sat in their control chairs watching the Second Captain displays, waiting for the indication that the torpedo was detecting its target.

"Detect and homing on the target, sir."

"Very well, Mr. First." Tanaka scowled. The force should have been ordered to attack days before, not now that the aircraft-carrier force was within spitting distance of the Home Islands. As soon as the American submarine was put on the bottom, he would run at maximum speed to intercept the aircraft carrier. He wanted that carrier.

"Any detection of our weapon by the target?"

"Not yet, Captain," Mazdai said. "He hasn't changed speed or course."

"Very good."

The crew waited, the second Nagasaki ready for employment.

Keebes yawned, drying off his face. It was only a little after 1900 local time but he was tired. He considered going to the wardroom to screen a movie with the off watch officers but decided to hit the rack.

He was half-asleep when the circuit-one blasted over his head.

"TORPEDO IN THE WATER! TORPEDO IN THE WATER! MAN BATTLESTATIONS!"

Keebes ran to control.

"Sir, incoming torpedo bearing north, I've got it in the edge of the starboard baffles, running at flank speed."

"Set up to counterfire down the bearing line, Mr. Becker," Keebes said, staring hard at Becker, seeing his panic right below the surface. "Come on, line-of-sight mode on Pos Two, bearing north, set the range at five miles. That's it." Keebes stepped up on the periscope platform. "Attention in control, snapshot tube three, assumed target bearing north. Ready, Mr. Becker?"

Jensen arrived in control barefoot and in boxer shorts, putting on his wire-rimmed glasses, his contact lenses obviously out for the night.

"Ready, Captain."

"Snapshot tube three!"

Becker fired the tube-three torpedo at the phantom target, the one Keebes had guessed, at least to get a torpedo out there. The torpedo launch transient didn't seem as loud this time, perhaps because it caught Keebes by surprise.

"Set up tube four for another snapshot!"

Keebes intended to keep pumping them out. He could always get a reload, but if he got hit by a Japanese torpedo his own weapons would be useless on the bottom of the sea. And if he kept shooting torpedoes, the crew would be distracted by the activity, since the only thing he could do as a torpedo closed in on him was run from it, as Becker already had done.

Either the torpedo ran out of fuel, or they died. There was nothing more he could do.

"Snapshot tube four," Keebes ordered. The second counterfired torpedo was fired. "XO, get a SLOT buoy loaded, put a message in the disk that we're being fired on and get it out to Fleet command."

The sound of the torpedo's sonar came through the hull then. The high pitched squeal of it was horrible to hear. And if the torpedo was so close that he could hear its pinging . . . He tried to keep his face impassive, but what he was thinking was that he was not ready to die.

They had been right in the fleet briefings. There was no running from a Nagasaki torpedo.

The sound of the torpedo sonar changed from a high-pitched ping to a siren sound, no longer transmitting and listening, just transmitting. It had to be extremely close. Keebes glanced at his watch. It told the date as well as the time. Christmas was only four days away, his kids' toys would be opened with him . . .

"Set up for a snapshot, tube one," he ordered.

But the explosion came then, the deck of the *Cheyenne* ripping open, the lights going out, the blast wave bending Keebes, head first, into the steel of the overhead. The hull came completely open, the torpedoes two decks below went up in sympathetic detonation with the Nagasaki warhead explosion. The hull of the *Cheyenne* came apart in two pieces, though there was little left of the bow section, and the middle where the sail had once been was blown into fragments by the huge torpedo warhead and the other warheads' explosive charges.

The aft section of the ship dived for the bottom, going down in a thousand fathoms of water, the aft-section hull imploding at crush depth of slightly more than 2000 feet.

When *Cheyenne* hit the sandy bottom it was little more than twisted high tensile steel sheeting. The sail landed intact a half-mile to the south of the stern section. The bow, the sonar sphere and the tunnel that led to it went into the sand six feet. The bottom between the bow and stern section was littered with wires, valves, computer cards, glass, books, severed body parts and boots. A small piece of debris the size of a baseball bat, pinned under a heavy technical manual, was hit by another falling piece of debris. The debris, a sheet of glass, knocked the manual aside, and a cylinder began to rise, to float to the surface. It had been the SLOT buoy, the one-way transmission unit that Jensen had been coding the message into when the torpedo hit the ship.

Forty feet to the north, a body was pinned below a section of jaggedly ripped steel. The torso had a set of gold submariner's dolphins pinned to it and an embroidered patch below the pin. The letters on the patch spelled the word KEEBES.

## SS-810 *Winged Serpent*

"Sir, the enemy submarine is down. We've confirmed the breakup of the hull." Mazdai made the report from the sensor consoles at the aft port corner of the room.

"Status of the weapons he counterfired?" Tanaka asked, standing on the periscope platform.

"Both far off to the west, Captain. One is shutting down now, probably out of fuel. The other is circling, confused."

With the Destiny's double-hull design, Tanaka thought, he could probably take a direct hit from one of the small American torpedoes and keep going. His ship systems would be hurt but he would not have a hole in the inner hull.

"Let me know when the second unit shuts down, and keep the Second Captain looking for other American submarines. Have a track calculated for the trip to the east side of the islands."

"Yes, Captain. Sir, second torpedo unit has shutdown. It looks like it is breaking up, imploding as it sinks."

"Make your course 250 degrees true and take ship speed to full ahead."

"Yes, sir."

Tanaka stared at the electronic chart table, adjusting the scale to show the entire Home Islands, the location of the American aircraft-carrier battle group pulsing in blue about sixty miles from Tokyo Bay. *That* was where he had to get. But at least his orders were different now. He had permission to do his job—unrestricted submarine warfare against the American fleet.

Because after the supertanker exploded, no supply ship would dare cross into the exclusion zone until every last ship in the American task force was on the bottom.

**JAPAN OPAREA**
**FIFTY NAUTICAL MILES EAST OF POINT NOJIMA-ZAKI**
**USS *Ronald Reagan***

"Admiral?" Paully White was at Pacino's stateroom's open door.

"Come on in, Paully."

"Intel photos, sir." White put the photos down on the small table in the center of the stateroom. "Supertanker went down hard. Two hits. Look at this. The oil slick is washing toward Japan now."

"Not pretty," Pacino said heavily. "What about survivors?"

"No lifeboats ever came down. No one got out of the ship alive."

"Did we get a situation report from the *Cheyenne*?"

"No, sir. We should have heard an hour ago, but if I know Keebes, he probably just wanted to get out of the area before he transmitted anything about the sinking."

"Any word from President Warner?"

"White House has been informed. No new orders."

Pacino thought about Wadsworth. The CNO was probably blaming him for the supertanker. Of course, stateside, its sinking was probably seen as a sign that the US meant business, but to Pacino the blockade had failed if the first ship tried to break through. He told himself that no other ships would try that, at least not for a while.

"Admiral?" The enlisted messenger stood at the doorway.

"Yes, what is it?"

"Flash message for you, sir, downloaded to your WritePad."

"I'll get it."

Pacino had turned off the unit to recharge the battery. Now he turned it on and heard its urgent alarm calling him to get his E-mail. There on the screen he saw a fragmented message:

202037 Z DEC
FLASH FLASH FLASH FLASH FLASH FLASH FLASH FLASH
FM USS CHEYENNE SSN-773
TO CNO WASHINGTON, DC // COMPACFORCE // COMUSUBCOM
SUBJ NAVY BLUE / OPERATION ENLIGHTENED CURTAIN SECRET
//BT//

1. UNDER ATTACK FROM SUBMARINE UNIT OF JMSDF.
2. POSITION APPROXIMATE AT

"That's it?" Pacino said.

Paully White scanned it, looking at his watch.

"That message is a half-hour old yet it's marked flash. And it's partial. The time on the date-time group is just about an hour after *Cheyenne* sank the supertanker. You don't think—"

"It's right there. In black and white. The *Cheyenne*'s been attacked and it's on the bottom."

The phone rang. Pacino answered it, listened and stood. "Aye, sir."

"Where are you going?"

"Bridge. Admiral Donner wants answers."

"Good luck, sir." And added, "You'll need it."

# CHAPTER 22

The Destiny III-class submarine *Curtain of Flames* was, on the outside, identical to the sister ships of the Destiny II class. The difference was the interior, forward of the high fin. On the Destiny II-class vessels the inner hull extended fifteen meters forward of the fin, housing the command module, a three-deck-tall compartment that accommodated the crew. The upper deck was laid out to contain the control room, the radio room and the senior officer's staterooms. The middle deck contained the mess room and galley and the remainder of the staterooms, while the lower deck contained electrical equipment and the computer modules of the Second Captain, with an emergency diesel generator on the aft part of the lower deck.

The Destiny III-class command module, by comparison was only five meters long, allowing for a doubling of the weapon loading, since the empty space opened up by abbreviating the command module allowed the insertion of the additional weapons. The command module of the Destiny III class remained three decks tall but all the space was devoted to a new computer system. The middle and lower decks housed the conventional part of the unit, including the power supplies and the lower tiers of the processing, the distributed control system serving as a kind of brain stem for the upper functions residing in the layered neural network and the DNA soup processors, which were contained in the upper deck in large shock-proof environmentally controlled cabinets. The DNA, cellular material removed from the brains of dogs, resided in special vats, the networking of the vats allowing the DNA processor to act in parallel at much greater speeds than the electronic tiers of the unit. The integration of the computer system resulted in what had come to be called a "mental processing suite," the term computer no longer sophisticated or accurate enough to describe the functions of the system.

The mental processing suite of the *Curtain of Flames* had driven the ship from Yokosuka, from which it had been towed by the Destiny II-class ship *Winged Serpent,* to its dive point, where it submerged after a self-check of all ship systems, into the Pacific. Its mission had been coded into the processors and double-checked.

The mental processing suite routinely recorded its memories of the mission into a history-module bubble memory. In the event of the loss of the ship during combat, it would physically jettison the memory from the ship for the use of the Maritime Self Defense Force's later evaluation.

In order for the history-module bubble memory to receive the mental processing suite's memories, the suite would dictate relevant observations into the history module. As important events occurred during a mission the suite would think into the history module, recording formal observations into what the system called a Deck Log. Informal observations, such as the unit's estimates of mission completion, estimates of unit survival, opinions of the mission, were considered just as relevant, and were also recorded into the Deck Log, differentiated somewhat from the official entries. The formal observations were recorded in machine language, other observations were written in more conventional if contracted Japanese. The dual memory traces comprised a complete record of the mission, and in the event of the loss of the ship could be useful in further development of the submarine-cybernetic system.

# CHAPTER 23

**NORTHWEST PACIFIC**

The computer-driven, unmanned Destiny III-class *Curtain of Flames* rolled in the swells at mast-broach depth, watching the American task forces' highest value target, the USS *Ronald Reagan.*

The mission: sink the aircraft carrier. The programming was simple—twelve Nagasaki torpedoes were to be targeted for the carrier. When they were launched, the *Curtain of Flames* was to ensure that the carrier sank; if it remained floating another six torpedoes would be launched, and would continue to be until the American ship was dead.

The probability of the submarine's mission being successful depended on the presence or absence of American submarines in the area, since the computer-driven submarine was not able to fight other submarines. The subroutines for sub versus sub actions were too complex to be uploaded into the mental processing suites of the Destiny III class. The programs were being worked on, but as yet Destiny IIIs had continued to lose in exercises to Destiny II manned submarines. If the carrier were unescorted by American attack subs, the *Curtain of Flames* counted on surviving. If it were accompanied by a sub escort, all the *Curtain of Flames* could hope to do was get out all its torpedoes at the carrier prior to being attacked. Once engaged by an American submarine, it would be totally vulnerable.

## SUV-III-987 *Curtain of Flames* Official Deck Log of Underway Mission Number 118, Commencing 20 December

*Mission 118 Official Deck Log Entry 27: Current position—thirty kilometers west of island Onahara-jima, forty kilometers south of the mouth of Tokyo Bay. This unit is at mast-broach depth observing American aircraft carrier, hull number CVN-76, as it steams eastward. Task force now reduced to ships needed to protect carrier. Other ships of task force split off to enforce blockade further around perimeter of Home Islands, the line the Americans have called exclusion zone boundary.*

*This unit steaming at bare steerageway, five kilometers per hour, the periscope using low light enhancement to view the night steaming of carrier. Ships visible are carrier at bearing one one five, cruiser at bearing one two one, destroyer at bearing one zero eight. Range to central ship, carrier based on periscope range marks at four kilometers. Carrier approach angle negative. The carrier is steaming away from this unit. Range can be made more accurate with use of laser periscope range. Will be done before launch of Nagasaki torpedoes nominated for carrier. To determine range now using laser range finder could give this unit away, and a destroyer would come and attack this unit.*

*Not a satisfactory way to begin attack. Orders received by this unit on the UHF antenna. JDA has ordered this unit attack task force with primary target identified as aircraft carrier. If aircraft carrier sinks, this unit authorized to use remaining torpedoes on the other ships of carrier task force. Other Destiny III-class submarines have been assigned those targets, so this unit will wait to see reaction of task group when coordinated attack begins.*

*Coordinated attack to begin at time twenty-one thirty hours Tokyo time. Event clock being reset for coordinated attack, now reading episode time minus four minutes. Time to apply power to torpedoes.*

*Nagasaki large bore torpedoes in tubes one through twelve are warmed up, power applied to computer power supplies now. All twelve computers have satisfactorily turned on and now executing self checks.*

*While self checks are in progress this unit is lowering periscope. Tubes being flooded so that outer doors can be opened. All twelve torpedoes report water in tubes is not causing power supply or signal feed shorts. All tubes report flooded.*

*This unit now risks noisiest maneuver, opening of outer doors of torpedo tubes. Outer tube doors coming open. Unit risks look at task force. The periscope comes out of water. Water washes off lens. Unit sees task force, which continues steaming east away from this unit, range approximate at six kilometers. Not a problem. Nagasakis can run at 100 clicks, can pursue a wake for an hour putting effective range at 100 kilometers. This unit able to shoot using over the horizon targeting data from overhead Galaxy satellite. Odd thing that Americans have not shot down satellites.*

*The carrier looks different. It is turning to its right. It is coming around, to try to attack this unit? This unit watches, puts torpedo attack on hold as new course and speed of carrier are predicted. No torpedoes to be launched if target is wiggling or zig zagging, according to tactics files. This unit lowers the periscope and checks status of torpedo tube outer doors. All now open, all torpedo units reading back nominal, self checks all back showing satisfactory units, gyros on all twelve units spinning at full revolutions.*

*At event time minus two minutes all torpedo fuel tanks are pressurized. At minus one minute fifty seconds gas generators on all tubes are armed, mechanical interlocks removed to allow tubes to fire torpedoes as soon as this unit's software decides to shoot. Torpedoes now fully ready to fire. All that remains is to wait for event clock to come down to time zero and to ensure that carrier, the target, is on its new course so its position at future time can be calculated. The point is that torpedoes are not aimed at target. They are aimed at point in space where carrier will be in future when torpedoes and target occupy same space at same time.*

*Episode elapsed time minus one minute. This unit extends periscope and finds target steadied up on course southwest. Approach angle shows carrier approaching this unit. This unit watches and determines that carrier's course remains steady. Weapon control unit is calculating torpedo launch courses and speeds and presenting to this unit's upper functions for check This unit reviews calculations. They are acceptable.*

*Episode elapsed time minus thirty seconds and this unit decides to confirm the range to the carrier with brief pulse of laser light. Light bounces back and shows carrier to be 6756 meters away. Light confirms weapon controller's estimate of target speed.*

*Episode elapsed time minus ten seconds. Calculations to target are sent to each torpedo and locked in. Torpedoes know where they are going. They no longer need this unit. Signal and power feeds to units now disconnect. All twelve units now independent of this unit.*

*Episode elapsed time minus five seconds. Initial torpedo launch will commence with tube one's gas generator ignition in three point five seconds. Tube two will be next after ten seconds, then three and so forth.*

*Episode elapsed time minus one second. Tube one's gas generator ignition sequence is started. Gas generator lights off, pressure at aft end of tube rises to ten atmospheres, continues to rise, pressure pushes on aft end of torpedo. Fifteen atmospheres in tube, now eighteen. Pressure in tube declines back to seawater pressure. Torpedo unit one is away.*

## USS *Ronald Reagan*

Pacino found Admiral Donner on the bridge in his customary starboard wing VIP chair.

"Sir, you called."

The ship was rigged for night wartime steaming, the nav lights out, the bridge lit only by two weak red lamps. It was all Pacino could do to find Donner. The ship was also at full antisubmarine warfare alert, which Pacino found comical, since by itself the carrier was helpless against submarines. Only the ships of the task force could help her, and most of them had gone to the northeast or southwest to patrol the exclusion zone boundary, leaving the *Ronald Reagan* with a token force—the cruiser *Port Royal,* an AEGIS-class unit that was excellent at fighting incoming aircraft or missiles and adequate at antisubmarine warfare, the towed array sonar systems and her LAMPS helicopters the main means of defense, and the destroyer *John Paul Jones,* the Arleigh Burke-class ship that was now refitted to handle its own LAMPS helicopter. Pacino noted that none of the helicopters was now flying. He would take that up with Donner. It was also time to think about bringing one of the submarines back in close to act as their escort. In Pacino's opinion, the carrier position was also too close to the islands.

"Have you heard about the *Cheyenne*?"

"Yessir."

"What do you make of it?"

"Officially, I can't say until we can vector one other submarine to the area. I think it's more important that the other sub, the *Pasadena,* be recalled to protect the carrier, even if it means leaving the Sea of Japan open for now."

"You said officially. What do you think unofficially?"

"I think the Japanese MSDF subs put the *Cheyenne* on the bottom."

"So the way you see this, you were right all along. The Japanese are fighting back."

"Admiral, I don't form opinions so that they will confirm my earlier predictions. I'm calling it the way I see it."

"I'm sorry, Patch. I have to say that I agree with you. I'm just worried about Warner."

"Why? What's the president going to do?"

"If word gets out that we lost a submarine? In exchange for a tanker? We'll be relieved the same day."

"Sir," a young lieutenant commander said, coming up to the admiral, "we've got a detect of a laser off the starboard beam. I'm calling battlestations."

Before the admiral could respond, the officer of the deck's call blared out over the ship's circuit-one announcing system.

"MAN BATTLE STATIONS. MAN BATTLE STATIONS."

The ship's general alarm went off while Pacino and Donner moved to the center of the room.

"I'm laying below to ASW Control," Donner said.

Pacino nodded, deciding to remain on the bridge.

Laser detect, Pacino thought. That meant a submarine was out there. A submarine that was not a friendly.

**SUV-III-987 *Curtain Of Flames* OFFICIAL DECK LOG OF UNDERWAY MISSION NUMBER 118, COMMENCING 20 DECEMBER**

*Mission 118 Official Deck Log Entry 28: Current position—thirty kilometers west of island Onahara-*

*jima, forty kilometers south of the mouth of Tokyo Bay. This unit is at mast-broach depth observing the American aircraft carrier hull number CVN-76, as it steams southwest on a pace pattern. Episode elapsed time is plus forty-five seconds. Tubes one, two, three, four have been fired. Torpedoes one through four are on their way to the aircraft carrier the target.*

*Episode elapsed time plus fifty seconds. Tube five is launched, the torpedo now away. This unit keeps the periscope up.*

**USS *Ronald Reagan***

Pacino stood on the bridge feeling helpless. The men in ASWC, the combat-information center for antisubmarine warfare, would fight the ship, fight the task force. He stood behind a row of video consoles and watched, the ASW Control scenes of little value to him but the sound being piped in telling him the story. Paully White appeared.

"Admiral," he said in his high-pitched voice, "I couldn't find you. You weren't in ASW Control or flag plots—"

"This is as good as ASW Control. We can get the audio feed."

"They'd better launch the Vikings and the helos or we're in deep shit," Paully said.

"I think they're setting up to do that now. Looks like we're turning to the south so we can launch aircraft. And check out the *Port Royal* and the *Jones*. Their helos are taking off now."

"All I can say is that those choppers should have been up a long time ago."

"Ditto."

"They don't listen to me, Admiral. They just tell me where to put my submarines, your submarines, and ever since they sent *Pasadena* and *Cheyenne* to the other side of the world, I'm pretty much irrelevant. I told the captain he'd better get one of the subs back but he didn't want to hear it. Same story you got from Donuts up here."

"Careful, Paully. Admiral Donner isn't fond of that moniker."

White pulled out a cigarette. "Ah, he's a sweetheart, he just don't know dick about submarines."

"I'd say that's why—"

The audio feed from ASW Control grabbed Pacino's attention.

"Did you hear that?"

"No, sir, what?"

"They called torpedo in the water."

**SUV-III-987 *Curtain Of Flames* OFFICIAL DECK LOG OF UNDERWAY MISSION NUMBER 118, COMMENCING 20 DECEMBER**

*Mission 118 Official Deck Log Entry 29: Current position—thirty kilometers west of island Onahara-jima, forty kilometers south of the mouth of Tokyo Bay. This unit is at mast-broach depth observing the American aircraft carrier hull number CVN-76, as it steams southwest on a pace pattern. Episode elapsed time is plus three minutes. All torpedoes are away.*

*This unit is watching to see what the target will do. It looks as if target is turning toward the south, which would correlate with target understanding it is under attack since torpedoes are chasing it that way. But carrier steadies up on what looks like a course of due south, and if it knew the torpedoes were coming it would run to the southeast. Sonar bearings to the torpedoes indicate they are tracking the target in passive mode, following the carrier as it maneuvers based on the noise it is putting out into the water.*

*Episode elapsed time four minutes. First of twelve Nagasaki torpedoes detonates under carrier's stern.*

*The explosion, viewed at night, is spectacular, the ball of flame rises in large mushroom cloud above deck of the ship. Second torpedo hits twelve seconds later impact on starboard forward quarter. This explosion darker cloud, more water flying up. Third torpedo hits under ship's control island on port side. Destroyer steaming with carrier erupts into flames, one of other unit's torpedoes hitting it, or this unit's with a torpedo drawn off course. This unit will count to confirm all twelve torpedoes hit carrier.*

## USS *Ronald Reagan*

Pacino and White could only grab handholds after the first explosion rocked the ship, tossing White to the deck and Pacino into the radar console. After that they stayed away from the windows and held onto the handhold near the helmsman's console.

"Have you still got power?" Pacino asked the officer of the deck.

"We're slowing down." He reached for a phone. Before it got to his ear the second torpedo exploded, forward and starboard. The ship lurched to starboard and rolled back to port. One of the bridge wing windows shattered, glass scattering onto the deck.

"We need to get to radio and see if we can get a message out to Warner—"

"Sir, it's being taken care of," the officer of the deck said.

The next torpedo exploded much closer, this detonation right under Pacino's feet. He saw the aft bulkhead of the bridge coming at him in slow motion, tried to lift his hands to shield his face but wasn't fast enough. The wall hit him in the nose, the room got dark, the sounds faded. For a fraction of a second, as Pacino sank into a dark place, he could hear alarms and shouting and glass shattering and the next explosion, but then he was slipping deeper down into a place of liquid warmth. It was almost peaceful and pleasant as the world vanished.

# CHAPTER 24

**ARCTIC OCEAN, UNDER THE POLAR ICECAP**
**USS *Piranha***

The ship was now under the icepack, the groaning and creaking of the ice above, the knowledge that if they needed to come up in an emergency it would be impossible, the possibility of getting stuck between a shallow ocean bottom below and a deep raft of ice above. Navigation under the ice got steadily worse. The inertial nav systems had bugs that crept into the electronics, the system getting progressively more corrupt the longer it went without a fix from the navigation positioning satellite overhead. But there was no way to come to the surface to get the nav fix; the ice overhead was almost 200 feet thick. The charts here were spotty; only a few submarines had ever tried to make the passage from Atlantic to Pacific during the winter, and those that did were not in a hurry. From what Bruce Phillips had been able to read, the four ships that had made the passage all the way had had to turn around for several dead ends. The passage would consume time, and Phillips did not have time.

The BSY-2's SHARKTOOTH under-ice sonar bleeped eerily in the corner of the room, the forward and upward-looking unit augmented by a sail-mounted camera to scan the icepack ahead in addition to a bow-mounted video unit. The ice was close here, within forty feet of the top of the sail. And the bottom was a mere fifteen fathoms under the keel. It would only take a small inverted ridge to catch the ship.

And without the ability to go to the surface above,

Phillips had no idea what was going on with Operation Enlightened Curtain. For all he knew the operation was over. Or maybe Pacino needed him now, right now, and that thought sent a pulse of adrenaline into him.

"Off'sa'deck, increase speed to standard."

Joe Katoris, the main propulsion assistant, looked up from the forward-looking under-ice sonar, a scared look on his skinny face.

"But sir, we could overrun our sonar and visual. We can't—"

"You'll do fine, Katoris, now just increase speed. There are no state troopers down here."

"Aye, aye, sir. Helm, all ahead standard."

Phillips stood at the console behind Katoris, staring over his shoulder at the video displays, scanning the SHARKTOOTH sonar for ice rafts ahead.

The ridge that came down ahead blocked the way. The sonar showed it just before the bow-mounted video camera picked it up. Katoris's eyes were wide as he froze.

"Helm, back full!" Phillips shouted, feeling the deck tremble beneath his feet, the ridge ahead still looming in the sonar and video screens.

## SUV-III-987 *Curtain of Flames* Official Deck Log of Underway Mission Number 118, Commencing 20 December

*Mission 118 Official Deck Log Entry 39: Current position—thirty kilometers west of island Onahara-jima, forty kilometers south of the mouth of Tokyo Bay. This unit is at mast-broach depth observing the American aircraft carrier, hull number CVN-76, as it takes the last of the twelve torpedoes launched against it.*

*Ship is taking on water, continues to settle, torpedoes pounding into it. Carrier was a survivable ship, this unit thinks, because it took hit after hit and remained afloat. For a moment this unit thinks even with twelve Nagasakis hitting it carrier will remain afloat. But hull starts listing more, center settling further into the sea. Helicopters lift off deck. Large boats lowered into water. This unit trains periscope to bearings to destroyer and cruiser to see if sinking from their hits. Cruiser is bow down, sunk to the aft superstructure, screw pointing up to sky, ship sinking lower. Only tip of destroyer's bow above water.*

*Periscope trained back on carrier. More helicopters leave, then return. This unit not certain regarding reason for this action. They are hovering over deck of carrier, listing now to forty-five degrees. Picking up survivors? Carrier capsizes, forward and aft hulls roll to port, only keel sticking up, bow and stern sinking into water. This unit turns periscope to find destroyer. It is gone. This unit sees cruiser sink. Periscope trained back to carrier. It is almost gone. A man stands on hull near fracture. Jagged line traverses keel, cuts ship in half. Man stands on hull shaking fist. He must not know that the suction of a hundred and five thousand tons of ship sinking will drag him to the depths with the vessel.*

*Hull goes under water, man going with ship. In ultrahigh optic power, no sign of man shaking fist. Surface of ocean quiet, oil fires going out, sounds from under water violent. This unit listens to sounds on sonar, finally single crash as hulk of carrier hits rocky sea bottom two kilometers deep. Even now, some compartments must have stayed intact, air trapped aboard, men inside trapped. Could explain banging noises that continued for next four hours, banging growing faint, less frequent.*

*Sun rises over Pacific, sea quiet again.*

## Arctic Ocean, Under the Polar Icecap
## USS *Piranha*

The ship had been able to pull back from the ridge, but now there was no place to go but back. It was like finding a way through a cave, Phillips thought. When one path didn't work he had to backtrack to a common branch and go another way. It could take forever. A claustrophobia seized him, a driving urge to get the hell out of the Arctic and back to open water. He knew what he needed. He looked over at Katoris.

"Hover here and wait for me."

He went to his stateroom. Deep in his locker he found the bag that he'd packed when he'd thought about this situation two weeks ago. Then, it was just brought along for good luck. Now he'd have to execute his wild scheme. He withdrew the bag and found the dirty jeans. He pulled them on. They were loose over his butt. He took off his sleeved T-shirt and put on the dingy sleeveless one, stuffing his pillow underneath the generous cut of the material so it looked like he had a beer gut. Next came the work boots, the tool belt and the worn leather gloves. Phillips looked at himself in the mirror. Not quite right yet. He took some soap and a razor and cut the soap into dust, smeared it over his face, took some dirt from behind the door hinges and smeared that on his face. Better. The week's growth of beard helped too. Finally he put on the old yellow hardhat, the outfit complete. He opened the door to the control room and strutted in.

All eyes were on him as he walked up and stood on the conn. Even Whatney, who had lived with Phillips for the last two years and thought he'd grown used to his stunts, stared at him.

"Gentlemen," Phillips said, "the Bruce Phillips construction company is here. Let me amend that. The Bruce Phillips demolition company. Did I ever tell you guys I worked during summer leave with a wrecking ball in center city Philly? No. Well, you know it now. XO, do you have any idea what I'm going to do now?"

"I'm afraid, sir, that I do."

"Officer of the Deck, do you?"

"No, sir."

"How about you, Dive?" Phillips asked the diving officer.

"Yes, Captain. You're going to do some demolition work on the ridge ahead."

"That's exactly right. We're here to do some demolition work. Since you got that answer right, Dive, how am I going to do it?"

"Torpedo, sir?"

"Dive, do I look like a wimp to you?" Phillips puffed out his fake beer gut.

"Sir, I'm not sure what you look like."

"I look like a real man. And do real men use wimpy torpedoes?"

"No, sir," Whatney said.

"That's right." Phillips reached for the microphone for the circuit-one. "ATTENTION ALL HANDS. THIS IS THE PRESIDENT OF THE BRUCE PHILLIPS DEMOLITION COMPANY. WE'VE ENCOUNTERED A WALL DOWN HERE THAT WE'RE GOING TO BLOW THROUGH. WE'RE GOING TO USE A VORTEX MISSLE TO BLOW A *PIRANHA*-SIZED HOLE TO DRIVE THROUGH. WHEN WE'RE DONE YOU MAY ALL COME TO THE CONTROL ROOM ONE BY ONE TO THANK ME. UNTIL THEN, FASTEN YOUR SEATBELTS."

Phillips put the microphone in the holder and squinted at the crew. "Get the weapons officer in here—ah, here he is now. Weps, I didn't think you would hold out long after that."

The weapons officer, a lieutenant named Tom McKilley, worked for Scott Court. McKilley was a redhead, although his hair was trimmed too close to his round head to see that. The Irishman was fond of Ray Ban sunglasses, cigars and a new BMW sport coupe. Just before Phillips had arrived, McKilley had married a beautiful blonde woman, a marketing executive who worked in D.C., the two commuting between D.C. and Norfolk, seeing each other when they could. As far as Phillips was concerned, McKilley was too shy, but any man who smoked cigars—and could prove he did it before Phillips arrived aboard—was okay with him.

"Weps, the show is all yours. I want you to put a Vortex right into that ice bank ahead."

McKilley didn't say a word, he just plopped down in the weapons-control console. The console powered up, the displays rotated through as McKilley powered up one of the forward Vortex missiles.

"Bow cap is opening, okay, the missile is clear forward. Aft breech door is jettisoned. The missile tube is clear."

"Status of the missile?" Phillips asked, still wearing his hardhat and construction worker outfit.

"Power is go, missile is armed. Distance to ridge ahead?"

"Range is . . ." Phillips stepped to the SHARKTOOTH console. "Two hundred yards."

"Too close, sir," McKilley said. "I need at least a mile standoff, preferably two."

"Come on, Weps, I can't do that. It'll take forever. And there's no room to turn around, so I'd have to back up for a mile. Just override the interlock and shoot the bastard."

McKilley turned in his control chair to face Phillips. "You don't understand, Captain. This thing is as powerful as a small nuke. If we fire from here we'll go up with the ridge. And the last thing we want is to have a big hunk of the icepack fall down on us when that explosion goes up."

"Okay, okay. Helm, lower the outboard and train it to one eight zero."

The outboard, a thruster that could lower from the bottom of the hull at the lower level of the aft compartment, was used for maneuvering in close to piers. Phillips intended to use it to drag the ship backward.

"Outboard's down, Skipper."

"Very well, start the outboard."

In the video displays the ridge ahead grew smaller as the ship backed up.

"Sir, we have room to turn around now," Katoris said from the SHARKTOOTH panel.

"Helm, stop the outboard, train to zero zero zero and raise the outboard."

"Aye, sir, outboard coming up. Outboard is up."

"Ahead one third, right twenty degrees rudder, steady course north."

Phillips watched as he withdrew along the track he came in on. He looked up to see Roger Whatney's face staring at him.

"What is it, XO?"

"Sir, could I have a word with you?"

"Sure, XO. Officer of the Deck, keep driving us back, I'll be in my stateroom for a few minutes." Phillips led Whatney to his cabin and shut the door behind him. "What's going on, XO?"

"Sir, I was going to mention this when we were in open ocean so it wouldn't distract you. But I just found a report about the Vortex missiles in the computer systems of the ship. Sir, this missile's bad news. It blows up its launching tubes."

"Yeah?"

"Well, sir, I'm not sure I'm all too enthusiastic about using a weapon that's a suicide machine. The test submarine sank when they fired the test missile. I saw the video, sir. The tube blew right open and the missile vaporized the forward half of the ship."

"Roger, listen to me. All that's true, but that's why we've got these tubes on the *outside* of the hull. The back tube cap comes off and the missile exhaust just blows astern. There's no pressure boundary to rupture. Those things are more guidance cylinders than weapon tubes."

"I thought of that, Captain, but it wasn't just the pressure. The exhaust itself is white-hot. It could melt clear through our hull. These external tubes haven't been tested."

"Well, XO, they're about to be. Now get back in that control room and put your goddamned warface back on. I don't want the men to know you're nervous about this."

"Yessir."

Phillips walked back into the control room, tried to

reassure himself that Pacino had fixed the problems with the missile, or else they wouldn't have been sent out with it.

In any case, they'd soon know.

The ship had finally put several miles between itself and the ridge. Phillips turned the ship around and again faced the ridge.

"Ready, Weps?"

"Yessir."

"Okay, here it is, men. Firing point procedures, Target One, the ice ridge ahead, Vortex unit one."

"Ship ready," Katoris said.

"Weapon ready," McKilley said.

"Solution ready," Whatney said.

"Hit it," Phillips said, wondering if those would be his last words.

"Excuse me, sir?"

"Oh, right, fine, shoot on generated bearing."

McKilley hit the firing trigger and the noise from outside blasted into the ship. Phillips held his ears, realizing he had just launched a solid-fuel rocket with its engine little more than twenty feet away. The video screens at the bow went to white-out, the rocket motor exhaust blinding them.

"Dammit, the video's probably a goner," Phillips said, a smile coming to his lips as he found Whatney's face in the room. The missile had worked. It had launched without killing them. Now if it could just do its work on the ridge ahead.

"I'm dropping the unit-one guidance tube," McKilley said.

"Jettison the tube."

"Tube one disconnected."

A click and a slight bang and the guidance tube outside the hull for the Vortex missile disconnected from the ship and fell away.

The noise of the weapon was still loud but it was fading now.

"Impact in three, two, one. . ."

Phillips watched the bow video display, which had

refocused on the sea ahead, no longer blinded by the missile exhaust.

The explosion was so violent it threw Phillips against the chart table, gashing his forearm. The lights flickered. Phillips's ears rang. The video display had whited-out again, only now coming back to normal.

"Well, XO, let's go back and see if there's a *Piranha*-sized hole up ahead, or if we made it worse."

"You think it could be worse?"

"Sure. This is a cave. We might have caused a cave-in. No way to tell until we see it."

It seemed to take forever for the ship to move back to where they had been. When they got to the ridge Phillips stared at the video screen, amazed at what he saw. The ridge was gone, and there was a half-mile-wide patch of open water above. The heat of the fireball had vaporized ice two hundred feet thick.

"Bring us under the open water, Katoris. I want to grab our radio traffic and tell Pacino what's up."

Katoris gave the orders. *Piranha* came slowly up to periscope depth while hovering, the periscope mast able to receive the satellite transmissions. Phillips looked out the scope, saw the water around the ship begin to freeze in the arctic cold. It was only a few minutes before Katoris was ready to go deep, and already the water had skinned over to ice a quarter-inch thick.

Back deep, Phillips watched the video and sonar screens as Katoris drove them on. He was afraid that there would be another ridge, or that the missile had blown up prematurely and the original ridge would be waiting for him, but the ice overhead seemed thinner. And then the ocean floor below got deeper, falling away under him to form an arctic trench. Phillips looked at the fathometer and the SHARKTOOTH and realized he could make twenty knots for the next few hours. He gave the orders, the ship accelerating.

Soon he'd be out in the Pacific, with a chance to hit the Japanese Maritime Self Defense Force. Or so he thought until he saw the message the ship had received while at periscope depth. A bead of sweat ran down his forehead, and suddenly Phillips realized he was out of uniform.

Slowly he walked to his stateroom, handing the WritePad to Whatney just before he shut the door. He took off the construction worker's duds and slowly put his poopysuit back on.

He could not believe it. The entire USS *Reagan* carrier-action group. Sunk. Down. Every goddamned ship blown away except for one mid-sized radio command and control ship, the *Mount Whitney,* which had picked up survivors. No one knew why the Japanese had let the *Mount Whitney* go, except perhaps because it had no weapons, no gun-mounts or torpedoes or missiles, just radio antennae. Maybe that last was the point—they wanted Washington to listen to what had happened from their own people.

# CHAPTER 25

**NORTHWEST PACIFIC**
**USS *Mount Whitney***

"Admiral? Sir? Can you hear me?"

Pacino's head was swimming. He tried to open his eyes but saw nothing. He put his hand to his head and felt the gauze wrapping around his face.

"Where?"

"Sir—" It was Paully's voice. He sounded okay. "We're on the *Mount Whitney,* the command and control ship. For some reason the Japanese spared it and let the helicopters drop us here."

"What—my face?"

"A little glass in the eyes. Your right eye is actually okay but the left got surgery this morning. Also a bad concussion. You've been in a coma."

"How long?"

"Day and a half."

"Jesus, we've got to get moving! What's the deal with the battle group?"

"Sit back down there, Admiral. I'm afraid the blockade is history."

"Any orders from Warner?"

"She made a statement that the Japanese sank our surface ships but she said that the force commander in the Pacific had a fleet of American submarines headed for Japanese waters to neutralize the threat."

"Donner. Where is he?"

"Admiral, you're the PacForceCom now. Donner never made it out of the *Reagan.* In fact, everyone in ASW Control bought it. One of the torpedoes detonated right against the hull there. We were just damned lucky we made it out."

"How did we do that?"

"Just lucky I guess."

"Don't listen to him, sir," a female voice said.

"That's Eileen, your nurse."

"Admiral," the nurse said, "Commander White pulled you out of the bridge, down four levels to the flight deck and out to the port side, then flagged down one of the helicopters that was waiting to get survivors."

"Sir, I just did it because you were the only other guy on the stinking carrier wearing submarine dolphins. I couldn't let you go down."

"We lost Donner. What else?"

"Sir, they got every single ship. Every one in the battle group except *Mount Whitney,* and we're hightailing it out of here at flank. No one knows when they'll hit us but everyone is wearing lifejackets."

"How many survivors?"

"Couple hundred."

"Paully, there were six, seven *thousand* men in the battle group."

"I know, sir."

Pacino's mind tumbled with the news. He had been right, but he hadn't thought they'd try to sink the whole battle group.

"It's worse, sir."

"Worse?"

"The two other carrier groups that sailed out of Pearl last week. *Abraham Lincoln* and *United States.* The two Nimitz-class carriers. They sent Destiny III's out into a Pacific deep penetration. The robot subs had the carrier groups targeted—"

"Wait, slow down. Where are the *Abe Lincoln* and *US* battle groups?"

"Same place the *Reagan* battle group is, Admiral."

"What about their submarine escorts?"

"That's the only silver lining. And also the reason Warner hasn't thrown her hands up yet. The two subs, the *Tucson* and the *Santa Fe,* did well. *Tucson* was assigned to the *Lincoln.* When the fighting started her captain vectored in on the source of the torpedo shots and determined that there were four submarines sent in to get the battle group. Not one of them seemed to care, they just fired away, oblivious to the *Tucson.*"

"Her captain, John Patton, right?"

"Right. Patton unloaded a torpedo bank into the first Destiny sub and blew it to the bottom. Then he had to drive fifteen miles to get to the next, and four torpedoes later the next sub was down. By then the *Lincoln* was dead in the water, listing, internal explosions going off, not a pretty picture. The third took an hour to find and put down, and by the time he zeroed in on the fourth it was out of torpedoes."

"How did we know those were Destiny III robot subs?"

"The fourth Destiny just hung out at periscope depth watching the show. Patton and the *Tucson* fired a single Mark 50 at it and it came to the surface. By this time Patton was pissed. He wanted some prisoners. The whole force was sinking, and the *Lincoln* went down right then. Patton surfaced and took a Zodiac boat to the Destiny. He and ten guys went over there with MAC-11s and 9-millimeter automatics and some acetylene torches and he cut into the hull, fired a magazine into the ship and went inside. By now you've figured out what he found—a computer. The forward space was all of ten or twelve feet long, three decks tall. The space was just a place for the computer consoles. There wasn't a human aboard. He checked out the other compartments, all but the reactor compartment. The core was still at power, so no one in there would have made it anyway. The robo-sub apparently works shooting at surface ships, but not so good against other submarines. I think we can count on the OpArea having only Destiny IIs, which might be good news since there are fewer of them."

"Maybe. Or maybe bad news since the Destiny IIs will be much more capable against our subs than the Destiny IIIs."

"Anyway, Patton radioed Pearl and had an oceangoing tug get underway to meet him to pick it up. He went and picked up survivors, about seventy-five men, and had to meet the tug halfway to drop them and the Destiny off, so he'll be late getting to the OpArea."

"I take it the same thing happened to the *United States* and the *Santa Fe*?"

"Joe Cosworth, the skipper, did okay. He actually sniffed out one of the Destinys before it started firing. He engaged it, shot at it and it put a torpedo in the water, but aimed in the opposite direction. Joe fired at the Destiny, but the Destiny just fired at the *United States*. The Destiny didn't even know he was there. Or if it did, it didn't care. Joe put it down with one torpedo. But there were four more ships he had to find and sink. By the time the fifth Destiny was destroyed, the *United States* had exploded and gone down. Joe got more survivors, though. His boat was filled with them. He's surfaced now, he's got a couple hundred men on the deck and a couple hundred more below. He's trying to keep them alive and meet the rescue ship from Pearl. I think he'll be even later to the OpArea."

"What do you make of all this, Paully?"

Pacino was thinking Paully White was the best deputy he'd ever had. Sean Murphy was good but could he brief like this? Which reminded Pacino he'd have to get some messages off to Sean.

"Well, Admiral, I think the Destiny III was designed as an antisurface-ship killer. It's not much on antisubmarine warfare. I'll tell you why, too. Fighting in a sub-versus-sub environment must be too tough to program. They can teach this computer how to attack a surface battle group, because when you get right to it, that's easy as bowling. You put out some weapons and the pins go down. Killing another sub, one that knows you're there, is damned hard. Maybe they just haven't been able to program that. Or maybe these boats were only loaded with antisurface-ship torpedoes. Maybe they just don't have an ASW torpedo. But I think it's the first reason. The Destiny IIIs are too dumb to go up against another sub. A Destiny III is something to be afraid of if you're standing on the deck of a surface ship. Underway submerged, no problem. Now the Destiny II class, that's something to stay awake over. The Japanese are good, damned good, and with their Two-class ships up there in the OpArea, we've got our work cut out for us. The Two class, I think, has an acoustic advantage against the 688 boats."

"How do you know?"

"We got more data from the loss of the *Cheyenne.* The *Pasadena* was nearby. She tried to get in close and target the Destiny but the Destiny just faded away, disappeared. Too damned silent."

"At least she was quiet enough that the Destiny didn't hear her."

"I guess."

"But now we've pretty much put the Three-class ships on the bottom, so the OpArea should be safe for a battle group if we have sufficient submarine escorts, is that right?"

"Technically, yes. Politically, no."

"Go on."

"From an operational point of view, sir, you're right. The OpArea is trouble for a battle group, but a looser exclusion zone wouldn't be a problem as long as you have an escort submarine. But we don't have any more carrier battle groups in the Pacific. The others are all in the Atlantic for that African flap. We're missing about five carriers and seven amphib helo carriers. They all had gone through the canal on the way to Africa, and when they were on the way home the Japanese thing hit us. They're on the way now but they're about three weeks away."

"Why so long?"

"Panama Canal problems. An oil tanker exploded in the western mouth of the entering locks. Sank in shallow water. They'll need to pull it out of the way and that'll take a salvage crew a few weeks."

"How did that happen?"

"Some say a Japanese commando unit blew it up. It was positioned perfectly to block the canal. And it's prevented all but two of our Atlantic coast subs from getting through. They're all going around the horn now with our missing carrier forces."

"What about the French and British. The *Ark Royal* and the *De Gaulle?* They were in Guam."

"They told us the blockade was our decision, they weren't consulted on it, and they won't support it with their hardware."

"Not the real reason, I assume."

"Hell, no, sir. They're scared shitless that their carriers will be blown to the bottom. A great way to lose votes at home."

"Looks like the aircraft carrier is as obsolete now as the battleship was at the start of World War II."

"I think the carrier has some good years ahead of it still. It just needs some help from guys wearing dolphins, guys like us."

"Okay, so tell me about President Warner. What did I miss?"

"Well, for one thing, she wants a videolink with you as soon as she gets up. It's three in the morning her time, so by seven tonight our time we'll need to brief her. She's still saying the blockade will be enforced by units of your submarine force."

"Where *are* the units of my submarine force?"

"I've called them all up to periscope depth and asked them that question. We've got about eight Los Angeles-class ships in close to the OpArea, one Seawolf class, and the rest, the other twenty-one 688s, are still on their way, more than two days' steaming out of the OpArea. Like I said, the other carrier groups and the Atlantic subs won't be here for three weeks. Oh, and your Brucey Phillips called in from the Arctic. He had to blow a hole in the ice with a Vortex missile to get through. So he's down one Vortex. But otherwise he's okay. Damned lucky he came over the pole, because if he'd taken the Panama Canal we'd be waiting for him till mid-January. As it stands, he should be here in another two days."

"So we wait until we have all thirty of the Pacific units, plus Bruce's *Piranha,* then coordinate them, then stage them so we all penetrate the OpArea at once. Anything submerged that isn't American goes down."

"Sounds obvious, doesn't it?"

"Of course it's bloody obvious."

"Which is why we aren't doing that."

"Paully, what is going on here?"

"Sir, President Warner is what's going on. She wants the OpArea secured *today,* meaning tonight our time, and she wants the blockade back in force."

"That means we have to clear out the OpArea of—how many Destiny IIs?"

"Between eighteen and twenty-two. Depending on force readiness."

"Say twenty-two. That's, hell, eight of ours to twenty-two of theirs."

"Nine, counting the *Barracuda,* the Seawolf class ship."

"Tough odds but maybe we can live with them."

"Warner says we have to live with them."

"So, Paully, tomorrow is Christmas Eve. We've got till close of business Christmas Eve to get the curtain back up around Japan."

"Right. With all of nine fast-attack subs."

"We'll just have to do that—but with eight of them."

"Why only eight?"

"Paully, you and I are about to make the USS *Barracuda* our new flagship. If I'm the PacForceCom, I can do this any way I please. Right?"

"You are going to piss off one Capt. David Kane."

"Kane saved my career once," Pacino said. "The least I can do is thank him in person."

"He's not one to enjoy having his submarine commandeered by staff types."

"I know how he feels, but that's the way it's going to be. By the way, get out a message to Sean Murphy and CB McDonne back at USubCom. Tell Murphy to get the Panama Canal cleared and do what he can to get the Joint Staff to secure that area."

"Anything else?"

"Yeah, get this damned bandage off me. You said I had one good eye, right? Get me an eyepatch for the bad one."

"Oh, this is going to be great, Admiral. You'll look

like a pirate when you get to the *Barracuda.* Should I get you a parrot too?"

"I already have one, Paully. Want a cracker?"

"Oh, very funny. Sir."

# CHAPTER 26

**ARCTIC OCEAN, UNDER THE POLAR ICECAP**
**USS *Piranha***

"How long to the start of the Bering Strait Trench?"

It was nice when Scotty Court had the conn. He could be both officer of the deck and the navigator. Phillips felt that the more pressure the navigator was under, the better. The control room still blurped and wailed with the eerie sounds of the SHARKTOOTH under-ice anti-collision sonar. Phillips stared at the console, wondering if the Japanese had the capability to go under the icecap. Probably not, he decided. Why would they, considering their scope of operations.

"Captain, looks like another six hours."

"At that point we'll have enough depth below and clearance above to make, what do you think, Nav, twenty-five knots?"

"Well, Skipper, speaking as the ship's navigator, I'm not comfortable with anything over twenty knots. Too much risk of collision with an ice raft or a ridge like the one you blasted through. But speaking as the officer of the deck and the ship's operations officer, I don't see any reason why we should go any slower than thirty knots. We'll have an eight-hour transit at thirty knots to the marginal ice zone. Once we have some open water overhead, I don't see any reason for speed restriction at all. We've got an OpArea to get to, and we need to get there now."

"You know, Court, if you ever want to be a skipper of one of these things, you're going to have to learn to make the big decisions. If you want to run with the big dogs, you gotta bark like one. And bite, too. So can the equivocal bullshit and give me a straight answer."

"Thirty knots, Captain. When we're in the marginal ice zone, gun it."

"Absolutely, Mr. Court." Phillips clapped the navigator on the shoulder. "I don't care what they say about you, Scotty, you're okay."

"Thanks, sir. I think."

"I'm going to hit the rack, Mr. Court. Think you can get us through this maze all by yourself?"

"I'll try, sir."

"I'm just a phone call away, Nav."

Phillips opened the door in the aft bulkhead of control and stepped into his stateroom. He sank into the high-backed leather swivel chair and stared at his WritePad. He turned it on and reread the message about the sinking of the battle groups. He went to his locker and pulled out an old-fashioned paper chart of Japan, and taped it to his conference table. He stood over it for a long time, firing up a fresh cigar. After a while he got a pencil and marked in the boundary of the exclusion zone, the Japan OpArea. He stood over it, continuing to stare down at it.

What would he do if he were the fleet commander? There must be some two dozen 688 ships he could coordinate and deploy into the OpArea. Coordination was the key. He would hit the Japanese with everything he had, all at once. It would be the only way to survive, especially since the Destiny IIs had the tactical and acoustical advantage.

The tactical advantage was theirs because they knew where the intruder subs would be coming from and when. The acoustic advantage belonged to them because they were three to seven decibels quieter than the Improved Los Angeles-class ships. The quietest sub heard the intruder first and could set up to put a torpedo in the water before the intruder knew what was happening.

So how could the American force beat that? Maybe by entering in superior numbers, two US boats for every Japanese boat, so that if a Destiny fired at one submarine, the noise of the torpedo launch would alert the other American ship. Hell of a way to win a war, Phillips thought. Maybe the Destiny ships would need to reload torpedoes and would go back into port, and the US force could catch them coming out.

Still, the chances looked slim. The only hope was the stealth of the Seawolf-class subs and the power of the Vortex missiles.

But there were two dozen Destiny submarines and only nine Vortex missiles.

### NORTHWEST PACIFIC
### USS *Mount Whitney*

Adm. Michael Pacino lingered in the door of sick bay, saying goodbye to the doctor, then spending a few moments more with Lt. Eileen Constance, the nurse who had attended to him during the ten days he had spent recovering from the *Reagan* sinking. Finally he checked his watch, blinking as he realized it was hard to see anything with his left eye obscured by the patch. The *Mount Whitney* doctor had given him the black eyepatch until the eye healed.

"I've got to go," Pacino said. Eileen asked if he would come by before he got on the helicopter for the personnel transfer to the *Barracuda*. "We'll see," he said.

Pacino struggled down the passageways, the eyepatch making navigation difficult, finally arriving at his temporary stateroom that he and Paully White were assigned. He opened the door, saw Paully, whose jaw dropped just before he erupted into laughter.

"It's not funny. The bad eye hurts," Pacino said.

"Sorry, boss, but I just couldn't help it. You need a spyglass and a hook for a hand, a tricornered cap, and you're ready."

"What I'm ready for is to get out of here." Pacino went to the locker and took out the wetsuit, took off his uniform and struggled into the wetsuit. Paully White cursed getting into his. By the time Pacino was suited up he was sweating and seasick. The suit was tight and constricting and hot. As long as it had taken to get into it, it would probably take longer to get out of it once he was aboard the *Barracuda.* Pacino glanced at his watch again. It wasn't quite time yet—the *Barracuda* and the *Mount Whitney* needed to close the range between them or else the chopper wouldn't have enough fuel.

Pacino sat at the temporary stateroom's conference table and unrolled his large chart-sized electronic display, which was a WritePad blown up to ten times the regular size. The chart display was selected to a large area view of the Japan OpArea. Pacino had made half a dozen marks on it, showing the present positions of his eight Los Angeles-class submarines. Going through each position was a line segment indicating his idea of where he wanted that ship to go. Pacino glanced at the chart from a few feet away, frowned and erased the arrows through the ship's present positions.

"Trouble?" Paully asked.

"It's not making sense," Pacino said. The heat of the wetsuit, the strain of putting it on in the stuffy stateroom while the ship rolled in the swells, the stress of being ordered to win a war that might not be winnable were all building into a world-class migraine headache. "Look, Paully, trying to attack the MSDF sub force with eight subs is a mistake. And geography is killing us too. The backside, the Sea of Japan, is too remote, yet that's where the Russian resupply ships would be. Warner wants results in one day—"

"Typical."

"—so I'd have to put something together for the Pacific side. That would leave the Sea of Japan with no US submarines. Which means that the Russians could run out the so-called blockade and Warner gets mud on her face."

"I say don't worry about the Sea of Japan," Paully said, stabbing his finger on the chart. "The Russians aren't going to resupply from the east or the west—not after the *Cheyenne* put that supertanker on the bottom."

"Go on."

"Well, we'd be in big trouble if we hadn't shot at one of the Russian ships, but we did. We sank the first guy dumb enough to run the blockade. We blew him to the bottom. They lost ten men, the whole crew."

"They shouldn't have had to die. The *Cheyenne* crew would have had to live with that the rest of their lives—"

"Hey, they're dead, too."

Pacino shook his head. The blockade had become a war and it was out of control. And he was the man responsible to the president to control it. By comparison, it had been so easy and so simple to just command a submarine, with all the relevant information at his fingertips. Now there were so many unknowns for the enemy as well as his own forces that his tactical decisions were going to come down to a series of guesses. He tried to remind himself that so much of his past success was based on hunches and guesswork, and that that was why he was here today. If his past intuitions in combat had been flawed he would be dead at the bottom of the Arctic Ocean or the Bo Hai Bay or the Labrador Sea. *Trust yourself,* he commanded himself.

Paully was saying something.

"Say again, Paully."

"Okay, sir. We sank the supertanker *Petersburg.* Russia isn't going to screw with another ship through the blockade—I'm amazed the *Petersburg* ran the blockade in the first place, because there's no insurance for anyone running a blockade. Lloyd's of London just laughs. You're on your own."

"I thought they would insure anything."

"Oh, they will. The insurance premium for a billion dollar ship with, say, three hundred million dollars in crude would be, oh, about 1.3 billion. It doesn't make any sense to insure it. Like I said, you're on your own. The Russians had to pay for the loss of the *Petersburg.* That's a couple billion dollars in anyone's currency. You've spent your life welded into big sewer pipes, you don't know squat about what makes the world go round. It's money. Listen to me. A couple billion had to hurt and hurt bad. So the Russians, they're not going to be anxious to lose another vessel. Yeah, the Japanese sank our battle group. But the battle group didn't sink the *Petersburg,* our *submarine* did. And submarines are invisible. So no Russian merchant ship is gonna cross that line because for all they know we've got more submarines out there."

"Paully, Russia's money was an investment in a relationship with Japan. The Russians might try again now that the battle group is gone. They might try to escort in a convoy with Russian navy vessels, maybe even an Akula nuclear submarine."

"No way, sir. The Russian fleet is too poor to use the fuel to go to sea. They can't send a submarine out, there's no food for the crews. Admiral, don't you read the NewsFiles? The Russian navy hasn't paid their officers for three months, and their sailors—the ones who are left—have been working for free for six months. The sub-trained ratings were tilling fields to try to get food to be able to go to sea, and the harvest this year was squat. This is not about charity to Japan, Admiral. This is about yen and rubles and pounds and dollars. The Russians are too poor. *That's* the reason they were helping the Japanese in the first place. Now that you sank their tanker they've got a great excuse to do nothing. 'Hey, we tried but they sank our ship, and the water's full of subs, so we can't risk any more.' Now the Russians can sit this out and still get credit for trying to help."

Pacino's headache was worse, and he had no idea where Paully's tirade was going. White's tone would be considered disrespectful by some officers; Pacino was grateful for it. He was blessed with an aide who would tell him the truth without the sugar coating.

"So don't worry about the Sea of Japan. Leave the *Pasadena* there as insurance. Put your subs on the southeast, the Tokyo side."

Pacino sat back and rubbed his eyes.

"Great. So we leave the west side alone. What about the Pacific side?"

"Sir, your vectors show the eight sub force spreading out."

"Yes. They operate independently."

"I think we should wolfpack them in on the north and south corners of the OpArea. Two or three subs within ten miles of each other. One will serve as a tripwire for the other. If one gets attacked, the other can back him up from a different bearing. We know the Japanese can kill one of ours alone. Why not change the equation?"

Pacino glared at White. "So you're suggesting we rewrite the Approach and Attack manual, abandon forty years' worth of nuclear submarine tactics, techniques that have been tested in the Bahamas test range in years of sub-versus-sub exercises, years of computer simulations against the Destiny class—abandon it all and go back to World War II U-boat tactics. Is *that* what you're saying?"

White said nothing.

"Well?"

"Yessir. That's my recommendation."

For the first time since Pacino came in with the eyepatch he smiled at Paully, then held out his hand.

"Good. It's a great idea. I'm going to call it Tactical Plan White. If it works I'll make sure you get the credit for it."

"And if it fails, you'll get to take the heat."

Pacino looked up. "If it fails it won't matter." He pushed the chart over to Paully. "Show me where you'd put the boats."

"Nine boats, eight with *Pasadena* holding down the Sea of Japan. That's four packs of two, call them A, B, C and D. A and B start here in the southwest OpArea. C and D begin farther north. A and B move north and C and D come south down the coastline, linking up outside Tokyo Bay. By that time the OpArea is secured."

"There's no D. Remember, we're keeping *Barracuda* out of the wolfpacks. I want her center stage, right here. We're going to be at periscope depth trying to run the show."

"That almost works out, sir. We could put the *Buffalo, Albany* and *Boston* up in the north, and *Atlanta, Jacksonville, Charleston* and *Birmingham* down south."

"The Yankees against the Rebs."

"Easy to remember, anyway."

Pacino grabbed the WritePad and began a tactical employment message. Each ship was given a position and a time to be there. The subs were to link up with their wolfpack partner in the Pacific, then enter the OpArea. Pacino wrote that each ship was to report to him using SLOT buoys, the one-way radio buoys that could be launched from a signal ejector at depth and would then rise to the surface and transmit, allowing the subs to stay deep.

"What do you think?" Pacino asked Paully.

"Transmitting, even SLOT buoys, is dangerous. The Japanese will be onto us."

"I'll tell them to program coded SLOTs with prewritten messages. Then at midnight and noon they'll put them up, and on the *Barracuda* we'll know what's going on."

"Coded SLOTs?"

"Code 1 means 'no contact,' code 2 means 'pursuing contact,' code 3 means 'I'm under attack' and code 4 means 'we sank a Destiny.' "

"Not much meat there, Admiral."

"We can't micromanage the skippers. We just need to know if they're still alive."

Pacino modified the message, then attached the electronic file depicting his marked-up chart. "Too bad we lost the USubCom authenticators when the *Reagan* sank. Now our people will just have to trust it's us sending the message."

"No, sir. We'll have access to *Barracuda*'s authenticators. They'll have everything we had on the *Reagan*."

Pacino nodded, sent the order. The WritePad transmitted the files to the megaserver in orbit, which relayed the data to the Navy's western Pacific ComStar communications satellite and from there to the subs nearing the OpArea.

"Time to go, Paully. You got everything?"

"I'm loaded. The chopper is waiting on the aft deck. You want to say goodbye to the ship's captain? He asked me to tell you he sends his luck. Hugs and kisses, all that good shit."

"No time."

Pacino pulled out his waterproof bag, which was a carbon fiber canister with a gasketed screw top. He rolled up and stowed the chart pad and the WritePad inside, along with the uniform he'd come with and some new ones. He still had his solid gold dolphin pin and his admiral's stars from the uniform he'd been wearing when the battle group was attacked.

"Let's go."

They walked down the crowded passageways of the *Mount Whitney,* their wetsuits creaking and squeaking. The ship's halls were busy with cables and junction boxes and pipes, but nowhere near as crowded as a nuclear submarine. The surface ships wasted space and volume everywhere, so much so that it was hard for Pacino to walk their passageways without thinking of the waste, but soon he would be aboard the *Barracuda* and it would all fall into place—

But would it? He felt a dread come into him then, settling onto his spirit like a carrion bird on a carcass. Suddenly the war seemed to become sinister and alive, a beast too big for him, and for the first time in memory he felt unequal to the task. In the past he'd taken his abilities to the limit. On the *Devilfish* he had once been faced with sinking under the polar icecap with a dying nuclear submarine or trying to emergency blow through ice a hundred feet thick. He had had nothing to lose in aiming for the ice—either his crew would have died if he did nothing, or they had a chance, however slight, to live if he took a huge risk. It hadn't been a choice. Now, his decisions would affect several thousand men with several thousand families, and maybe even the nation. If he prevailed, America would again be the big kid on the block. If he lost, the US would go the way of Napoleon's France or Hitler's Germany or Sihoud's United Islamic Front of God. The pressure was too much, he could feel it crawling down his throat, a cold claw on his heart. Every decision would inevitably send men to their deaths. He tried to tell himself to stop such thoughts and calm down, but the battle coming up in the next hours would determine a judgment of his entire life.

Before, at sea, in command, he had coped with the pressure by simply telling himself that he knew his crew had taken risks to come to sea with him and that they trusted him. And that if he lost, he lost his ship and his men and that was it. But there were other ships, other captains, other days for them to fight.

Here now, in the Pacific outside of Japan, there was only himself and his fleet, two-thirds of it late, the other third already committed by an overly aggressive commander-in-chief who might relent when he confronted her—but who might not. And this battle was not just for his life, his crew's, his ship, it was for a whole fleet of ships, his country's future. If he blew this . . .

Pacino knew he would be sailing into darkness, not only blind but dumb, not able to tell his ships his orders unless they came out of the depths to hear him—

Paully's voice interrupted, his words focused on the irrelevant, the nurse who had attended Pacino when he was injured, Paully, of course, unaware of Pacino's thoughts.

"Admiral, you really should take a few minutes with Nurse Eileen. She tended to you when you were out of it!"

Pacino kept walking. His headache was pounding harder.

"Admiral, I think she'd feel real bad if you just jumped into a helicopter without thanking her."

"You're right," Pacino said finally.

As they walked by sick bay Pacino stopped. "I have a migraine. I'm going to grab some aspirin or something before we get in the chopper. You wait here."

Pacino walked into the door to sickbay. Lt. Eileen Constance was doing computerwork in her office. She wore her regulation whites, her face tanned with no makeup, her hair long and blonde. She had been a nurse for eight years, most of it on the hospital ships, but she had wanted to be a flight surgeon and had put in for medical school. Her application to the University of Florida had been accepted and she was only waiting here on the *Mount Whitney* as a nurse until med school commenced in the fall. Pacino had learned about her career ambitions while flat on his back in sickbay after recovering from the eye surgery. When they had removed his bandages he had seen her for the first time and felt his heart sink. She was too beautiful, out of his league. It hurt just to look at her.

"Hi, Eileen, thought I'd stop by and say thanks. I appreciated . . ."

She looked up, apparently surprised. "Admiral." She stood up. "How is the eye? You look like you're in pain." She put her hand on his forehead.

"Headache."

She gave him two pills and a bottle of spring water. He swallowed, his eyes on her. He moved closer to her, knowing he shouldn't. She smiled up at him.

"Well, since you just came to say goodbye, I'll say good luck. Be careful on the personnel transfer . . . and give them hell."

"Thanks."

"And come back in one piece, okay?" She paused. "Do you think we'll ever see each other again?"

Paully's knock came at the door. "Time to go, Admiral."

"Tell them to start the engines," Pacino shouted through the door.

"I've got to go," Pacino said.

"Please be careful, Michael." His first name from her lips, when no one called him anything but "sir" or "admiral" or "Patch" or Donchez's "Mikey" sounded strange but wonderful.

The sound of the helicopter's jet engines spooling up could be heard dimly through the bulkheads, the noise swelling as the turbines whined, moaned, screamed. The sounds of the rotors came next, the chopper starting the main rotor.

Paully knocked again. "Chopper's *ready,* sir."

Pacino turned back to Eileen, grabbed her shoulders, pulled her close and kissed her. In a way it seemed absurd, a cliche, the warrior off to war, kissing his woman goodbye. Well, hell, so be it.

He pulled away. "Bet on it, I'll see you again."

He stepped out the door to the passageway, shutting it behind him. Paully followed him to the aft helodeck, and as they opened the watertight door to the helodeck Pacino noticed his headache was gone.

He stepped into the Sea King helicopter and sat by the hatch, looking at the ship. Paully waved orders at the pilots and the rotor outside roared, the chopper shaking with the power of the rotating blades. The helicopter lifted off the deck, climbed to the southeast and then turned and sped away, the *Mount Whitney* vanishing far below.

# CHAPTER 27

**NORTHWEST PACIFIC**

Pacino pulled his mask off his neck, spat into it and rubbed the spit across the lens until it squeaked. Satisfied with the antifogging technique, he pulled the mask back down over his face and let it dangle at his throat. He clamped the regulator into his mouth and tasted the coppery air from the tanks on his back. The regulator worked. He spat it out, the rubber taste lingering.

"Okay," he said to Paully White, "you got your waterproof bag?" Pacino checked his as Paully confirmed his own items on the checklist.

"Yeah."

"Tanks?"

"Check."

"Regulator functional?"

"Yes."

"Gage?

"Full."

"Weights?"

"Tight."

"Mask?"

"Yeah."

"Flippers?"

"Tough to put on with all the other equipment."

"Let's get this thing on the hump."

"Sirs! Drop zone in two minutes," the chopper copilot shouted back. The *Barracuda* was four miles ahead, only its periscope mast protruding from the water. Pacino checked the Rolex, knowing the ship had been submerged at periscope depth, hovering motionless, for the last fifteen minutes, since he and White had been late getting off the deck of the *Mount Whitney*.

## USS *Barracuda*

Capt. David Kane sat at his stateroom's large conference room table. The captain's cabin on the Seawolf class was done perfectly, he thought. A large rack, a conference table that could comfortably seat a half-dozen men, a large leather swivel chair that could roll between the conference table and his desk, the wheels of the chair locked unless he pushed the travel button. Set into a soffit in the centerline bulkhead were four widescreen video monitors, the first monitoring the navigation display of the ship's position, the islands of Japan in the upper right corner, the boundary of the OpArea flashing yellow, now only a hundred nautical miles to the northeast. The second display showed a view of the control room in one window, the maneuvering room aft in the other. The third was also a split-screen view, the left half selected to the view out of the type-20 periscope, the sea quiet, nothing to see but the dividing line between the waves of the deep blue ocean and the light blue sky, the right half of the screen displaying the broadband sonar waterfall screen that showed the ocean empty of other ships within the audible range of the BSY-2 combat system. The screen could also display the combat-control system's dot-stacker computer display, useful when they were trailing an enemy submarine—the captain could look up and see the solution to the target with a glance, eliminating a hundred phone calls a day when in trail.

Kane was showered, shaved and dressed, the arrival of the Pacific Force Commander announced on a flash message he had gotten from the *Mount Whitney* the night before. He was particularly bothered by this, the arrival of a meddling admiral onboard his submarine, turning his command of one of the newest Seawolf-class submarines from independent action to little more than a flagship. The arrival of an admiral at sea was always bad news, he thought. His authority as commanding officer would be under constant scrutiny and evaluation in front of his observant crew. In his own memory every time one of his commanders had taken aboard an admiral, that admiral had become a sort of proxy captain. The captain of a ship was one of the world's last dictators, but in the world of instantaneous communications the surface-ship captains were no longer fully in charge. They took their orders by the ream from the carrier captains, from the battle-group commanders, from Pentagon bureaucrats, even from the president. But submarine commanders were different. They were submerged below the sea where radio signals couldn't penetrate—except for slow, uncertain and rarely used extremely low frequency signals—in a tactical employment in which they were prohibited from talking and listening. Sub skippers were chosen for their abilities to operate independently, they were where there was no boss, no appeal, no help. The ultimate authority aboard was with the skipper. The ship was *his* ship.

But if a captain of a sub were a god, an admiral was some kind of celestial being that pulled the god's strings. Crewmembers stared at his stars, awed by a force considered more powerful than the ship's captain. And when an admiral was seated next to the captain, and the captain spoke, he was as often as not met with a "huh?" as the subordinate stopped looking at the admiral. A flag officer could only be considered bad news.

And in this case, Adm. Michael Pacino was doubly bad news. Kane had rescued Pacino in the Labrador Sea from the wreckage of the *Seawolf,* but by that time he was unconscious, never recovering until months later in the hospital, long after Kane had ceremoniously scuttled the *Phoenix.* But Kane had heard rumors and stories about Pacino, the folklore that Pacino had lost his first ship, the *Devilfish,* in the Arctic Ocean under the cover of an airtight top-secret classification. There was something about that that bothered Kane, particularly since it had been Donchez who had always protected Pacino, and Kane had never approved of Donchez. Pacino was not only an unknown, he was a commander of unprecedented power in the reorganized submarine force. Before the reorganization, the force had been split between Atlantic and Pacific fleets, each running a very different navy, the cultural gap as wide as the one between New York and Honolulu. Pacino had been named by Admiral Donchez, then the chief of naval operations, as head of the newly formed Unified Submarine Command, which sacked ComSubLant and ComSubPac, the admirals in command of the Atlantic and Pacific fleets, uniting the organizations under his single command. And the fleet seemed to align itself to Pacino like iron filings to a magnet. Pacino had a stranglehold on the skippers of the fleet. No one came to command without being put through a test with him watching in the submarine control-room simulator in Norfolk. The simulator tests were renowned for their realistic, harsh battle scenarios. One captain, who had passed the attack-simulator test, had walked from the room and collapsed in exhaustion, waking up in a hospital. Pacino's setup was absolute—flunk that test and either lose command or say goodbye to the possibility of ever having it in the first place. Up to then Kane was the only commander grandfathered, excused from Pacino's combat test, having served honorably aboard *Phoenix* and then appointed to command the *Barracuda*, but since he had taken over, several incumbent captains at neighboring piers had been fired by Pacino for lack of aggressiveness in the attack simulators. Kane felt Pacino was building a force of submarines commanded by men who were loyal to him, who had his stamp of approval, men he had made. Well, he had been one of the few holdouts from the fleets before the reorganization. Finally, three weeks ago, Pacino had sent him the message to report with his officers for an evaluation in the control-room simulator, the trial that would determine whether he would keep his job commanding the *Barracuda*, but before he could show up for the trial, the emergency orders had come in to put to sea for Operation Enlightened Curtain.

And the fact that Pacino had decided to give him the trial in the attack simulator meant that his position was not as secure as he'd thought. All his effort in the Muslim war had been for nothing, because Pacino had called him to the evaluation and would replace him if he didn't perform against whatever computer game Pacino programmed into the simulator. It was almost as if he would have to go to another Admiral Rickover interview. He tried to remember Rickover's words to him—*I expect you'll prove yourself to be one of the best nuclear officers who's ever been in the program.* But where Rickover was near-neurotic about reactor safety, Pacino was off the deep end for blood-and-guts aggressiveness. Rickover wanted brains, Pacino wanted balls. Kane had passed Rickover's test but a doubt had developed whether he would pass Pacino's. And Pacino's test was, he felt, one that he shouldn't have to take—he'd been in command for almost five years now, on the verge of selection to flag rank himself, and now a man his own age who had lost two submarines, would pass judgment on whether he was good enough to keep his command. At least that's the way he saw it, and he'd built resentment against Pacino ever since that message ordering him to the test. Well, now the admiral would get a chance to see him perform for real, that is, if the admiral allowed him to enter the OpArea in an offensive capacity. He worried that Pacino would want to remain outside the OpArea and watch the sea battle, turning the *Barracuda* into a flagship no more offensive than the *Mount Whitney.* Well, Pacino was here now. The waiting was over.

The periscope view had stopped turning circles viewing the horizon and was centered on a section of the sky, the crosshairs of the reticle framed on the clouds above the horizon. Nothing was visible until the officer of the deck changed the optical power from low to medium. A small dot could be made out floating above the horizon. The screen jumped a second time as the power was switched to high, the dot growing into a small image of a helicopter, the image bouncing in the view. Again the image jumped as the OOD clicked in the power doubler, and the chopper could be seen approaching, the block letters above the cockpit barely readable as US NAVY.

Kane walked out to the control room, where Lt. David Voorheese was hugging the periscope monitor.

"Status, OOD?"

"Hovering at periscope depth at the rendezvous point, Captain. I finally have visual on the helicopter."

"Flood the forward escape trunk."

"Aye, sir, flood the forward escape trunk," Voorheese repeated back. "Chief of the Watch. Flood the forward escape trunk."

Kane looked up at the control room's periscope-view monitor, the screen set up in the overhead of the room above the attack center. The helicopter now filled the high-power view.

"Do a horizon scan, Officer of the Deck," Kane ordered Voorheese. Fixating on the helicopter could make him miss an oncoming merchant ship appearing on the horizon.

"Aye, sir."

"Off'sa'deck, sir, forward escape trunk flooded," the chief of the watch reported from the forward port wrap-around ballast-control panel.

"Open the upper hatch," Kane commanded. "And find the helicopter again."

Voorheese gave the order to open the escape-trunk upper hatch, then turned his attention back to the periscope, the view in low power showing the approaching helicopter, the image shift to high power revealing the markings on the chopper's sides, the door open, the feet of two men sticking out. The admiral and his aide, done up in scuba gear. Typical, Kane thought. It seemed overly flashy, intended to wow the crew. An admiral swimming aboard in scuba gear was as radical as the queen of England wearing a thong bikini.

Pacino moved up to the chopper's open door, dangling his flippers over the sea, some fifteen feet down. White moved up next to him.

"The periscope is in sight, Admiral. We're setting up now."

Pacino checked Paully, who looked pale behind his mask. White had told Pacino it had been years since he had been diving. Pacino had been away from it for ten years, but how hard could it be?

The chopper slowed and hovered, the sea below deep blue with whitecaps from the stiff breeze. Pacino looked out at the sea and the sky, his habit to enjoy his last air before going into a sub still compelling. He took a breath, aware that he'd be breathing canned air for the next weeks. He exhaled, clamped the regulator into his mouth, tested the air and nodded at Paully. He pulled the mask onto his face, careful not to disturb the black eyepatch over his left eye. Going into the water with full scuba gear could be tricky, he remembered. The idea was to make water entry without losing equipment.

"Ready when you are, Admiral," the copilot shouted.

Pacino waved at the pilots, put his left hand on his mask and regulator, his right on the strap for his canister, looked down at the water, bent low at the waist and leaned out over the water until he fell out of the chopper.

The freefall into the sea was busy with sensations, the violent wind from the rotors of the gray-and-black Sea King machine floating above him, the sea careening toward him, his flippers breaking the surface, the sea coming up to splash into his face, threatening to knock off his mask. Pacino's instinct took over as he went underwater, the brainstem telling him not to breathe. He had to force himself to take the first breath from the tanks. He looked for Paully, swimming back to the surface to find him. When his mask broke the surface he could see the helicopter flying away, its noise gone ever since he'd hit the water.

Paully was on the surface. Pacino looked for the periscope, finding it silhouetted against the sun. He nodded to Paully and they swam on the surface until they got to the periscope. Pacino then jackknifed his body so that his head went down, the mast of the periscope extending into the darker depths. He kicked his fins, swimming downward, the air flowing naturally now. The feeling of incredible freedom flooded him, the sea around him now welcoming instead of nightmarish. The water was pleasantly warm against his skin inside the wetsuit.

Pacino's ears were now compressing in the pressure, the pain coming slowly, then urgently. He grabbed his nose through the rubber of the mask, clamped his nostrils shut and blew against his sinuses until his eardrums blew back out, equalizing through his Eustachian tubes, the pain gone.

Pacino's fingers traced the cold metal of the sail trailing edge and he swam deeper into the sea until the sail ended on the surface of the deck. Again he checked for Paully, who was behind him, then put his hands on the surface of the deck. The ship felt mushy, foamy, the rubbery tiles of the acoustic absorption material making the surface less able to reflect the sound waves of an active sonar pulse from a surface ship. He made his way aft, beginning to wonder if he had missed the hatch opening in the hull. He could see some ten feet in any direction but the surface above was not visible. There was plenty of light, but he couldn't see distant objects, the world ending ten feet away in a blue haze. The odd visual effect combined with the floating feeling of neutral buoyancy sometimes made divers experience the same sensations of vertigo that pilots suffered. Pacino remembered the disastrous flight to the *Reagan.* He watched the stream of his exhaled breath, the bubbles floating upward in the same direction he had assumed it to be. He looked back toward the sail, the structure beginning to vanish in the visual haze. Had the crew failed to open the hatch? Then he looked ahead and saw it in the haze. He swam toward it, the hatch larger than he'd recalled, the circle of it perpendicular to the hull surface, the steel ring of the hatch some three feet in diameter. In the surface of the hull the hatch opening was a gaping maw of darkness. Pacino reached the hatch and grabbed it, motioning Paully into the interior.

On the screen the helicopter hovered overhead, the scuba-equipped inhabitants of the chopper dropping into the water, the chopper immediately turning and flying off, leaning far into the direction of flight, the aircraft's bottom side and rotor circle all that was visible as it accelerated away. Voorheese did a surface search near them, the divers already underwater or too close.

"The XO at the hatch?" Kane asked.

"Yessir, with the Chief of the Boat."

"Very well. I'm going to upper level. Put the chief of the watch on the phones, and when I give him a double click have him announce the admiral onboard."

Voorheese acknowledged and Kane left the room, climbed the forward ladder to the upper level and walked aft along the paneled passageway to the hatch to the escape trunk.

"They in yet, XO?" Kane asked his executive officer, Comdr. Leo Dobrowski, an older and more senior officer than many captains. Leo had had an extended shore tour at the War College finishing a doctorate in international relations, which had set him back, but he would be in command of his own submarine within a few months—that is, if he passed Pacino's simulator test. Dobrowski was of medium height, in good shape, a full head of hair cut into a flattop, making him look somewhat tough. He was a serious man. In fact, the only time Kane could remember Dobrowski smiling had been at the ship's softball and football games. Off the ship, the XO was actually funny and full of laughter. Aboard, he wore his serious expression. Kane was grateful to have him.

Paully disappeared into the darkness, his fins trailing. Pacino followed him, lowering himself in feet first, watching the light above as he came down into the chamber of the ship's escape trunk, a large airlock that could hold ten men. Finally Pacino's flippers touched the deck of the bottom of the escape trunk, the circle of light seeming far above him. He looked down at shoulder-level and found the diver-control panel, put his hand on the T-lever and pushed it horizontally to the end of a track, then pulled it upward to the stop. The lever was built into the hydraulic-control valve for the hatch operating hydraulics.

The hatch came down, the circle of light being eclipsed by the dark circle of the inside of the hatch.

Pacino watched as the light vanished, the hatch clunking down on the steel of the hatch ring of the hull. As the trunk plunged into darkness, Pacino could hear the control ring rotating until the hatch was completely secured. They were now inside the USS *Barracuda,* although a dark and flooded part of it.

"They're in, sir," Dobrowski said, looking at the status panel, the red circle labeled as the upper hatch changed to a green bar, indicating the hatch was now shut. "Draining down now."

Kane waited for the lower hatch to open, turned and instructed the crew to form up behind him. He'd be damned if an admiral would come aboard without a regulation greeting. He picked up the phone to control.

"Chief of the Watch? Get ready to make the announcement. I'll click when he steps into the upper level."

With no further action, a blasting noise sounded in the trunk and a light came on high up in the overhead. Pacino could see the surface of the water coming down until the surface of it came to his chin, his mask clearing like a periscope breaking the surface, the trunk looking different through an atmosphere of air than it had under water. The water drained quickly, the air in the chamber foggy, until the water was gone, puddles remaining near Pacino's fins. He pulled his mask off, adjusted his eyepatch, dropped his regulator, then pulled off the fins, glancing at Paully to see that he too was removing equipment. Pacino dropped his lead weight-belt, his tanks and his equipment canister, now wearing only his wetsuit. In the dim light of the trunk he could see the hatch to the ship set into the side of the huge trunk, dogged mechanisms that slowly began to rotate, the air between the trunk and the interior of the hull equalizing in a short hiss of air. The mechanism stopped and the hatch came open to the exterior of the trunk. The light of the hull was bright compared to the interior of the trunk. Pacino stepped down two steps to the deck to find himself in the wide upper passageway of the forward compartment.

Standing in front of him were a group of poopysuit-clad men—one of them Capt. David Kane. As Pacino extended his hand to Kane, the ship's announcing circuit blasted throughout the ship.

"COMMANDER, PACIFIC FORCE COMMAND, ARRIVING!"

Pacino smiled at Kane, Kane's hand dry and hard. Kane was one of the skippers Pacino had not screened in the training command but he was certifiably excellent. Pacino had decided to bring him into his training simulator to show some of the younger skippers how a torpedo approach was done—Kane would open some of the kids' eyes. Kane's face was deadpan.

"Welcome aboard the *Barracuda,* Admiral Pacino."

# CHAPTER 28

**NORTHWEST PACIFIC**
**USS *Barracuda***

Pacino looked at the greeting party formed up behind Captain Kane, the spotless deck, the shining bulkheads. He took a deep breath, the smell of the submarine what he'd expected, the scent a mixture of cooking odors, mostly grease, sewage from the sanitary tank vents, body odor, ozone from the electrical equipment, oil from the lube oil systems, amines from the carbon dioxide scrubbers. It was strong but faded into the background after a few minutes.

Pacino looked into Kane's eyes, thinking the man was a Hollywood version of a nuclear-submarine commander—tall, tanned, high cheekboned, blue-eyed, trim, assured.

"Finally I get to meet Capt. David Kane in person," Pacino said, his smile genuine. He then turned to Paully White: "Captain Kane rescued the survivors of the *Seawolf.* If it weren't for this man I'd be long dead. And, Captain, I don't know that I ever properly thanked you for that. I wanted to present your Navy Cross but I couldn't walk at the time. Captain Kane, this is Comdr. Paul White. Paully was the *Reagan*'s sub ops officer. He pulled me out when I was out cold on the deck and the carrier was going down. I think it's damn good luck that I have two men who've saved my life on the same ship."

Kane's expression was blank. "Well, sir, let's get you to the officer's head and out of the wetsuit."

Pacino looked down at his feet, where a puddle of seawater had built up. Kane led him and Paully to officers' country, where the stainless-steel room had two shower stalls and two commodes, amazingly roomy compared to the older 688-class layout, Pacino thought.

"When you're done here, sir, my messenger will take you to your stateroom."

Pacino peeled off the rubbery wetsuit, dumped it on the deck and stepped into the shower. Soon the traces of the sea were gone, he dried off and opened his waterproof canister, pulling out his own black coveralls, a gift from the Royal Navy during a coordination meeting in London. His name was embroidered above the left breast pocket. American-style submarine dolphins were embroidered in a patch above the name, and Pacino's two admiral's stars were sewn onto the collars. The shoulders were graced with patches, the left an American flag, the right the emblem of the Unified Submarine Command, the symbols designed by Pacino and a commercial-artist friend. The USubCom patch featured a Jolly Roger flag flying above the sail of a submarine, the skull and crossbones standing out on the field of black, the banner reading UNIFIED SUBMARINE COMMAND across the top of the Jolly Roger.

Pacino emerged into the passageway, and the messenger took him aft down the centerline passageway to a steep staircase to the middle level. Back along a dogleg to another centerline passageway, forward again to a door marked EXECUTIVE OFFICER. Pacino knocked and entered. The stateroom, vacated by Dobrowski for them, was simple and small. Against the far bulkhead two racks were set into a curtained area, one rack above the other. The aft bulkhead was taken up by a fold-down desk and two chairs. The forward bulkhead had cabinets and drawers set into it, a small sink area and the door to the common head shared with the captain's stateroom. Pacino unpacked his canister into one of the lockers, tossing his WritePad down on the desk. Paully was sitting at one of the chairs, looking up at Pacino expectantly.

"Have we got a ship-control readout?" Pacino asked.

Paully nodded. "It's in the corner inside the lower rack."

Pacino craned his neck and squinted his good eye. A

small panel with three dials glowed in the darkness of the rack interior. The readouts were course, speed and depth. The ship was heading 330 true, the direction of the OpArea, the depth was 654 feet, the speed 44.8 knots—flank speed. Pacino rolled out his chart electronic pad, wondering where they were.

"We've got about twenty minutes before we have to talk to the president," Paully said, looking at his watch.

"We need to bring Kane into the loop," Pacino said. "But let's be careful. I don't want to call him to this stateroom—that's a power play. We should do this in his stateroom, with him at his command seat. I want you to be particularly respectful of Kane, Paully—this is a guy who's not too happy with us aboard. When Kane talks, you and I listen hard. We don't make phone calls to his officer of the deck. We don't ask his officers tactical questions. We don't even ask the nav tech the ship's position. Our information has to come through Kane. And for that to work, Kane's got to be on the team."

Paully found the phone, the special command circuit between the conn, CO's stateroom, the XO's stateroom and maneuvering. He buzzed the captain's stateroom, listened, then spoke quietly, looking up at Pacino.

"Captain Kane would love to speak with us in his stateroom. He said to pop on in through the head door."

Pacino remembered how uncomfortable he had been as a submarine skipper when an admiral, even though it was Dick Donchez, had been riding the ship at sea. The situation was miserable, all he could wait for was the moment the admiral left. But though he could empathize with Kane now, nothing he could do short of leaving Kane's ship would make the situation completely comfortable for Kane, but as he had said to Murphy a lifetime ago, they would all need to operate outside their comfort zones. He knocked on the door to the commanding officer's stateroom. Kane's voice was muffled as he called Pacino in.

"Thanks for the reception, Captain Kane," Pacino said. "That shower made me a new man. Your ship is impressive."

Kane stood, offering Pacino his command chair. Pacino waved Kane into it, sitting in a seat at Kane's right against the bulkhead.

"Great layout," Paully said. Pacino poured a cup of coffee, admiring the ship's emblem on the cup, the snarling fish swimming past the sail of a submarine, and felt the old urge to command his own ship again.

"The video camera is above the status panels on the centerline soffit, Admiral," Kane said. "I'll pipe the Oval Office into the central screen."

"We've still got a few minutes," Pacino said. "I wanted to brief you on what our approach is going to be. Paully, roll out the chartpad and show Captain Kane what we're suggesting."

White dropped his semisarcastic style and slipped into a crisp just-the-facts briefing, showing Kane the OpArea and the deployment of the seven attack submarines on the Pacific side, where he envisioned the placement of the *Barracuda.* If Kane was upset by the *Barracuda* acting as a standoff command and control ship, he didn't show it. But there was also no enthusiasm on his face either, which might have been due to the commitment of the seven ships against the entire Japanese Maritime Self Defense Force submarines.

"Sir," Kane said to Pacino, "we've got the better part of a squadron of submarines steaming two days to a week behind us. There were boats out of Pearl that couldn't get out of repair for a weekend and worked to get going for a few days before they deployed. Before I'd put a half-dozen 688s into the OpArea I'd recommend a coordinated attack with the other two-dozen ships. We could put that together by, say, the day after tomorrow. We could go into that OpArea and clean it up."

"I know," Pacino said. "But the president wants to see results by Christmas. That's hours away. I can't wait a week. The blockade has to go back up now."

"I think the wolfpack idea is a good one, but seven ships, sir, that's just—"

"Unavoidable," Pacino finished for him. "But I'm going to see if I can buy some time with President Warner. We should get to setting up the videolink now."

Kane hoisted a phone to his ear. Within seconds the deck inclined upward as the ship came shallow, preparing for periscope depth. Minutes later the ship rocked gently in the swells near the surface, the radio antennae raised so that they could transmit to the ComStar satellite. Kane spoke into a phone again, probably to radio, Pacino thought, to set up the videolink. The central screen went blank, then deep blue with a countdown of time on it, the numerals slowly rolling down from two minutes. Pacino laid out his chart pad and WritePad on the surface of the table, waiting for the videolink, preparing his argument to Warner.

When the numbers rolled down to zero the seal of the president of the United States flashed briefly on the screen, followed by the appearance of three people at a table, blue curtains behind them. Pacino recognized the situation room of the White House basement and realized that things must be even worse than he thought. The situation room in the basement was almost never used by Warner. In the center of the screen was Warner herself. She looked rested and calm, her eyes wide and blue, hair neatly coiffed, makeup light. She wore a cream-colored suit, a simple string of pearls, her hands on the surface of the table. On her right was Adm. Tony Wadsworth in his service dress blues, gold stripes up to his elbows, rows of ribbons under a gleaming surface-warfare pin, a deep frown etched in his face, his eyes black and angry. To Warner's left was Richard Donchez in a blue pin-striped suit looking as if he'd lost another ten pounds since Pacino had last seen him. Donchez looked emaciated, weak, like he didn't have much time left. Pacino vowed he'd see him first thing when this was all over.

"Can you hear us, gentlemen?" Warner asked. There was a slight disconnection between the image and the voice, as if the video-link were some old foreign film that had been dubbed. Just one of the problems with the massive amount of data that had to be transmitted for a videolink. It would probably be another five years or even a decade before videolink technology was good enough to replace voice-only telephones.

"Good morning, Madam President," Pacino said

crisply. "You're coming through fine. Can you hear me?"

There was a delay as his transmission made its way to the other end—another damning trait of videolink hardware that would need to be upgraded. The one-second delay made it impossible to speak in real time—if someone tried to interrupt, it wouldn't be heard until another sentence down the road.

"I hear you fine, Admiral Pacino. You know Admiral Wadsworth and Mr. Donchez. Who do you have with you?"

She probably didn't give a damn who was with him, he thought as he hurried through an introduction of Kane and White.

"Well, let's just get to it, shall we? Are your forces in the exclusion zone yet, Admiral?"

Pacino described his status and his intentions, watched Warner's face, her brow crinkling in annoyance as he tried to persuade her to give him three more days. Wadsworth's face was a thundercloud. Donchez's expression was unreadable. He spent half the time scribbling on a WritePad in front of him.

"Admiral, I don't have three days, I don't have three hours. I need some Japanese submarines sunk in the next two days. If you're not done with that in forty-eight hours I'm going to withdraw the blockade and meet with Kurita. You have forty-eight hours to put those submarines on the bottom. I want a report at seven A.M. my time on the twenty-sixth and I want good news."

Donchez's face seemed to carry a warning. Pacino could hear his WritePad's electronic alarm beep once, announcing the receipt of an urgent electronic mail.

"Madam President, could I mute this for just a few seconds?" Pacino asked.

"Certainly, Admiral. We'll wait."

Pacino nodded at Kane, who pressed a function key on his seat arm, and the screen displayed the words OUTGOING AUDIO/VIDEO MUTED.

"We're in deep shit," White began. Pacino held his palm up to Paully without looking at him, his concentration on his WritePad. He flashed his fingers through the software buttons until he got to the E-mail function, the flash transmission blinking on the menu. He selected it, the E-mail sent from Donchez just a few seconds old. He skimmed it, then read it again. The text was short and simple, in Donchez's trademark telegraphic style, all in capital letters

> MIKEY, URGENT YOU GET WHATEVER SUBS INTO OPAREA YOU CAN NO MATTER THE RISK. WARNER UP AGAINST FULL BLOWN MEDIA ATTACK. CONGRESS VOTING DAY AFTER CHRISTMAS TO PULL PLUG ON ENLIGHTENED CURTAIN. SINK MSDF SUBS BY THEN OR WITHDRAW. WADSWORTH PROPOSES RELIEVING YOU IMMEDIATELY ON DEC 26 IF NO RESULTS. GET IN, ATTACK, GET OUT. GIVE WARNER SUNK DESTINYS SO HER NEGOTIATION WITH KURITA WILL GO IN OUR FAVOR. SHE MEETS KURITA REGARDLESS OF RESULT, SO KILL HIS FORCE. URGENT YOU COME HOME IN ONE PIECE. NEED TO TALK TO YOU ASAP. UNCLE DICK.

Pacino stared at the WritePad, then saved the message and pushed the WritePad aside. Warner had a prearranged meeting with Prime Minister Kurita. It wouldn't matter if the entire US submarine force arrived on December 27, it would be too late. Modern warfare happened very fast, with information flowing almost faster than it could be generated. Twenty years before, Pacino might have been given two weeks or a month to get ready for the blockade. Look at how long the army had had to prepare for Desert Storm in Saudi Arabia, dragging equipment and men into the desert for six months before the shooting started with the Iraqis. Look at how long the air force had taken to set up for the bombing of Chah Bahar, Iran. Three weeks to assemble the bombers and plan the mission. The invasion of southern Iran had taken two months. But now the world political stage called for immediate victory. Battles were no longer exclusively in the hands of the generals and admirals, the politicians were deeply involved. And yet that wasn't new . . . hadn't Jimmy Carter tried to micromanage the failed Desert One rescue of American hostages in Iran? Hell, it went all the way back to World War I, the only obstacle to the commander in chief taking tactical command being his information-and-command systems. In the past the speed of information flow had mostly limited the president to the back seat, the field commanders in wartime making the immediate decisions. But now here he was taking rudder orders from the president when he should be given a free hand. He'd been unable to convince her to use the most elementary fighting tactic, the massing of force against the enemy. Wadsworth hadn't been helpful, and all Dick Donchez could do was tell him to follow his orders or he would be fired.

"We ready to reconnect?" Pacino asked the group. They nodded. "Turn it back on."

Pacino looked up at the screen. "Madam President, we'll engage the MSDF submarines and report back in forty-eight hours."

"Good luck, Admiral," Warner said, holding her palm up to Wadsworth, who obviously wanted to say something.

The connection was cut off at the other end, the presidential seal appearing, then the screen went blank.

"Cut it," Kane said into a phone. "Go deep and flank it."

The deck inclined, downward this time, to a steep ten degrees as the ship dived for the depths.

Pacino stared at the chart for a moment, then told Paully to present the plan one last time. Pacino barely listened, the plan rolling through his head at every waking moment. By the end of the presentation Kane and Pacino had no changes to make. The submarines would deploy as he'd indicated.

# CHAPTER 29

**East China Sea**
**Forty Kilometers Southwest of Miyanoura**
**Dake Island**
**SS-810 *Winged Serpent***

Comdr. Toshumi Tanaka flashed his fingers over the keyboard of the Second Captain console set up in his stateroom. The upper console displayed the navigation chart, showing their progress from the Sea of Japan through the Korea Strait southeast through the East China Sea past the southern tip of Kyushu. In a few more kilometers they would emerge into the Pacific on the southeast side of the Home Islands. The nav display also projected the *Winged Serpent*'s future track, following the coastline separated by seventy kilometers, northeast toward Tokyo Bay, where off the mouth of the bay south of Point Nojima-zaki a replenishment ship would take station at anchor. The *Chrysanthemum* would be standing to, looking like an old rusty tanker flying a Liberian flag, her name painted in English in uneven rust-obscured block letters. But all resemblance to a merchant tanker ship would end there. If *Winged Serpent* had not gained contact on the American submarines by then he would continue up along the coast of the Home Islands until he reached the Shibotsu-jima island at the far north point of Hokkaido Island. There he would turn the ship back southwest and patrol farther from the coastline, 150 kilometers distant, steadily working his way deeper into the Pacific until he had contact. Nothing could stop him now. The orders had taken forever to come but finally he was at sea doing what he was born to do.

Unrestricted submarine warfare against all units of the American navy. He would paint the sea bottom with their blood. He would remain at sea until the food was gone, and beyond, until the last Nagasaki had been launched and had hit its mark. Then he would sail only for the rendezvous with the *Chrysanthemum,* reloading torpedoes, food and bottled water. He would give the crew and his officers twenty-four hours with the replenishment ship's prostitutes, comfort women, and they would be back ready for battle. The thought of indulging himself with a comfort woman did not cross his mind. He could only focus on one thing—righting a wrong.

The lower console of the Second Captain was a text display of intercepted radio messages from the Americans, with some probable decodings. They weren't assured of being correct. Many times the names for things came through but numbers were problems. Typically numbers, such as the latitudes and longitudes of positions, were double or triple encrypted. The first encryption was electronic, converting the raw-form message into meaningless electronic symbols that were then sent over the radio circuits. A second encryption could be done with the radio transmission itself, in which several dummy messages could be transmitted at once on separate frequencies, the real message cut into the text of the various dummy messages so that the actual radio transmission jumped frequencies, the receiver on the other end decoding all half-dozen messages and discarding the portions of the dummy messages that had no meaning, retaining only the vitals of the actual message. Even then a third encryption could be done at the point of receipt, where numbers that came out of the system were altered by the message reader. A one could become a three, a four a six, with a constant added on or multiplied with the "raw" number. Sometimes numbers were subtracted. Sometimes they were inverted and the nearest whole number used, sometimes multiplied by pi, then the third decimal figure the result of the convolution. This could go on to the point of absurdity, but in any case there had been so many cases of latitude and longitude distortion from messages that were broken that Tanaka no longer trusted them.

It was the verbal content of the messages that intrigued him. The term "wolfpack" recurred several times. Tanaka reclined in his seat, recalling the rich history of submarines, when in the last great war the Nazi submarines would gather together to attack convoys. If one was too far away, the other boats might be better positioned—the old vintage boats too slow to chase a swift convoy, relying instead on positioning themselves in the paths of the surface ships. In addition to positioning, two boats had twice the torpedo loadout of one. Finally, if one were to come under attack, a second boat could vector in and counterattack out of nowhere. There was one case that came to mind when the destroyer *Aggressive* was closing in on the damaged German *Unterseeboot U-458* to ram and sink her, and the undetected *U-501* was submerged at a right angle to *Aggressive*'s assault, delivering three torpedoes to the attacking destroyer, breaking her in half and sinking her just a few hundred meters before she would have overrun the *U-458.* Both U-boats had escaped.

So now the Americans were going to gang up for safety from the aggressions of the Destiny class. Tanaka tapped through some sequences, coaxing the Second Captain to extrapolate the positions of the *Winged Serpent*'s sister ships, the Destiny IIs. The Three-class ships were virtually useless in a fight with a submerged enemy. Most of them were probably already sunk, dead and gone, their poor programming inadequate to the task of fighting a true antisubmarine-warfare attack-submarine. But the Two-class ships would be there patrolling the waters surrounding the Home Islands, preparing themselves with the same intelligence data that he had. He considered putting up a message to the other ships in his Two-class squadron but decided against it. The commanders knew what they were doing.

Tanaka closed out the lower display and dialed in the sonar computer-screened data, the computer looking for preset characteristics, filtering the ocean's noise through the system's knowledge of what the American submarines sounded like. The raw data coming in from the sea was voluminous and random, but a man-made ship made pure tones, tonals and specific transient rattles. Bangs and flow noises and squeaks. The computer could be used to filter out the meaningless clutter of the seas and look only for noises that matched pure tonals, the regularity of a screw thrashing through the seas, the noise of a hatch slamming, a sewage pump putting water overboard, a torpedo tube flooding. The Two class' Second Captain combat control system had catalogued over ten to the fifth transient and tonal noises, and although that sounded like a lot it was a thousandth of a percent of the random noise of the sea.

With the Second Captain on the case, *Winged Serpent* could not fail. It would be, Tanaka thought, as if he were a Wild West gunman going up against blind men.

**ALEUTIAN TRENCH, BOUNDARY OF THE BERING SEA AND THE PACIFIC OCEAN**
**USS *Piranha***

Bruce Phillips leaned the captain's chair far back in the dark of the wardroom, the large-screen flat panel displaying a classic Arnold Schwarzenegger movie, the bulging muscles of the protagonist exposed, tensing as his arm lifted a hefty weapon and he began firing a machine gun into a crowded city street. Phillips shoved a handful of popcorn in his mouth, listening to the comments of his wardroom as the bullets flew. The phone rang from the conn. Phillips pointed the remote at the flat panel and the action froze, plunging the room into silence.

"Mindless violence," Phillips muttered in mock disgust as he hoisted the phone to his ear. "Captain."

"Off'sa'deck, sir. We're leaving the Aleutian Trench now, sir. We're officially in the Pacific."

Phillips looked over at the speed indicator, the readout showing forty-three knots, the deck vibrating slightly from the turbulence of the seawater flow over the Vortex tubes, particularly since the ship's hydrodynamics had become uneven with the loss of the number-one Vortex unit.

"How long to go at flank?"

"Arrival in the northern quadrant of the OpArea is slated for thirty hours from now, sir."

It wasn't good enough, Phillips thought.

"Put this on the status board and pass it on to your relief, Mr. Porter—we won't be coming to periscope depth until just before we penetrate the OpArea. And I want us running at flank until then, to hell with navigation errors. In fact, put that in the ship's deck log, that I ordered us to blow off going to PD until we're at the forty-fourth parallel. That gives us forty-three knots all the way. What's that do to the time?"

"Takes it down to about twenty-six hours, Captain."

Still not good enough.

"Off'sa'deck, send the engineer to the wardroom." He hung up the phone, clicked the remote and the bullets continued to fly onscreen. He watched a few moments until he saw Walt Hornick's head appear at the round red window to the centerline passageway, then got up and walked out into the brightness of the passageway.

"I'll buy you a cup of coffee, Eng," Phillips said, walking the engineer across the passageway to the opening to the crew's mess. He poured the engineer a cup of fresh steaming coffee, a glass of bright red Kool-Aid for himself, the mixture so sweet he had to wince to choke it down. He steered Hornick to a dinette table in the far corner, pulled out two cigars, one for Hornick, one for himself. He noticed the engineer didn't flinch this time as Phillips stuffed the stogie into his mouth and lit the end.

"Well, Eng, before we get into this I want to ask you a question."

"Yessir."

"Have I ever meddled with your department? Micromanaged you? Given you rudder orders?"

"No, sir." Hornick seemed confused.

"But I have given you goals to achieve, right? I've

told you the big picture of what I've wanted and left it to you to get it done, right?"

"Yessir."

"How do you feel about that, Eng?"

"How do I *feel* about it, sir?"

"Yeah. How does that feel? I'm assuming you haven't been treated like that before."

"You're right, Skipper, I haven't. Captain Forbes before you was the ship's real engineer. I just took orders from him and tried to satisfy him. He was never satisfied. I had a letter of resignation written, I was going to resign my commission and go into business with my father-in-law but Forbes left before I could submit it."

"Where's the letter now?" Phillips puffed and looked at the smoke drifting into the overhead.

"I tore it up after we did that emergency startup of the reactor, Skipper."

Phillips looked at Walt Hornick, the slightest hint of a smirk on his face.

"So how do you feel about this patrol?"

"I'm fully committed to the ship's mission."

"And how does your engineering plant relate to that mission, Eng?"

"Sir, we're a steam-making service. You want RPM, we're in business to give it to you."

"Then I want to tell you about a problem I have." Phillips withdrew his WritePad computer from his shirt pocket and put it on the surface of the dinette table's checkered oilskin tablecloth. He clicked into the software, finally displaying a small chart of the northwest Pacific, looking down on the earth as if from low orbit. "This is our position." A small dot pulsed brightly east of the Kamchatka peninsula. "This is where we need to get to, here east of Hokkaido Island at latitude forty-four north. By the book that's thirty hours away. I did my part by ignoring the regs to come to periscope depth every eight hours, so for the next twenty-six hours I'll continue deep. I'm only allowed to ignore the PD requirements if I'm under the icecap. But I'm willing to risk the creeping nav errors in the inertial system to get there faster. It might be a stupid decision—it's deep out here, but I could still hit a submerged peak at the Kuril Island Ridge as we cross the fiftieth parallel. But here's the situation, Eng, I won't lie to you. Admiral Pacino's going into the OpArea with just a couple of submarines and he's going to try to duke it out with the whole Maritime Self Defense Force's Destinys."

"You know that for a *fact,* sir?"

"We got an intel brief at the last periscope depth. Pacino called for our position and everyone else's and ordered the initial task force of subs into the OpArea. Only seven ships, not counting the *Pasadena* in the Sea of Japan. Which means he needs some serious help."

"Wow."

"Which means I need to deliver *Piranha* into the OpArea now, not twenty-six hours from now. So, do you have any . . . recommendations, Eng?"

Hornick had come a long way since Phillips had arrived at Electric Boat. He smiled slightly, his eyes slits against the smoke of his cigar clenched between his teeth.

"As a matter of fact I've been working up something for you, Skipper. I think I can do better than the forty-three knots we're doing now. We're seeing a lot of drag from the Vortex tubes out there in the potential flow field around the hull. But we have a hell of a lot of unused reactor power. I did some research into the design calculations of the power train, from the propulsor to the thrust bearing through the reduction gears to the main engine rotors and casing, including the journal bearings. I followed the design upstream through the steam headers to the steam generators, and back the other way through the condensate system, looking at pumps and maximum flow rates. The steam generators' ability to put out dry steam at rates greater than designed was catalogued in the files, and I took it back into the main coolant loop to the core, looked at core metal temperatures and control rod binding at this age in core life."

Phillips hadn't the slightest idea what Hornick was talking about. He had just asked him what time it was, and Hornick was building him a watch.

"And?"

"And, sir, I found out that the power plant is designed for conditions at the end of its life, thirty years from now, when the core is full of fission-product poisons, the metal is neutron embrittled, the steam pipes have some slight stress corrosion cracks, the condensers have tube leaks, the feed pumps have seal leaks, the main coolant piping is slightly clogged with corrosion products, the steam generators have lost 5 percent of their tubes and the generator's chevron moisture traps are eroded and half gone. So that running the ship at 100 percent reactor power will be safe thirty years from now, the designers limited us up front."

"So, are you saying you have some kind of, what? Hidden reserves of power?"

"Sir, by my calculations we could take the core to 200 percent power with some modifications authorized by you."

"Like what?"

"I can run in battle-short mode long enough to reset the trip points for the nuclear instruments. That way the plant won't trip out until it sees 230 percent power. We'll be raising average coolant temperatures to get better power from the steam, which isn't all that safe but it will work. Also, I'll have to restrict access to the aft compartment, we'll have much higher radiation readings."

"Will we have permanent damage to the core?"

"Yes, sir," Hornick said as if it were obvious. "We'll have some slight fuel-to-coolant leaks, fuel-element failures, and main coolant radioactivity will escalate by a factor of ten to twenty. You won't be able to walk through the tunnel without your hair standing on end. And when this mission is over we'll have to shitcan the reactor and decontaminate the entire reactor compartment and every piping system inside it. Other than that, nothing should break. We'll be able to double thermal power going to the turbines."

"How does all that relate to velocity?"

"Well, sir, doubling shaft horsepower won't double ship speed. With parasitic drag, to double velocity would require you to quadruple your power. So by doubling power we'll only have 41 percent more speed. That's about sixty-one knots."

"You're kidding me, Eng."

"We won't know till I crank it, sir, but hell, I say go for it."

"Admiral Rickover will spin in his grave." The father of the nuclear navy, Phillips knew, was such a stickler for reactor safety that he would probably haunt the ship.

"Sir, his tomb was empty three days after he died."

Phillips laughed. "Okay, Eng. What the hell order do I give you to make all this happen?"

"Well, why don't you say, 'Engineer, elevate reactor limits to 200 percent.' Then, when you're ready to give it the gas, order the helm to go to emergency flank."

Phillips gave the order, Hornick vanished aft, still puffing on the cigar. Phillips walked into control, briefing the OOD on what the engineer would be up to.

As the ship accelerated to emergency flank, the velocity indicator passing forty-five, then fifty, fifty-five knots, on to 59.8, slowly increasing to sixty, topping out at 60.6 knots, the deck shook steadily. Everywhere that Phillips walked, the ship trembled, the vibration irritating but then, who cared as long as the ship could make the speed? He peered over the chart flat panel and calculated the time to the OpArea. With their newfound speed they would be in the OpArea in slightly over eighteen hours.

Hornick showed up on the conn, the deck still trembling.

"Anything you can do about the vibration, Eng?" Phillips asked.

"Sorry, sir. I made sure it wasn't the thrust bearing or the drive train. I think the shaking is from the Vortex missiles. Some kind of turbulence from hauling them through the water at the speed of a torpedo. Plus we're unbalanced with the first one gone."

"Think the shaking will hurt the ship?"

"The electronics should handle it," Hornick said. "It's the crew I worry about. Bad for crew fatigue."

"THIS IS THE CAPTAIN," Phillips said into the circuit one microphone, his voice booming through the ship. "WE ARE RUNNING FOR THE OPAREA AT EMERGENCY FLANK. YOU'LL ALL BE HAPPY TO KNOW WE'RE BREAKING A US SUB-

MERGED SPEED RECORD AT OVER SIXTY KNOTS. THAT IS WHAT IS RESPONSIBLE FOR THE DECK VIBRATIONS, WHICH COULD LEAD TO CREW FATIGUE. FOR THE NEXT EIGHTEEN HOURS ALL OFF-WATCH PERSONNEL ARE ORDERED TO THEIR RACKS. GET SOME SLEEP, GENTLEMEN. ONCE WE'RE IN THE OPAREA THERE WON'T BE MUCH SLEEP FOR ANY OF US."

Phillips clicked off, looked at Hornick, then at his watch.

"Eng, I think I'm going to follow my own advice."

"Aye, sir. I'll be aft. I want to make sure the protection circuitry modifications go down okay."

Phillips was asleep within thirty seconds of hitting his pillow.

**NORTHWEST PACIFIC**
**SOUTH OF SHIKOKU ISLAND**
**SS-810 *Winged Serpent***

Tanaka walked into the crew messroom. All fourteen junior officers and Hiro Mazdai were now present. In a corner of the room the Second Captain displays rotated through the navigation, sensor, ship control and weapons-status panels. There was no one in the control room during the briefing—the Second Captain had complete control. While they were in the waters where Tanaka expected to see contact with the enemy submarines, he would need to brief his officers, and the sooner the better.

The officers stood at attention as he walked into the oblong room, its central feature the long narrow conference table. Tanaka waved the men to their seats and poured himself a cup of tea, then sat at the head of the table, consulted the notes on his personal computer pad, looked up.

"Officers, I will be brief. Item one—the history to date. The Three-class ships sent into the deep Pacific have experienced success. The surface-action groups being sent here have been attacked successfully. Three aircraft carriers and their associated ships have been put on the bottom. I believe few of the Destiny III submarines survived the encounters, the escort submarines are assumed to have sunk them. So at this point we have only Two-class submarines to defend the waters of the Home Islands.

"Item two—our history of encounters with the American attack submarines. The information received to date shows that the only submerged encounter between a Two-class ship and an American submarine was our own attack of the vessel that torpedoed the supertanker. Either the Americans are at a severe disadvantage or that ship was poorly trained. For now I want to remind each one of you that our success against the first American could have been more from luck or a bad day for the Americans than our own skill or ship quieting. So we will maintain absolute ship silence in our future encounters, and whenever we detect an American we will assume he has detected us.

"Item three—the collected intelligence about American intentions. Mr. First will post the electronic chart display. We believe that the Americans will enter our close-in waters in pairs or threes. These are known as wolfpacks, although we may think of them as being more like frightened teenagers pairing up before going into a dark forest. This will prove most helpful to our tactics, because we will be more efficient at killing them. They will be clustered, so once we detect a pair we will shoot torpedoes at them both, putting down two with the work of sinking one. In addition we will know that all submerged contacts we see will be hostile, while the American commanders must keep in mind that another friendly submarine is nearby, which will make them hesitate when they launch their torpedoes. We believe they will split their force between north and south of our waters and work their way to Tokyo Bay in their attempt to sink our force. Then they could go up Tokyo Bay and cause some damage, making their position much stronger. We will concentrate on preventing that.

"I expect that their forces will arrive in two waves, one now, the second in three days as more of the Pacific hips arrive in zone. Our tactics will be to try to sink he initial task force, reload torpedoes, then rescour the one for Americans. My intuition on this matter is, I elieve, sound since I have spent more time in the vicinty of the *gaijin* than anyone here.

"That is all, men. If any one of you has questions, ubmit them to Mr. First and he will bring them to me."

Tanaka left the room, his officers coming to rigid atention as he left. Mazdai hated that he was cold with he younger officers, Tanaka thought, but their genea-ion was, he felt, soft, compromising. Perhaps he could et through to them by example. Perhaps his hatred of he Americans would be contagious.

Regardless, he was determined that the mission ucceed.

# CHAPTER 30

**NORTHWEST PACIFIC**
**TWENTY MILES SOUTHEAST OF**
**POINT MUROTO-ZAKI, SHIKOKU ISLAND**
**USS *Birmingham* SSN-695**

Comdr. Robert Pastor had rigged the ship for ultraquiet three hours before crossing into the Japan OpArea. The rig was designed to maximize ship quieting so that the sonar system could more easily hear into the sea without the interference of noise made by the *Birmingham* herself. Pastor walked through the ship from the shaft seals as far aft as a man could go to the goat locker forward checking the rig, and found the wrong reactor circulation pumps running—the engineering officer of the watch had one, two, three and four on, when the pump combination three, four, five and six was much quieter. Forward, in one of the crew-berthing spaces, he had found a boombox going, the volume down but music pouring out of it anyway. One of the navigation technicians was trying to fix a spare electronic cabinet in the nav space aft of control, which Pastor immediately stopped, the crew prohibited from doing maintenance during the rig for ultraquiet.

Pastor, on sneaker-clad feet, was of medium height, slightly paunchy but with Midwestern good looks, a healthy hairline, a thick mustache, blue eyes clear and penetrating. His expression rarely changed from a glare or a smirk, the glare normal, the smirk a sign of approval. Pastor had been in command for only a year and was still finding himself, his command style, but so far the ratings were good. He had passed Admiral Pacino's attack-trainer test, having put an Akula Russian submarine on the bottom at the same time he was under attack by a destroyer unit of the Royal Navy—in Pacino's wild scenarios *anyone* could be the bad guys. Pastor was considered a tough captain, a disciplinarian, a by-the-book man so long as it made sense to go by the book. He was good to his officers, took them out for dinners, which came out of his pocket at a thousand dollars a shot, until Admiral Pacino ordered him to put those expenses on the ship's account, telling him they were rewards for good performance. When Pastor had said that the men brought wives and girlfriends, Pacino had told him it was the least the captain could do for them in exchange for all their long hours and weeks away.

Pastor had been thinking lately about what he would do when his command tour was over, something that every nuclear sub skipper asked himself. Command of an attack sub was the end of sea duty. The day they turned command of the sub over to someone else was a dark day in the lives of most skippers, not unlike giving a daughter away at a wedding. They would be proud to have done a job well, the ship, like the daughter, an accomplishment, but now someone else would be in charge of her. Pastor saw nothing that interested him after command, not in the Navy's bureaucratic quagmire in Washington, not in the shore-training commands, not in the surface navy. A new program had been commissioned to allow sub skippers to take command of a deep-draft oiler or supply ship as a stepping stone to commanding an aircraft carrier, from which a man could make flag rank. But that would take another fifteen years of going to sea on surface ships. Besides, Pastor now had two lovely daughters, six and eight, growing up in a world that was becoming more bizarre by the minute, and Pastor was beginning to think that all the sea duty, all the time away from home was beginning to affect the girls.

Pastor shook his head and brought himself back to the supervision of the ship's rig for ultraquiet. As he walked the ship he switched lights in the spaces from bright white to red—the red lights kept awareness for the rig foremost in the crew's minds.

In the goat locker, the chief's quarters, he found a grizzled, veteran chief taking a shower. He felt like killing the man. The rig specifically prohibited showers, laundry and cooking, all of which made unnecessary noise. It didn't matter how hot and sweaty the men got, the rig was the rig. Pastor chewed the chief out as quietly as he could, then continued on his rounds.

He returned to the control room. "Weapon status," Pastor asked the young officer of the deck, an academy grad named Mark Strait, who was the sonar officer.

"Sir, we've got all four tubes loaded. One and two are flooded with outer doors opened, torpedo power applied and units warmed. Units in three and four have been powered down from before. We'll shift in another hour."

The maximum readiness rig specified open tubes, weapons powered up with their gyros spinning, ready to fire at any time. That way if Pastor found a target they could program the torpedo in seconds and launch. The only trouble was that the torpedoes could not remain powered up for more than an hour at a time or the gyros would overheat, and sometimes in the middle of tracking a target the outer doors would have to be shut, the weapons powered down, the alternate tubes opened to sea and their torpedoes spun up. The operation could take ten or fifteen minutes, which meant that long without the ability to shoot at the target.

Pastor leaned over the central firecontrol display, the one known as position two, selecting it to line-of-sight mode. The way he figured it, he would have all of one minute to identify the target, put its bearing into firecontrol, set the bearing and assumed range into the torpedo, and fire before the target knew he was there. Maybe less. *Birmingham* was not a new boat, and the newer Improved 688-class ships were much quieter, but then if Pastor felt his ship shouldn't be here in the OpArea, ready for combat, he wouldn't be in command of her. Admiral Pacino would replace him with someone willing to take the risk and fight.

Pastor looked over at pos one, the console furthest forward, selected it to geographic plot mode, a God's-eye view of the sea, showing the coastline of Japan, their wolfpack partner ahead and to the east, the USS *Jacksonville,* the two submarines steaming on a parallel course up the coastline searching for Destiny submarines. The *Jacksonville* was the same vintage as the *Birmingham,* both at the tail end of their service lives. Pastor stepped to pos three, the third console aft, and selected it to line-of-sight mode with the target selected as the *Jacksonville,* just so that he could see where *not* to put a torpedo in case things got confused. That done, the firecontrol system was as good as it was going to get with no hostile contacts.

Satisfied with the status of the control room, Pastor moved on into the sonar room through the forward starboard door of control. Sonar was lit with blue fluorescents, its screens multicolored displays, the room's light ghostly after the red of the control room. In charge of sonar was Petty Officer Hazelton, a skinny curly-haired farm boy from Iowa who loved to torture city kids with stories of butchering pigs at pig roasts, his stories of behind-the-barn sexual encounters equally lurid. In spite of his youth and odd interests, Hazelton knew the sonar suite. And Pastor, a sub captain who believed that sonar was the center of the submerged universe, knew more sonar acoustic physics and equipment knobology than many chiefs.

"Permission to take a console," Pastor asked Hazelton, the formality in reference to the fact that Hazelton was in charge in sonar, and even the ship's commanding officer needed to ensure that taking a console would not interfere with the sonar search. Hazelton replied in the affirmative, handing Pastor a headset. Pastor strapped it on, adjusted the microphone and looked down on his dual-screen console display.

The upper screen was selected to the waterfall display of short- and medium-time broadband noise. It was a way of "seeing" what the ship's spherical array heard, but with this display the user could listen to all directions at once and look back in time to compare this second's noise with last second's, this minute's noises with the minute before. A noise was shown with a spot of light, the brightness in proportion to the strength of the sound. As time went on, the noise heard at that instant moved down the screen to be replaced by new display traces, the noises falling down, a noise of a ship drawing a vertical line down the waterfall of the random-noise display.

The lower screen was a number of graphs, the vertical axis of each graph sound intensity, the horizontal axis the frequency. The ship was searching for specific tones put out by the Destiny II-class, the intelligence tipping them off to search for a signature around 150 hertz, most probably generated by the ship's turbine generators.

Pastor slouched deep into the leather of the seat and listened to the various traces down the display, investigating each one for a man-made sound, selecting a narrowband processor on the traces he couldn't confirm as biologics, as fish. He trained the cursor to the bearing of the *Jacksonville,* the trace very slight on the waterfall display. He could just make out her screw turning if he concentrated on it. The *Jacksonville* would be more detectable on narrowband, but as long as he knew she was there, there was no sense wasting narrowband processing time on the friendly sub.

Whenever Pastor operated a sonar console he thought about his family. He wasn't quite sure why, except that perhaps it was that the sounds of the ocean sounded like his wife's stomach when she was pregnant, the lazy Friday nights spent with him lying with his head in her full lap, her perfume caressing him, the sounds of her abdomen soothing him, the occasional kick of the baby pressing against his ear. The first child had almost killed Carol, the emergency C-section taking place at the last minute, the surgeon losing Carol's heartbeat, spending endless minutes trying to revive her. Pastor had stood in the operating room, wearing his scrubs, open-mouthed behind the surgical mask as they carted away his newborn baby daughter from the room, the baby's mother clinically dead. Over and over they tried to start her heart but all they could see was the flat line of the heart monitor. Pastor, trained to handle pressure, had not been up to seeing his wife lying there dead, her abdomen cut open. Finally a nurse realized he wasn't part of the team and had ushered him out of the room, and it was like he had been drinking all night—his memory trace just stopped. He never lost consciousness but it was almost as if the mental pain had been too much for him. He came to an hour later in a waiting room outside intensive care. He stood, as if lost, and asked about his wife. At first the nurse looked at him blankly, then waved him to a room. Carol's face was as hollow-eyed as a corpse, her skin as white, her hair wild, but when she opened her eyes and looked at him she had never seemed more beautiful to him. He had hugged her as hard as he felt she could handle, tears of relief coming from his eyes, shaking as he felt her hand patting his back. She had said only two words—"the baby?"—and Pastor had stood upright, at a loss. He had never asked about the child, and had kissed Carol's cheek and said the baby was fine. He practically ran from the room to see the child, a normal and healthy seven-pound girl, short brown hair curled around her sleepy eyes. The baby accounted for, Pastor hurried back to Carol, but she was out cold and would not wake up for a day and a half, and when she did she remembered nothing, not even asking him about the child.

After that episode with tiny Adrianne, Pastor was unwilling to try again, but she had insisted, and two years later he had sweated out another pregnancy with Carol, this time twins. But that pregnancy had gone sour, too, one of the twins dying in utero, requiring them to induce labor, endangering the life of the healthy fetus. The living newborn was ten weeks premature, tiny, struggling for life. Carol had trouble coping, the dead twin constantly on her mind. As Darlene grew up, her name given her before birth, Carol insisted she saw an apparition of the dead twin Danielle. It had been a tough year, the first after Darlene was born, but that was five years ago, and it had been over a year since Carol had seen the apparition of Danielle playing with her living twin. Pastor had wanted Carol to get psychiatric help but she wouldn't hear of it. At least things were calming now, Pastor thought.

He moved the sonar electronic cursor over to a new trace and listened hard. The groan of a whale could be heard in the distance, the sound eerie, surreal, echoing through the depths of the sea. Pastor continued his search, wondering if they would ever detect anything in the OpArea. The size of this chunk of ocean was huge in square miles, an area the size of California and Nevada combined, and so far there had been exactly nothing. The officer of the deck in the control room turned the ship in a baffle-clearing maneuver to train the spherical array on the ocean that had been astern of them, in the blind spot behind the screw, although Pastor had ordered them to "drag the onion," deploy the teardrop-shaped AN/T-47 caboose array that was designed to look aft, but he agreed with the OOD's decision since the caboose was crude and small, only a supplement to occasionally turning the ship to see behind them. But for ten minutes after the turn there was still nothing. The OOD returned to base course and followed the coastline to the northeast.

The sea was absolutely empty. Aside from the *Jacksonville,* there was no one there.

**NORTHWEST PACIFIC**
**EIGHTY KILOMETERS SOUTHEAST OF**
**POINT MUROTO-ZAKI, SHIKOKU ISLAND**
**SS-810 *Winged Serpent***

Tanaka joined the watchstanders in the control room after viewing the scenario develop on the Second Captain, the sounds of the two American submarines on the sonar sets for the last twenty minutes. Hiro Mazdai had been frantic, asking Tanaka to call battlestations immediately and fire four Nagasaki torpedoes at the contacts. Tanaka looked at him, knowing the Americans were nearly blind. He had insisted to the officers that they treat the Americans with caution, and caution might seem to dictate that the enemy submarines be fired at immediately upon detection ten kilometers before. But to Tanaka the height of fear was not equivalent to caution. Firing Nagasakis blindly was foolish and had no meaning. He wanted to sneak up on the Americans, determine their range, speed and course precisely, then put the four Nagasakis out, two per submarine, when he knew exactly where in the ocean the enemy subs were. *That* was caution.

He also refused to man battlestations. That just made noise and put the crew in a trigger-happy mood. They needed to be able to fight a prolonged war from their normal steaming watch sections, he insisted. They were panicky now with the first American in their sights, but there would be more, many more, perhaps another dozen or two dozen, and Tanaka would train the officers to consider this almost routine. Precise, controlled, cautious, planned, and routine. This was a time for the mind, not the stomach, he told Mazdai.

The conning officer, Lieutenant Commander Kami, had driven the ship slowly closer, keeping his eye open for a maneuver by the Americans. Not that he was concerned if the American submarines fired at him. Their torpedoes were of little consequence. The Destiny II class had a computer-controlled SCM sonar system in the bow and the stern. The SCM, sonar countermeasures, was an electronic ventriloquist that could confuse any American torpedo. When the torpedo pinged a sonar pulse at them the SCM ventriloquist sonar would hear it, electronically modify it and send out a return pulse precisely shifted in frequency, distorted and sent early, all arranged to arrive so as to confuse the pinging sonar system. Any incoming torpedo that encountered their SCM system would turn in circles, as confused as a blind sheepdog, or blow up in the middle of the sea. And even if one of their inferior torpedoes did close range in spite of the SCM system, the Two class could take a hit of that size and not sink. It would take several direct hits to put a Two class, with its double hull, down for good. A single direct hit would be an inconvenience, perhaps even shut down the Second Captain for a few scary moments, but beyond that there was little to fear from the Americans.

Finally it was time to attack. The ship was in position, the targets' locations and speeds and courses absolutely known to the Second Captain, the Nagasaki torpedoes warm and ready to fire. Tanaka considered giving the order to fire from his stateroom but rejected the idea. He put on his uniform tunic, buttoned the high collar, straightened his hair and proceeded to the control room.

The eyes of the men met his, and to his disgust they all showed fear. Even Mazdai seemed nervous.

"Mr. First," Tanaka said, "launch Nagasaki torpedoes one and two at the southwestern American, torpedoes three and four at the American bearing west, presets as indicated in the Second Captain."

"Aye, Captain," Mazdai said, looking grateful to finally be doing something.

The torpedoes were away.

Tanaka did not stay to monitor their progress. He walked back along the central passageway to his stateroom and sat down at the Second Captain console to watch the torpedoes as they sped to the targets. He selected the upper display to the sonar-detection system, already forgetting about these first two Americans, concentrating instead on finding the next American boats.

**USS *Birmingham***

Pastor was still on the sonar console when the trace showed up on the screen. He placed the electronic cursor on it and listened. It was definitely man-made, a tremendous whooshing noise.

"We've got something here," he told Hazelton. The sonar tech put his cursor on it.

Pastor noted that the trace diverged into two, then three, finally four. Two of the traces moved across the screen as they were going quickly across *Birmingham*'s bow. The other remained at a constant bearing.

Hazelton clicked his boom microphone to the control-speaker circuit. "Conn, Sonar, torpedo in the water, bearing zero seven zero! I say again, torpedo in the water—"

Pastor threw his headset down and ran through the door to control, where he found the officer of the deck standing on the conn with his hand in his pocket and his mouth open, paralyzed by what the instructors at Prospective Commanding Officer school referred to as the "aw shit factor." It wasn't that Strait was panicking, his mind was simply overwhelmed, overloaded with data. He had to take in the notion of the incoming torpedo before he could react to it, and this was so far outside his experience level that it could take up to three seconds for him to process the information.

Pastor had no such time lag. He was full of adrenaline as he went to the conn. "All ahead flank! Maneuvering cavitate! Right fifteen degrees rudder, steady course two five zero! Dive, make your depth one thousand feet! Ready the Mark 21 countermeasure in the aft signal ejector! Load the forward signal ejector with SLOT buoy marked 'code 3.' "

For the next thirty seconds Pastor kicked his crew, getting them over the shock, getting them *moving.*

Thirty seconds after that there was no more to do. He had bumped reactor power to 100 percent at flank speed, he had dived deeper to 1000 feet to keep the screw from boiling up sheets of bubbles that would add to their noise signature, he had launched a countermeasure that simulated the sounds of the ship and he had turned and run from the torpedo. All that was left was to launch the signal ejector's radio buoy that would notify Admiral Pacino they were under attack. He hesitated, knowing that to launch the radio buoy was an admission of defeat, that that could be the last thing anyone would ever hear from the USS *Birmingham.*

"Launch the SLOT buoy in the forward signal ejector."

"Launch forward signal ejector, aye, sir," Strait said, punching the red mushroom button, the radio buoy now away.

Pastor leaned over the pos-two display; the junior officer of the deck was trying to rig a solution to the firing submarine, assuming it had fired from the bearing that the torpedo was first detected. But when that assumed solution was compared to the bearing to the *Jacksonville* set up on pos three, any torpedo *Birmingham* fired at the enemy would pass right by *Jacksonville* first. Pastor was not about to give up trying. Just because the firing Destiny submarine was on the other side of *Jacksonville* did not mean that he couldn't fire. It just meant that the torpedo would need to remain in transit mode until it was on the other side of the friendly submarine. There was a problem—his knowledge of the position of the *Jacksonville* was based on her preattack position. Just as he had maneuvered *Birmingham* in response to the torpedo, he knew Jack Stolz would be maneuvering *Jacksonville* to get away from the torpedoes launched at her from the Destiny. That was what those other two contacts had been. Still, he might be able to get a solution on the *Jacksonville* and avoid putting a torpedo in her.

He set up pos three in dot-stacked mode, all the while dimly aware of his crew filing into the room for battlestations, the immediate action they took when a torpedo in the water was called. Someone handed Pastor a headset. He put it on, still adjusting the knobs on pos three, anchoring *Jacksonville*'s position at the time it zigged, maneuvered away from the torpedo. There was a minute or two of data that was garbage since that was during the time that *Birmingham* was also maneuvering. Sweat poured off Pastor's face and dripped onto the console. He wiped it away, concentrating as hard as he ever had in his life on the firecontrol display in front of him, trying to visualize the sea above, the location of the hostile sub, its position relative to the *Jacksonville,* where *Jacksonville* would turn after the torpedo was fired at her.

The tactical problem was turning into a nightmare, and suddenly it began to matter less when the sounds of the torpedo sonar pulse cut into the control room, the sonar noise as loud as a referee's whistle blown a foot from his ear, the sound piercing and painful. It kept up, a short blast every fifteen seconds, each one closer. Pastor sweated over the solution to the *Jacksonville,* finally felt comfortable with it. He glanced down at the pos-two screen, the assumed solution to the firing ship based on the bearing to the incoming torpedo, then compared that with the solution to the *Jacksonville*.

"Snapshot tube one," Pastor called. "Alter presets to set in a ten-thousand-yard run to avoid homing on the *Jacksonville*."

Pastor waited. At least he was going to get a shot off at this bastard. The pinging of the torpedo blasted into the room, getting closer with each ping, until he could hear the screw noise of the incoming torpedo.

"Weapon ready, sir," the weapons officer shouted over the latest ping.

"Fire," Pastor ordered. He realized that he hadn't heard a ping in the last few seconds, only the sound of the torpedo's screw noise. He watched as the weapons officer rotated the trigger to the standby position.

Still no ping from the torpedo. A moment of hope. It would be too good to be true, he thought, getting to counterfire at the Destiny and having the Destiny's torpedo be a dud.

As the weapons officer pulled the trigger to the fire position, Pastor abruptly realized it was Christmas Day and his children on the other side of the world would be awake, opening their presents. The sound of the torpedo-ejection mechanism blasted into his eardrums as the torpedo in tube one was launched, the *Birmingham*'s answer to the Destiny's Nagasaki weapon.

"Merry Christmas, Destiny," Pastor said, as another booming crash hit his eardrums.

The second noise was the sound of the first Nagasaki torpedo detonating on the top surface of the hull, the explosion ripping down from aft of the sail, blowing a hole in the hull big enough to drive an eighteen-wheel truck into the ship. The hull rupture was located just aft of control, and the ripping metal and wave of water, the pressure of it enough to cut a man in half at that depth, slammed into Pastor and sent his body hurtling forward to the bulkhead at the ship-control panel, ripping his flesh and bone. The force of the water blasting into the hull at a thousand feet beneath the surface was enough to bend the hull to a thirty-degree angle, not quite enough to break it in half.

The second, redundant Nagasaki hit them, and this explosion did fracture the hull already weakened by the first detonation, the aft end of the ship separating, both hull fragments drifting to the ocean bottom 2000 feet farther down. The hulls hit the rocky bottom, groaning and creaking and breaking apart still further, littering the bottom with broken pipes and tanks and pieces of equipment. There were no recognizable bodies.

Seven miles to the northeast another hull hit the rocky bottom and disintegrated, two of its weapons detonating as it hit the bottom. The USS *Jacksonville* had arrived at its final resting place.

Three thousand feet above the remains of the *Birmingham,* the SLOT buoy reached the surface, extended a whip antenna and transmitted *Birmingham*'s last message to the US Navy ComStar satellite, then flooded and sank, coming to rest near the screw of the ship. Several hours later, when the bubbles had died down and the reactor metal had cooled, the ocean bottom was, once again, quiet.

# CHAPTER 31

**NORTHWEST PACIFIC**
**120 KILOMETERS SOUTHEAST OF**
**POINT MUROTO-ZAKI, SHIKOKU ISLAND**
**SS-810 *Winged Serpent***

The buzz of the phone rang in Tanaka's stateroom. It was Mazdai in the control room.

"Sir, the torpedo fired from the first target went far off course and just shut down. It seems to be sinking and imploding now. The threat is gone."

There never had been a real threat, Tanaka thought, concentrating on his sonar screen, looking for the next contact.

He had put the phone down and continued looking at the display, his aggression seeming to fuel him. He wasn't hungry or thirsty. He wanted blood, the Americans' blood. He stared at the console a full five hours before the next contacts came, another two American ships, both of them 688-class ships as the first two had been.

An hour after that Tanaka had made a second quick trip to the control room, four more Nagasakis had been launched and two more hulls were wreckage at the bottom of the sea. Tanaka then called one of his officers to paint small American flags on the bulkhead in the control room to show the sinkings they had made. With the sinking of the first ship in the Sea of Japan, this now made five flags for the officer to paint. Five ships. Perhaps another two dozen to go before Tanaka could rest. The ship carried only twenty-one weapons. He had launched ten. It was time to stop doubling up. He had been launching two weapons at each target to insure that if one failed, the other would score a kill. But now with the success rate this high, and the use of torpedoes this swift, he would only launch one per target. Which gave him eleven more targets.

The *Winged Serpent* continued northwest, hunting.

### Northwest Pacific
### USS *Barracuda*

The afternoon watch on Christmas Day passed without incident. The ship had been at periscope depth for most of the day. The men were happy; they had received their familygrams, transmitted by USubCom headquarters, each man aboard allowed one short transmission from his wife or kids or girlfriend or parents.

Pacino's familygram had come in from Tony on the WritePad. The youngster was almost a teenager, twelve years old, missing his father, but then, Pacino being away had been almost normal. All the sea duty had kept him away from the boy for too long. And now, nearing the end of his naval career, Janice had left him and taken Tony with her. The familygram from Tony was brief and gut-wrenching. Pacino put it down on the fold-out desk, staring off into space, missing his son, missing his old life, wanting to toss the football with Tony, race against him in the Go Karts, hang out with him at the amusement park, cruise the beach with him in the sports car. All the things they'd done in the past, but hadn't realized would vanish into the past. It had seemed that Tony would always be there, and now he was living somewhere in New Jersey, over 300 miles away from Virginia Beach, which was over 13,000 miles from this Japan OpArea.

The WritePad's annunciator alarm went off, beeping into the quiet of the stateroom. Pacino silenced it before it could wake up Paully, who was asleep in the upper rack, having been awake for more than twenty hours and only agreeing to go to bed when Pacino had ordered him. Pacino knew he should hit the rack himself but couldn't seem to slow down his mind. He stroked the software keys of the WritePad, going deeper into the software until it displayed the E-mail he'd just been beeped for, and realized it was a second familygram, this one from Eileen Constance—

> MICHAEL, JUST WANTED TO WISH YOU LUCK. I CAN'T WAIT TO SEE YOU AGAIN. MERRY CHRISTMAS. LOVE, EILEEN.

He wasn't sure how he felt about it. It seemed like Eileen was going too fast. But so was he. He'd found himself thinking about her, missing her, then trying to dismiss it. It was, he told himself, a physical attraction that had pretended to more in the thick of impending combat. And even if it did build into a relationship, she was so much younger and would be going to medical school in Florida while his HQ was in Norfolk. And what if she wanted children? Wasn't he too old for that? And then he had to laugh at himself for crossing so many bridges before the road was even built.

A knock at the door, a radioman offering Pacino the ship's secure WritePad. He signed for the messages, which were then automatically transferred to his own WritePad. He punched the surface of the notepad's display, read through the first four messages, and his heart sank. From the *Birmingham* in the southwest OpArea, code 3—*I'm under attack*. From the *Jacksonville,* also in the southwest OpArea, code 3. From *Charleston* and *Atlanta,* both farther north in the southwest OpArea, code 3. The southern forces, all four boats, had been attacked. And in all probability were down. Another knock at the door.

The radioman again. Again Pacino signed for the messages, transferred the electronic messages to his own WritePad, then waited for the radioman to leave. The three messages were from the northern task force, the *Buffalo, Boston* and the *Albany.* All code 3s. Pacino rubbed his eyes, knowing what he needed to do, at least in the short term.

A half-hour later he and Paully White were in David Kane's stateroom.

"We need to get the Pearl Harbor ELF facility to call all the OpArea submarines to periscope depth," Pacino said. "I'll write the subs a message for their broadcast, ask them to transmit that they're okay. I'll need your permission to transmit, Captain."

Kane nodded. "Absolutely, Admiral. Need any help with the messages?"

"No. It'll only take a few moments, I'll take them to radio when I'm ready."

A half-hour later the Pearl low-frequency radio facility had transmitted each of the seven submarines' ELF call signs, the powerful but slow radio waves penetrating deep into the Pacific, calling the subs to periscope depth, where Pacino's message waited for them.

Pacino waited an unbearable hour. He had gotten one message back, from the *Piranha,* which was almost at the boundary of the northern OpArea. Pacino stared at that, wondering how the hell Bruce Phillips had gotten south that fast. He reread the latitude and longitude, which correlated with the alphanumeric grid coordinate Phillips transmitted. Phillips said he was definitely close to the northern OpArea. But looking gift horses in the mouth was not Pacino's style.

He showed the results to Paully and Kane, and it was Kane who suggested they call the deep-Pacific boats, still on the way in from Hawaii, to periscope depth and see how they were doing. It took an investment of another ninety minutes, but as midnight neared, Pacino's electronic chart had plotted the positions of the Pacific submarines, the other twenty-one of them. The early wave would be there in another thirty hours. The later wave, the lagging ten boats, would take an additional twenty-five to thirty. Warner's time constraints, however justified, had resulted in the loss of the ships Pacino had sent in as a stopgap.

Back in Kane's stateroom Pacino paced the deck. "What now?"

"Maybe we should request a videolink with Warner," Kane said.

The time that Warner had wanted an update was over twenty hours away.

"And ask what? What we should do? Captain Kane, we've just sent seven subs into the OpArea. Seven subs sank. Or if they didn't, all seven of them mysteriously failed to come to periscope depth when called."

A knock at Kane's door, the radioman again. Pacino perked up, wondering if at least one of the 688-class ships had come to PD and transmitted that they were okay. Pacino signed for the message and searched his WritePad for it, his heart sinking as he scanned it.

He checked his watch, the time nearing midnight Christmas Day.

"It's from Wadsworth. He wants us to set up a video-link," Pacino said, handing the message to Kane.

"When?" Paully asked.

"Now," Pacino said.

Pacino took a deep breath and let it out. He knew what Wadsworth would say, and he also knew what he would do. He spoke for a few minutes, and Paully took off to the control room and picked up a phone to Pacino in Kane's stateroom.

Kane and Pacino sat at the conference table as the radioman set up the videolink. There was no seal of the president this time, just Tony Wadsworth's big face on the screen, his frown deeper than usual.

"Gentlemen," Wadsworth said, "President Warner asked for a status report. We have heard exactly nothing from you, Admiral Pacino. Should I take that as good news?"

"I wouldn't assume that, Admiral," Pacino said, staring hard at Wadsworth, the phone to the conn in his hand under the table.

Forward in the control room, Paully White approached the officer of the deck, Lt. Chris Porter, the sonar officer, who was dancing with the fat lady, spinning the periscope through an endless surface search while the ship stayed at periscope depth to monitor the communications with the other submarines.

"The captain said he wanted you in on the videolink," White said to Porter.

"I can't do that," Porter said. "I've got the watch."

"Skipper asked me to relieve you," White said. "I'm qualified on the Seawolf class."

"You haven't stood any watches since you've been aboard," Porter said.

"That's because the admiral's been running me like a plebe."

"Yeah, that's true."

"Anyway, you'd better give me a turnover and get in there."

"How do I know the skipper wanted this? He didn't call me."

"He's in a videolink with the fuckin' Chief of Naval Operations. He sent me out here. *Okay?*"

"All right, all right. Ship's at all ahead one-third, turns for five, depth eight zero feet, no contacts, low power on the horizon."

"I relieve you. Now go on."

"I stand relieved. Helm, Quartermaster," Porter announced, "Commander White has the deck and the conn."

"This is Commander White, I have the deck and the conn," Paully said loudly, taking the periscope, pressing his face toward it.

Porter moved through the aft door of control, the front of his uniform dark with sweat from the periscope watch. As he entered Kane's stateroom Kane waved him to a seat, intent on the video monitor.

"We called all seven ships to periscope depth," Pacino was saying. "None of them replied."

"And what do you make of that, Admiral Pacino?" Wadsworth's expression was even colder, more hostile, if that were possible.

"Well, sir, I think it's bad news."

*"You're goddamned right, it's bad news!"* Wadsworth

swallowed, glaring. "Pacino, we sent you there to do a job and you botched it. You were to send in your boats to try to make a difference. All you did was lose your entire force. I'll be calling Warner now to tell her the news."

Pacino had been waiting for Wadsworth to take a breath; interrupting on the videolink was nearly impossible because of the lag in reception. Finally he had his chance.

"Maybe we should talk to President Warner right now, Admiral Wadsworth. I think she'll see this for what it is. We knowingly committed a small number of subs to the OpArea when we knew it would be best to mass force against the enemy. We failed to do that, and I mean *we* as in you *and* President Warner and me. Are you reading me, Admiral Wadsworth? What's indicated here is a commitment of the entire submarine force to the task, not sending them in piecemeal."

"Admiral Pacino, are you finished?"

"Yes." Pacino would be damned if he'd call Wadsworth "sir."

"This is a direct order. You're relieved as commander Pacific forces. You are to withdraw your forces immediately, return to base and stand by for—"

Pacino clicked twice on the phone handset to the control room.

In control, Paully White heard the double click in his headset, snapped the periscope grips up, lowered the periscope and shouted, "Emergency deep!"

"Emergency deep, aye, sir!" from the diving officer.

The helmsman took the bowplanes to full dive and put a ten-degree down-bubble on the ship, rang up all ahead standard while the sternplanesman put his planes on full dive. The chief of the watch at the ballast-control panel flooded depth-control one, making the ship hundreds of tons heavier in a half-second. He stabbed a toggle switch, lowering the BIGMOUTH radio antenna and at the same time reached up to the circuit-one microphone.

"EMERGENCY DEEP! EMERGENCY DEEP!"

The depth indicator unwound. The speed increase,

taking the down angle and flooding depth control to make the ship heavier had all combined to take the ship from periscope depth to deep at 200 feet in a few seconds, the maneuver intended to save the ship in the event the conning officer saw a close surface ship bearing down on them when they were at periscope depth.

"All ahead full," White ordered. "Dive, make your depth six hundred fifty feet. Helm, right two degrees rudder, steady course zero three zero."

Soon Porter came back to the conn, looking shaken.

In Kane's stateroom Wadsworth had been talking so fast his mouth was a blur on the screen when the sound of the circuit one rang throughout the ship sounding EMERGENCY DEEP and Wadsworth's eyes grew large just before his image winked out for good. They had left the surface, where their periscope and radio antenna had them plugged into the world of the Pentagon and the Oval Office, and now *Barracuda* was deep, the radio waves gone, on her own. For the moment, anyway.

"Maybe we should call President Warner," Kane said as Paully White came back in.

"You can bet that Wadsworth has already taken care of that," White said.

"So we can assume we're on our own now," Kane said.

"I think that's safe to say," Pacino muttered.

"So what now, Admiral?"

"Now we put *Barracuda* on the case. We'll go north into the OpArea here and see what luck we have against the Destiny class using a Seawolf class and some Mark 50 torpedoes."

"Admiral, those were the same weapons used by the 688s we lost."

"We don't know if they bagged any Destinys though."

"What about *Piranha*? She could be a big help to us."

"She'll be coming in from the northern tip of the OpArea. We're here just to the east of Tokyo Bay. I say we sweep north until we link up with *Piranha*. She'll come south and shoot her way toward us."

"Maybe we should radio the *Piranha* so Brucey Phillips knows what to do," Paully put in.

"I don't think that's a good idea," Kane said. "After the collision with that fishing boat at periscope depth the antennae are out of commission."

"*What* collision?" Paully was mystified until Pacino spoke up.

"The one that made you do the emergency deep, of course. Paully here has had so little sleep that he forgets colliding with that fishing boat . . ."

Paully smiled, catching on.

"So how will *Piranha* know what the deal is?"

"Bruce Phillips will know," Pacino said. "Believe me, he'll know."

"Sir," Kane said, doubt in his voice, "I'm not so sure I'm okay with disobeying an order, even one from the Wadsworthless."

"Kane, listen to me. Wadsworth knows me. He knows I'll disregard that order. If we can put some Japanese subs on the bottom, between us and Bruce Phillips, two Seawolf-class ships, Wadsworth will forget about this order."

Kane said nothing. What the hell could you say to an admiral willing to cut his own throat?

"Okay," Pacino said, clapping his hands. "Now, let's get this bucket of bolts positioned in the OpArea and go to work."

# BOOK FOUR

# *BARRACUDA*

# CHAPTER 32

**NORTHWEST PACIFIC**
**JAPANESE OPAREA, TWENTY MILES EAST OF POINT NOJIMA-ZAKI**
**USS *Barracuda***

"Any activity?" Pacino asked Kane in the control room. Kane was looking up at the sonar display above the pos-two console.

"Nothing."

"They'll turn up."

"Hope so."

"How are the weapons?"

"I've got all eight loaded with Mark 50s. All eight tubes have outer doors open, and the upper four have torpedo power applied. I can get four out within thirty seconds of contact."

"I'd think about warming up at least two more," Pacino said. "If the gyro temps get too high you can always shut them down, but—" He realized he was interfering, doing what he swore to Paully he wouldn't do. "I'll be in my stateroom," he said. Kane watched him leave, then looked over at the officer of the deck, Lt. David Voorheese.

"Warm up the fish in five and six," Kane ordered quietly, looking aft toward Pacino's commandeered stateroom.

**Northwest Pacific**
**Japanese OpArea, Off Point Erimo-misaki,**
**Hokkaido Island**
**USS *Piranha***

Comdr. Bruce Phillips walked into control wearing a multicolored cotton poncho, a dusty flat-brimmed leather cowboy hat, faded tight jeans, cracked and dirty cowhide cowboy boots and a leather gunbelt with two pearl-handled Smith & Wesson revolvers protruding from the poncho. A hand-rolled cigar was clamped between his teeth, the dirt of a week smeared on his hands and unshaved face.

"Sir," Peter Meritson said, looking up at Phillips as he mounted the periscope stand, "your boots are violating the rig for ultraquiet. They're clumping all over the place."

Phillips stopped his pacing and glared down at Meritson, the sonar officer crisply turned out in his pressed blue coveralls, flag patches on the sleeves, his hair perfect, his face a pleasant triangle that the girls went crazy for, his silver double bars and gold dolphin pin gleaming in the light of the control room, his shoes new black cross-trainers.

For a full thirty seconds Phillips stared down hard at the younger man, then blew a smoke ring in Meritson's face. He looked around the control room, the displays humming, the fans muted, the section-tracking team members murmuring to each other softly.

He clumped into the sonar room, the sonar chief set up in the second control seat of the four-console row. He leaned over the chief's shoulder. Master Chief Salvatore Gambini sat at the display, his full headset on, his bifocals poised on the end of his nose. Phillips clapped his hands on Gambini's shoulder. Gambini was an older Sicilian, a full head of gray hair combed back on his scalp, his face open and fatherly, wrinkling into smile lines, his dark eyes the kind that penetrated. If he liked what he saw, his smile lines crinkled. If he didn't, his face might as well have been embalmed.

"How you doin' today, Sal?" Phillips asked. He was not one to call a chief, or an officer for that matter, by his first name, but he had made a connection with Gambini that went beyond any professional relationship. Gambini's file had been rich with detail, perhaps too rich, much of it entered by Admiral Donchez himself. Gambini was too old for the submarine business, having served in attack submarines for a long and distinguished career. He was now fifty-one and technically not physically qualified in submarines. He had had a bad heart attack during shore duty while teaching the kids out of high school the science of sound propagation and the BSY-2 combat-control system's sonar suite. The result had been an emergency quadruple bypass, more than enough to cashier him from the service, except Gambini's mind had been too valuable to lose. He had been assigned to the old Pacific Fleet Submarine Command HQ before the submarine force reorganization, before the Muslim war, serving as the command master chief to ComSubPac, the commander of the Pacific Fleet's submarines, Admiral Donchez. He and Donchez had hit it off, talking over beers in a backstreet bar away from the base. Gambini and his wife Maureen were prominent at SubPac, giving frequent parties at their seaside home. It had been evident that the two of them were one of those rare married couples who were inseparable, two halves of one soul. At one of the Gambini parties Maureen had buttonholed the admiral and whispered in his ear about how much Gambini missed the submarines. Donchez had used his powers, being the bureaucracy's equivalent to a 500-pound gorilla, to reinstate Gambini's submarine qualification. Gambini was entirely too senior to go back to sea, especially in submarines, but the reinstatement meant he could at least ride submarines to help train their sonar crews.

Donchez would move on from SubPac to become the Chief of Naval Operations, and Gambini left HQ to stay home with Maureen when she was diagnosed with brain cancer. The doctors gave her only a few months to live. Gambini's face became hollow, his clothes hung on him. The cancer progressed. Gambini was beside her night and day as she slowly slipped away, finally becoming a different person, no longer able to recognize her husband or their three children. It was a Thursday night when she came out of the coma long enough to look at Gambini, this time with recognition. She had gripped his hands, hard, just before she shut her eyes for the last time. The moment of lucidity had been so brief, so startling and unexpected, and so close to the end, that Gambini had said he wasn't sure if it had really happened, but a nurse in the doorway had also witnessed it.

After her burial Gambini had been lost. He couldn't eat, sleep or work. On the rare occasions when he showed up at HQ he stared into space or put his head on his desk. Donchez's replacement, Admiral Carson, had convinced Gambini to retire. The same year Donchez—then the number one admiral in the navy, the Chief of naval operations—on a trip to Pearl Harbor stopped over to see Gambini. One dinner with the man was enough—Donchez pulled the strings, and Gambini was sent back to sea as a sonarman, a trial assignment to the *Piranha* since the *Piranha* was a new construction ship not expected to spend much time at sea the first year of its commissioning. At first Gambini had been slow to adjust to shipboard life, but it had been a key that unlocked a vital part of himself from his prison of grief. Within four months of the assignment Gambini was back, almost. Weekends and holidays remained black times for the master chief, typically finding him on the ship, but the worst day was the first anniversary of Maureen's death.

When the ship was bumped up in readiness condition by Admiral Pacino, Gambini was supposed to be separated from ship's company and assigned back to Electric Boat. Official Navy orders remained paper, even in the era of electronic communication. They had arrived by courier the week before *Piranha* was to sail for the OpArea.

Comdr. Bruce Phillips had signed for them and promptly fed them into the shredder. *Piranha* sailed with one unauthorized enlisted man, the best sonar tech in the US Navy, possibly in the world.

"Captain, I'm doing better today that I guess I have a right to," Gambini said.

"Master Chief, don't feel guilty for feeling good. And if you have to feel any guilt, feel it for not finding me a Destiny target."

"Don't you worry, sir, we'll get him."

"What's that on the display?" Phillips was not one of the submarine captains who knew it all, nor was he one who didn't but claimed he did.

"I've got six frequencies I'm looking for, Captain. The graphs, they're the frequency tones that Destiny should put out."

"How do we know what he's going to put out?"

"Good question, Skipper. We don't know and we goddamned well should."

Phillips bit his lip. Not good. Usually a submarine they were searching for was catalogued with the tonals it put out and the transients it was known to put out. This data came from a sound surveillance done by a US sub that shadowed the new target submarine on its sea trials, listening and recording while the new sub went through its paces. Then, armed with the tonals the target emitted, later searches for that sub class could concentrate on just the tonals he put out, rather than guessing or looking at a whole range of frequencies. It was a paradox—to find a sub you had to know exactly what you were looking for. It was like walking through a dense forest and trying to identify a specific bird out of the noise of all the animals and insects and wind through the trees. If the bird's song was known, finding it would be easy.

"We had a sound surveillance of the old Destiny One class," Phillips said.

"Right. That's what this is based on."

"So we never did one on the Two class."

"It was scheduled for the *Barracuda* to do this next month."

"That was crappy scheduling. Who left us with this bag of cow manure?"

"Admiral Pacino, sir. He decided he wanted the surveillance done by a Seawolf class instead of one of the newer 688s. But *Barracuda* was the only Seawolf in the

Pacific, and we were still unavailable at Electric Boat and in the wrong ocean."

"So what is this graph?" Phillips pointed to the screen. On the graph the trace of the incoming sound looked like a fat lopsided finger pointing upward.

"This one is looking for fifty-eight to sixty-two cycles per second."

"There's a spike there. That's a tonal coming in. What is it? Is that him?"

"No. That display is trying to catch Destiny's electrical grid. If his sound signature is like the Destiny I class, he puts out a sixty-cycle tonal that comes from his grid frequency. Problem with that one is that *we* put the same tonal out there, so it's hard to tell if that's my ship or the bad guy's ship. Every once in a while I pick up this phone and call the boys back in the teapot, and they shift our electrical grid's frequencies around. If the spike moves, that's not a Destiny, just the *Piranha*."

"Did you call on that one?"

"Just before you came clomping in with those shit-kickers."

"What happened?"

"The nukes changed their frequency and my tonal spike moved with it."

"Okay, so that's not him. What about this one? 155 cycles. There's a hump on that one."

"A hump but not a spike, sir. The system looks out at the ocean, and not the whole ocean, just a slice of it, and looks for this one frequency. The ocean's so full of noise that there's noise at every frequency. The sounds in this range are more concentrated in the middle of the frequency gate, that's all."

"I don't know, it looks like it's growing."

The hump in the center of the graph from 153 to 156 cycles per second was growing taller. Gambini watched it, slurping coffee from one of the dirtiest coffee cups Phillips had ever seen. Phillips leaned over, watching it.

Aft, in the control room, Lieutenant Meritson stood before the attack center on the starboard side of the conn, hands on his hips, looking up at the sonar display screen. Meritson, in addition to being this watch's officer of the deck, was the ship's sonar officer. He squinted hard at the screen center, at the frequency graphs that Gambini was examining in sonar. Meritson frowned at the graph, watching the spike in the center grow.

"Chief of the Watch," he said quietly, not moving his gaze from the sonar screen.

"Sir?"

"We got a phonetalker set up in every space?"

"Yessir. It's part of the rig for ultraquiet."

"Good. Get on the phones to every phonetalker. Get them awake. On their feet. Get a report from every watchstander. I mean it, I'm gonna need those guys in about two minutes."

"Aye, sir." The chief of the watch spoke into his boom microphone, sounding irritated. "All spaces, Control. All watchstanders report status of rig for ultraquiet."

The chief listened as his phonetalkers reported in one by one.

"They're all alert, Officer of the Deck. What's on your mind?"

"Chief, in about one minute the captain's going to come crashing through that door and he's going to man battlestations."

In sonar, Phillips glared hard at the screen, dumping his old cigar and finding a new one, this one as homespun as the previous stogie. He lit it, not with his lighter but with a wooden match, in keeping with his 1859 El Paso outfit.

"Captain?"

"Yes, Master Chief?"

"I think we've got a bite on the line. Be careful that you don't spook him, okay, sir? It would be nice to set the hook."

"What are you saying?"

"I think that . . . is new sonar contact Sierra One, possible submerged submarine."

Phillips felt a chill crawl up his spine, shivering in the air conditioning of the compartment.

"Is this him?"

"I think so."

"Destiny II?"

"I think so."

"Any bearing?"

"I'm getting a weak signal. Don't do anything yet. I'm shifting to the forward beam."

"The end beam is terrible. You'll just pick up our noise."

"No, not the end beam, just a more forward-looking one. Hold on."

"I'll be right back. I've got things to take care of. Master?"

"Yes, Captain?"

"Set the hook. I want this son of a bitch."

**NORTHWEST PACIFIC**
**JAPANESE OPAREA, FORTY-FIVE KILOMETERS EAST-NORTHEAST OF POINT NOJIMA-ZAKI**
**SS-808 *Eternal Spirit***

The *Eternal Spirit* sailed at a keel-depth of 200 meters, speed ten kilometers per hour. Her crew, a dozen officers of the Japanese Maritime Self Defense Force, comprised some of the best in the squadron. The commanding officer, Comdr. Soemu Toyoda, was a Tokyo graduate and widely regarded as the flotilla's captain to beat. His ship had been neck and neck with the *Winged Serpent* for the flotilla's battle quality award, something Toyoda coveted.

Toyoda was reading in his stateroom's bed, the reading lamp the only illumination in the room. The report he was studying was an evaluation of the Destiny II class versus the Destiny III class, the leadership of the MSDF trying to decide the future of the force. Toyoda was forty-five years old and had spent his entire career at sea in submarines, first in the *Harushio*-class diesel boats built by Mitsubishi and Kawasaki, the ships streamlined and formidable-looking on the outside but crippled by the lack of a nuclear reactor. Batteries and a stinking sulfury diesel were no match for a nuclear power plant.

Toyoda had been an engineering consultant for the construction of Japan's first nuclear submarine, the Destiny class. At first the project had been exciting, Japan taking the next step in the technology curve, although the project had required the nation to take the next step, the embracing of nuclear technology for the military. After Hiroshima and Nagasaki were bombed by nuclear weapons at the end of the war with America in 1945, the very idea of using nuclear science was repugnant to an entire generation of Japanese. But one generation gave way to another, the younger generation tired of hearing about the holocaust of nuclear destruction. This generation had felt responsible for Japan's emergence into the world scene as an economic contender. Products labeled "Made in Japan" went from being scorned to being state of the art. The generation after them went further, not happy with economic prominence but intent on economic domination, taking over one world market after another until the trade sanctions by the West had put a stop to that ambition. But a generation's ambition couldn't be turned off like a switch, and within two decades a desire to rule the world's markets had given way to an unspoken desire to rule the world itself. Full circle.

The Destiny submarine had been launched and found to be better than expectations. The ship was built for export sale, Japan five years before intent on meeting the spirit of its military-banning constitution if not the letter. But when the trade war escalated, Japan realized the West was more enemy than ally, and it stood alone with the might of Russia and the two Chinas facing it to the west, the new regime of terror in India, and the country's leadership had called on engineers like Toyoda to manufacture its own military hardware. Admiral Tanaka—Akagi Tanaka, not his arrogant social misfit son Toshumi—had asked Toyoda to take a building-yard assignment to command the first Destiny II-class submarine, built by Japanese for Japanese in the Yokosuka shipyard. The ship was named the *Eternal Spirit* and was world class. More than world class, a world beater. Toyoda took the ship to sea on its initial sea trials. A week later he wrote a memo to the elder Tanaka that with a supersub like the Destiny II, Japan could again rule the seas.

In the next five years the yards had pumped out Destiny IIs as if war were imminent. Toyoda had been pleased, watching the Maritime Self Defense Force move from a second-rate navy to a killer force. It was two years before that the development divisions of the MSDF made their most crucial mistake. Toyoda sat back against the fluffed-up pillows of his bed, continuing to contemplate the report. Two years ago the hull of the *Divine Firmament* was ripped open and the command module compartment amputated except for a few meters, just enough to contain the cabinets of a new computer system designed by a prominent research scientist named Onasuka, a biocomputer pioneer who took the previous technology of the Destiny II ship control system, the Second Captain, and modified it. The Second Captain was already in the forefront of computer technology, able to run the ship in the absence of the crew for routine straight-line steaming, but was not able to fight the vessel in combat. It was a layered neural network floating on a conventional distributed control system. Onasuka took the neural network and replaced the upper functions with parallel processors, multiplying the processing speed by a factor of ten thousand, with the use of biological DNA soup processors. The soup processors were composed of genetic material taken from the brain stems of small animals and cultured into the liquid soup that functioned as a biological process-control module. It was revolutionary and radical. The *Divine Firmament* was renamed the *Curtain of Flames* and became the first Destiny III class.

And the unit performed admirably, if expensively. The Destiny III was matched against various Destiny II-class ships in exercises. The Two-class crews were literally fighting for their jobs; to lose an exercise against a Three class would signal the admirals that the time had come for the computer to replace manned crews. Unfortunately, although the manned crews invariably came out on top in combat, the MSDF leadership had still decided on committing the fleet to the Three class. Perhaps it was all the promises they had given the government, or the men standing to make a profit from the computerization. Whatever the reason behind the decision, the MSDF admirals had decided on the Destiny III, spending the next two years building nothing but Three-class ships, neglecting even to maintain the Two-class vessels.

The result had been disastrous, Toyoda thought. The intelligence message on his personal pad computer told the complete story. The Three-class computer-driven ships had triumphed in sinking the enemy surface fleets, but in the process they had been sunk, smashed to bits by the fleet-escort submarines. After spending the time and resources to build more than a dozen Three-class ships, they were now gone, not responding to their orders to transmit their locations to the Galaxy satellites. And now the defense of the Home Islands was left to the Two-class submarines, which were capable but neglected for two years by the shipyards of Japan.

There were dozens of American submarines sailing for the Home Islands, and only a limited number of torpedoes on the Destiny II-class ships deployed to guard Japan. What would happen when those torpedoes were gone? Less capable American submarines would survive to fire overwhelming numbers of torpedoes at the Two class. The American torpedoes were small and slow and relatively ineffective, but ten of them together could certainly sink a Two class, double hull or not.

If the leadership had built more of the Two class and less of the Three class. But there was no sense thinking that way.

Toyoda got up, put on his shoes and took his evening walk through the ship, going first into the control room, where his first officer Ryunosuke Kusaka presided over the modified battlestations section watch. Toyoda waved Kusaka over to the forward door of the room, where the other officers in the watch section couldn't hear their conversation.

"Any contact?"

"No, Captain. You know I would have called you if there were."

"It just seems odd. The computer files—are they se correctly?"

"Sir, the Second Captain is scanning the sea for the known characteristics of all flights of American 688 class with a secondary scan in action for any units of the British Royal Navy or the French Navy. There has beer nothing, nothing at all."

"Maybe our job is over, maybe the enemy will pul back."

"I think there will be more action, Captain. I feel it."

"I feel it too, First. They are out there and they're coming for us."

"Yes, sir."

There seemed little more to say. Toyoda left and too the stairs to the middle level and the messroom. He wa amazed at the officers awake in the messroom, some o them studying for the next rank, some writing haiku some in a lively discussion that died when he came in Toyodo thought of the loneliness of command, that h had no one to confide his own thoughts to. He smile at the men, wondering why these off-watch men didn' sleep. In another six hours they would be on watch wit him in the control room. Probably they were awake fo the same reason he was—tension. He spoke a few words wondering if Toshumi Tanaka—the lead commandin officer of the flotilla and a flaming maladjusted marti net—ever took time to speak to his men. Not that i mattered, Toyoda thought. He said good night to th men and returned to his stateroom.

He shut the door behind him, deciding to take a last loo at the Second Captain's sonar displays. The computer filtered data was empty. He scanned the raw unpro cessed data, realizing there was too much to examin and what there was was random. He was reminded of time in his youth when he had been in love with th television set and his parents were gone and a thunder storm had knocked out the cable system, but he had no accepted that, and in his desperation to watch televisio he went through every channel, looking for a show. H flipped through channel after channel, seeing nothing bu snow, but sometimes seeing a shadow of a face, a hin of printing, a glance at people walking, but then the snow would prevail, leaving him wondering if he had just imagined it. The raw sonar data was like that, all random noise of every frequency and tone and duration. Looking for the noise made by a machine in that mess was like looking into a rainy jungle for a camouflaged soldier. He snapped off the console and got back into bed.

# CHAPTER 33

**SS-808 *Eternal Spirit***

Comdr. Soemu Toyoda pulled his uniform off, draped it on his chair and climbed into the bed wearing only his shorts. Back in the control room the first officer had orders to continue to patrol the waters offshore until contact was gained on the next enemy sub. Toyoda's *Eternal Spirit* had already put three enemy vessels on the bottom, each of them easily detected on sonar, but since then the sea had been empty. Completely empty. Toyoda wondered why, if there were no more enemy ships, there had been no word on the radio command and control circuits about what was going on. It seemed odd, but then so had this entire mission.

He turned off his reading lamp, feeling tense and nervous. There was something not right about the situation but he couldn't put his mind on what it was. He shut his eyes and tried to think about the woman he had met just prior to sailing. Her name was Suni Ariga and she was half his age and beautiful, vital in a way he wasn't, mysterious and sexual. She had made it very clear from the start that she wanted him sexually, and it was strange—her generation was so different from his own, so willing to say what they wanted. The young women were entering the work force and threatened to knock on the door of the military someday. But it was the women's sexuality that was so difficult to accept, centuries of courting rituals being washed down the sewer pipe with other Japanese customs as the television set homogenized the world, the Western influence spreading more by the hour.

He returned his thoughts to Suni, seeing her face, remembering how her eyes had looked into his, how her mouth had moved on his chest. He could feel himself getting hard and tried to ignore the feeling, one welcome in the company of an aroused woman but very unwelcome alone inside a ship filled only with men at war.

USS *Piranha*

Bruce Phillips came into control, his cotton poncho flying in the breeze of his passage, his boots clumping on the deckplates, coming to a halt in front of Meritson.

"Man silent battlestations!"

Meritson snapped his fingers at the chief of the watch, having anticipated Phillips' next action.

There was no circuit-one announcement. The word went out on the phone circuits to the watchstanders in the spaces, each of them wearing cordless phones that put them in touch with the control room. The forward compartment phonetalkers woke up the section's duty messengers, who went through the berthing compartments and woke up the crew. Men jumped out of their coffinlike racks, curtains sliding aside. They climbed into their coveralls, grabbed glasses, shoes, all in the tight dimly lit spaces that were a challenge just to walk through much less dress in. In twenty frantic seconds seventy men rocketed out of the berthing rooms, coverall uniforms wrinkled and stale with sweat, hair spiked from sleep, eyes puffy, all business.

Those seventy men dispersed, some heading aft, others forward or below. In the control room two dozen watchstanders came silently in. Phonetalkers strapped on headsets. Plotting officers took their stations at the plot tables snapping fresh sheets of tracing paper over the flat panel displays. The row of consoles of the BSY-2 attack center filled with officers, each trained to manipulate his panel in a unique way, each dancing with the computer to a different song but on the same dance floor. The arriving helmsman waved out the watch section's helmsman, the new arrival the ship's best, the regular watch helmsman getting up and muttering what the ship's course and depth were, the battlestations helmsman sliding into the control seat, the yoke of the controller slipping into his hands.

On the conn Scott Court, the navigator, took over the officer of the deck watch from Meritson. Their conversation was short as Meritson gave a rapid data dump in Court's ear:

"Target One confirmed Destiny II bearing two zero six on towed array narrowband's 154 Hertz, bearing ambiguity resolved, own ship on one four five, depth eight hundred, speed all ahead two-thirds with turns for eight, ship rigged for ultraquiet, we've got a layer at 110 feet with a good sound channel between seven hundred and nine hundred. We've got weapons one through four up and warm, outer doors open, target solution programmed but weak. The Mark 50s are backups to the Vortex battery. We've got Vortex unit two coming up to speed now, gyro readback due in forty seconds."

"I've got it, get the hell out of here. I relieve you, sir," Court said to Meritson.

"I stand relieved, sir. Helm, Quartermaster, Commander Court has the deck and the conn."

"This is Lieutenant Commander Court, I have the deck and the conn," Court announced to the room, his voice quiet.

Meritson slipped into the seat at position two in the center of the attack center. He had already configured the display for dot-stack mode on Target One. He leaned back in the leather seat, looking at the upper and lower display, his fingers resting on the two circular knobs and the fixed function keys, feeling the fit of his function. He was a biological link in the submarine's machine, the best man for this job. He was plugged into the tactical situation, the pos-two battle stations operator one of the most prestigious positions on the ship. He and the BSY computer were a two-brain team charged with finding the target, predicting exactly what he would do in five minutes' time in the face of uncertain and conflicting data. Without his work, the captain would be helpless

Meritson smiled to himself, his mind becoming one with the BSY system, his senses reaching out into the sea with the sonar gear, the target in the palm of his hand.

Roger Whatney, the Royal Navy lieutenant commander and executive officer, walked quickly into control, strapped on a one-eared headset and tested the phone circuit with his south-of-England accent. Whatney was the firecontrol coordinator, the owner of the "solution" to the target, the output of Meritson's pos-two console meshed with the manual plot's backup solution. Whatney would function as the captain's auxiliary brain, a sounding board, fully empowered to disagree with the commanding officer where the target's motion was concerned although the captain could override him with a gesture.

Next to Meritson, on the console further forward, position one, Joe Katoris seated himself and put on a headset. Katoris would back up Meritson, doing his own dance with the computer, trying to outdo Meritson's solution, and in place to track the secondary target should another Destiny or other hostile target appear on the scene. His other function was to return the console to geographic mode so Phillips could see a God's-eye view of the battle zone, then toggle back to his dot-stacker mode when Phillips no longer needed the geo plot.

On the console next to Meritson aft, position three, was Ensign Braxton, his display a hybrid, able to stack dots or do a line of sight mode on friendly contacts, if *Piranha* had had a wolfpack partner or surface action group to be careful of. He was the safety man, there to remind Whatney and Phillips of friendly ships and keep the torpedoes away from them. And if a hostile ship surprised them he would track it for a quick reaction shot.

Aft of Braxton in the fourth console Lt. Tom McKilley, the weapons officer, was at that weapons-control console, a larger version of the first three units, this one with a full computer keyboard on the lower section on the right. The upper display was filled with colored windows that displayed weapon status, one window for the torpedoes, another for the Vortex units. The lower part of the console to the left of the keyboard was dominated by a large stainless steel gleaming lever with a suicide knob on it, a semicircle engraved onto the surface of the console, the word STANDBY written at the nine o'clock position, the letters spelling FIRE at three o'clock. The lever was the firing trigger for the torpedoes and missiles. At one point DynaCorp had experimented with a simple covered square soft-feel function key for the firing mechanism, but the submarine captains had complained bitterly, the firing trigger dear to them, the wimply fixed function key an insult to John Wayne macho submariners who tested it. They demanded their World War II trigger back and soon got it.

McKilley brought up the Vortex window and monitored the gyro spinup and data readback for unit number two, the forward upper missile on the port side. He jettisoned the missile cap forward and the blast cover aft of the missile tube, the tube now open to the sea fore and aft. He went through the software screens, testing the missile, finally satisfied.

On the conn Scott Court in his starched and creased coveralls turned to scruffy Bruce Phillips in his cowboy boots, still wearing the flat-brimmed leather hat with a headset crammed underneath it, his dingy poncho covering his chest, the revolver handles protruding from the hip openings.

"Sir, battlestations are manned."

Phillips leaned over the conn rail, squinted his eyes, put out the cigar. He looked down on the watchsection. "Attention in the fire-control team. We got ourselves a bad guy at bearing two one zero and we're going to kick him in the tail. You cowpokes got all that? Firing point procedures, Target One, Destiny II class, Vortex unit two."

"Ship ready, Captain," Court said.

"Weapon pending, sir," McKilley said.

"Solution pending, sir," Whatney said. "Recommend maneuver to course three zero zero to get a range to the target."

"Status of the weapon, Weps? Why are you pending?"

"Sir, I need the solution range."

"Why?"

"If he's too close the detonation takes us out with it. Remember the icepack, sir? This thing has a kill radius of about two miles."

"Oh, hell, Weps, he's way the hell out there, and besides, that's my problem. Solution status, Coordinator?"

"Sir," Whatney said, "I've got a bearing, but that's it. It's not a firing solution."

"Okay," Phillips said, loud enough to stop all talking in the room, "listen the hell up. The next man in this watchsection who tells me we need the range to Target One gets a spur in his ass. Straight up the hole. Goddamnit, men, this isn't like shooting a ridge, this is a fucking . . . Japanese . . . submarine. Okay? You *got* that? Now, dammit, firing point fucking procedures, Vortex two, Target Goddamned One. What's the status?"

"Ship ready, sir," Court said.

"Weapon ready, sir," McKilley snapped.

"Solution ready, Skipper," Whatney said.

"Shoot on generated bearing!"

"Standby," McKilley announced, pulling the trigger to the left.

*"Fire!"* Phillips called.

The noise of the missile launch was deafening, but this time Phillips had his fingers clamped into his ears for the thirty seconds it took the unit to clear the immediate vicinity. He looked up at the sonar screen watching the track of the missile, wondering if he were about to go up in smoke himself. Even if he were too close, inside the blast zone of the missile, there was something satisfying knowing that he would at least go down scoring a major hit on one of the Destinys, but then he thought of Abby O'Neal and regretted the thought. He wanted to live through this, and knew only his ship, his crew and his instincts could hope to win this fight.

He waited, one second running into the next, the noise of the Vortex missile long gone. As the silence lingered he wondered if it had been a dud, a dud that had provoked a Nagasaki counterlaunch. Even if it did, he decided, he would not run. He would stand his ground and keep firing Vortex missiles until one hit the target. Hell, a Vortex missile might even target an incoming Nagasaki—wouldn't that be a trick, a weapon that homed in on and destroyed the enemy's weapon. Still he waited, and still he heard nothing.

Finally: "Sonar, Captain, line up the BSY in active mode and report when you're ready," he said into his headset microphone.

The Vortex missile blew through the water at terminal velocity, over 300 knots, the waves high above flashing by in a blur. The solid-rocket fuel burned rapidly, the missile getting lighter with each passing second. The unit's blue laser seeking device scanned the water ahead in a wide cone, the need for last-instant depth and course corrections vital to success.

When the target appeared in the blue light shining through the water, the computer realized the target submarine was far below it, deeper by some three hundred feet. The aft nozzle rotated and sent the missile into a dive as it corrected its course by a few tenths of a degree. The target size grew from a speck to a huge blur in milliseconds, and the missile's warhead of seven tons of high molecular density PlasticPac detonated and ignited the sea around it to a temperature approaching the surface of the sun.

Toyoda in the *Eternal Spirit* was still in his bunk thinking of Suni when the missile arrived. The hull ripped open, and the *Eternal Spirit* became a huge teardrop-shaped mass of vaporized iron and steam rising toward the ocean surface above. The steam formed smaller bubbles, the ocean condensing the steam into smaller bubbles and eventually collapsing them from the pressure and near-freezing ocean temperatures, the sea boiling with loud noise for the next thirty hours.

"We're ready to go active, Captain," Gambini's voice reported from *Piranha*'s sonar.

And just then the ship shook to a violent ear-splitting explosion as the Vortex missile detonated on target. On the sonar screens, all screens of the broadband system went completely white, the sonar blue-out complete, so much noise in the ocean that there was nothing to hear. The explosion went on for a long time, roaring and ebbing and roaring again.

"Officer of the Deck," Phillips said to Court, "secure battlestations. I'll be in my stateroom." He clomped out of control and disappeared into the door marked CO STATEROOM.

# CHAPTER 34

**EIGHTY MILES EAST OF HITACHI, JAPAN**
**USS *Barracuda***

In the sonar room just forward of control, Chief James Omeada sat at his console glaring at the sensors. He checked his watch. In two minutes Lt. Chris Porter would come barging in to ask the usual questions—"Any contacts?" and "You usin' the right search plan?" and "What's the status of the BSY?" Omeada and Porter had worked together as sonar chief and sonar officer for almost two years. Secretly Omeada liked and admired Porter, but for reasons long forgotten he was crusty with the young chubby officer, regularly throwing verbal barbs at him, especially in front of the other enlisted men, which most officers would strongly object to. At first Porter had taken the insults, since most of them were based on Omeada's correct assertion that sonar officers didn't know squat about the BSY-2 combat-control system, the combined firecontrol, sonar suite and navigation computers. Sure, they knew how to play with their little knobs in the control room and stack their little dots, but the real work of nailing down an enemy sub was done in sonar, and Omeada felt Chrissy needed to know that. However, inadvertently Omeada had created himself a monster. Chris Porter had taken aboard each insult about his dangerous lack of knowledge, withdrawing from sonar to study. The next day he'd be back, exploring the same question he'd asked the day before, but now armed with knowledge and often challenging Omeada's own knowledge, more than once sending the sonar chief to the tech manual. It was almost spooky how Porter did it—he sure as hell didn't spend any extra time on the ship. The sonar officer was notorious for leaving the ship at five P.M. every day, no matter the crisis, and at sea, he rarely missed sleep, reliably counted on to be in his rack when he wasn't standing officer of the deck watch.

In fact, Porter slept so much that Omeada had taken to calling him Bunky. Porter hadn't reacted, had never threatened Omeada in spite of his elevated rank. He took Omeada's taunts as if he himself were just another of Omeada's seamen striking for sonar technician. Porter's acceptance of Omeada's criticism and the way he responded to it by learning rather than resenting had gained Omeada's unconditional respect. This was something that had never happened to him, respecting an officer. The other chiefs in the goat locker gave him tremendous grief about it. After all, Omeada had spent years putting down officers and their lack of knowledge coupled with the fact that they got all the credit, all the glory, all the medals *and* all the money. Omeada, in his defense, kept saying that Chrissy Porter was different, that he was "heavy," submariner's respectful term for knowledgeable. The other chiefs had just laughed and made noises about Omeada and Porter having some kind of weird thing going on. Now that it was Omeada's turn to take the heat, he learned a lesson from Porter and accepted it, and soon the sarcastic taunts of his fellow chiefs died down.

Omeada was still amazed, after twenty years of frustration with officers, how much he did admire Porter. So much so that he felt dutybound to disguise that feeling in front of the men, doubling his cuts at the twenty-six-year-old lieutenant. As for Porter, an odd thing had happened to him during the course of their association—he became bitingly sarcastic, to the point that the other officers accused him of being Omeada with lieutenant's bars, which he met with Omeada-style wit.

In addition to the growth of their professional relationship, Omeada could now closely predict Porter's rhythms. Of course, it helped that Porter was a soul who loved routine, always coming on watch at midnight, going off watch at zero six hundred hours, sleeping until he could no longer sleep, then coming into sonar to check the status of the equipment prior to taking his watch. Porter would be coming into sonar now to get his prewatch brief in about ten seconds. Five seconds. Two. One. Zero.

"Hello, Chief," Porter said. Porter, of medium height, paunchy with pasty skin, a five o'clock shadow, a double chin and a receding hairline, looked fifteen years older than his age. "Any contacts?"

"A thousand of them, Bunky. All over the map. All high-value Destinys. I just forgot to tell control about them."

Porter leaned over a console and punched some soft-touch function keys, flipping the display through several channels, spending only a moment looking at each.

"You usin' the right search plan?"

"Oh, my God! I knew we forgot something. The search plan. Williams, get the damned plan entered in."

"Come on, Chief."

Omeada pointed to the computer running in the corner of the room. Porter flipped through the windows, seemed satisfied with the plan.

"What's the status of the BSY?"

"Broke-dick, sir. Down hard. I just neglected to tell control."

"Chief."

"Nominal, okay? Jeez, you're worse than my mother-in-law. Although, come to think of it, you do kind of look like her. She's got a gut just like you."

"We can't all be skinny and beautiful like you, Chief."

"Don't forget young-looking. With silky skin."

"And great legs."

"I try."

A serious look crossed Porter's face. "I've got a feeling about this watch."

"I don't want to hear about your feelings, sir. This isn't an encounter group."

"Oh? You wouldn't know it from all the moaning and groaning in here. Let me know what you get. Today's the day."

"Have a good watch, sir," Omeada said. Porter stared at him for a moment, realizing it was the first statement made in a month by him without sarcasm. It seemed to confirm Porter's feelings. Today was the day, this was the watch.

Porter took a detour from his usual prewatch tour and went below one deck to the torpedo room, went forward past the shining green-painted Mark 50 torpedoes stacked neatly on the hydraulically controlled racks. He stopped at one of the torpedoes and touched its flank, its surface cool and smooth. Stenciled on the side were the words "MK 50 MOD ALPHA WARSHOT." Porter walked again to the forward bulkhead to examine the tubes. All eight had large white phenolic tags with red letters proclaiming "WARSHOT LOADED." Porter stood there for a moment, then walked back up the ladder to the upper level, arrived back in control and nodded to Lt. David Voorheese, the man Porter would relieve as officer of the deck. Porter scanned the status boards, the navigation plot, took a final look at the sonar display and told Voorheese he was ready to take the watch.

"Nothing going on. The OpArea's empty, Captain's racking, XO's got the command duty officer, the place is dead. Midwatch as usual."

"Captain's night orders?"

"Same as last night's. Find the Destiny. Don't wait to shoot at him while you're manning battlestations."

"Hell, maybe I'll just shoot his ass and let you guys keep sleeping."

"Fine. You got it? I'm tired."

"One more thing. Where's the admiral?"

"He haunts the place, hangs out in sonar or the crew's mess. Guy works the crowd a lot. Never seen a guy with two stars shoot the shit with a third-class petty officer for a half-hour."

"That shows you he's got nothing to do. You know these riders. No responsibility, no worries, just leave the driving to ship's company and watch movies, eat ice cream and sleep, maybe diddle themselves while looking at some of that Tahitian porn we picked up the last run."

"If I had nothing to do I'd get about twenty hours of sleep. Well, the engineer calls."

"You working aft tonight? We're rigged for ultraquiet. You can't take anything apart, Voorheese. Hit the bunky, man."

"Good point. Helm, Quartermaster, Mr. Porter has the deck and conn. See you, buttface."

Porter raised his voice. "Helm, Quartermaster, log that Lt. Christopher Porter the third has the deck and conn for the midwatch on December 26, the watch in which we expect to put at least one Destiny submarine on the bottom of the Pacific."

**100 Kilometers Northeast of Hitachi, Japan**
**SS-810 *Winged Serpent***

Lt. Comdr. Hiro Mazdai heard the dressing-down that the captain was giving one of the junior officers. Mazdai was in his first officer's stateroom, trying to concentrate on the chart of the offshore waters, but only hearing Tanaka raging at the officer about his failings and how weak he was. In Tanaka's view everyone but himself was weak.

The captain was driven to find and sink the Americans. For the sake of his own sanity Mazdai wished he'd get it over with, put them on the bottom so this mission with Tanaka could come to a conclusion.

**Seventy Miles Northeast of Point Oshika-hanto**
**USS *Piranha***

Bruce Phillips picked up the phone from a sound sleep. He listened for fifteen seconds, said, "Man silent battlestations," and tossed the phone on his desk, then headed out for the control room.

"Gambini's got another one, skipper," Scott Court said.

"Very well," Phillips said, putting on a headset. "Sonar supervisor, Captain, report status of the contact."

It took only forty-five seconds for Phillips to plug into the tactical situation. Target One was a submerged Destiny class off the point of Oshika-hanto, contact faint on narrowband, bearing nailed down at one nine seven degrees true, with little else known.

The limiting factor on the attack was the time for the Vortex missile to get ready. Within two minutes from battlestations being called, the missile was away. Phillips took a digital stop watch from his vest pocket. The time of flight of the Vortex through the water was less than five minutes, putting the target some twenty-five nautical miles away.

The explosion from this Destiny was as spectacular as the first, the noise easily audible to the naked ear. Phillips nodded, returned to his stateroom, Court looking after him.

The cloud of steam and vaporized iron of the Vortex fireball had once been the Destiny II-class submarine *Winter Dragon.* The crew of the *Piranha* would never know that.

*Piranha* sailed on southward, closing on Tokyo Bay.

## SS-810 *Winged Serpent*

Comdr. Toshumi Tanaka sat at the Second Captain console in his stateroom, eyes bleary, dark circles under his eyes. He had stayed awake all through the previous night and on into the day, and was still awake now well after midnight. His consumption of tea had been a record, but nothing next to the amphetamines the Yokosuka doctor had given him. The uppers kept him going after all these hours, letting him stick at the console. He hadn't eaten, slept or spoken to his crew for almost thirty hours, with the exception of Lieutenant Ito, who had come into the stateroom to give his view of the American forces' deployment. Tanaka had ripped into him for thinking he could express himself any way he

felt to the ship's commanding officer. It was somethin
that would happen on an American ship, he had said. It
had never seen discipline before, not from his parents o
his teachers or his previous commander, Tanaka tol
him. The younger generation was soft. Weak.

Which was why he insisted on standing watch at hi
own Second Captain. He believed he couldn't trust th
officers. The Americans had probably been lost while h
was on the last sleep cycle. Well, not this time. He woul
not sleep until he had a detection on the screen.

He stared at the console as the clock ticked into th
night.

## USS *Piranha*

The third and fourth Vortex missile launches had gon
off much like the first two—a faint narrowband detectio
on 154 Hertz on the towed array sonar, a sniff of th
enemy, battlestations silently manned, the Vortex missil
warmed and ready while the battlestations team was sti
relieving the watches, Phillips in the control room, th
missile roaring away, then exploding, the shock wav
and noise of the explosion deafening.

The last two Vortex missiles had blown up Destiny I
hull numbers SS-807 and 814, the *Godlike Snowfall* an
the *Heavenly Mist.*

Phillips proceeded to work his way south, on towar
Tokyo Bay, uncertain what the hell he would do whe
he got there.

## USS *Barracuda*

The ship was dead quiet, the way Porter liked it. Ther
was something special to him about the midwatch, th
officers in their racks, the captain and admiral sawin
logs, the enlisted men bedded down, every space de
serted except for the watchstanders. Porter scanned th
sonar repeater screen, able to send it through every dis

play that Chief Omeada had forward in sonar. Nothing on the displays. The sea was deserted.

Or was it? He felt an electricity, the same he had felt before on both good and bad occasions. He'd felt it the day before he got his acceptance letter from the academy. And the Thursday night before the Friday he met his first serious girlfriend Diane. He'd begun to think this tingle of premonition could only mean good things, but he'd also felt it the week before he and his roommate Todd had gone skydiving. He had piled into Todd's '02 two-seat T-bird with the retro tailfins and they had gone out to the field, packed their chutes, saddled up and gone up in the Cessna. As usual, at 14,000 feet he and Todd had left the plane, goofing off all the way down until the altimeter buzzed at 3000 feet and he pulled the ripcord, the mattress-shaped parasail deploying above him and jerking him up by the crotch. He smiled with the sheer joy of flying without wings—until he saw Todd in trouble.

The trip down from 3000 feet under canopy took him six minutes. It took Todd seventeen seconds. Todd's main chute had deployed automatically instead of by his ripcord, the altimeter rigged to do that at 900 feet in the event that the jumper failed to pull before 3000 feet, but it had malfunctioned, and at the time Todd was doing body barrel rolls, still goofing off, so that the main chute wrapped around his neck and extended up into the slipstream, his rolling body turning the silk of the parachute into a death shroud. He fell like that, choking on the cords of the chute wrapped around his throat, looking like a tumbling cocoon, until he impacted the ground on a patch of concrete driveway.

After that the tingle was on Porter's black list. The next time he felt it was the October of his first class year at Annapolis. For two days he sweated, wondering what would happen this time, until the company commander had called him to his office for a phone call. *Who died?* was all Porter could think when he picked up the phone. The voice at the other end said his grandfather had passed on after a stroke hit him an hour before. They buried his grandfather in his native Wyoming, in a graveyard with cactus and sagebrush, the walks made of river stones, facing a mountain ridge. It had been a beautiful ceremony, and Porter had to smile at the memory of his grandfather's jokes. He had thought that had been the meaning of the tingle, but the feeling of premonition stayed with him even the day after the funeral, up to the moment they read the will. Grandfather had left Porter a defunct gold mine in South Africa, a bit of a family joke, but the week before his death the old man's mining company had found platinum in the mine. Porter's net worth grew from a few thousand dollars—the price of his five-year-old sports car—to several million overnight. Actually, by the year before, the estimate had been found to be low, the mine potential estimated in the hundreds of millions of dollars. None of that changed Porter, none of it seemed to reach him. No one outside the family even knew about the mine. Porter didn't really believe it until he made a trip there to see it with his own eyes. But the role of rich kid wasn't of interest. He was, he thought, put on earth for something different and it had nothing to do with money.

The next and last time Porter had felt the odd tingle was days before, when *Barracuda* had been heading for the Japan OpArea. Something was happening to the ship. Hours later the message came that the ship was to rendezvous with a helicopter to receive a visitor, Admiral Pacino himself. Kane had been angry, his kingdom invaded, but somehow Porter felt this was the positive side of premonition. Whatever, in the admiral's presence he felt it biting at him.

And now, timed with the takeover of his watch, the old tingle was hitting him full force. This was the day. This was the watch.

If only he could tell if it was a good portent, or a bad one.

## SS-810 *Winged Serpent*

Lt. Comdr. Seiichi Kami had the section-A watch in the control room. For the last two hours, since midnight, he had stared at the same consoles, looking at the same displays, all of them empty. The hours since the sinkings of the first Americans had been filled with both boredom and tension. Boredom because the screens were empty. Tension because the Americans still hadn't given up. The Americans, Kami decided, were doing this on purpose, trying to exhaust them before coming back into the area with more submarines.

He thought about his newborn son Kosaku waiting for him at home. He had never spent much time thinking about his MSDF duty, but now that Kosaku was here he found himself jealous of every moment away from him. He was thinking that MSDF duty was no longer for him; the other men seemed somehow different from who he was, they no longer had much in common.

Kami stared now at the sonar data screens, the data filtered by the computer, and seeing nothing, sat down in the deep cushioning of the control seat to continue to watch and to wait.

## USS *Barracuda*

Lieutenant Porter stood on the conn and snapped his fingers at the chief of the watch, calling for coffee. The sonar display was selected to the thin wire narrowband towed array sonar, the beam looking forward as the ship continued to sail northeast. The sonar repeater was selected to the time-integration feature of the narrowband sonar, the graph of 152 to 155 Hertz in screen center. Chief Omeada had just zeroed the frequency bucket, wiping out all previous data. Now the computer was going to wait and collect sound in that specific tonal range, display noise that it received at a higher level vertically. The graph was almost like the bottom of an hourglass, the sand representing each piece of sound at a particular frequency. If the graph line rose horizontally with time, the line flat, then there was no one out there. If the graph line became a spike with a narrow peak at a particular frequency, there was a pure tone out in the

sea constant with time. And the sea did not generat
pure bell tones that lingered as time passed. Only ma
chines did.

Porter received his coffee and slurped it, the tingl
running through him as he stared at the sonar screens
If only he could detect the Destiny and beat out Omead
he would never let the chief forget it.

He flipped through the sonar displays, but seemed t
feel a resonance of the tingle at the time-frequency dis
play. He watched the six frequency buckets on the screen
barely blinking, until his scalding hot coffee was gon
and the frequency at 154 cycles per second had spike
into a narrow finger of sound.

The Destiny was out there and by God he had foun
it. He put down the coffee mug and ran toward the doo
to sonar, colliding with Omeada, who was running ou
of sonar into control.

"We've got him," they said at once, rubbing thei
foreheads from the collision.

# CHAPTER 35

**USS *Barracuda***

Admiral Pacino woke up from a sound sleep at the prodding of Paully White.

"Sir, it's two A.M. Kane's manning battlestations. We've got a Destiny."

"About time," Pacino muttered, slipping into coveralls and leather deck shoes. He rubbed the sleep from his eyes, feeling the gauze of his injured eye, wondering when if ever the eye would heal. He pulled on the eyepatch as he left the stateroom, careful to avoid the rushing watchstanders.

The large control room was packed. Kane stood on the conn with his officer of the deck, Scott Court. XO Roger Whatney stood below between the conn platform and the attack center. The consoles of the attack center were filled with officers, adjusting their solutions, trying to find one that fit the data to the Destiny.

Kane nodded curtly at Pacino and Paully, then addressed the watchsection. Pacino strapped on a battle headset so he could listen to the conversations in the room. Again he felt he was watching from the sidelines, and with it the thought that this action *should be his.* He shook his head to concentrate on the battle in front of him.

"Attention in the firecontrol team," Kane announced from the conn. "We have designated the sonar contact as Target One, Destiny-class submerged submarine. We now hold Target One weakly on the thin wire towed array forward-looking beam, his 154 Hertz tonal coming in clearly. We hold him at bearing west, approximately two six five. There's no broadband from this bearing.

This isn't much to go on but we will be putting out multiple salvos of Mark 50 torpedoes on the bearing to the target. That's all, carry on."

## SS-810 *Winged Serpent*

Tanaka looked at his watch. It was after two in the morning and he had been staring at the Second Captain screen for what seemed forever. He was tired and frustrated. He told himself he would watch the screen for one more hour, then go to bed in spite of the Americans out there, the pounding of his heart from the uppers, the shaking of his hands, and the acid in his stomach.

The mission had gone on too long. The Americans and their waiting game had finally gained them an advantage. He swept the heavy green-shaded lamp to the deck, brought his hands to his face, his hands shaking. He desperately needed sleep but there was too much of the amphetamines in his system. He was feeling closed in by the ship, by the mission, by the lack of contact with an enemy.

When would it end? And how?

## USS *Barracuda*

"Firing point procedures, Target One, horizontal salvo, tubes one through six, one quarter degree offset, twenty-second firing interval," Kane announced to the control room. There was no sound in the room except the whining of the gyro and the low rush of air from the air handlers.

"Ship ready," Jeff Joseph, the battlestations officer of the deck, reported.

"Weapons ready," from the weapons officer.

"Solution ready," the XO finished.

"Tube one, shoot on generated bearing," Kane commanded.

"Set," pos-two operator Lieutenant Porter said.

"Standby," the weapons officer called and rotated the stainless steel trigger to nine o'clock.

"Shoot," Kane said.

*"Fire!"* weapons said, pulling the trigger to the right.

The launch sound blasted into the control room, high-pressure air venting from the downstream side of the ram that pressurized the torpedo tanks. Pacino felt his hearing was half gone.

"Tube one fired electrically, sir," the weapons officer called.

"Conn, sonar," Chief Omeada said. "First fired unit, normal launch."

The second torpedo was fired, the control-room crew reading from the same script, then again for unit three, until six torpedoes were fired. Kane powered up the weapons in tubes seven and eight and opened their outer doors while having the torpedo-room crew reload one through six. It took a few minutes, but seven and eight came up to speed and were ready to fire.

Kane shot them, a total of eight torpedoes traveling through the sea, intent on hitting the Destiny that he had estimated to be twenty nautical miles away. Impact would be at a point somewhat closer than the Destiny was now, since he was getting closer with time. The impact point was about seventeen miles to the west, with calculated time for the torpedoes to reach impact point eighteen minutes from now. If they had fired a Vortex missile, Pacino thought, impact time would be more likely only four minutes. Anything could happen in eighteen minutes.

"Attention in the firecontrol team," Kane said. "With eight fish on the way, we wait to see what Target One is going to do. He may counterfire, and if he does I intend to cut the wires in all tubes and run east. Otherwise, we'll sit and listen."

## SS-810 *Winged Serpent*

Tanaka craved sleep but he knew if he went to bed all he'd do would be to listen to the complaints of his body.

He grabbed the water carafe and drank out of it, the water running over his chin—and when he put it down he saw that the Second Captain display was full of broadband noise, pulsing broadband noise.

He sat back down and scanned through the screens, his jaw falling open as he realized what was happening. A half-dozen American torpedoes were screaming in toward them. How long had they been in the water? Why hadn't anyone detected the American who fired them? What happened to his officers in the control room?

And how the *hell* did six—no, seven—no, now it was eight!—torpedoes get launched at them?

He grabbed his uniform tunic and ran out of the room to control and found his first officer Hiro Mazdai crouched over the Second Captain display being run by the mechanical officer, Lieutenant Commander Kami.

"What's going on? What are you doing? Man full battle-stations and get the weapons in tubes eleven and twelve warmed up. Open the outer doors! Why didn't you detect the Americans?"

Tanaka came up closer to first officer Mazdai, who had stood at attention. Tanaka slapped him hard; a red welt appeared on his cheek.

"You have brought dishonor on my ship, Mr. First. One more mistake and I will relieve you. Permanently. Is that clear?"

"Very clear, Captain."

"Now get those tubes ready to fire!"

"Yessir."

**USS *Barracuda***

"Any activity from the target yet?" Kane asked Omeada in sonar.

"Nothing yet, Captain. I don't think he can hear us yet."

"He sure as hell should hear our torpedoes—"

A low rumble could be heard through the hull, just

barely audible. Kane looked up at the sonar screen, which had been selected to the broadband waterfall display ever since battlestations were manned. A large white patch appeared at bearing north, the sound intense from its reading on the screen, the white patch of sound spread out over ten degrees of azimuth.

"What the hell was that, Chief?"

"Something blew up from the north, Skipper. Could be a nuclear blast from what I can see."

"Good God," Kane said to Pacino. "You don't think they have nuclear torpedoes, do you?"

"No. They don't need to. The Nagasaki is the most destructive torpedo in the world right now. If our Mark 50s could do what it does, we'd have no problems."

"So what was that noise?"

"That, Captain Kane, was one of ours."

"But we don't—"

"Just fight the ship against the threat at hand." Kane didn't need to worry about the explosion from the north. It was Bruce Phillips shooting a Vortex missile, putting down another Destiny II.

Paully White looked up at Pacino from the control room deck and mouthed the word, "Brucey." Pacino just nodded.

**SS-810 *Winged Serpent***

"What was that?" Tanaka yelled at Mazdai. "What was that sound? What does the Second Captain show?"

He received no answers from the man or the machine. Perhaps it had been the detonation of a Nagasaki torpedo against a distant American, perhaps one of the northern deployed units.

"Status of the tubes?"

"Weapons are warm. We still have no sonar data on the launching ship."

"You *still* have no contact?"

"Nothing, sir. The sea is empty. Look for yourself."

"The sea is not empty, Mr. First. We are looking for

the wrong thing. The computer is filtering out the noise we seek."

"No, sir, it is correct. The American Los Angeles-class ships—"

"This is obviously not an LA-class vessel. It is something else, British or French."

"No, the computer was looking for them also."

"Then maybe the American Seawolf class. We're not filtering for that." Tanaka knew time was ticking but he had to solve this problem and solve it now.

"Seawolf class had three ships. One sank from a flooding or torpedo accident. The other is on the US east coast being built. The third was in Hawaii but it never got underway. The Galaxy satellite photos showed it pulled into a maintenance barn. It never emerged."

"It might have sneaked out during a storm or with a cold reactor submerged or any of a hundred ways a sub can be sneaked to sea."

"We would have known—"

"Obviously, First, we *didn't* know! Now reset the filters for the Seawolf class and find this submarine. I want torpedoes in the water in two minutes."

**USS *Piranha***

Bruce Phillips stood on the conn and heard Gambini's voice calling in something from sonar.

"Say again, Master Chief?" Phillips said.

"We've got distant noises that I'm classifying as torpedoes, all concentrated on a bearing set to the south. I am not, repeat, not, calling torpedo in the water."

"I'm confused. What's the deal?"

"Sir, the torpedoes appear to be . . . Mark 50s. This may be a battle with another US unit and the Japanese. All I can detect are the torpedoes, they're the loudest, but there must be something going on to the south."

"Attention in the firecontrol team. After we launch this Vortex at Target Five we'll clear datum to the south at emergency flank. There may be someone down there vho needs our help. Firing point procedures, Target 'ive, Vortex tube six."

The launching litany continued for the sixth time since he first Destiny was shot. With the missile that Phillips iad launched at the arctic ice ridge, after this one was one, he was six missiles down, four to go. The launch equence went as the previous five had, ending in a deafning roar of the Vortex rocket motor ignition, the noise asing as the missile flew underwater downrange, then he second deafening transient as the missile hit the fifth )estiny and exploded.

"Helm, left five degrees rudder, steady course south, ll ahead emergency flank," Phillips ordered.

*Piranha* came up to emergency flank turns, almost ixty-one knots, her deck shaking hard as the main engines shrieked aft, the steam flow-rate twice the maxinum allowable.

**S-810 *Winged Serpent***

'Sir, may I remind you that we still have eight incoming orpedoes and we have not evaded them? Shouldn't we urn the ship and run?"

Tanaka glared at Mazdai. "Don't ever again advocate urning and running from the enemy. I'll kill you." He ent back down over the console and bit his lip, the ilters for the Seawolf class now entered into the Second Captain's processors. All there was to do was wait to ollect the data. The American was out there and he vas dangerous. He had the acoustic advantage, he hadn't hown up on the Second Captain system with the Los Angeles-class filters set up, so he had to be a Seawolf. Yet how did he get by the Galaxy satellites? It didn't nake sense but the proof was in front of them, the Second Captain beginning to show data coming through the ilters. The screen annunciator went off, confirming the ounds of the Seawolf-class submarine. Perhaps they lidn't have the acoustic advantage after all, Tanaka

thought, perhaps it was just that the Second Captain wa
looking for the wrong sounds.

This battle might yet be turned around.

"Sir, what are you going to do about the eigh
torpedoes?"

"I'm going to let the Second Captain take care of
as soon as the two Nagasakis are away. Now let's maneu
ver the ship to get a range on the Seawolf out there
And then we can launch."

## USS *Barracuda*

"Still nothing from the target, Captain," Omeada's voic
said in Kane's headset. The Destiny hadn't counterfired
hadn't maneuvered, just kept going as if he didn't car
that he'd been shot at, or didn't know. But it was on
thing not to hear the *Barracuda.* It was another not t
hear eight loud Mark 50s.

"That's a fact, Captain," executive officer Leo Do
browski reported from the attack center. "Contact ha
maintained course and speed. He doesn't know we'r
here, or our torpedoes."

"Very well, then, we'll keep waiting."

Pacino glanced at Paully White, an uneasiness fillin
him.

## USS *Piranha*

Bruce Phillips stood over the chart, his pointer shakin
over its surface with the vibrations of the deck. Th
speed indicator showed a velocity of sixty-two knot
now, since all but four of the Vortex tubes were gone.

At this rate, assuming the noises they had heard were
at the limits of sonar detection, fifty miles, the ship
would be in the vicinity of the battle in another forty-
five minutes.

Phillips looked up at the overhead, wondering if tha
would be enough.

## SS-810 *Winged Serpent*

"Finally," Tanaka said as the first leg of data was in on the American Seawolf. Now he could turn the ship to get a parallax range. "Left minimum rudder, ship-control officer, come to course north."

Tanaka watched the data fall into the Second Captain, waiting tensely, biding his time. All the while the incoming eight American torpedoes were soaring in at them, arrival time could be as soon as five minutes. The thought occurred to him then that the SCM, the sonar countermeasures feature of the Second Captain, might malfunction and he would have to eat his words about being able to take torpedo hits and survive. Of course, if that should happen, he would not long be embarrassed. He would be on the sea floor, dead.

"Tube status?"

"Ready to open the outer doors. Tubes eleven and twelve are flooded, weapons warm. The enemy location and velocity are locked in, gas generators ready to arm an outer-door opening."

"Good, open the outer doors."

## USS *Barracuda*

"He's maneuvering," Kane said quietly to Pacino, his hand covering his boom microphone. "He knows we're here."

"Getting a range on you," Pacino said. "He'll be opening his outer doors soon and then we'll have company, Nagasaki torpedoes. Have you got the ship positioned so we can hear the target without our torpedoes masking him?"

"We're going north at full speed. I don't dare flank it or our noise signature will double."

"Just keep your bearing separation in mind—"

"Conn, Sonar," Omeada's voice called on the battle circuit, "we have transients coming from Target One. I'm calling torpedo tube doors coming open."

"Very well, Sonar," Kane replied into his headset looking at Pacino. "Helm, all ahead flank."

"Ahead flank, aye, sir, maneuvering answers, all ahead flank."

"Helm, right one degree rudder, steady course zero two zero."

"Rudder right one degree, sir, passing zero one zero to the right, ten degrees from ordered course . . . steady course zero two zero."

The deck trembled slightly as the ship accelerated, the reactor circulation pumps aft—huge pumps, each the size of a compact car—started up, their 1500 horsepower motors spinning the rotors, pumping the coolant water through the core so the reactor power could double from 50 to 100 percent.

"Any minute now, sir," Paully said to Pacino.

## SS-810 *Winged Serpent*

"Shoot," Tanaka commanded. The torpedo in tube eleven left the ship under the force of the gas generator's steam pressure, the torpedo's engine starting and spinning the pumpjet propulsor of the Nagasaki torpedo to full revolutions. The Nagasaki dived to 400 meters and sailed on toward the target.

Tanaka remembered what he had been thinking about using only one torpedo per American submarine, but this was a special circumstance. The Seawolf-class ship would be a threat on an even playing field with the Destiny II class, and a single Nagasaki could not be completely trusted to tear it apart. A second torpedo launch was the safe thing to do.

"Tube twelve," Tanaka said. "Shoot!"

The twelfth Nagasaki launched by the *Winged Serpent* departed the bow of the ship, starting its engine and accelerating toward the target.

"That should take care of the Seawolf," Tanaka said, his mood improving. "Now for the incoming eight American torpedoes." He concentrated on the Second Captain console, switching it to the ship-control and weapon-evasion screens. He found what he was looking for, the function that would turn control of the vessel over to the Second Captain and allow it to use the massive computing power to ping out with the ventriloquist SCM sonar system.

Soon the Seawolf-class ship would be on the bottom, the *Winged Serpent* able to continue in its search of the offshore waters for any remaining Americans. When the American sank he would go to bed confident that the worst threat in the Pacific had been neutralized.

There was even more good news here, he realized. With the most formidable ship in the American submarine force on the bottom, how willing would the Americans be to send in an inferior Los Angeles-class ship? So this was it, the concluding battle of the American blockade.

The Second Captain took command of the submarine then, distracting Tanaka from his thought as the ship went into a violent maximum-rudder/maximum-speed maneuver to try to get the range of the incoming torpedoes. The deck abruptly tilted twenty degrees to the right, almost throwing Tanaka into a row of Second Captain consoles. He grabbed a handhold to steady himself, watched the computer driving the ship. The ventriloquist SCM sonar system kicked in then, which meant the Second Captain's calculations were complete and it could begin its work of confusing the incoming torpedoes.

Surely the system could fool two, perhaps three torpedoes—but eight? A terrible moment of doubt, but he shook it off.

**USS *Piranha***

Bruce Phillips was back in his submarine coveralls. Scott Court was stationed as officer of the deck with an augmented section-tracking team.

Phillips strapped on the battle-circuit headset in time to hear the sonar chief saying something about torpedo

pings and odd sonar groaning sounds coming from th
southwest and more pings in a different frequency fron
the southeast. Phillips checked the bearing separation
realizing that he was closer to the action than he'd origi
nally thought.

"Man silent battlestations," he told Court. "One las
time."

# CHAPTER 36

**USS *Barracuda***

"Attention in the firecontrol team," Kane said. His voice was steady, authoritative, but Pacino knew he was probably more frightened than he'd ever been in his life. "We're running from two Nagasaki torpedoes fired by the Destiny II class astern of us. The torpedoes are on the edge of our port baffles. I intend to jettison the caboose array to gain some speed, then turn fifteen more degrees westward. We have countermeasures loaded in the forward and after signal ejectors and we'll launch those at the appropriate time. Carry on." Kane turned to Jeff Joseph, the skinny, odd-looking navigator and officer of the deck. "Make that happen, OOD. Cut the wires, shut the doors and jettison the caboose. Move it."

Pacino bent over the plot, wondering about the *Piranha*.

**SS-810 *Winged Serpent***

Tanaka held onto the handhold, his knuckles white as the ship executed the second loop of the figure-eight maneuver, the computer trying to determine the range to the incoming torpedoes. Finally the maneuver was complete, the ship now heading south at maximum turns.

The SCM sonar countermeasures were making so much noise and the pump jet propulsor was putting out so much turbulence that the rear-facing passive sonar system was unable to detect the arrival in the area of the second Seawolf ship.

## USS *Piranha*

"Captain, Sonar," Gambini said to Phillips, "here's the picture. At bearing one nine eight, south-southwest, we have Target Seven, Japanese Destiny II class. Target Seven is turning max revs getting out of town because at bearing south I've got multiples Mark 50 torpedoes, all of them in pursuit of the Destiny II. At bearing one seven five, south-southeast I have at least two Nagasaki torpedoes in pursuit of the contact at bearing one six zero, southeast, which I'm classifying as a US Seawolf submerged submarine, designated Friendly One."

"Skip the Friendly One bullshit, Master," Phillips said. "Call it the *Barracuda*."

"Aye, sir. So what we have here is that the Destiny II and the *Barracuda* have fired at each other. Tough to say who shot first, but since the *Barracuda* got off eight shots I'm guessing she fired first."

"Doesn't matter," Phillips said, staring at pos one, the geographic plot, the God's-eye view of the sea. The three ships, the Destiny, the *Barracuda* and the *Piranha* formed a triangle with *Piranha* at the top, coming in from the north. At the bottom left the Destiny was running southwest away from eight Mark 50s. At the bottom right the *Barracuda* was sprinting to the northeast trying to get away from two Nagasaki torpedoes. An image came into his mind of the *Barracuda* being chased by two sharp-teethed black muscular dogs. He had to do something.

The first order of business was the Destiny II.

"Attention in the firecontrol team. One crisis at a time. We're going to put Vortex unit seven down the bearing line to Target Six, the Destiny bearing south-southwest. Let's get that out of the way now. Firing point procedures, Vortex seven, Target Six, bearing one nine eight."

"Ship ready."

"Weapon ready."

"Solution ready."

"Shoot on generated bearing."

"Set."

"Standby."

"Shoot!"

*"Fire!"*

The roaring of the missile ignition was once again deafening. The watchstanders had all plugged their ears with their fingers as the solid-rocket-fueled underwater-missile launched and sailed off to the south.

"Attention in the firecontrol team," Phillips shouted over the roar of the missile. "I intend to try to do something for the *Barracuda.* Everyone just hold on for a second."

Phillips leaned over the weapon-control console, where round-headed Tom McKilley sat looking up at him.

"Weps, is there any way we can program the Vortex to detonate at a particular bearing and range without it homing on a target?"

"You mean disable the blue laser and have it count seconds until it's at a certain bearing and range to own ship, then go off?"

"Right?"

"Skipper, I don't know, but I'm sure as hell going to find out," McKilley said, reaching to the overhead for the technical manual.

"Don't you have its tech manual on the outline software?"

"Yessir. One moment." McKilley was becoming flustered, flashing through the software to the help-screens, going through one after the other. It had been two minutes since the missile launch and still no explosion.

Phillips looked back at the geographic plot, deciding to work on the range to the *Barracuda.* To do it would be violating yet another hallowed submarine tactic by using active sonar. Active sonar was the practice of pinging a noise into the sea, waiting for the ping to bounce off the object of interest and return to the listening sonar set. The time delay and the sound velocity determined the two-way-trip length, which divided in two was the range to the contact. It was a tactic unused for decades. A stealthy submarine attempting to remain undetected would never ping out a noise. It defeated the purpose and besides, passive listen-only sonar could be just as effective, although it took the ship longer to determine the range to the contact.

But the entire ocean knew *Piranha* was there—hell, he'd just launched the loudest weapon ever known to man. Another noise in the form of a ping would make no difference and would save time to getting the *Barracuda*'s exact location in the sea. The only problem was that active sonar was subject to interpretation just as passive sonar was, the human brain definitely part of the combat-control system. And the sonarmen were generally not too great at active sonar, an unpracticed art. Still, if anyone could do it, Gambini could.

"Master Chief, I want an active range to the *Barracuda.* Can you do it?"

"Yessir. It'll just take a moment to line up."

"Ping when you're ready and step on it, Master. Weps! What's the status of the answer? Can we put an explosion at a preplanned point in space?"

"Still trying to find out, sir."

Phillips bit his tongue, knowing that yelling at the lieutenant would make him feel better but would only mess up McKilley's efforts. Nothing like the heat of battle, Phillips thought. There was something about pressure that made most human minds start to go to hell. The fluster factor was with them now. The simplest things could become immensely complicated under pressure.

Phillips took a deep breath and waited.

The Vortex missile speeding toward Target Six should have had an unobstructed shot at the target, but the Mark 50 torpedoes shot by the *Barracuda* were sent off course by the ventriloquist sonar set of the *Winged Serpent.* The torpedoes were all lagging by several miles, directly astern of the Destiny II ship, their sonars convinced that the target was 4000 yards closer than it actually was because of the Destiny's rear-facing active sonar sending false pulses that mimicked the Mark 50s' pinging sonar sets. The Mark 50s all tried to slow down and detonate where the Destiny should have been, but when the weapon computers said the Mark 50s should be right on top of the target, they instead found only empty ocean. The sonars tried again, pinging out to the target, hearing now that it was straight ahead, then speeding up and positioning themselves where the target should have been, only to meet nothing.

In spite of a Mark 50's ability to do seventy knots, they followed the Destiny in a tail chase at fifty-five knots, a constant distance behind the Destiny as it evaded to the southwest. After a few miles down the track, the Mark 50s would run out of fuel and sink.

From the viewpoint of Vortex Seven's blue-laser sonar, eight Mark 50 torpedoes and their combined turbulent wakes met the target parameters for a valid submerged target. The Vortex got within twenty yards of the aftmost torpedo before exploding into white-hot plasma, destroying every single torpedo.

Still, the Destiny II-class submarine did not escape undamaged. The blast effect and underwater shock wave hit it hard.

## SS-810 *Winged Serpent*

The explosion from the stern took Tanaka by complete surprise. The detonation extinguished the lights and killed the Second Captain, and the ship went into a dive since the computer no longer controlled the ship's attitude.

"Override in manual!" Tanaka ordered the ship-control officer. "Bring us back up, two hundred meters. Kami, get down to the lower level and reinitialize the Second Captain. Mazdai, help him while I try to see what else is damaged."

There was no questioning Tanaka's frantic orders.

Kami and Mazdai rushed out of the room. Emergency battle lanterns flickered in the space, then came alive, lighting the compartment in a ghostly incandescent glow, patches of light and darkness spreading throughout the ship.

Tanaka cursed, wondering how one of the torpedoes had managed to get in. Without the Second Captain he was blind, deaf and dumb. And defenseless. Computers? They were as unreliable as humans.

## USS *Piranha*

"Captain, I think I can do this!" McKilley nearly shouted in triumph. The only problem, Phillips thought, was that by now it was probably too late. The torpedoes in pursuit of the *Barracuda* were catching up—the detonation of the first-fired Vortex came then, the noise rumbling through the hull, marking the death of the Destiny submarine.

"XO," Phillips ordered Whatney, "get ready to recommend a detonation point for the next Vortex so we can put a blast zone around the Nagasaki torpedoes homing on the *Barracuda.* And bear in mind it would be nice if we could avoid putting a friendly submarine on the bottom."

"Aye, Captain."

"Attention in the firecontrol team, we're taking an active bearing and range to the *Barracuda* so we can put a Vortex out there that can screw up the Nagasakis following her. Carry on."

"Captain, Sonar," from Gambini. "We're ready."

"Go active, Master Chief."

"Active, aye sir."

The BSY-2 sonar suite was configured so that the spherical array in the nose cone could transmit an active pulse out into the water. The array was capable of putting out so much sonic power that water would actually boil on the surface of the fiberglass nose cone when the pulse went out. Gambini hit the cover of the active key, the switch configured so that no one could just accidentally hit the key, then punched the key. The pulse went out, not as deafening as a torpedo launch or a Vortex ignition, but loud, the sound reverberating throughout the ship. The pulse traveled through the water, going south and reaching out to the USS *Barracuda,* still running from two Nagasaki torpedoes. The pulse hit the hull of the Seawolf-class submarine, which was wrapped in tiles, anechoic coating especially designed to avoid returning an active sonar pulse. But like any kind of shielding it did not make a return pulse impossible, it simply lowered the intensity of the return pulse.

The listening spherical array of the BSY-2, quiet since the pulse, strained to listen for the return. Unfortunately the sea around her returned the sound, some from the waves overhead, some from bubbles in the water, a pulse coming back from the Nagasakis, one from the *Barracuda,* many from the biological content of the water.

In sonar, Gambini tried to correlate the active return signals the BSY-2 had collected to the passive listening set and the towed array's narrowband detect of the Seawolf-class ship. There were all three indications at the bearing he knew to be the *Barracuda.* The range cursor on that one ping return, just a blob on the video screen, read a distance of 7.8 nautical miles.

"Conn, Sonar, range to *Barracuda* is sixteen thousand yards."

"Go, XO," Phillips ordered. "Come on, come on!"

"Aye, sir, recommended Vortex detonation at bearing one seven five, range twelve thousand yards."

"Weps, one seven five, twelve thousand yards."

"That's too close, Captain," McKilley objected. "The blast zone will kill the *Barracuda.*"

"So will the Nagasakis. Enter the goddamned bearing and range."

"Aye, aye, sir."

"Firing point procedures, phantom target, Vortex unit eight."

Phillips collected his reports and ordered the Vortex to fire. The ignition again blasted his ears, and as the missile left the ship, he said a silent prayer for the *Barracuda.*

### SS-810 *Winged Serpent*

"Second Captain is reinitialized, sir."

"Open tube doors thirteen and fourteen, programmed to the bearing of the launch of that weapon. Get them out on the bearing now, immediate enable, safety interlocks off."

"Yessir," Mazdai said, flashing through the software displays of the weapon-control consoles of the Second Captain. "Ready to fire."

"Tube thirteen, fire."

"Thirteen away."

"Tube fourteen, fire."

"Fourteen away."

"Excellent."

### USS *Barracuda*

The ship continued on its run from the Nagasaki torpedoes.

Pacino and Paully looked at each other. It was grim, the same scenario that Pacino had put Bruce Phillips through.

There had to be something they could do. Shut down the ship, scram the reactor, emergency blow to the surface, ping active sonar at the Nagasakis, anything. But there was nothing he could do without being in command, and Kane was too intense to reach without shaking him by the shoulders. Besides, if Pacino thought he had a clear course of action that would save the ship, he would be happy to dress down Kane in front of his men, but Pacino knew his guesses were no different than Kane's. On second thought, all they could do was wait—

The detonation erupted into control, throwing bodies forward into the equipment like dice against the border of a crap table. Pacino went into the pole of the number-one periscope, shoulder first, ribcage next, knees last. He slipped down to the deck, but the deck had become a bulkhead as the ship rolled far to the left, so far that the decks had become vertical. He slipped down the deckplates, conscious enough to see the blood pooling beneath him, hearing the screams of the wounded and dying, feeling the ship try to right itself, the deck coming back to being a deck, but when it was done with the recovery, he realized that it was not level at all. The ship had taken on a steep down angle, the lights off, the blood running downhill.

*Barracuda* was busy dying.

## SS-810 *Winged Serpent*

The detonation from the northeast—the Nagasaki torpedoes hitting the first Seawolf-class ship—blew the *Winged Serpent* into a tailspin as the Second Captain lost control of the X-tail aft. The computer then regained control, but Captain Tanaka had been thrown to the deck. He picked himself up and looked up at the sonar console. The Nagasakis launched against the intruder to the north were still tracking. The first target was now gone, its sonar signature lost in the fireball of the Nagasakis. Tanaka smiled.

*Winged Serpent* was winning.

## USS *Piranha*

Phillips learned almost immediately that his prayer should have been said for his own ship, the *Piranha.*

"Conn, Sonar, two torpedoes in the water, bearing two zero zero! Both of them Nagasakis."

"Shit," he said. "Attention in the firecontrol team, apparently Target Six isn't as dead as we thought he was. And I'm not running, I'm shooting." He paused, noting the eyes of the crew on him. "Firing point procedures, Target Seven, Vortex unit nine."

The combat litany rolled through the room again until the Vortex roared off into the darkness of the sea, its destination the Destiny that had caused all the hell.

## SS-810 *Winged Serpent*

"Sir," Mazdai reported from the sonar panel, now that he was back from recovering the Second Captain, "we've got another strong broadband contact. This is some kind of torpedo, sir. We'd better evade it."

"No, First. The SCM will take care of it. Prepare to engage the Second Captain in ship-control mode. We've evaded eight torpedoes before, we'll evade one more now—"

"But sir—"

"Mazdai!" Tanaka was furious, even raising his hand as if to strike Mazdai, but then they both froze, hearing the sound of a submerged rocket motor. There were no words capable of describing the power of that roar as the missile came shrieking in toward the *Winged Serpent.*

The Vortex missile detonated, raising the temperature of the vicinity around it to that of the sun's surface. Toshumi Tanaka was vaporized, the atoms of his body so elevated in temperature that they lost their electrons and became a plasma, glowing brilliantly in the depths of the sea.

Nothing was left of the ship, its steel becoming a plasma of iron and carbon atoms. The Second Captain died along with every living being aboard, the computer able to watch itself die, its consciousness much quicker than the processing of the human mind. It sensed the collapse of the hull, the propagation of the plasma front, the sequential vaporization of its process-control modules, watching the plasma eat it alive, finally howling in electronic pain as the plasma devoured it. There was nothing left then but a cooling bubble of gas and a shock wave of a pressure pulse moving through the ocean. An external observer would never have suspected that one of the world's greatest designs had passed with nothing left to mark its passage.

## USS *Piranha*

XO Roger Whatney looked up at Phillips.

"Sir, now that the missile is away, maybe we should evade those Nagasakis."

Phillips looked down at Whatney and thought about Pacino's simulation in Norfolk. He'd be damned if he'd experience in reality what he'd experienced in that simulator, running from the Nagasakis and dying on the run. He would die with his boots on, his Vortex battery empty.

"No, XO. Goddamned if I'm going to run." Phillips raised his voice to the men in the room. "Attention in the firecontrol party. We're going to do the same thing for ourselves as we did for the *Barracuda.* Helm, right two degrees rudder, steady course two three zero, all ahead two thirds. Mr. McKilley, give me a phantom target straight ahead, range four thousand yards."

"We won't make it, sir."

"Five thousand yards and that's it."

"Aye, sir."

"Firing-point procedures, phantom target at five thousand yards bearing two three zero, Vortex unit ten."

The reports rolled in, and Phillips called for the launch. He put his fingers in his ears one last time, feeling sad that the last Vortex was gone. If only the icepack hadn't eaten up the first missile, he would still have a ticket home.

## USS *Barracuda*

Admiral Pacino pulled himself to his feet and made his way to the conn. He and four other men remained conscious, one of them Paully White, the other the helmsman, the third the executive officer, Leo Dobrinski, the fourth, the chief of the watch at the wraparound ballast-control panel. The survivors seemed to have picked at random. Dimly Pacino registered that David Kane was collapsed on the deck of the conn. He bent down, fighting his dizziness, and rolled Kane over. Kane's face was shattered, blood coming out of his nose. Pacino put his face down near Kane's and heard rattling sucking breathing. Kane must have taken a hit in the chest as well as his face. Pacino lowered him to the deck. The ship was dying, he reminded himself. *Save the ship, save the plant, then save the men,* his old mentor Rocket Ron Daminski, long dead now at the bottom of the Mediterranean, had taught him back on the *Atlanta.* It sounded coldblooded but it made sense. A dead ship ensured a dead crew.

Kane was wounded and down. Pacino was the senior submarine-qualified officer aboard. Navy Regs said he was now in command. Ironic. All the time since Seawolf had gone down he had missed command, and now it was his—a submarine crippled, drifting, probably flooding and sinking, hit by a Nagasaki torpedo, an enemy Destiny out there to be fought, a ship's company that probably numbered more dead than living. Get with it, he ordered himself, and stood upright on the conn.

"This is Admiral Pacino," he said in a ringing, probably foolish sounding voice. "I now take command of the USS *Barracuda* in the absence of her commanding officer in accordance with US Navy regulations." He paused, wondering if anyone would dispute his claim, but all he saw were the eyes of Paully White and Leo Dobrowski, both ready for orders.

Pacino reached for the circuit-one microphone.

"ALL STATIONS, THIS IS ADMIRAL PACINO. CAPTAIN KANE IS WOUNDED. I HAVE ASSUMED COMMAND. ALL STATIONS REPORT DAMAGE STATUS IMMEDIATELY."

"Paully," Pacino said, "get the reports off the battle circuits. Helm, keep this damned thing level." Pacino pulled the 1JV phone from the conn cradle. "Maneuvering, Captain. Maneuvering! Pick up if you hear me." There was nothing.

"XO," Pacino said to Dobrowski, "lay aft and get the reactor back up."

Dobrowski was gone before he had finished the order.

"Goddamnit, Paully, what's on the phones?"

"There's no one reporting, Admiral. We're it."

"Get into sonar and see what you can do. Just stay on the phones."

White ran into sonar, leaving Pacino with the helmsman and the chief of the watch.

"Get the battle lanterns going, Chief. Mark ship's depth."

"Sir, we're at one thousand feet and sinking. Speed is one knot, we're showing no power and I have all ahead flank rung up."

Were any more torpedoes coming in? He was helpless if they were. If the ship sank any deeper he'd have no choice but to surface the ship. He grabbed the 1JV phone to maneuvering.

"XO, what's the status?" Pacino shouted into the phone.

"Sir, it looks like the plant scrammed on shock. I'll have to do a fast recovery startup but I'm all by myself! I can't do this by myself."

"Hold on, I'll send Commander White aft."

"Paully!" Pacino shouted into his headset.

"Yessir. Sonar's down and Omeada's dead. So are the other guys, there's blood everywhere—"

"Paully, get aft now and help out the XO. I want power yesterday, you got it?"

White rushed out of sonar and ran through control, one hand up at Pacino as he rushed by on the way to the aft compartment.

"Depth thirteen hundred, sir!"

Crush depth was coming up in another six hundred feet. If Paully and Dobrowski didn't get power up by then, he would have to emergency blow, and then it would be all over, the Japanese air force would blow the *Barracuda* to the bottom. Assuming another Destiny didn't do the job for them.

The tenth and last Vortex launched by the *Piranha* detonated two and a half miles from the firing ship. The blast effect and fireball reached out to the surrounding waters propagating outward spherically, the immediate blast zone a mass of high-energy steam and plasma, the effect further out a pressure shock wave moving at sonic velocity through the water. The Nagasaki torpedoes launched against the *Piranha* were on the *Piranha* side of the Vortex blast zone, the weapons passing each other on the way to their respective targets. But it hardly mattered, the blast and shock passing through the speeding torpedoes, vaporizing the one furthest behind, smashing the structural framing of the torpedo in the lead, the latter self-detonating in an explosion that was designed to rip open an enemy submarine hull but just dissipated outward in the waters of the Pacific.

The threat of the Nagasaki torpedoes was eliminated, but the effect of the saving Vortex missile had to be endured. The shock wave hit the *Piranha* like a huge fist. The reactor scrammed, tripped out, the shock of the blast knocking all but a handful of men to the decks and spilling their blood.

In the aftermath of the battle there were two submarines left, one crippled and sinking, the other shut down and whole but in deep shock. If that were all, the two submarines might have recovered without incident.

But that was not all.

Ninety kilometers to the south the Japanese Maritime Self Defense Force Destiny II submarine *Spring Sunshine* made its way northward, its Second Captain reporting on the many explosions from the battle zone.

# CHAPTER 37

JSS *Barracuda*

'Sir, depth is eighteen hundred, a hundred feet from rush depth."

Pacino had no choice. He had no reactor, a sinking ubmarine a hair's breadth from crush depth and a crew of only a half-dozen functioning men. It no longer mat-ered who waited for them on the surface or who lurked n the area with armed Nagasaki torpedoes. The choice: Certain death from the pressure of the deep, or possible ife from the safety of the surface. Pacino chose the urface.

"Chief of the Watch, emergency blow forward."

The chief stood and reached into the overhead for he chicken switch, the lever that would admit ultrahigh pressure air directly into the main ballast tanks forward. He pushed the lever upward, and an immediate loud roaring nvaded the silence of the dead control room as the air illed the forward ballast tanks.

The depth indicator didn't stop its downward drift, the gage now reading 1815 feet, only eighty-five feet above crush depth. Around Pacino the sounds of the metal of he hull protesting and groaning could be heard—the prelude to a hull failure.

"Chief, emergency blow aft," Pacino commanded. The chief pushed the aft lever forward, the roaring noise dou-bling as the aft tanks were being evacuated of seawater. The ship was now tons lighter, even at this depth.

The depth gage continued its downward drift, at 1825, 1830, 1840, until it froze at 1860, the depth staying con-stant. Pacino thought that crush-depth figures were subject to some errors, that no one really knew what pressur the hull would collapse at until it actually did, but the the deck slowly inclined upward, and the depth indicato clicked up one foot. Just one, but that was enough. Th gage began to click some more, the deck inclining up ward as the ship began to rush toward the surface, th digital indicator showing the vessel picking up speed.

"Keep the ship flat if you can," Pacino told the helms man. If the up-angle was too much, the ship would com up and dump the air from the ballast tanks, then sin back down again.

The depth gage unwound, and even with full plan angles the helmsman couldn't keep the deck level. Pa cino grabbed a handhold as the deck inclined upwar past thirty degrees to forty-five, the deck becoming mor of a wall than a floor. The gage whizzed through th numbers—500 feet, 450, 300, 200, 100, until the ship ca reened from the deep and leaped from the sea, only th pumpjet aft remaining submerged as the ship rockete through the waves, froze in space for a long moment then crashed back down into the sea.

The depth gage came back down, 100 feet, 200, bu then the downward plunge stopped and the ship agai climbed back to the surface, bobbing in the waves, roll ing slowly to port, then to starboard.

"THIS IS ADMIRAL PACINO," Pacino said on the circui one, his voice booming through the ship. "WE HAV EMERGENCY BLOWN TO THE SURFACE. CONTINUE TO BRIN BACK THE REACTOR."

Pacino raised the number-two periscope to see what wa around them there on the surface; the sea was empty.

It might take hours to recover the plant and resub merge the ship. He wondered how long it would tak the Japanese to realize he was there for the taking.

**USS *Piranha***

"Where are we now?" Phillips asked.

"Normal full power lineup," Walt Hornick's voice sai

on the phone circuit. "We should have full propulsion in about one minute."

"Very well. Nice recovery, Eng. You'll get a medal for this." If they survived, Phillips thought.

Five minutes later full propulsion was back on-line and *Piranha* was back.

"Master Chief. What do you hear?"

"Sir, the news is mixed. The Destiny is gone, but the *Barracuda* did an emergency blow to the surface."

"Damn. How far, XO?"

"Geo plot shows them about six miles from here, Skipper. Bearing one one five."

"Helm, all ahead flank, right full rudder, steady one one five."

The deck rolled as the large rudder order was followed, the ship's speed accelerating to forty-three knots.

"What are you thinking, Captain?"

"If the *Barracuda* is on the surface they could be in trouble, especially if the Japanese come to call. Helm, all ahead emergency flank."

It took six minutes to reach the *Barracuda*'s position. Phillips came shallow and slow, cleared his baffles and ascended to periscope depth at the walking pace of five knots. When the periscope cleared, he could see the *Barracuda* rolling in the waves, no men on her deck.

"Conn, Sonar, new contact, submerged Destiny II class, bearing one nine zero, contact is distant, designate Target Seven."

"And we're fresh out of Vortex missiles."

"What now, Skipper?" from Whatney.

"We surface and get the *Barracuda* crew out of there," Phillips said.

"But sir—"

"But nothing. Admiral Pacino's aboard. You ever consider what would happen to us if he got taken prisoner? Mr. Court, take us up and bring us alongside."

The next hour was like a drunken memory to Pacino. The *Piranha* surfaced almost right next to them, thrusting up against their hull, lines coming over, men with safety harnesses crawling over the hull. Pacino ordered the hatches opened, and the *Piranha* boarding party came aboard. He felt himself getting dizzy as they carried out the men. He sat at the pos-two control seat and put his head on the console, the dizziness overwhelming him. Finally he felt strong hands drag him up by the arms, and he was lifted up the ladder, feeling himself go more limp.

In a blur he found himself carried aboard the *Piranha* and lowered down the ladder into the hull, conveyed to a pile of blankets in the crew's mess. He saw a face hovering over his, a voice saying *Good Lord, he looks white, must be internal bleeding,* and he sank in the cold and the dark and knew no more.

**USS *Piranha***

"Diving Officer, submerge the ship to eight zero feet." Phillips was on the periscope, watching the empty *Barracuda.*

He knew what he had to do now, with the incoming Destiny II submarine. There was little choice.

It seemed to take forever for the ship to get down. Once it did, he was ready. The torpedoes in tubes one, two, three and four were flooded, open to sea and warmed up, all of them programmed with the location to the *Barracuda.* There was no way he'd let the Japanese have such a prize, a technological wonder. He would sink it before he'd allow that to happen.

"Conn, Sonar, Target Seven, Destiny II-class submarine, continues inbound, signal-to-noise level increasing."

"Sonar, Captain, does he know we're here?"

"Don't think so, sir."

"Let me know." Phillips took his face from the periscope. "Attention in the firecontrol team. I intend to put four torpedoes into the *Barracuda* to keep it out of Japanese hands, then hightail it out of the OpArea and head to the deep Pacific. With luck we can be gone before Target Seven, the next Destiny, knows we're here. We'll be doing a periscope approach on the *Barracuda.* Firing-point procedures, tubes one through four, Target Eight, surfaced US submarine."

"Ship ready, sir."

"Weapons ready, sir."

"Solution pending, sir."

"Final bearing and shoot, USS *Barracuda.*"

"Ready, Captain."

Phillips pressed a red button on the periscope grip. "Bearing mark."

"Two seven six."

"Range mark, three divisions in high power."

"Range fifteen hundred yards."

"Set."

"Standby."

"Shoot one," Phillips commanded.

"Fire one."

"Tube one fired electrically."

The other three torpedoes were launched then, Phillips's eye on the periscope lens. The torpedoes hit one after the other, the black rising clouds of spray and smoke from the explosions spectacular. There was not much of the ship to see on the surface to start with, only her sail and the top of her hull normally exposed, 90 percent of her below the water, but after four torpedo hits, the ship settled and sank quickly.

Nothing was left of the *Barracuda* except a white foam on the surface.

"Dive, make your depth six hundred feet. Helm, right five degrees rudder, steady course east, all ahead emergency flank. Lowering number-two scope."

Phillips stood and leaned on the conn rail. He stayed and watched the chart and listened to Gambini's reports on the Destiny II class, Target Seven, but the Japanese submarine had apparently never detected them. He seemed to be heading for the sound of the explosions coming from what used to be the *Barracuda,* but by the time he got there, the *Piranha* was long gone.

Phillips watched as the ship crossed over the boundary of the OpArea and headed east, the vibrations gone now

that the Vortex tubes were no longer there, all of then
jettisoned after the firing of the individual weapons.

A few hours later, Phillips slowed to flank, and si
hours after that, turned off the reactor circulation pump
and coasted down to full speed. He came to periscop
depth, transmitted a situation report and a request t
the *Mount Whitney,* and went back deep.

He took one trip up to the crew's mess, a makeshif
sickbay for the men pulled off the *Barracuda,* and foun
the unconscious form of Admiral Pacino.

"Well, Admiral, you don't know it, but you saved ou
lives with your little control-room simulation-trainer. I
not for you I'd have run from those Nagasakis. If no
for you I wouldn't have had any Vortex missiles. Yo
kicked their asses out here. I just wanted you to know
that."

Phillips stared at Pacino for a long time, the man'
skin white and unhealthy-looking, the eyepatch stil
strung across his bad eye, his lips swollen and chapped
Finally he walked away. As he did, a slight smile seemed
to come to the admiral's lips, although no one was
watching to be able to say either way.

Twelve hours later the ship surfaced a second time and
discharged the patients, Pacino among them, into the
Sea King helicopters for medevac to the *Mount Whitney*
Pacino didn't wake up as he was loaded, and was still
unconscious as he was unloaded from the chopper and
hauled into sickbay. It would be two days before he
opened his good eye.

# CHAPTER 38

Pacino slowly became aware of his surroundings. The sound of the air rushing around him, the feel of the bed, the slicing, throbbing pain in his side, the bandages there, the sheets covering him. His lips were dry. But strangely, the sensation of the bandage over his left eye was now gone. He had gotten used to that sensation but now it was absent.

He tried to open his eyes, the lids coming open, but the world appeared as if seen through Vaseline. He blinked but still couldn't see clearly. Finally a white shape appeared over him.

"Admiral." A woman's voice.

Eileen Constance.

"I got your note when I was at sea," Pacino said, his voice a hoarse croak. "Thanks . . . thank you."

"You're very welcome."

"Are my eyes okay?"

"They'll be back to normal in a few days. You have some drops in them."

"My side . . . ?"

"We did surgery, you were bleeding internally."

"Were you there?"

"I assisted. And I can tell you that even flag officers are made of snakes, snails and puppy dog tails. Don't laugh, it'll hurt your incision."

"So . . . what happened?"

"We operated and—"

"No. Japan."

"You don't know. Of course. You and the *Piranha*

sank all but two of their operational submarines. Som of the others had to return to port because of failure but of the ones that worked, only two survived. Presi dent Warner received Prime Minister Kurita in th White House yesterday. He offered a full apology fo attacking Greater Manchuria and invited the UN an US forces into Japan. The Destiny subs are now unde UN guard, the FireStar fighters have been flown to th Philippines and all the radioactive weapons are in th custody of the US Army."

"I missed a lot," Pacino's lips tried to smile.

"I was watching the news. I put some of it on a disk in case you want to look at it later."

"Your word's good enough."

"President Warner wanted to know when you cam to. She sent this note. Want me to read it?"

"Sure."

" 'To Vice Admiral Michael Pacino'—"

"She got my rank wrong."

"You're always the last to know, Admiral. Your thir star came in with the note. You're confirmed by Con gress. Warner struck while the iron was hot. Should I b jealous of you two?"

"Just read the damned note," Pacino croaked, but hi chapped lips were smiling.

" 'To Vice Admiral Michael Pacino—thanks to you courage, tactical foresight and strategic brilliance, th United States has prevailed in this struggle with Japan A grateful nation could never fully thank you enough but as a measure of our esteem I have nominated yo and Congress has confirmed you as Vice Admiral Unite States Navy. In addition, your name has been submitte by me personally for the Navy Cross, third award. Wit fondest wishes and hopes for your full recovery, I remai your grateful commander in chief, Jaisal Warner, Presi- dent.' Personally I think the Medal of Honor would b more appropriate," she added.

"Why?" Pacino frowned, the expression adding t his headache.

"Ask Paully White. By the way, he's okay. So is Cap-ain Kane, although he had a nasty collision with a ulkhead."

"How many men did we lose?"

"There were forty-two survivors from the *Barracuda.*"

Pacino bit his aching lip. That meant some eighty men ad lost their lives aboard the sub, in addition to the ther eight 688-class subs lost in the OpArea. He ouldn't help wondering if it had been worth it, but then ealized there was no telling what Japan would have become or would have done if not for Operation Enlightened Curtain.

"What now, Admiral?"

"Maybe I'll retire to Florida. Where did you say you were going to med school?"

Her kiss felt good, but he was already sinking into a eep sleep even before she pulled her lips away.

'he USS *Mount Whitney* steamed on, Pearl Harbor ound, the sun setting in the Pacific astern of her, the ash of green its last salute as it vanished below the orizon.

# EXPERIENCE HEART-STOPPING ACTION-ADVENTURE FROM BESTSELLING AUTHOR

# JACK DuBRUL

**The Medusa Stone** 0-451-40922-1

Ten years ago, the spy satellite *Medusa* burned upon reentry—but not before its sensors revealed a secret buried deep in the earth, hidden for thousands of years from the eyes of humanity. A priceless discovery that some would die to find—and kill to possess....

**Pandora's Curse** 0-451-40963-9

During World War II, in a secret Nazi submarine base, boxes made from looted wartime gold were hidden away. These "Pandora's boxes" contained an artifact so lethal that whoever possessed them held the power to unleash hell upon the Earth. And now they have been found by a man who will use them to hold the world hostage—unless Philip Mercer can stop him.

**"A master storyteller...the finest adventure writer on the scene today." —Clive Cussler**

*COMING IN DECEMBER 2002:*

RIVER OF RUIN 0-451-41054-8

To order call: 1-800-788-6262